JOSEPHINE AND HARRIET

Betty Burton is the author of the novels *Jude*; *Jaen*; *Hard Loves, Easy Riches*; *The Consequences of War*; *Goodbye, Piccadilly*; *Long, Hot Summer*; *Falling in Love Again*; *The Girl Now Leaving*; *Not Just a Soldier's War* and *The Face of Eve*, as well as a collection of short stories, *Women Are Bloody Marvellous!* She has written for television and radio, and won the Chichester Festival Theatre Award. Born in Romsey, Hampshire, she now lives in Southsea.

D1335376

By the same author

Jude
Jaen
Women of No Account
Hard Loves, Easy Riches
The Consequences of War
Goodbye, Piccadilly
Long, Hot Summer
Falling in Love Again (Rose Quinlan)
The Girl Now Leaving
Not Just a Soldier's War
The Face of Eve

SHORT STORIES
Women Are Bloody Marvellous!

BETTY BURTON

Josephine and Harriet

HarperCollins*Publishers*

HarperCollins*Publishers*
77–85 Fulham Palace Road,
Hammersmith, London W6 8JB

www.harpercollins.co.uk

This paperback edition 2004

2

First published in Great Britain by
HarperCollins*Publishers* 2004

ISBN 0 00 719263 0

Set in Sabon by Palimpsest Book Production Limited,
Polmont, Stirlingshire

Printed and bound in Great Britain by
Clays Ltd, St Ives plc

This book is for Sheila Burton.

Acknowledgements

Much of the truth that lies at the heart of *Josephine and Harriet* was unearthed by ace researcher Elizabeth Murray. Thanks to her.

Thanks also to my editor, Susan Opie, and copy editor, Penelope Isaac. They took my script by its shoulders and shook it until it made sense.

Harriet ran home as fast as her young legs could carry her.

Alarmed – but without reason.

Embarrassed – but not knowing why.

Fearful of the vicar, because what she had done might have been sinful.

Scoldings from Mam were always over before the sun went down. 'Sleep not on thy wrath.'

Punishments from Pa could be worked off in extra chores, or, 'Sing to me my little throstle and we'll call it quits.'

But sinning?

God dealt out punishments for that, and not until you were dead.

She didn't believe that she had sinned too much, not yet, but by the time she was dead, she might be weighed down with sins.

She might end up at the left hand of Jesus, with the goats.

The coin that was clutched in her hand became hot and sweaty. Perhaps if she threw it away then the sin would go with it. No. It was money, and money was fair short at home. For the life of her, the seven-year-old couldn't decide. 'Tell the truth and shame the Devil.'

So, when she reached home, she opened her palm to her mam.

'Oh, and where'd y' get that, me girl?'

'Gaffer gid it me.'

Her mother turned. She was making flour and water 'floaters' to put into knuckle-bone broth, flour hanging like rags from her fingers. 'Is that so then?'

Mam's look was enough. She was trying to be like always, but by Mam's straight face Harriet knew that something serious had happened. Money was always trouble with Mam and Jesus. He didn't like rich men, He turned over the money-lenders' tables in the temple, and He was sold out by Judas for pieces of silver. There hadn't seemed to be anything wrong about standing on a stool in Gaffer's workshop and taking a ha'penny for singing a song.

But, clearly, even if she wasn't sure what, she had committed a sin, and she did not want to confess it to her mam. She fed a few coals into the fire under the stewpot as a good deed.

'And why'd he give ya a whole ha'penny then? Has he give you money before?'

'Naw, Mam.'

2

Mam turned her back on her child and plunged her hands into the flour and water, gathering it into a ball. 'Well then?'

'I sang to him.'

'Oh.' Her mam chopped the ball of dough into little 'floaters' and put them aside to dry out a bit. 'Is that all?'

'Yes, Mam, I sang him the Easter song, just that one, no more.'

'Oh. Well, my pet. It's true that you have a sweet voice, but it's as well not to get paid for a gift of God. And don't go inside Gaffer's door if y're on y'r own self. You understand that?'

'Yes, Mam.'

'No harm done. Put the ha'penny in the jar and it'll add to fair money when time comes round.'

The coin was dealt with, but Harriet Burton knew that she had sinned. The greater sin was not in letting Gaffer touch her, but telling her mam a barefaced lie, and the day would come when she would pay for it.

Harriet placated people; that was how she made her way in the world.

Like me, please.

Like me, I'm not really a bad girl.

Nor was she.

Josephine Thomson, the other young woman involved in this story, also, as a child, had an experience that would follow her into womanhood.

Only she of her entire family had survived the ravages of a contagious fever that spread like wildfire.

3

She was saved by a visit to Hani's remote home village – Hani being the Thomsons' living-in help and friend, and teacher to the children. But saved for what? To succeed? To live up to the belief her father had had that women were as capable as men of making 'something of themselves'? But what was this Something? She was almost twenty before a talent was revealed; unfortunately it was not a talent that English provincial society expected women to possess.

Josephine Thomson's early years living far from England, with parents who hardly differentiated in the upbringing of herself and her twin brother, had given her a liberal view of what women should expect for themselves. This view was confirmed when tragedy forced her to come to live in England under the care of an intelligent and powerful uncle and his wealthy high-society wife; she also held quite advanced views on the capability of her own gender. Even so, Josephine's aunt believed that women's lives were improved by marriage to a loving man, as her own had been.

Josephine grew into blooming, ambitious womanhood with cobwebs of guilt clinging to her subconscious.

Christmas Eve 1872

Harriet Burton. Pretty, dainty, probably a few years older than she appeared. Not much of her native Norfolk dialect left since she had become a Londoner.

As her first-floor tenant tripped lightly downstairs, Mrs Wright waylaid her in a friendly manner, and asked cheerfully, 'Off then, Miss Burton? You look very nice.'

'Thank you, Mrs Wright.'

'Did Mr Wright remind you about the rent?'

'He did, but he didn't have need to. I realize I'm a bit behind, but, like I told him, I'll have it tonight when I get back from the theatre.'

'You got a booking then?'

'I think so. I'll know when I get there.'

'Good luck, then. Christmas Eve don't hardly seem the time when your sort of songs is best appreciated. No choruses, is there?'

No choruses . . . absolutely no choruses. Harriet Burton's act was simple: a pretty woman who sang sweet, sentimental ballads. No choruses. Her name was never high on the list of acts at the Alhambra Palace.

'True, but it's a time when a deal of drink is taken, and the audience does incline to get sentimental. They don't necessarily care about choruses.'

'Hard, though, working the Palace. I know what it's like.' Mrs Wright nodded at herself, having been on the halls before she got lucky and became a landlady.

'Ah well . . . when needs must . . .'

'I hope you got your boots on, it's snowing like anything.'

'Is it?' Harriet looked down at her pretty embroidered shoes. 'I'd better go back and change.'

On her second appearance outside the Wrights' apartment the singer was wearing her old boots, the embroidered shoes tucked into a dolly-bag, along with her little pots of eyes and lips. Through the hall-door window she saw that big snowflakes were beginning to lie. 'I'm off then. I'll say hello when I come in. I might be late.'

'That don't matter – you know Mr Wright likes to see who's coming into my house.'

Mrs Wright held that if any blame for vice on the streets of London be laid at anyone's door, it should be at the doors of men who used the girls – but men got off scot-free. Having narrowly escaped life on the streets, she did what she could to redress the balance by letting rooms to girls who were decent but down on their luck. So, 12 Great Coram Street was not a brothel, nor even a house of ill-repute – nowhere near that, because Mrs Wright took nothing extra from her girls if they brought a man-friend to visit. Just the rent when it was due. Her girls looked after her in other ways: a bit of fruit here, a tot or two there, a few hot pies . . . Little treats, free tickets to the shows – but no money except the rent.

Number 12 Great Coram Street then was a lodging house for young women. Like the rest of the long, brick-built terrace of iron-railed, large houses, it comprised a large basement kitchen and scullery, ground floor accommodation for the Wrights, and three other floors of rooms rented out to young women. Mrs Wright would never take men as boarders. Although there was a turnover of young women, they remained her girls.

Josephine Thomson. In her twenties, a journalist on the staff of The News, *one of the new-style and outrageous 'rags', as they were known. In her professional life, Josephine Thomson became Jemima Ferguson.*
When a church clock struck twelve, Josephine collected together the piece she had ready for her editor, Mr George Hood. Her career in journalism had started with contributions to the *English Woman's Domestic Magazine.* She chose her name because she had read an article concerning women's rights by an American woman whose name was Ferguson. To have used the name Thomson could prove awkward for her family, in particular her uncle James, who had brought her up as a daughter. Uncle James was Detective Superintendent

James Thomson – Thomson of the Met., well known far beyond his Bow Street manor for his modern ideas of policing, and his determination to transform the police from a body of men who were shown little respect by the public into a well-trained, well-equipped force. A man with such revolutionary ideas made enemies, so Josephine did not intend making matters worse by having the name Thomson tagged to any piece of mud she might throw in her columns.

Being ambitious and sure of herself, she had made this decision long before her name ever appeared attached to a column. A good decision on her part, now that she had joined *The News*. This had transformed itself by quadrupling a two-page Sunday rag into a daily paper that 'tickled', in Fleet Street terms.

> Tickle the public, make 'em grin,
> The more you tickle, the more you'll win,
> Teach the public, you'll never get rich,
> You'll live like a beggar and die in a ditch.

The News lived and expanded following this philosophy. Women columnists tickled the public, as did murder and scandal. Josephine liked to be given assignments where she could stir consciences and create indignation. Mostly it was here-today, gone-tomorrow journalism, but Josephine believed that constant irritation made people want to scratch – eventually. Once she began working in Fleet Street, she learned how to give an edge to her 'women's articles', and tried to give something more insightful than a paragraph or two of fact. Of course, the real plums were given to the men, but she had an ally in the editor, Mr Hood. It had been he who had 'stolen' her from *The Echo* a couple of years ago. That was when *The News* had transformed itself by bringing in Oxbridge men to try to give it some gravitas, but degrees in literature hardly ever gave those men a taste for the kind of 'tickle' that sold the paper: this came from the editorial talents of George Hood.

Josephine had 'tickle' in bags-full. Although that endeared her to her editor, it never brought her the plums she was ambitious for. However, she had faith that the future belonged to her and women like her. Her time would come.

Today, instead of handing the pages she had finished to the youth whose job it was to get them to the editor, she decided to take them herself to Mr Hood. Quickest way to get his approval – or not.

She would have given much not to have come into *The News* office today. She felt as though she might have caught a cold, the weather was worsening under a snow-laden sky, and the stove in her office had sulked.

But, when she had been offered a post as a 'filler' columnist – as opposed to the reviewer and fashion writer she had been with *The Echo* – she determined to prove herself equal to the Oxbridge men with their decent offices and time for lunch. This, of course, meant that, like other women in the profession, she had to be better than they were. Which was why she turned up regardless of colds, chills and freezing offices.

Josephine Thomson had determined to report on the lives of women, to be an investigator and reporter. And heaven alone knew there was much material here in London. The piece she had just completed was good. Mr Hood would like it. Death by starvation of an educated woman who had been unable to find work of any kind. Josephine – having picked her way through the apathy of other lodgers in the rooming-house, who themselves had come and gone as unrecognized and worthless as the woman known only as Jane – had pieced together the last weeks of Jane's life. Josephine's passion was evident in every seven-word sentence and five-line paragraph – the preferred style of *The News*.

As she made her way through the buzz of reporters at work and the familiar smell of cigar and tobacco smoke – and this morning wine, too, she was aware of the looks she got. They were not friendly. The male reporters who resented her most were those 'men of letters', 'Oxbridge men', men who had been persuaded to join *The News* for much the same reason as Josephine: to change the formula and appearance of the 'old rag', to give it a bit of dignity and gravitas and, in Josephine's case, to broaden its outlook. George Hood had warned her that in entering the world of male professional writers and male opinions, she had a hard furrow to plough. This, of course, did not daunt Josephine one jot. Her parents – missionaries of unorthodox views – had taught her and brought her up no differently from her twin brother.

The Thomson twins had a great sense of their own self-worth, while also valuing other people.

As always the door to the editor's office stood open. The name 'George Hood', and his title painted on the glass panel, was therefore not revealed until one was inside the room. 'Miss Ferguson, come in.'

'My piece about that woman Jane.'

'How many words?'

'Seven fifty. I know you wanted five hundred, but . . .'

He held out a hand for the copy, read swiftly, then nodded. 'But?'

'That's as spare as I can make it without it becoming . . . well, trivial.'

He read it over again quickly. 'I agree. We'll run it in the next edition.'

Josephine warmed with gratification. 'Anything else for me?'

'Not today. Going to your family?'

'Yes, I can't foresee a Christmas when I won't.'

'Was that a sigh?'

'No . . . well, yes . . . probably.'

'Families, eh? Can't do with 'em, can't do without 'em.'

'That about sums it up for me – not that I don't love them dearly.'

'What do they think of you? I mean, working here, it's not the most usual job for a young woman of your education. They must have very advanced views.'

Avoiding his eyes she answered reluctantly. 'They, um . . . they have no idea what I do.'

11

'I'm sorry, bad thing intruding on private life. I had assumed . . . sorry.'

'I left home some time ago. I have rooms, I share with another young professional woman. I have no parents.'

'Oh.'

'It's all right, I was orphaned when I was quite young, my uncle and his wife took me in and educated me. I am like a daughter to them – an only child, in fact. I owe them everything. I love them, too. They would never understand this world – well, my aunt wouldn't. My uncle knows it but wouldn't approve.'

George Hood pondered for a few moments on this uncle, but no ideas came immediately, nor could he think of a Ferguson who might fit the bill. 'What do they suppose you do with your time?'

'Write,' she smiled. 'I show them the pamphlets I have written up for one or two historical societies, and I have contributed to a London guide. My aunt is quite proud of me. Her friends ask me to produce little collections of kitchen receipts.'

A faint flicker of amusement crossed his face, and he arched his brows. 'Do they pay you?'

'They do. My aunt insists upon it, she tells them that they would not expect to get their hats trimmed free. Actually, they pay me quite well. Some of them have their collections printed up in little booklets of ten pages or so.'

'Do you get signed copies?'

'Actually, I do, I have quite a collection. It's a very good disguise for the work I do here.'

Now they both laughed outright. 'Miss Ferguson, you are a wonder.'

'I know, Mr Hood. I just need to prove that to the male reporters. They think I'm a joke.'

'I don't, and I am the only one who matters here. I brought you in because I had noticed your pieces for *The Echo*.'

'And you offered me a good arrangement to come to work on *The News*.'

'Just be patient, Miss Ferguson. Of course there is prejudice against women in professions.'

'Why "of course"? There doesn't have to be.'

'There doesn't have to be prejudice against producing newspapers every day of the year, but there is, and we can only chip away at rusty minds.'

Five years ago, the only females working on newspapers were in America, and mostly were daughters of owners and editors. Josephine might be a 'filler' writer, but at least she'd had no preferential treatment because she knew the right people. She had come to *The News* on merit. George Hood had noticed her work with *The Echo* and asked to meet her. The deal he offered was better than she could ever have expected. She had been bold in asking for more important assignments than 'Just for Women' pieces.

'Get you off, then.'

'Can I ask you something, Mr Hood?'

'Ask away.' He made a point of editing her piece as he talked to indicate that he was a busy man.

'When am I going to be given a chance to do

13

something that will get me on the front page? I can judge my own work, and I know that it's good. I like doing social conditions, but—'

'But nothing, Miss Ferguson. You are everybody's favourite She-Radical.'

'Everybody's what!'

'*The News*'s She-Radical.'

Josephine stiffened and drew back.

'From me, that is a compliment, Miss Ferguson.'

'I had no idea . . . I'd prefer to be thought of as a journalist, not a "she" anything. A journalist . . . a reporter like the rest. Do you have any He-Reporters, He-Overseas-Correspondents? Or . . . or He-Editors for that matter?'

'I like what you are . . . you wear your allegiance on your sleeve. Everything you write shouts Injustice, Unfairness, Favouritism. Readers warm to your indignation.'

Josephine stood there, speechless after her outburst. She took her work seriously, and put a lot of effort into her research.

Dropping his blue editing pencil, he got out of his seat and came out from behind his large desk.

If he patted her shoulder, or said one sweet word to placate her, she would walk right out.

He went to the window and looked down. 'When you come in tomorrow, I'd advise you to carry a shovel and get in some dry wood for that stove of yours.'

Josephine shook her head and wondered where her outburst had got her.

14

'Now don't get huffy at what I am about to say. You didn't apply to work on *The News*, we enticed you away. You were wasted on *The Echo*, filling their ladies' corners. *The News* is just finding its feet. One or two of the American dailies have got splendid women on their staff writing and reporting, the best ones being good writers. This business needs all the good writers it can get; if the Man in the Moon lands on Earth, what good is it if the reporter who sees it can't paint the word-picture for the rest of us?'

Josephine could only shrug her shoulders. He was stating the obvious.

'This piece,' he leaned over and picked up her Jane story, 'is a beautifully-written obit. to this woman. On this one page you have distilled the tragedy of a woman's life. You can *write*, Miss Ferguson . . . Jemima. You have an instinct that any of our BA and DLit word machines would give a lot to have. I'd swear none of them could whip up a storm and prick consciences in the same way as you have in Jane's story.

'I'll tell you something,' he continued, grinning and tapping the side of his nose, 'confidential. Now, the word "blood". Do you think there is any better description of . . . well, *blood*?'

'I don't. In any context it is the word I would use – life-blood, bloodstained, bloodshed . . . It is an evocative word.'

'Not the "crimson stream of life"?'

Smiling, she said, 'No, never the "crimson stream of life".'

'A dog's tail – a "cordial appendage"? An oyster a "succulent bivalve"? And coffee . . . oh yes, let coffee be "the fragrant berry of Mocha". You may well laugh, Miss Ferguson, but my blue pencil has often been needed to make our Oxbridge men into journalists. You, Miss, never use two words where one will do – and that one word will be choice.'

'So why am I not being given the chance to report on parliamentary debates, or something like that?'

Folding his arms across his chest, he looked her directly in the eyes, 'Is that what you *really* want? To sit in the House listening to men ("the male of our species") who, you will quickly learn, you are worth two of, day in, day out, writing up their boring speeches so that they sound profound for their constituents.'

'But those reports are prominent, and the correspondent's name is prominent too.'

'So?'

'So, people in power, MPs, members of the House of Lords, people who can change things . . . they read those articles and editorials.'

'Sorry,' he grinned, 'editor's job is taken.'

'My "Jane" will be read with breakfast and be gone by dinner.'

'And what do you suppose happens to the great chunks of editorials? Do you suppose that when the master throws down his newspaper, that his wife and subsequently his servants rush to read a report on a speech made in the House of Lords by Lord Tom Noddy on the price of pig iron?'

Josephine grinned in spite of herself.

'No, no, the great newspaper readers of this nation are those who turn to the tickle and titbit pieces – and that is not to say that tickle can't have serious content. *News* readers will remember "Jane's" life and death. There will be people, maybe just a few, who the next time they are about to turn a woman away because of some prejudice, will be a bit more understanding.'

'So, what are you saying, Mr Hood? That I must not aspire to the front page?'

'I am saying no such thing. You must aspire to the front page. To your own by-line. I am confident that you will have front page—'

'Even though I wear skirts?'

'The day will come when skirts will no longer excite comment in our world. Don't worry, it will come for you. It is a matter of finding something that will launch you. Something current, something we get before the opposition . . . and something that shocks the socks off our readers. And it will be something that the "Young Lions" won't have the passion or experience to handle. You will know when it comes, and so will I. Now, ' "Starved to Death in a Garret". Good, honest-to-God writing, but I shall alter that title, and make it a paragraph heading.' Josephine frowned. 'Don't worry, your words are safe. What I propose is placing it on the Obit. page, black-border it.' He squared his thumbs and fingers. "Jane" and her dates, by Jemima Ferguson.'

Taking a deep breath, Josephine let it out expressively.

'That's marvellous, Mr Hood. You're the best editor in London.'

'I know, that's why I get paid such a large salary and work such long hours. Now be off – and take this with you,' and handing her an envelope said, 'A bonus, a Christmas box . . . recognition that *The News* is pleased that you are with *us* and no longer with the opposition.' Returning to his desk he started marking up her work again. 'And don't forget what I said about a shovel and some dry sticks tomorrow.'

'Christmas Day tomorrow, Mr Hood.'

'Ah, yes, but I shall be here – at least for as long as I can to escape a house full of aunts and cousins and grannies.' He grinned. 'News editors have similar privileges to doctors and cabbies – a reason to be at work when families get too much.'

'You really love your work, don't you, Mr Hood?'

Spreading his hands, indicating the untidy office, he said, 'What is there not to love? Ambition fulfilled.'

'Merry Christmas, Mr Hood.'

'Thank you, Miss Ferguson.'

Back in her office, she opened the envelope. Twenty pounds! More than some could earn in a year.

She walked through the bustling streets where an icy wind whipped skirts and coat-tails, and flakes of snow were blown into corners of buildings where they settled in little pyramids. Christmas. She had always loved those few days of magic, ever since she had lived in England. Several family traditions had emerged from a single event – like Hani and Cooper, her aunt's general factotum, going out in the early hours to visit the flower market, and coming back with Cooper pushing a handcart laden with a tree and great bunches of chrysanthemums, holly, mistletoe and ivy. As a child 23 December had been the accepted beginning of the Christmas holiday. Uncle James kept well out of the way, coming home only when it was time to trim the tree – at least, coming home when his duties allowed. There had been times when he had sent a police messenger to say that he would be late but to wait for the tree. Aunt Ann would say, 'Wait for the tree, wait for the tree, does he think we can go many more hours with a naked tree?' But usually he came. Now Josephine was the one not to be there on the 23rd. It was still, in her mind, the start of Christmas, but she was creating her own traditions.

Yesterday evening had been the most enjoyable since she had left her uncle's Thames-side house at Chiswick to set up a home of her own. Boot Street was a world away in style from the sylvan area of Chiswick. Josephine's rooms – a few steps away from the very old timbered and jettied 'Boot Inn' – overlooked a busy street of shops, inns and dining rooms. She leased an apartment in a sub-stantial building that had been built in the time of King George; since its heyday as a town house, like most of the houses in the street, it had had its ground floor made over into shops. Josephine's independence consisted of four large first-floor rooms fronting the street. The lease was cheap and the entertainment constant: London life passed back and forth all day and much of the night. Two of the large, high-ceilinged rooms she sublet to

Liliana Wilde, a painter; they shared a kitchen and other facilities at the dark back of the house. Liliana also had rooms on the Left Bank of the Seine in Paris, and divided her life between the two.

Yesterday evening Josephine and Liliana and ten of their friends had gathered in the public dining rooms that were next door and up a few steps. There they had shared a long table and a feast of roast beef and rich pudding. Later they had retired to Josephine's big first-floor room, where, due to the lack of many comfortable chairs, they had sat on cushions on the floor, eating fruit and sugared plums and drinking coffee made in the French manner by Liliana. The aroma of ground coffee beans drifted along the hallway, mingling with cigar smoke – some of the women smoked small cigars, not because they particularly liked the experience, but because it was outrageous. Josephine's friends enjoyed rejecting conventions, not for the sake of it, but so that they would not let prejudice or snobbery preclude experience. Josephine didn't particularly enjoy the cigars, but she did like Scotch whisky – not often the chosen drink of women brought up in high society as she had been. Most of all she liked the freedom to do as she chose within her own rooms.

The first time they had organized this pre-Christmas gathering, there had been only Jo, Lili, her brother David and Christine. David Wilde was a 'notorious' preacher, and Christine Derry an art-lover, who held shows of paintings and sculptures in her Bloomsbury home. Liliana, David and Christine were all dissidents of a kind – not revolutionary, but unwilling to accept everything that society deemed acceptable. One of the men had met the reformer Edwin Chadwick and persuaded them to read his treatise, 'London Labour and the London Poor'.

Josephine had been very influenced by this, for although – like all of her 'comfortably off' friends – she saw poverty at almost every corner as she went about London, she had not understood its nature: that destitute people were part of the same society in which she lived, and that quite minor events, such as a girl not being given a 'character' from her mistress, could push her over the line and onto the streets. Any children she might have would never know anything else. But, although Josephine and her friends were often very serious in their talk, they also knew how to enjoy life.

She was able to make most of her purchases in Boot Street, where she was greeted as a valued customer and friendly neighbour. When she went into the interior of 'Zammit – Silversmith', the owner opened his palms and greeted her like a relation. 'Miss Josephine!' He grinned, showing teeth ground down from years of gritting them in concentration while practising his craft. 'You were right, look, my first modern piece, you remember I said that the colours . . . oh, the oddness . . . Egyptian, you said, soon all London will be asking for copies of the jewels of the ancients . . .' On and on he went, relating his protests and her insistences, until he unwrapped a piece of suede revealing a row of large squares of colours, silver-set and linked.

'Mr Zammit! That's absolutely beautiful, more than I imagined.' She ran a finger over the smooth surface of the small tiles of stone. 'Jasper?' He nodded. 'Hardstone? Obsidian?'

Nodding, he gently polished where her finger had touched the vivid stone. 'And not one piece of jet. A few people have seen me working upon it and agree with me that exotic pieces like these will become popular. I have got the boy to go to the museum and make drawings. I will show you when I have finished the drop-earrings in the style of miniature oil jars – amphorae, so he says.'

Josephine paid him, much less than his beautiful work warranted, but he insisted that he would gain when other women saw the bracelet and coveted one like it, so she purchased pairs of filigree earrings in more conventional style for her aunt and Hani.

Liliana as usual was engrossed in her work, the room fuggy with the smell of oil paints, turpentine, and wood smoke from a small log that had fallen from the fire and lay smouldering on the tiled hearth. Josephine was about to admonish her friend when she was shocked into speechlessness at seeing the portrait that Lili was in the act of signing in tiny letters. Liliana turned and beamed, 'Christmas present, Jo. Merry Christmas.'

Josephine stepped forward to look at the small portrait – of herself. Not a formal pose – Josephine had never sat for Liliana, and Liliana hardly ever painted portraits – but a half profile, head slightly tilted, captured as though Josephine had turned, leaned back and was about to ask a question as she sat at her desk.

'Say something. Do you like it?'

'Of course I like it, Lili. I love it . . . you have made me look quite beautiful.'

'Good Lord, woman, you *are* beautiful. I *have* got you, don't you think?'

'Definitely me, I wonder what I was asking you? How did you manage it without me sitting for you?'

'Josephine, when you are working away at that desk, you don't know what is going on around you. In effect you have been sitting for me from the day you took me in. I don't suppose you even realize how many times you look over your shoulder like that to call out to me.'

'Liliana Wilde, you are so talented. Is Christine going to put it in her show?'

'If you agree, it's yours now.'

'Of course I agree. It's the kind of thing that will get you commissions. Thank you, Lili.' She handed Liliana the jeweller's box. 'Merry Christmas. I wish I could say this is my work. But it *is* my design . . . Mr Zammit took a lot of persuading.'

When Liliana saw the variety and colour of the linked tiles, she drew a breath of surprise. 'Jo! *Your* design?'

'With a little help from some ancient Egyptians.'

'You should give up scribbling for a living and set up with Mr Zammit.'

Josephine glowed with pleasure. It was always difficult to choose gifts for an artist. She had, some months ago, dealt with her feelings of guilt at spending her money so frivolously.

David Wilde had helped her with that. 'Josephine, if

23

you continue to rub your conscience sore every time you spend for pleasure, then there is nothing for it but to disown what your parents left you, wear a blanket and sandshoes and carry your begging-bowl as some Eastern priests do. Of course, you might then add to society's problems. I believe that your friends would prefer it if you go on being the generous, considerate person that you are and enjoy the life God has given to you.'

When Liliana had said that her brother David was a preacher, Josephine's prejudice created in her mind a sober, opinionated man, but that was before she met him, before she had heard him say anything. Then, like the scores who went to listen to him speak in the open air of London's Hyde Park, and the hundreds who attended his meetings at St Giles (meetings, not orthodox Christian services, talks not sermons), she became charmed by his voice and manner. He certainly held strong opinions, and saw it as his duty to express them. For the most part his views turned out to be quite in line with Josephine's own. He was amiable, funny, the tone of his voice as easy to listen to as a professional singer, and the sincerity of his beliefs simple and honest. This ideal man might have become self-satisfied, except that he had Liliana for a sister, and Liliana had been keeping him in his place since she was four and he eight.

Also, he had enemies. Churchgoers who did not necessarily live very Christian lives, factory-owners who did not like what he had to say about the way they acquired their wealth, and most newspaper-owners.

The 'Rabble Rouser' or the 'Ranting Priest' was always good for several column inches. Fleet Street saw him as fair game to hold up to ridicule. Water off a duck's back.

David's words had been nice to hear, but Jo guessed that she would never be easy living comfortably whilst London teemed with hardship.

Detective Superintendent James Thomson of Bow Street 'E' Division. Well-known in the Metropolitan Police area for his advanced views on police methods. He firmly believed that the force would not be efficient and strong until the public respected the men they wished to protect them. This meant training – both police and public. He also believed that the future of detection must be in applying scientific methods at all scenes of crime, and ordered that there be no big boots until he himself or Sergeant Kerley had been called. Such attention to detail was almost unknown in a high-ranking officer.

Josephine's famous uncle, James Thomson, festooned with little parcels, put the key in the lock of his own front door and went to step inside, only to be greeted by his wife's firm voice, 'Boots, boots, James.' Handing her his parcels, he hooked off his elastic-sided overboots, only to be stopped again by Hani's soft voice, 'S'ippers, s'ippers, Mister James.'

Ann Martha Thomson, shutting the inner hall door against the icy blast that had accompanied James's entrance, then offering her pretty pink cheek for a kiss, asked, 'What's all this, James? Home so early . . . have Londoners stopped knifing one another?'

'What then, shall I go out and find a felon to keep me busy for an hour or two?' James Thomson at home was a genial and comfortable man to be with. James Thomson, Detective Superintendent Thomson of the Metropolitan Police, working out of Bow Street, was something else. There were times when he carried shreds of his profession home with him. Then he would shut himself away in a small room that was his own only because Ann Martha could see no use for it as part of her well-kept home. An iron stove, an old, large wooden table, an armchair and an old rocker.

'No, James, I am pleased that you will be here to welcome Josephine. I have one or two purchases still to make, and in any case I like to be out when it's snowing.'

'And nothing to do with the new fur-trimmed cloak and hood?'

Ann tripped lightly up the thickly carpeted stairs. 'Oh James, how well you know me!' Almost immediately she returned, now wearing the said cloak. James, seated on a bench inlaid in the new style, watched as she swooped around the hallway trying to produce the effect she hoped gusts of wind would have on the fur. 'Doesn't it just ripple beautifully, James?'

'Beautifully, Ann. It is amazing how rippling a few dead animals can be.'

'James!'

'Don't take on – I'm teasing. The cloak is beautiful,

much better on you than on the nasty little foxes. You have saved the lives of many chickens. Now go and enjoy the snowstorm.'

'You heard what I said about Josephine, you haven't forgotten?'

'Is it likely?'

'It's not unknown for you to doze.'

'I keep him 'wake, Miss Ann.'

Mrs Thomson smiled warmly at Hani. 'I'm sure you will,' and brushed a kiss on her husband's cheek, wafting a cloud of perfume around him. He had never discovered what it was, something discreet and elegant, probably very expensive – like Ann herself – lingering on the senses.

The warm tone of this little scene was unforced and quite usual. Detective Superintendent Thomson, Ann Martha and Hani. Harmonious under one roof where there was respect and a mutual caring. There used to be a fourth – Josephine. The light of all their lives.

It was Christmas Eve and they were each busy in their different ways, keen to shower her with affection as they had years ago when Hani had brought the orphaned child to London.

The interior of the Alhambra Palace was in direct contrast to the afternoon darkness and windy blasts of snow outside. Inside it was close and fuggy, lights burned around the walls, and spots lit up the stage. From time to time, the audience, some seated at tables, laughed and applauded. It didn't matter at what, the noise and music were at one with the atmosphere. Gaiety and Christmas cheer enveloped everyone as they entered, whether by the front of house or the stage door . . .

Young Man, age unknown. By the cut of his clothes, and the style of his hat, not English. Dark-haired. Not tall, but not short. Occupation unknown, but he appears excessively interested in the women who, between acts at the Alhambra Palace, often kept company with any man who appeared not to have a partner. He could make a single glass of beer last, taking sips of that as he took sips of the women.

Watching the parade of women – 'actresses', as some called themselves and some were – the young man was enjoying himself, a dark beer in one hand, a cigar in the other.

Back at the hotel on the far side of London, his wife would still be enjoying her fury but having to swallow it in the company of their fellow countrymen.

Until this morning, it had been weeks since he'd had satisfactory marital relations with her. Marital relations was her phrase, his own was coarser, something else to add fuel to her fire of resentment. Well, she was the one who had suggested the venture. If she regretted it, it was now far too late. No going back. Even though there had been a hiatus and they found themselves unexpectedly in England, there was still no going back.

Soon after their arrival at Kroll's German Hotel and their bags were taken up, she had slipped the latch against him. The latch had been as easily overcome as she had herself. He had thrust his strength, first against the fastened room and then against her body, and gained easy entrance to both. He had pushed her onto the bed, lifted her skirts and opened his trousers. Straddling her face, he had forced her to look at his erection. 'No more excuses. We can enjoy ourselves for as long as we like. The bed is sprung, the walls are thick and the room next to this is mine.'

For many days now she had pleaded menstruation as the reason. Before that it had been fear of an untimely pregnancy, and always the claim that, aboard ship, the walls to the cabins were paper thin and that she would never be able to face other passengers who might overhear the crudity of his love-making.

Not here, she said. When we get to our new country.

No, no, not now, she said.

Not tonight. Wait a little.

Others will hear us.

Be patient, she said.

Wait until we have a room to ourselves.

At the last moment he withdrew, spilling semen over her, and saw that this time she was actually telling the truth about her long-lasting menstrual condition.

It was then she had spat at him. 'Brute!' Literally spat. 'Lecher!' He had slapped her very hard on her buttocks, had felt neither brutish, debauched nor lecherous – only extraordinary. Standing where she was forced to look at him, he used her petticoats to wipe away her blood. Its intensity of colour on the white petticoat had excited him into erection again, making him feel doubly powerful.

This time he expelled himself inside her, confident that there could be no pregnancy whilst she bled.

He would never again accept that as an excuse. Wallowing in her blood was more exciting than he could ever have imagined.

Thoughts of how it would be when they were once again en route for Brazil, and yet again when they arrived and he was leader and responsible for the future of an entire colony of souls and bodies, including *hers*. All of them relying upon him to create a future. *She* of all of them was entirely reliant upon him. If she did not like the life he intended for them, to whom could she complain? She could write all the letters home she liked; he could let them go, or not, as he pleased. It was her extravagance and love of position and high-life that had brought them to the very edge. Only his own wits and shrewd planning had brought them back from the brink. She used to be outrageous and funny, daring him, drawing him into her fantasies of love. Love! He realized too late that she wasn't capable of love. Only of sexual excess – but on her terms. All those, 'No, no, not now. Not tonight. Wait a little. People will hear what we are doing. Wait until we have a room to ourselves.'

Well, that morning they had had a room to themselves, and in a moment of revelation he realized that he had been master all along. He could do as he pleased. She could not leave him; she was attached to him now. She had burnt her boats along with his. She could go nowhere, except with him.

His hand warmed and his heart swelled at the memory

of that subduing slap. All that he wanted from her was passivity. He would give her pleasure, he liked to do that, but only when she was passive. In their early days together, there had been such fever in her. He had loved to take her almost to ecstasy, but then withhold until she had performed some novelty on him, and then, if she would only lie quietly, he would give her satisfaction.

He felt the beginnings of arousal as he remembered how submissive she had become this morning, how explosively he had ejaculated.

A new actress came in.

At the side of the bar, the young man watched as she took off her boots, gave them to the barmaid, who stowed them behind the bar and slipped on some pretty embroidered shoes, after which she bought a tot of something and stood for a while, chatting to the barmaid in a low voice. He could not hear what she said, but was pleased to see from their glances that he was their topic.

Harriet said, 'Haven't seen him before, Tryphena, have you?'

Tryphena Douglas gave a section of the bar counter a hard polish. 'No, and I can't say as I mind if I don't see him again. He's been hanging on to that drink for an hour. I don't mind them hanging around, except if they don't shell out for a drink or two. Anybody'd think I was a charity.'

'He doesn't look too bad to me.'

'Full of himself.'

'Aren't they all?'

'Harriet, love. Don't get yourself all upset. Have you heard from him?'

'Oh yes, he writes regular, describes all the goings-on aboard ship, and the ports where they have to stop off. Last letter, he said the temperature was over one hundred.'

'And do you reckon you'd like that?'

'Of course I will, and it's not as hot as that where we shall be. He says the temperature is lovely, like summer all the year round. Can you imagine that? Not having to huddle around half the year trying to keep out the chill; always wearing lawns and silks.'

'When do you think he'll send for you?'

'As soon as he gets settled in a bigger house – the one he had before was just a bachelor place.'

Tryphena, worldly-wise, thought, Oh yes, he's sure to do that, just like he's sure to marry you. Harriet Burton wasn't silly, just too trusting of any man who was kind to her. And here she was, calling herself 'Clara' once again, 'Clara' because the man who arranged bookings for her said that was a better name for a performer. Here she was, back on the halls, doing her singing act because another man left her. Here she was, 'Clara Burton', bottom of the bill, Christmas Eve, looking for a man who would buy her a meal and a few drinks. 'See you later, Harriet. If you ask me there's something queer about a chap who wears a hat like that.'

True, it was a strange style. Harriet caught his eye, still

smiling at Tryphena's comment about the hat. Young, not bad looking, decently dressed. Tryphena said that he was careful, but he looked as though he could afford a bit of supper, and the rent she owed Mrs Wright. She had made her pick. He would do.

As he made his way to the bar, Harriet smiled briefly, shyly.

Like me, please like me. I'm not a bad girl.

The young man indicated to the barmaid that he would buy Harriet a drink. He had made his pick. She was the one. She would do. A pretty head held erect on a delicate neck. A submissive type, he could see that. And, by the look of the boots hidden behind the bar, she would not be the sort of London woman he had been told about, who would fleece a man of his last coin. He had never had an Englishwoman before. The idea appealed to him very much, although he couldn't explain why that was. Perhaps it was merely that she wasn't the one to whom he had somehow found himself married. Well, not actually *found* himself married. He needed a wife. There was no way that he would have been appointed to start a colony had he been an unmarried man.

The Thomsons' servants had been told not to pull curtains across the windows yet. 'It looks so welcoming and seasonal to see lamps glowing in every house.' As well, Ann Martha Thomson did not mind too much if passers-by caught glimpses of her art, which was the creation of beautiful interiors.

Josephine, who had come across London in an omnibus, alighted at the end of the square, not that there was much chance of Aunt Ann seeing her niece using that form of transport. Jo was very much her own woman now that she had her own accommodation, but it did no good going against Aunt Ann's wishes that Jo should always travel by cab. She did a deal with a street urchin to carry her bags from the bus to the house.

'Ha'penny *and* a bag of hot ches'nuts.'

'Lord save us, you drive a hard bargain.'

'I wouldn't have the strength to lift yer bags, miss, 'less I have a bit of something warm in me belly.' He could read her like a book. He knew she was soft.

Jo carried the chestnuts inside her muff to make sure that he kept his part of the bargain.

One day . . . one . . . day I'm going to write about these little lads. 'Here, give me one of the bags.'

'Not likely, you said a whole penny.'

'You'll get it. Come on, your arms will snap off.' As he still appeared reluctant, she bent down and said quietly, 'I can easily carry them myself, but I don't want my auntie to know I came here on a 'bus, because I shall get a good ticking off if she finds out.'

The boy found that reasonable.

Just before they reached the house, she gave him the penny, put chestnuts in both side-pockets of his man-sized jacket then, slipping her black fur muff from its cord, she placed it on his head. The boy jumped back, 'Here, what d'you want to go and do that for?'

'Keep your head warm.'

'You're right, it is that, but it must look pretty daft. Never heard of a chap wearing a muff on 'is head.'

'Do you know what a Cossack is?' He shook his head, wondering what this queer woman would come up with next.

'They are soldiers who live in Russia, where the snow gets as deep as houses. If they don't keep their heads warm, it freezes their brains, so they wear fur hats. In fact if they saw you wearing that, they would think you were one of them.'

He didn't know whether to believe her or not. But the hat felt a treat, the smell and warmth of the chestnuts seemed like it was pouring down his neck. 'Somebody will think I pinched it.'

'If any person says it's not yours, tell them Miss Josephine Thomson gave it to you – and if they need proof, then you just bring them to this house, and I will soon tell them to recognize the truth when they hear it.'

He grinned at her, showing a few half-grown second teeth.

Dear Lord forgive us! Working on the streets and still with baby teeth in his head.

'What's your name?'

'Who wants to know?'

'Me, because I am a polite person and I like to give people a name when I am speaking with them.'

'What's yours?'

'I've just told you.'

'Oh yes, Josafeen. I never knew nobody called that.'

35

'Well you do now. Now, come on, tell.'

'Micky Smiff . . . *th*.'

'Is it Michael, really?'

'How d' you know that?'

'Because I'm quite old, and I've picked things up over the years. My head's full of bits of information like that. Can I call you Michael?'

'You can, but I don't expect you'm be likely to see me again. Well, not unless you gets off the bus at Coram's Fields or round there. That's my patch.'

'If I give you another penny, will you promise not to spend it today?'

He didn't reply at once. 'If you *gives* us a 'nother penny, then it's mine.'

Jo nodded.

'Then you can't tell me what to do with it – because it's mine.'

It was too serious a statement for Jo to smile at. 'You're right, Michael. I have absolutely no right to interfere in your life or the way you spend your well-earned money.'

She handed him his penny and moved towards the glass porch of her aunt and uncle's house. The lamps within sparkled the glass panels, making her wish that he would go so that she could pull the bell. She didn't want him to watch her welcomed and disappear into the orange glow. Consciences were not salved by pennies and chestnuts.

'Miss, why do you think I ought to hold on to one penny?'

'I suppose I thought you might go throwing it around and somebody might wonder how you came by it and make trouble for you.'

'It's all right, some days I can make as much as thruppence. It's the hat that I'll have to be careful about.'

As he disappeared into the falling snow she watched as he cracked open a chestnut, threw it in the air and caught it expertly in his open mouth.

Frank Kerley. Detective Sergeant, Metropolitan Police Force, 'E' Division, Bow Street, London. An exact 5 feet 11 inches, fair skinned, light haired, broad and healthy at thirty-eight years old.

The Kerleys' house was up three steps. One of a long terrace of well-kept homes of lower middle-class families. Door brasses polished daily, lace curtains regularly washed and starched, and windows cleaned of London grime every Friday.

Today, Frank Kerley noticed that, instead of the healthy aspidistra which was usually placed centrally in the front window, Elizabeth had stood a small fir tree bedecked with baubles and tinsel and small gifts wrapped in red paper. She had done the same every year since Christmas Trees became popular. In the hallway she would have hung a large bunch of mistletoe, and behind every picture and mirror would be sprigs of holly. As he entered, he was not disappointed. Home for Christmas. He wished himself a bit of a good time for himself, Elizabeth and Frances this

year. A plain-clothes detective sergeant in Superintendent Thomson's hand-picked company of men, Sergeant
Kerley was well aware that wishing had nothing to do
with being home for Christmas. But still, delegation
being the super's philosophy, unless some particularly
heinous crime was committed during the next couple of
days . . .

Elizabeth Kerley's heart lifted when she heard the
jangle of Frank's keys, the creak of the front door
followed by a resolute cleaning of snow from his boots
on the coconut mat. 'Are you there, Elizabeth Kerley?'

'You know I am, Francis.'

'Well, come here and let's see if this mistletoe works.'

She appeared from the kitchen, her face alive with
pleasure, her apron showing signs of baking. 'It works
all right, I tested it on the milkman.'

They kissed one another as they had always kissed,
with passion and deep affection and good humour.

Harriet Burton. Josephine Thomson. Detective Superintendent Thomson. Detective Sergeant Frank Kerley, and
a young man who thus far has no name – all with plans
for the Christmas holiday.

Harriet Burton appeared twice on stage that evening.
She decided that, instead of something from her usual
repertoire, she would sing a Christmas carol. It went
down well and the stage manager said that she could
have a second spot later. When she went back to the
bar, Tryphena, the barmaid said, 'Your bloke must be

keen, he's passed over two or three of the girls who gave him the eye.'

'Well, he's going to have to wait, I've got a second turn to do.'

'You'll be in the money, then.' She nodded in the direction of the young man who was now seated at a table. 'You could tell him to sling his hook.'

'I thought about having a day in the country tomorrow . . . visiting. And I still owe this week's rent.' Harriet smiled cheerfully at Tryphena. 'Anyway, if he really wants me, I reckon I'll get supper out of him.'

'I told you, he don't seem that free with his money.'

'We'll see.'

The Thomsons' house was pretty, in a pretty part of London, beside the River Thames. Built in modern times, it had the advantage of stylish detail that could be ordered from a catalogue, and a terrazzo laid by Italian specialist gangs who were working their way through England, creating – in halls and glass orangeries – elegant stone floors inlaid with classical patterns.

Everything had been new when Josephine landed up here as a child. It still looked as fresh today, but many things within had been changed. Ann Martha Thomson was a great lover of the latest innovation and of style. It was a wonderful home to enter, and although Josephine now had a modest place of her own, she still enjoyed returning to the home in which she had grown up.

Surprisingly it was Uncle James who opened the door to Josephine.

'Uncle James! What are you doing at home so early in the day? Has London gone all honest, or have you got all the villains locked up?'

'Josie! I am beset by women who talk as though I am never at home. Not too grown-up for a kiss?'

'I shall never be that, Uncle James.'

'Good. You certainly look grown-up. Your hat is white with snow. You should be using a muff over those thin gloves.'

'Muffs are for old ladies. Who cares about snowy hats? It's Christmas and I'm happy and absolutely ravenous for some crumpets and tea.'

The familiar clip-clop of heeled slippers and Hani's gentle voice. 'Almond cake too, 'osie.'

'Hani, Hani, my darling Hani.' Jo clasped the exotic little woman and started to hug the life out of her.

'Stop it, silly gir'.' Hani's normally impassive features creased with joy.

Of course . . . and almond cake.

All the traditional English foods.

Josephine, shedding her outdoor clothes, looked at herself in one of the many mirrors that Ann Martha used to bring lightness into every room, and approved of herself. The skirt of her new street costume was a great success: tiered pleating, along with the hemline which was well clear of the ground, allowed Josephine to walk quickly and with longer strides than Aunt Ann's springy paces.

James Thomson put a fond arm about his niece's shoulder and guided her up a few steps towards the orange glow from red coals and peach-shaded lamps that radiated from the front room and shone out onto the street. Hani started to pull the curtains across, but James halted her. 'A little longer, Hani, you know how Mrs Ann likes to look in upon her handiwork.'

'Also street-feefs see what you have.'

'Street feefs also know that "Thomson of the Yard" lives here, so stop worrying.'

Hani's position in the household had always been ambiguous. She was neither servant nor family, yet the household would not function as perfectly as it did, nor the family be as united as it was without Hani. Between leaving Malacca and arriving in England, Hani had been all the family that Josephine had. London had been a shock for both of them. Hani, not much more than a girl herself in those days, was the means by which the girl Josephine had come to accept that a dirty city in a cold country would be her home.

'Where is Aunt Ann?'

'Gone out in the snow to fly her new foxes.'

'Miss Ann Mar'a has new cloat. Is very fine, suit her very much.'

'Uncle James – has he been teasing her again, Hani?'

Hani wagged her head and smiled, 'I think she don't mind.'

'She loves it. It shows her I notice, and I should soon be told of it if I tried outright flattery.'

'Go wash hands, 'osie.'

Jo went, as she had always done, at Hani's firm command, answering back childishly, 'I'm not a child any more, Hani.'

'I say you wash hand. I bring tea. Quick now.'

'It's not tea-time yet.'

'Tea-time when I say, 'osie. You have more tea-time when MisAnn come home.'

Jo was glad to get rid of the smell of roasted chestnuts. Maybe, though, I should keep wearing the smell to remind me that there are children who don't have crumpets and almond cake. Jo's conscience often tried to guide her to the high moral ground, but her resolve was weak.

This troublesome conscience was a legacy from her father. From an early age she and her twin brother Joseph had had to learn how to deal with being privileged in a land where poverty lay outside the gate, along the dusty track, becoming denser as it infested the city streets. He had not lived to complete the job he had started, teaching his daughter how to cope with the world. But in many ways he lived on in his brother, James, alike physically and with a well-developed sense of duty. But Father could never have done the same work as Uncle James. Josephine was proud of Uncle James.

Maybe she should tell him that. Yes. And tell Aunt Ann that she loved her for having taken on such an angry child, and the stubborn young woman who would not leave the child in a strange country. The child soon settled, but Hani stayed on, each year saying that she must soon return to her home. It was pretty certain that

Hani would go home once Josephine was settled in a good marriage. Josephine had told her often enough that the love of her life was her work. Big joke, Josie, silly gir' must not wait long time, man not want old women for marriage.

As she washed her hands in the warm water that flowed from a tap, she looked into her own eyes, facing her in the mirror – a very modish mirror she noticed, new since she was last here. What else was new? She and Aunt Ann would take a tour later, looking at the changes made. There would be changes. There always would be whilst Ann was mistress of a London house.

Hani was here now, living in Uncle James's household. Under five foot tall, smooth skinned, delicately boned, beautiful as a moonflower, moving about as she had done in her parents' medical missionary compound in Malacca. Softly, unobtrusively taking care of the details of the household. Hani was as near to a mother as Jo had now, and Uncle James as near to a father. Ann Martha? Younger than her husband, perhaps more like an older sister to Josephine. An older sister with firm views on society and how one lives in it, and the proprieties to be observed to keep the wheels of social intercourse running smoothly. An older sister who was sensible enough to see that, as she and her husband's niece had dissimilar views on women's roles, their relationship would be all the stronger if Josephine were allowed to set up in rooms of her own.

During the time when Josephine had for the first time shown how serious she was about having rooms of her own, life in the Thomson household had been difficult. Josephine had reverted to speaking only Malay, until came a day when Hani had packed the small bag with which she had arrived, and walked into the room where the three Thomsons were sitting at breakfast.

'I go back where children know their place in family, and fathers are wise to let grown daughters go from home. This daughter is good. She not bring shame on us. Josie – you now speak English, I am not your language servant.'

This was probably the longest speech in English that Hani had ever made. It worked. Josephine took rooms, but on the condition that she let one room to another woman. Hani stayed on with the Thomsons.

On Jo's way to the sitting room, Aunt Ann swept in, a swirl of red fox and snow. 'Josephine! My dear girl, there you are. Now the celebrations can truly begin.' Aunt Ann pressed her cheek to Jo's with warm affection.

'Aunt Ann! That cloak! It is exactly your style.'

'You think so? I knew that you would think so. Your undiscerning uncle referred to dead animals . . . well, of course they *were*, but not any more.'

'Absolutely, they have gone to heaven and come back as beautiful trimmings to suit your hair and complexion.'

Aunt Ann kissed her again, and, as the soft fur brushed her face, Josephine understood its appeal, as little Micky Smiff had with the muff on his head. Perhaps there would come a time when Jo would be ready to step out in furs, but not yet, not for a hundred years or more. Until then she would stick to her high necks and plain and practical skirts and a wonderful cashmere shawl that she used daily.

'Where's Hani?'

'Where do you think, Aunt, in the sitting room, hovering over the chafing dish.'

'Oh, she has been so excited, click-clacking all over the house. She has emptied Covent Garden of chrysanthemums.'

Jo laughed, having already seen some of Hani's exotic arrangements of flowers and bamboo sticks.

'I will just take my things into the airing room and then I shall be with you. Josephine, dearest, I can't tell you how much we shall love having you with us again.' She spoiled it slightly by adding, 'If only for a short while.'

'I am looking forward to my visit.'

'Josephine, I should quite like it if you would use my name without the "aunt".'

'All right, Ann, so I shall. Maybe you could call me Josie.'

'I don't think so, dear, Josephine is such a beautiful name. Your parents chose it, so I think we should keep to it.'

Josephine went through into the glowing sitting room where the small woman, who still had only sufficient English on which to get by, said everything that was necessary with her eyes: *My dearest child, you are here, my life is complete, my heart is full and I shall not give one thought to the time when you leave again.* 'Crumpets, 'osie, eat.'

'I suppose you won't sit with us, Hani?'

Hani smiled. 'Is plenty butter, 'osie.'

As always, right from when Jo and Joseph were little, Hani had made the rules. Hani in the room attending to food and comfort, organizing every meal down to the smallest detail. With the family, but not of it. Nothing to do with status, as Father had once explained when the twins had said he must tell Hani that she should eat with them. 'Hani chooses to be with our family in her own way. Don't embarrass her by expecting her to change to our ways. Has it ever occurred to you that she might find our ways at the table strange, even unpleasant?' No, it never had. Hani was a law unto herself.

The Thomsons knew that Hani would not stay with them for ever. Josephine too wondered about that, now that she herself was in rooms of her own, but she didn't like to think about it. Recently, she had been turning over in her mind the idea of having Hani to live with her. There was a spare bedroom, but what on earth would she do when Jo was off and about, as she was most days, often working long into the evening in her office? Josephine had no idea of Hani's age: say she was seventeen when she accompanied Josephine to England, she could be approaching thirty now. Hani was probably still young enough to have a husband and children. In her own country, but not here. England, and London in particular with its grey pavements and solid brick buildings, seemed to be too heavy and dark for her.

Overcome with love for Hani, Jo jumped up and twirled Hani round.

'Oh Hani, Hani, Hani.'

'You tell 'osie stand in wall-corner till she know manner, Mister James, Miss Ann Martha?'

Four people woven together by tragedy and love. Jo leaving to set up on her own had pulled a thread, but it had held, and the three older members had not demurred when she left, but still waited for her to return. Hani kept Josie's room always ready for when she would want to come back and live in the circle again.

It would not happen.

'What y' got there, kid?'

A scabby hand reached out for Micky Smith's bit of fur.

'Get off, it's mine.'

'Let's have a look then.'

'No! You'll only take it.'

'I won't, honest.'

'Get out of my way. This is my patch.'

'I don't want yer bleedin' patch, I wants to have a see of that ear-warmer.'

'It's a sojer's hat.'

'Queer sort of sojer.'

A wide figure stepped in front of Micky's assailant. 'And you're a queer sort of feef. Get off and leave the kid to hisself.'

The aggressor sloped off.

'You all right, Micky?'

'Yeah, I'm all right. Here, Chink, want a couple of ches'nuts?'

Chink crushed the shells easily and picked out the

cooked centre. 'I tell ya', if he gets after you again, fake as if you're going to run off, then get your heel up under his bollocks, hard.'

The yellow-skinned youth and the skinny white boy laughed at the thought. 'OK, Chinky.'

'Anyway, what is that thing – did you feeve it?'

'Truth, it was give to me by a customer. Best thing I had in my whole life. You can try it if you like.'

'Nah, don't want to breed your fleas along of mine.' Chinky's eyes disappeared into thin lines when he laughed. 'Tell you what, though. If you was to turn it inside out, you'd have the fur against your ears which'd be warmer, and feefs like that one won't be so interested.'

Micky turned the hat. Yeah. It felt good. Chinky was all right. He was quite old, probably a man, but Micky couldn't tell with Chinks. Anyway, Micky knew that Chinky was all right.

A warm, wonderful smell of grilled chops and cigar smoke rushed to surround Harriet Burton as the waiter opened the door for her, reawakening her hunger pangs, which had been kept dormant for hours by a tot of Irish and a glass of stout. The stout had been only temporarily filling, and, although her hunger was for meat, she did not hurry as she followed William, the assistant head waiter, to a table close to the side, halfway down the room. She was a regular client here and, although he guided her to her usual table, he went through the motions of asking whether this position pleased her without reference to her young male companion, who followed in sullen silence.

She smiled directly at the waiter, as though he had done her a favour by offering this table. 'William, thank you, this is splendid.' He held the chair and she arranged her full skirts, then the waiter moved a chair under the surly-looking man.

Harriet liked William. Whenever she went to the Cavour restaurant he saw to it that she was served a man-sized dish. It was he who had recommended stout because of its nourishing qualities, and Harriet had very much taken to the taste of it. He also always referred to her as a professional soprano.

'What's on the board tonight, William?'

It was the usual fare, but he presented the food as something exceptional and to the occasion. 'Ah, madam, tonight we have some splendid grilled chops. Or, if you prefer it, steaks? Finest tenderloin. Then there is fowl also. Yes, the fowl is excellent. Succulent, roast or boiled, both hot or cold.'

She enquired of the young man, 'Boiled fowl would be nice, don't you think?' to which he acquiesced with just a curt, 'Cold for me.'

'The cold boiled fowl is particularly good, sir.'

'Thank you, William, and for me. Plenty of chutney and potatoes mashed with cream.' William smiled, nodding approvingly at her nutritious choice. 'And William, ask Oscar to fetch me a bottle of stout and serve it now.'

Oscar, the head waiter, always dealt with the drinks.

He considered the pretty singer an adornment to the establishment, particularly when she came into the dining room still wearing the fine feathers in which she performed on stage at the Alhambra. Not that she was ever in other than good gowns and accessories of quality. He flourished the bottle, making much of the pouring of the stout. This was the first time he had seen her without at least one piece of nice jewellery. He hoped that this didn't mean that she had been forced to pawn them.

Harriet liked it when there were men around her. She knew that she possessed an aura of fragility and femininity. She had a magnetism that drew them to her. Until recently, since she had come to live in London, she had seldom wanted for a protector. Not casual protectors, but men who were bachelors or widowers who set her up in comfortable apartments and bought her pretty clothes, jewellery and adornments, and who stayed for months, even a year or more.

But how they did all want to '*improve*' her. All of them, in one way or another, told her how they loved her. She was graceful and lovely, she was carefree, generous and good-hearted – all this and more. And then, to a man, they set about trying to change her, improve her. Her most recent protector had gone back abroad where he was to make ready a home for the two of them. He would be almost there by now, and it would only be a matter of a few weeks until she would be able to collect her own ticket from his agent.

Just at this moment, Christmas Eve, she was a bit down on her luck, owning more pawn tickets than pieces of jewellery, and she was hungry. The man who would pay for supper was perhaps terse and less generous than she was used to, but if she went to bed satisfied with meat and brandy, she could easily stand his silence.

'Isn't this good? The Cavour always has very good fowls. Are you enjoying it?'

'I like it. You eat it all, you do not waste what has to be paid for.' This was about the longest sentence he had put together. She could tell that he was a foreigner, but he spoke in a low tone, as if he didn't want to be overheard. She had wondered if he couldn't speak English, but so far he had managed to buy her a tot at the Alhambra, and then negotiate a half-sovereign to go to her room. But she had insisted, 'First, a decent supper, and you pay for the omnibus tickets.' He couldn't have pondered longer had it been a deal between nations.

She always included food in her negotiations with men. Why else would she go with a casual if it wasn't to keep body and soul together? Money they might try to get back, but they couldn't do that with a decent meal and a couple of drinks.

'Don't you worry about me wasting food. Look, I can't keep on chatting to you if you won't tell me your name. Go on, call yourself anything you like. Who's going to know?'

In a low voice, he said, 'You call me Karl.'

'Ah, ha.' Harriet playfully waved her fork at him. 'That's what I've been trying to place. First off I thought you were Dutch – Dutch sailors always like the Alhambra.' She leaned forward and laughed lightly, the mixture of rum and stout relaxing her and making it easier for her to flirt. 'They like the Alhambra because it doesn't matter if you don't know a word of English. A lot of the acts are dancers and conjurors and trapeze artists. But Karl's a German name. You're a German, right?'

'Is not necessary to speak so aloud.'

'I'm not, this is just normal conversation. Sorry, Karl, I . . .' She noticed he looked at all the tables near enough to overhear, but nobody was interested.

She hoped that when he had eaten a good supper and had a couple more drinks he would join in the party-like atmosphere that was gathering in the restaurant.

'Do you celebrate Christmas much at home?'

'We do.'

'Of course you do, it was our queen's husband who thought of Christmas trees.' She smiled at him. 'A good idea, it's really become the fashion.' Harriet lowered her voice and shielded her words by her glass. 'You know our queen married a German?'

'Of course.'

'Germans are very popular since he became her husband – prince consort, not king.'

'Oh yes. But he is now dead.'

'Terrible. Just over ten years now. But the queen still favours anything German, you know.'

'Does she? Are you not eating this?'

'Um . . . all right, you can have it if you like.'

He scooped up the large portion of forcemeat, transferred it to his own plate and served himself some pickles and more potato yellow with butter and cream.

At the end of the meal not a scrap of food was left. She hoped that he was satisfied that they had eaten everything he was going to pay for. William came to remove the dishes, and Oscar to ask how they would like their coffee.

Karl shook his head. Harriet ignored him. 'A large pot, if you please, Oscar. French roast . . . heavy cream, and brandies.'

Oscar didn't consult Miss Burton's friend, but went off quickly to give orders to the kitchen. The man had not been pleased. Oscar didn't want him as a regular, and hoped that the young lady's luck would soon turn.

Harriet waited whilst the young man carefully counted out the coins to pay Oscar's wife who was seated at the little desk beside the door. Oscar handed her the bag containing her evening shoes. 'Have you got another booking soon, Ma'am?'

'Yes, two in fact.'

'Good, so I hope you'll pay us a visit. Are you doing anything special tomorrow?'

'I thought I would have a day in the country. I have a sister who begs me to visit, so I think that I shall, provided the snow doesn't lie too deep.'

'I think the gentleman is ready to leave.'

'Let him wait. Did any man ever find it so difficult to buy two liqueur brandies?'

Oscar held open the exit door. 'Goodnight, Ma'am, and a Merry Christmas. Good night, sir.' He did not add his usual hope that sir would pay the Cavour another visit.

* * *

On the omnibus travelling to the whore's room, the young man was irritated with himself for having let her have a name: that had been stupid. He withdrew into himself, ignoring the chatter that went on between her and some other women she knew.

There was ice in the air when they alighted. Although they had travelled a fair distance, he had made mental notes so that he could find his way back to his hotel. She pulled at his arm. Apples this time. She was certainly proving more expensive than he had anticipated. Women were alike when it came to getting them to open their drawers. They always wanted something. Marriage was the biggest payment. This one had said a half-sovereign and supper, and he had agreed before he had calculated how much this was in English money. And now apples. He let her carry them.

'Here we are then.'

He looked up at the house. It appeared to be very respectable. As they entered, a woman looked out into the hallway, checking to see who was coming in.

'Hello, Mrs Wright, this is a friend, just coming in to have a night-cap. Haven't got a couple of bottles of stout have you?' Mrs Wright had. Harriet twiddled her fingertips at the friend, indicating that he should pay.

Mrs Wright craned her neck to follow the man's progress up the stairs to where he waited on the landing. With a sardonic look, 'Isn't he just the eager type?'

'I only hope he's just as eager to go home. If you just hold on a minute please, Mrs Wright, I'll be back down with the rent arrears. Meantime, here are some apples for being so patient. I'll just take a couple, one for myself for the morning.'

When Harriet Burton returned with the half-sovereign, she was quite gleeful. 'I thought I might have had to squeeze it out of him.'

'Tight?'

Harriet Burton grinned. 'As my pa would have said, "tight as a bull's bum in August".'

Mrs Wright laughed, 'Well, I can't say as I ever heard that, but you got something out of him. Just tell him he's got to be out before morning. No breakfasts, tell him. I don't run a hotel.'

'Don't want him gone more than I do. I'd like to have a good sleep-in tomorrow.'

'Breakfast won't be till late, we're just having a few drinks round the fire tonight. We'll give you a knock when breakfast is ready.'

'You're a gem, Mrs Wright, I never had such a good landlady before. You won't get trouble from me.'

Christmas Morning 1872

In the two hours he had been with her, the man had twice gratified his lust. The second time – after she had gone downstairs for more bottles of beer – he suspected that, although she had gone through the motions of response and made the sounds of pleasure, she had actually been half asleep and half intoxicated. He didn't mind at all, he was able to enjoy her without being called 'brute!' She even snored a little as he turned her face down and sat astride and entered her as he had never tried with his wife. There was blood on him as he withdrew. He mopped it with his handkerchief, recalling the earlier episode with his wife's petticoats.

When he turned her over again, she was as pliable as a rag doll. As he was bending close to see whether she was breathing, her eyes snapped open close to his own. 'Got your money's worth?' Her speech was slurred. 'Reg'lar ol' Jew-boy you are.' Briefly tugging at his member she opened her eyes for a moment and made horns of her fingers. Her head fell back onto the pillow and she closed her eyes, a faint smile on her lips.

In the glow of the small nightlight he looked at his pocket watch. He had spent more time here than he had anticipated, but it was worth it. The last mauling of her would stay with him. Once the Christmas holiday was over, he knew only too well that it would be a return to his own fists and fantasies, but he was going to take with him a fantasy that he had never expected to have any chance of living.

Through the fringe of her lashes, she watched as, with his back to her, he sat on the bed and checked his money and numerous things he carried in his pockets. He was going. Thank God for that.

She closed her eyes and let herself drift into a deep, warm sleep. She did not hear him take a bite from the apple, nor feel him pull the counterpane up to her chin, did not hear him pour water from the jug into the hand-basin and wash his hands, did not see him pull on his trousers and jacket. Nor was she aware that he took his overcoat from the back of a chair, or that he picked up his boots and locked the door from the outside and took away her key. Neither did she hear him go stealthily down the back stairs and let himself out of Number 12 Great Coram Street by the back door.

He did not try to leave by the front door, but easily found the kitchen where it was as dark as the back of an oven, except for the lighter black square of window. He knew from observing it last night that the door was next to the window, and steps led up to the street from there.

Dark as the back of an oven, and wonderfully warm.

The warmest spot was beside the iron cooking range, where the girl, Daisy, lay curled up, making the most of the last few minutes before she must do the front steps and start the fires. It was Christmas morning, so nobody would be about early. Some of the girls had brought a chap home and the missis and mister had been drinking late with some friends. The girls would have got their chaps to bring a bit of something for the missis. The girls knew how to keep the missis sweet, particularly if they was behind with their rent. Some of them remembered Daisy and left little presents for her, some wrapped sweets, a side-comb with a flower, even a pair of fancy knee-socks, two sixpences and a pretty bottle still half-full of scent – not that she could use it in the house in case it contaminated the cooking.

When Daisy heard the pump in next-door's yard going, she knew that their girl, Minn, would soon be starting on their steps. Poor little beggar, her missis was heavy-handed. Daisy was fourteen, which she knew was true because her pa had once took her to look at the Parish Register at All Souls.

The oven warmth and thinking of her pa acted on her like a sleeping draught, causing her to drift away again into that pleasant state of half-sleep. She had been really proud that day.

Pa had said, 'I brought you here, Daisy, so as you will

always know who you are and be proud of yourself. Your name is put down in this big book which anybody can see if they asks the verger.' Daisy had never learned to read very well, but the letters that made up her name she could always see as clear as day . . . if anybody would have asked, she could write it herself. Sometimes she did that on steamed-up windows.

Stretching her toes she felt the side of the iron stove. Still enough fire left from yesterday, no need for paraffin rag and sticks. That gives me another ten minutes, not having to fire the stove from scratch. As she was about to move from her little cubby-hole and start the day, she heard the back stairs creak. Oh, Lord, one of the chaps had stopped longer than the missis liked.

He crept quickly through the kitchen, found the doorbolt, slid it along carefully, left the door open a few moments as he put on his hat and coat, then closed it very quietly and walked off in the direction of the main road.

Daisy tied her sack apron round her waist and started her day.

The lamplighter had not yet started along this street, but the sky was already lightening and the reflection from the snow enhanced the appearance of daylight.

The young man remembered, it was the morning of Christmas. He looked forward to a fine breakfast at Kroll's Hotel.

Having pulled on his boots, he walked away, thinking that if he should take a cab, it would be best to find one well away from this area. He enjoyed taking chances, but not foolish ones.

Frank Kerley – on duty. His were the only big boots to enter the crime scene. Waiting for the arrival of his super, he examined the bedroom, making detailed notes as he went, using the formula that he and the super had worked out between them. It was unfortunate that the room had been entered, but there was likely to be no tampering of evidence – the witness had not stayed long enough. He had, however, vomited copiously on the landing and, as Kerley had forbidden anyone to come up to this floor until the chief arrived, the combined odour of last night's boozing and that emanating from the area of the bed was a thing to be stoic about.

Frank Kerley waited beside the body of 'E' Division's first reported murder victim of the day. Christmas Day. Harriet Burton: that much he knew. A singer.

She had come home last night in the company of a man who had left silently without leaving any sign that he had ever been here. Any sign, that is, if you discounted the bloody water, the bloody petticoat used to wipe a weapon, the bloody handprint on the mantelpiece. That is if you discounted the corpse lying like a sleeping woman. Having replaced the counterpane as he had found it, he looked down at the peaceful face of the young woman and felt unprofessional sadness for her.

A country girl, he guessed. A village lad himself until he was twenty, he was pretty sure that she had not been a product of London's mean streets, where so many limbs never recover from a childhood spent in choking air and being fed poor and adulterated food. She had the look of a girl who had not been many years away from fresh air, barley broth, the smell of gillyflowers, and haymaking and harvesting. Frank had been away for more years than he liked to think of, but those early years were the stanchions of his own childhood. The longer he lived away from it, the more he forgot that haymaking and harvesting were sunny and healthy only in his memory.

Perhaps in twenty years or so, he would return to Dorset and retire to back there in Gunville, the village he had left in order to better himself. He withdrew his gaze. Francis Kerley, you're soft as butter. He and the super knew better. DS Kerley could be as hard as nails.

And in his innermost heart, he knew that, having lived as many years breathing London's air as he had that of Gunville, he had become a Londoner. A star of the Met. A faint smile crossed his face. He had once allowed an aspiring young journalist to question him about his work. Not something he would normally think of doing, but she had just started out, and Elizabeth had told him straight that he should do it, he'd been glad enough of a bit of a leg-up himself when he was young. 'She's a woman in a man's world, it's not asking much to answer a few questions. And in any case, if it gets printed at all, it won't be anywhere prominent.' That proved to be so. *A Day in the Life of* was short and sweet and appeared on the inside back page of a London magazine next to a receipt for a summer pudding, but it had helped her get a regular piece in *The Echo*. There had followed a whole series of *A Day in the Life of*. *A Star of the Metropolitan Police* . . . She had written a note apologizing for that. 'Sergeant Kerley, I have no say in the titles of my pieces. I hope that you were not embarrassed by the title (and, as agreed, the article gives no clue as to the identity of my "star"). But you should not be, because in my mind that is what I believe you are. I have always been a great admirer of London policemen. Jemima Ferguson.'

He continued examining the room. Lifting small items with his pencil and allowing them to drop again as they had been. He made lists and diagrams, knowing that to miss an item might be to miss a piece of evidence that could later prove crucial. But the murderer appeared to have left nothing behind him, except, maybe, his teethmarks on the apple and a bloody handprint. The super might have something to say about that.

Harriet Burton appeared to have few possessions, unless they were elsewhere. Most were scattered on the one or two bits of furniture, or hanging behind the door. On and in the chest of drawers were much the same oddments that he might have found on Elizabeth's dressing table, plus a few that he might not. Elizabeth did not use rouge or eye-black – nor, as far as he knew, did she use contraceptive sponges, a small porcelain jarful of which were beside the hand-basin, soaking in vinegar. That was the one smell that always pointed to the possibility of a woman involved in prostitution.

He opened the drawers one by one, from each of which escaped the smell of faded lavender. Then the various decorated boxes in which she kept her haber-dashery and frippery: some good lace collars, a set of ornamental buttons, bits of well-chosen, cheap jewellery, nice-looking beads and ear-drops. But few of these things were worth more than a shilling or two, although her gloves, millinery and gowns were of good quality. A couple of pairs of light shoes, very pretty, nicely made and to Frank's taste – he liked a woman to have a shapely foot. Both pairs, as well as some newish embroidered eastern-looking slippers, were in good repair. The clue to her fortune was in the snow-damaged, badly worn, high-buttoned boots – the ones she must have worn last night, which were in need of repair; he had noticed them propped up against the skirting board on the landing. It was quite likely that the embroidered slippers had been gifts from a man, or men. The young woman might well have preferred the gift of a stout pair of boots, but men liked to give impractical chilly silk and beads. Poor young thing, such cold feet. Permanently cold now.

Although the room was stuffy with the smells of bed-ding and clothes, soap, scent, cosmetic powder, lavender and vinegar mingling with the vomit and blood, it had that chill about it which only comes with dampness and a habitual lack of heating, and is a hallmark of poverty. Without having uncovered the victim more than a few inches, Frank Kerley knew that her life's blood had drained away. Looking under the bed he had seen the shine of a small pool that had gathered there. The rest would have been absorbed by the feather mattress. Thank God for a cold night. In summer the room would already have been stinking and buzzing with blowflies. Frank had a great hatred for the creatures. Even so, he was forced to admit, many a corpse might have lain undiscovered had it not been for those grisly investigators.

Not wanting to proceed without the super, and having seen as much as he could without making too much disturbance, Frank Kerley lowered his large frame to sit on the edge of the bed, almost as if he were a visitor with a sick person. Holding the counterpane by his fingertips he, for a second time, pulled it away from the young woman, and for a second time observed the gaping wounds that transformed a peaceful sleeper into a gruesome cadaver. She lay on her back, hands on her breasts, legs apart, the skirt of her nightdress raised to the waist, revealing above an unremarkable black triangle the marked and crumpled belly of a woman who has carried a child full-term. Frank Kerley could not remember having seen a more macabre sight than this: a bloody corpse, knees bent, legs spread wide, laid out ready for sex.

Covering her again, he said, 'How much did he pay you to do this?' He laid a large warm hand on her icy wax brow. 'Here's a promise, Harriet, we'll get him if we have to go to the ends of the earth to find him.'

This was not his usual way with murdered prostitutes. He had seen any number. Such cases were usually easily solved: a blow on the head in the street, or a knife in the ribs in a back alley; clients intent on getting their money back, or lost in rage because they couldn't get hard and blamed the woman; sometimes pimps who had fallen for a girl and then went mad with jealousy. Many times it was pimps cutting a girl for holding money back, and as a lesson to the others of his string not even to think of it.

This was no sudden frenzy. This looked thought-out, maybe planned. Here was a violent death, yet no sign of it in her expression. She was asleep, but with gaping wounds slashed deeply from ear to ear, fine cuts done in one swipe in each direction. This had been carried out with a thin and very sharp blade.

A young uniformed constable lurked discreetly across the square that fronted a church whose bells were ringing out proclaiming Christmas. Mass was over, and communicants streamed out into the clear, cold London air.

Ann Martha Thomson, one arm linked with her husband whose other arm was linked with Josephine's, stiffened as she drew breath to speak.

'It's all right, my dear, I see him too.'

'Oh James! Even on Christmas morning. People are too bad.'

'And if they were not, my ever-forbearing wife –' he raised her finely gloved knuckles to his lips and engaged her with twinkling eyes – 'I should be unemployed and you would complain because I was always under your feet.'

Making their way to where the constable was standing with a cab at the ready, Ann Martha said, 'I know that you told me what the life of a detective's wife might be before we married, but James . . . Christmas morning?'

'Well, Constable?'

The man said in a low voice, 'It's murder, sir. Sergeant Kerley's at the scene, Great Coram Street, number 12.'

'Would you like me to call you a cab, Ann?'

'No, you go, James, we do know how to call a cab . . . and James, do try to get something to eat.' The ritual of Holy Communion was always performed before food was consumed.

As soon as the cab with the policemen pulled away, Ann Martha and Josephine walked to a cab rank close by. 'Do you mind if I don't go with you, Ann? I think I would like to drop in on the service at St Giles's and then walk back. I can do with some exercise if I'm to be fed for two days like a *foie-gras* goose.' Ann Martha stepped into the open-sided cab and, taking both of Josephine's hands, she squeezed them as she pressed her cheek to Josephine's, wafting her delicate perfume. She said, 'That man is becoming quite famous . . . or notorious. I do read newspapers, Josephine.'

'He speaks up for poor people, Aunt. He's bound to tread on toes doing that.'

Ann Martha noticed the flush rise and fall on Josephine's cheeks. They said the new preacher at St Giles was young and handsome. 'I doubt if James will be back for lunch, but I do hope that you will be: we have guests.'

'Of course, Aunt. I just want to—'

'It's quite all right, darling, you can tell me what the preacher has to say about Christmas feasting.'

Josephine felt herself flushing again. Clearly Ann Martha was aware of the attraction at St Giles, although not that he had been part of the Boot Street group enjoying her niece's hospitality.

'I'll be in time for the meal. Promise.'

As the cab drew away, Josephine was stepping into the next in line. 'Coram's Fields. I will tell you where to stop when we get there.'

As the cab door closed, so had Superintendent James Thomson's mind closed on domestic affairs.

'Well, Constable?'

'Murder, sir. A young woman. Sometime during the night. In her own bed. Sergeant Kerley's waiting. We was called in not more than an hour since. Mr Kerley sent me straight over to find you. The lady at your house said where you'd be.'

Something tried to click into place in James Thomson's fact-filled memory. 'Coram Street, rings a bell. Do you know anything?'

'*Great* Coram Street to be right, sir. It's on my beat. To my knowledge it's a respectable street, not every house occupied by a single family.'

'What then? Sub-lettings, that kind of thing?'

'I believe so, sir. I don't recollect any trouble in the area.'

'Ah, sub-letting . . . doesn't make our job any easier . . . that's the first step on the downward path. You'll see, in ten years, every house will be let by the room or by the floor. The shared services will break down. Inhabitants will stop taking a pride, railings will not be painted, and no one will care except the beat bobby who will want to carry a night-stick in daylight hours.'

'I hope not to be a beat bobby in ten years, sir.'

'Ambitious are you, Constable?'

'The detection squad, sir. I believe that to be the bright future of police work.'

'Good. Start on the beat, that's where a good detective gains experience. Now, when we reach Great Coram Street, I shall get out a little distance from the scene. In answer to the question you would like to ask, it's easier for one to slip through the gawping crowd if one doesn't arrive in a cab with a constable up front. You will be the distraction. Whilst you make a good show of opening the cab door, I will be inside in two ticks.'

James got out at the end of the street, and walked on. Dressed in his church clothes, he was able to make his way unobtrusively along Great Coram Street. As he did so, memories of walking this particular area came tumbling into his mind. There had been a time as a uniformed officer when he could have written a very detailed report on this street.

He could see where number 12 must be.

The houses were large, quite impressive, but not grand, having no rising entrance to the front doors, but just areas enclosed in black-painted iron railings. The generous-sized front doors were set in shallow archways, beside a pair of windows with fancy iron window-boxes. First floors: three full-length windows, some dressed with blinds and drapes, linked by wrought-iron balconies. Second floors: three four-paned sashed windows and, symmetrically above these, three smaller sashed windows with the six panes typical of nurseries and servants' quarters. Then flat, slate roofs and large blocks of chimney stacks with numerous pots, most of them sending coal smoke straight up into the windless air. The architecture of the houses composing the terrace held no secrets or surprises as to the layout of the interior. Any secrets were what went on within.

Quietly insinuating his way between the sensation-mongers who were being kept at bay by some of his big-boots Bow Street men – 'Keep back there. Keep back, nothing to see—' he reached the iron railings of number 12. At the exact moment when the cab drew up and his constable opened the cab door with a flourish, the superintendent slipped into the house, making a mental note to tell the ambitious young policeman that he did well. Praise booted a man forward much more successfully than criticism.

Josephine alighted at the opposite end of Great Coram Street, closer to number 12 than the police vehicle had ended up, her sensible cabbie knowing how the numbers ran. Having told the driver well done and giving him a generous fare, she was able to mingle with the crowd just as her uncle went into the house. Her disguise was simple. Her fashionable beaded velvet tam-o'-shanter was turned inside out and pulled well down over her ears, her jacket was clutched around her and her hands tucked under her arms so that she appeared huddled and dragged down by the cold, much like many of the women who had come here with just a shawl hastily thrown around their shoulders.

'What's goin' on then?' A lowered, husky voice, words running together, she used the language of the city which she knew from experience usually got a response. Nobody interesting ever responded to a 'toff's' voice.

Without taking their eyes off the door of number 12, several of the crowd offered certain knowledge.

'Murder.'

'Whatappened?'

'Woman done in last night. One of her lodgers, her "girls", she likes to call them.'

'Who?'

'Hatty Wright, she lets out rooms to actresses and that.'

'D'you think it's one of them who's been—'

'Done in?' somebody offered. 'Bound to be, innit? *She's* been at the door, and it's him what found the body, and as the son was sent to fetch the police, must of been one of the girls.'

Josephine huddled closer to her informants. 'They all actresses, then?' That question got quite a bit of response, but still nobody bothered to turn round to see who was asking, just in case something might happen should they take their eyes off the door for a moment.

'Yeah. She used to be on the stage herself one time . . .'

'Quite a bit ago by the looks of her.'

'Yeah, well, you got to hand it to her for havin' a bit of sense. Once girls starts losing their looks they got two choices, an 'usband, or the other thing.'

'Or do what Hatty Wright done and start a lodging house.'

''atty still looks good . . .'

'But fat, she run to fat and couldn't get in the box no longer.'

Josephine stayed quiet for a while, not wanting to appear more-than-averagely nosy. She wanted to know *what box*? She needn't have worried, people who have seen something – a bag-snatch, a horse dropping dead – love to prove they know everything about everybody and will tell anyone whatever they wish to hear.

''atty Wright used to be a saw-in-half woman and a knife-thrower's gal.'

Josephine said, 'Is that the truth? Never met one of them before.'

''Ang around and you're bound to see her come out.'

'A knife-throwing act? I shouldn't like that,' Josephine said, warming to the gossip.

'Fancy trusting a fella like that!'

The fact of murder didn't prevent a bit of harmless chat.

'She'll be loving all this, 'specially if she thinks she'll get her name in papers.'

And not only the landlady. Enjoying the notoriety that comes with crime as long as it is once removed, the entire street was loving it. Christmas morning and a murder right in their midst. Her own activity? Josephine didn't question it. She was at work. This could be what was needed to get Jemima Ferguson's name on page one of *The News*.

Mrs Wright waylaid the superintendent in her hallway. 'He's up in her room, sir, your sergeant. He said to look out for you because he wouldn't leave the dear girl unattended.'

'Good, that is the correct thing to do. As few people as possible should move about this house until the sergeant gives permission.'

'Oh yes, sir, Mister Kerley said that.'

'And if you could keep to your quarters until then, it would be a great help.'

'I've already given instructions to everybody. Mr Kerley said that once everybody was up and decent, that they come down here,' she gestured, 'into my apartments, which of course I gladly agreed to.'

'Good.'

'Anyway, sir, I assure you, sir, having seen the state of my husband when he came down, I don't think anybody's likely to want to go up there. I reckon it's not going to be easy letting that room again.'

James Thomson wanted no opinions of any sort, so just looked at her until she became embarrassed.

'I won't show you right up, sir, if that's all right. It's this way.'

Thomson followed Mrs Wright up the first flight of stairs, mentally taking notes as they progressed.

72

'I let rooms on a monthly rent but most of them pay weekly when they settle for any meals they have had, but I don't do a lot of that.'

Her full-skirted gown swayed as she led him. She was quite young, probably in her thirties, but with a full matronly bosom and the swell and roundness of a woman who had borne children, and would no doubt bear more yet.

She halted on the first landing, getting her breath. 'I hope nobody's going to ask me to look at her, sir. Seeing my husband's face was enough for me.'

'No, no, Mrs Wright. Possibly later, when she has been taken to the . . . hospital, my men will accompany Mr Wright for formal identification.'

'Wouldn't one of her own family do that?'

'If we can find one.'

'I know she's got a sister. She has mentioned her, though I never have seen her.'

A door opened and closed, and Frank Kerley came down the few stairs to greet his superior officer, nodding at the patch Mr Wright had deposited on the lower landing. 'Watch where you step, sir.' Stepping round it, Thomson thanked Mrs Wright, and allowed his sergeant to lead the way. 'Door's busted, sir. Wright, the landlady's husband, said he did it.'

'The door was locked.'

'Yes, sir, but it's queer. Locked on the outside, no sign of a key, and they don't have a spare.'

Thomson casually inspected the damaged lock. 'No other in the house to fit?'

'Most doors haven't got keys anyhow; some have got bolts.'

'So?'

'Looks like our man thought he might gain himself a bit of time by locking the room and taking the key?'

'And did it?'

'Save him time? Probably not necessary, by the looks of the victim, always supposing he left quite soon after the deed was done. I'd estimate that he left in the early hours, and nobody in the house stirred until breakfast, which was later than usual because of Christmas.'

James Thomson looked at his pocket-watch, and, not believing that it was only fifteen minutes since he had left the church, shook it. 'The victim's name is?'

'Harriet Burton. Miss or Mrs I'm not certain.'

'And she was found at what time?'

'There's still a bit of confusion about that, but breakfast was ready by about eight thirty. Mrs Wright had said that she would give the victim a call. She was planning to have a day in the country apparently – the victim, that is. Mr Wright knocked,' the sergeant indicated the broken door, 'and, not receiving any answer, went down to ask his wife what to do. I believe he must have tried the door-handle, but he doesn't like to say.'

'Why?'

'Don't want to be thought of as a landlord who'd go into a girl's room uninvited. Well, that's my theory . . . Anyway, Mrs Wright then came up and knocked and it was she who tried the handle; they looked for a key, but couldn't find one. They were both a bit concerned, so decided to use force on the door.'

'Didn't it occur to them that she might have gone out and locked the door behind her?'

'I asked that, but nobody gets in or out of this house without the Wrights knowing about it. You've seen the layout. Front door, there's a kind of warning buzzer beneath the mat.'

'But anyone who knew about the buzzer could let themselves out quietly, which means surely that they might have reasonably supposed that the victim had risen early and gone out.'

'It was a possibility, but she wasn't very well off for sensible footwear, as you will see, and Mr Wright noticed that her only decent boots were on the landing drying out.' He indicated the pathetic boots. 'Quite the detective, sir. It's my belief that the murderer must have gone out through the basement.'

James Thomson fell silent, looking around, up the next flight of stairs, down the ones he had just climbed. 'Hardly call them decent boots. What's in there?'

'Just a kind of ablutions cupboard: water tap, buckets, chamber-pots.' Kerley opened the door and held it. 'Not the most savoury of places. I haven't taken a close look, but I mean to when you've looked over the room.' Shutting the closet door and pushing open the busted one, he continued, 'By the time Wright broke in, I reckon she'd already been dead a fair few hours by then. She's covered by a lot of bedding, but the room's cold. After you, sir.'

*   *   *

Josephine didn't wait for the appearance of the landlady, but backed her way through the crowd and slipped unseen down the steps of the house opposite number 12. She knocked softly on the basement door, which was opened a crack by a pale-faced girl who blocked entry with her thin body.

'Can you let me in? I just want to talk to you for five minutes.' Josephine Thomson's 'toff's' speech was gone again; she was missing the odd 't' and running words together as she had previously.

'I can't do that.' The girl spoke in a whisper, her eyes darting upwards to the front entrance, half fearful, but still curious. 'Who are you, miss? I don't know who you are. What do you want?'

Josephine took the hint, speaking in a whisper too. 'Five minutes. I can pay you.' Josephine dipped into her jacket pocket and took out a florin, pressing against the door as she did so. The coin, which happened to be a bright and shining, newly minted one, caught the girl's attention. 'My name's Jemima, what's yours?'

Watching the florin as it threatened to return to Josephine's pocket, 'Why would you want to pay me all that money for five minutes?'

'Because you live opposite where all that is going on, and I want to know about it.'

'I don't know nothink.'

'I'm sure you do . . . what's your name?'

'Edith, miss.'

'Well, Edith, you must see more than most about what goes on in the houses opposite.'

'D'you think I got time to stand around peeping through the shutters like . . . ?' She jerked a thumb upwards, took Josephine's proffered florin and opened the door wide enough for Josephine to slip in. The girl gently closed the door behind her, then went to the bottom of a flight of stairs and listened. 'The master will give me a right beltin' if he finds you here.'

'Is he likely to?'

'Well, I suppose not. They're all upstairs watchin' out the front winda, but I'm on my own here till teatime. Cook had to go and see her badly mother . . . *they* didn't like it, but they know Cook will up and go if they don't be easy with her – they don't keep staff – the maids have been sent to morning service with the children. When they gets back, we has to send up something cold.'

'It's nowhere near dinner-time, I expect they won't want serving yet.'

'That's true, specially with everything that's been going on over there.'

'Do you know somebody was murdered in number 12?'

The girl's hand flew to her mouth and she stared at Josephine. 'I hoped she wasn't killed, I hoped she was just beat up. I guessed it might be bad because of the police and that, but I never thought murder.' Shaken, Edith lowered herself onto a wooden kitchen chair. Josephine dipped a beaker into a bowl collecting water from a filter. Edith drank without realizing it. 'Oh, miss, I never thought . . . He could easy come after me, I could be found dead.'

'Edith', Josephine touched the girl on the shoulder, 'whoever did this is probably far away by now. He's not likely to come back to this road again.'

'He could. He's a bold one, he is. When he gets to thinking about it, he might realize that anybody could have seen him: the streetlights was on, and he stopped to pull his boots on.'

Chilled and thrilled at the same time, Josephine said casually, 'You saw a man leaving number 12 then?'

Edith nodded uncertainly. 'Could ov, but he never acted like he was a murderer.'

'Were there people about?'

'Oh no, only me, and he wouldn't know I was looking. I never makes any noise in the morning, I'd get a right belting for that.'

'What did you see?'

'I see him come up the area steps. Then he bends down and does something to his boots, like straightening his socks, and off he goes.'

'You didn't notice which way he went when he left Great Coram Street?'

Edith shook her head. 'No, I only know he didn't go towards Marchmont Street.'

'So, once he reached the corner he might have gone towards Euston Road, or Southampton Row?'

'Could ov gone anywhere.'

How true. This was an area of crescents, squares, interlocking streets and roads. Euston Station, St Pancras, King's Cross, and the underground train stations and main bus routes were all within easy walking distance.

Once he turned the corner of Great Coram Street, he could disappear.

Edith's eyes kept flicking at the row of bells, any of which, Josephine knew, could jangle and bounce around at any moment, summoning Edith to above stairs. 'Look, they'll want me before long. If I don't eat my dinner now, I don't know when—'

'Edith, I am so sorry. Just tell me how he looked and I'll be gone and the florin is yours.'

'He was youngish, not that tall, he had on a short sort of coat – not a jacket, a real top-coat, but short. And he had on a round sort of hat, a bit like a billy-cock, only not the same. His boots, his coat and his hat . . . all queer sort of clothes, I'd say.'

'Foreign?'

Edith gazed off for a moment. 'Yes, I suppose that could be it. Yes, kind of foreign, I'd say. But, it wasn't that light.'

'Do you know anyone who lives there?'

'Only Daisy, who's the skivvy, like me. I know the missis is called Wright. Far as the lodgers go, they're just women lodgers. Though Daisy did say that one of the new ones was on the stage at the 'lhambra Palace – Clara Burton. I hope it wasn't her, because Daisy and me was hoping to go and see her next time we got an hour or two off at the same time. Clara said she could get us in cheap.'

'Thank you, Edith, thank you very much. I would be very grateful if you didn't mention to anyone what you have told me.'

Edith dipped thick bread into thick broth and snorted. 'I an't likely to do that. He'd have the skin off my back if he knew I even let you into the house. They wouldn't want to get mixed up in anything like that, especially if, like you say, it wasn't a bashin' but somebody was done in. Waa, miss, I just thought: I seen a murderer. Don't tell nobody, please, miss. I'd just as soon give you back your money.'

'I swear I won't tell a soul that you've spoken to me . . . In any case, I wouldn't want anyone to know how I got to know what you told me. I'll tell you something, Edith, I'd be in hot water myself if you told anybody I was here asking questions. If I were you, I would keep quiet about what you saw.'

'You don't think the police is going to start asking questions from everybody?'

'Ah well, the police is another matter. It's your mistress they will talk to if they talk to anybody . . . and even if they do ask you questions, you can just tell them the truth, like you told me, but you don't have to tell them that I was here.' Edith looked a bit doubtful, but she thought of a whole florin to herself, to spend it on anything she liked . . . 'All right, Edith?'

'Yes, miss. But you'd better get out before she rings that bell.'

Josephine had the great good fortune to be sneaking up the area steps just as the mortuary wagon arrived, compressing the audience, making it even denser.

Ann Martha Thomson stood in the bow window of her

'Divertimento Gallery', a room she had invented to delight herself and any of her friends who liked to gather there. The divertissements provided by Ann Martha were as many and varied as she could provide to indulge simple and innocent whims: arts and games, books, magazines, craft objects and small gardening experiments, such as growing little trees from pips, musical instruments and music boxes, pens, water-colour boxes, crystallized fruits and boxed chocolates.

It could not be truly said to be a gallery, but it was the wide, high window that bowed far out into the back garden that gave it the appearance of such. What gave the room its delightful ambience was the clear view beyond the walled garden across the River Thames as it flowed towards Chiswick. There was a public footpath at the bottom of the garden, hidden from their view of it and the public's view of the Thomsons'. From the gallery it was almost possible to believe that the house stood on its own beside river and fields. It was an illusion, of course, one had only to open the glazed doors and step onto the balcony to see the truth of that.

Ann Martha stayed inside the window this morning, drinking mid-morning café au lait. Hani had been in and out several times. She used the room to make her stylized flower arrangements, often of a single flower, a stone and a reed, which must surely be mathematically placed, because when Ann and her friends tried their own versions they could never get the proportions quite right.

Although Ann Martha gazed out, she was not taking

in how golden the undulations of the snowy fields were, lit by the far-off clear sun. Snow had frozen where it had fallen onto bare branches, and had finished the garden wall with a coping stone of white. She had intended to go down and look to see if the first of the chionodoxas had pushed through, but had been waylaid by her thoughts, not made less troubled by Hani.

'Why you let her go, MisAnn?'

'Do you think you could have stopped her? Our Josie has become very independent.'

'She come just for two short day, and first day she runs away. MistaJame, he does not know. Eh? When she come here, I tell her she had no bad manner when she live in this house. We both tell her we are cross. Eh?'

Ann Martha had given Hani the brief, sedate, one-armed hug that each understood to be as strong as any pressing of cheeks and clutching of shoulders. 'Hani, she is no longer our little girl. She has become independent. You would not like her to be a silly little miss gazing at herself in a mirror and making ribbon bows all day.'

'She think she can be like young man.'

'The world is changing, Hani. Many young women no longer look for an engagement ring. If they are intelligent and educated, they look around and see what domesticity can do to women.'

'It can do very well for MisAnn.'

'Perhaps she has taken you as a pattern to follow.'

Hani dismissed this notion with a puff of air. 'Because I not go home and find man?'

'Maybe because when she was an orphan child, you

were free to bring her here; there was no man to tell you what to do.'

Hani smiled wryly. 'Almost I was not free. This time when I take 'osie to my village, my father gave me to a man. If big fever did not happen, I should now be wife and mother to babies so.'

'Don't you want that?'

'Not first thing I choose now. First thing I choose is to live in London . . . live with you and MastaJame.' She sat neatly, her cup of jasmine-flower tea neatly placed on the saucer. 'You think I can live in London, MisAnn? I mean for all time? Not go back to my village?'

'Don't you want to go back?'

'To father to tell what I must do? To man who will not want old woman for wife?'

'Hani, you can't be thirty yet, that's not old.'

'I was, I think, thirteen year when 'osie came to my village, and my father gave me to village boy. I am *old*.' Looking over her cup at Ann Martha, she smiled, wrinkling her small flat nose, 'Also, I like red stone house like this, I like shop with windows, I like gaslamp, so. Snow, him I like, jus' for looking. En'lish man, some I like, big men like MistaJame men.'

Ann Martha laughed. 'Hani, you sly thing. So you are not totally opposed to domestic life – I mean, life with a man . . . a husband?'

'Not village man . . . too old for my village man now.'

Ann Martha had tried to keep the exchange light, but had come to realize that Hani was going as far as she was able to discuss her future. Hani had brought James's niece across thousands of miles when little more than a girl herself. Josephine had clung to her as to a life buoy during the first months; Hani had become an essential part of the household, almost part of the family. Ann Martha suddenly realized what a hole in all their lives there would be if Hani left them.

Her mind now off her earlier musings about Josephine, and what she was doing going to St Giles, Ann Martha took a seat opposite Hani, where they were at eye-level with one another, a feat not always achievable with the inches difference in their height. 'Are you saying that you want to make your future life here, in London?'

'Yes, it is what I mean. But I think, now 'osie is gone from here, you think I also must go?'

'Go? No, no, Hani. I have never given a thought to that . . . how self-centred we are. We don't want you to go. I can't remember how it felt before you brought Josephine here, but this is much more a home since you did.'

Hani, peering into her tea, sat still and quiet for some moments, 'Thank you, Miss Ann, I feel very good now. I still tell that girl she is doing bad manner not coming from church with you. Where she go? What she do with herself all time now she live in rooms. Rooms! What is rooms?'

'Rooms is where young people like to live in these strange times. Where they can make mistakes out of sight of fussy dragons like me and you.'

'Boot Street! I should like to see this Boot Street.'

'That is not a very good idea, Hani. If she thought that we were spying on her independent life, we might lose her altogether. We should go down and look to the cold collation, and I must prepare myself to tell our luncheon guests that their host will probably not be joining us, and his niece . . . ? Only the Lord knows what I shall tell them if she isn't here.'

'Maybe she will not be long away.'

'We can only hope, Hani.'

Having established from the ever-increasing crowd that the victim was Clara Burton, one of Hatty Wright's actresses, Josephine hurried away. In Tavistock Square, Josephine hailed a cab. '*The News* offices, please, cabby.' No directions needed: the offices of all the dailies were well known to cab drivers. She had bet on Mr Hood being in this morning, if only to check incoming stories and post. She told the cabby to wait for her. The nightwatchman said that Mr Hood had come in about half an hour ago and hadn't left. Her heels sounded, clacking up stairwells and through deserted corridors.

In the empty reporters' room she put down the outline of her report. George Hood appeared in the doorway. 'Miss Ferguson?'

'Yes, it's me, sir.'

'Where are the dry sticks?'

'I am quite warm enough without a stove. Look sir, I want you to read this. I know that it is going to become a big, big story. It's a big story which *The News* can publish first. Young actress, singer in the halls, meets a man, takes him to her room . . .' She looked up from her notes to see his expression.

'And?'

'He killed her, then leaves in the early hours of *this* morning. He was seen leaving the house, bold as brass, with the streetlights still burning. Just a few hours ago. Murdered on Christmas morning.' She paused. 'It's all there, isn't it, sir? And I know that I'm the first home with the story. When I left the scene, I saw none of the opposition in the crowd. But they won't be long.'

Hood looked over her shoulder at what she had written, hands clasped, thumbnails pressed against his lips. Hardly daring to breathe aloud, she waited, then jumped out of her skin when he spun round and clapped his hands loudly. 'Yes, Jemima Ferguson, it is all there.'

'If we could get it out today . . .'

'Even if our customers and advertisers are not particularly God-fearing people, they will cry stinking fish if we don't observe Christmas Day, more so than Sundays and Good Friday.'

'They expect cabbies and gasometer workers to work.'

'You should try debating that with a Tory MP from the Shires and see where it gets you.'

'I shouldn't mind doing that.'

Hood smiled and held up a placating hand. 'Let's hope that you will one day get that opportunity, but for now—'

'Would there be any objection to starting the presses at midnight? Boxing Day?'

'They would never believe that we did not desecrate this Holy Day, but . . .'

She could almost hear the cogs of his mind turning.

'A Special Edition. A single fold. There are any number of pieces already set that I held back from the last edition, and some ready for the post-Christmas edition. Pictures, too, as fillers. Did you say she worked at the Alhambra Palace?'

'No, I said that she was an actress, and my source said that she *thought* so.'

'Library picture of the Alhambra will do. Where did the murder take place?'

'Number 12 Great Coram Street. Everything I have so far is in my notes.'

Hood shook his head. 'What's her name?'

'That I don't know for certain.'

'Who is on the case?'

'Superintendent Thomson.'

'Very, very well done, Miss Ferguson. We have a busy few hours before us. You go back and find out as much as you can whilst I start calling in a few of our typesetters.'

'Christmas Day, sir?'

'Boxing Day – stretched a bit. Sworn to secrecy and big bonuses. They will come.'

'Thank you, sir.'

Again that loud clap of hands. 'Have you heard of Miss Barbara Baker?'

'The American columnist? I have. Certainly. Yes. She's my model.'

'Did you know that her father owns the paper she works on?'

'I didn't.'

'I'm not saying that he bought it *for* her, but the relationship cannot be to her detriment.'

'Even so, she is a very good reporter. And she is opening a door for women into a very male profession.'

He put a friendly hand lightly on her shoulder. 'As *you* are Ferguson. You have the instincts.' Narrowing his eyes and giving her a tight smile, '*And*, I suspect, you have the ambition of a young man.'

'It is true, sir, I am ambitious. Many young women are.'

'But not for a diamond ring followed by a quiet life in Kensington, eh?'

'That is a disease known as *terminal ennui*.'

'No boredom in this establishment, Ferguson.'

As the hooves of the cab-horse clopped its way through the sparsely peopled streets towards the Haymarket, Josephine laid her fingers on the place where her chief, Hood, had touched her shoulder. She smiled to herself. Jemima Ferguson, MP. Here was another bastion of masculine power to be breached. There must come a day when women would sit in the House of Commons; that was where changes to society could be made.

Josephine Thomson often had such daydreams.

It was not the bed with its covered human form that first caught James Thomson's attention, but a polished apple placed on the mantelpiece, its bright red skin glowing except for where a single bite had been taken. Close to the apple was a hand-print of blood where the killer must have grasped the mantelpiece for support.

'Get this over to that new department.'

'To make a cast, sir?'

'Long odds, Kerley, and I cannot detect any sign in the toothmarks of any missing.'

Kerley peered closely at the apple. 'Nothing lost in trying, sir.'

At New Scotland Yard, an embryonic department was working towards establishing scientific methods of detection. Plaster casts of footprints were not generally accepted as firm evidence, but might be used to prompt a confession.

His eye was now drawn to more blood. On the washstand a bloodstained hand-towel, the marks on which seemed consistent with someone wiping a dagger, stiletto or knife on it, and a china hand-basin containing bloodied water.

The superintendent now leaned forward to look at the victim, the head of whom was the only part visible, and was poleaxed to see the features of a woman he recognized. Quickly recovering, he said, 'Such a peaceful expression.'

Kerley didn't miss the super's sudden pallor. 'Yes, well . . . Are you all right, sir?'

'Thank you, yes, Sergeant. I took Holy Communion this morning and came straight here.'

'Ah, so you won't have eaten yet.' Frank Kerley hadn't much time for a religion that forbade its followers to eat a decent breakfast before pretending to eat the flesh and drink the blood of a god like heathens. He had brought with him to London his simple Wesleyan religion, but had lost it in a life amid a welter of violence and sordid acts. The super, he knew, was Roman Catholic and observed the rituals. How could a man of such superior intelligence believe in all that? A hearty debate on the subject would have been good, but their ranks were too distant for that.

Kerley waited quietly as Thomson turned full circle and methodically checked the room, his eyes flickering up and down, noting mentally not only the layout and furnishing but quite likely the small detail that Frank himself needed to write up in his notebook. His super had the ability to look at a scene and set it firmly in his memory. Frank preferred to have things down in black and white; things might get lost if you kept them in your mind.

'Who is she?'

'Harriet Burton according to the landlady. There's a letter – it's written and addressed but not sent – to a "Mrs E. Horwood, Grove Hill, Hurst Green", her sister.'

Thomson lifted a page of notepaper from the envelope, read it, then handed it to Kerley. 'Make a note of the address and go yourself to break the bad news. I will take the letter with me. Notice, she signs herself "C" Burton, not Harriet.'

'Might not be the same woman?'

'Doubtful . . . ask Mrs Wright, and about the sister before you go there. See what she knows.'

Frank Kerley observed his superior officer. He appeared

reluctant to inspect the body. Frank watched and waited until at last the super appeared to force his gaze to rest on the bed.

Kerley took a step forward.

'No! Not yet, Kerley. Did you find her tucked up like that?'

'I did, sir. Wright swears he didn't touch a thing, he saw the blood-print on her forehead, and the bloody towel and the water . . .' Frank flipped back pages of his notebook. 'Exact words, "I took one look, and she was that white I knew straight off she was a goner".'

'He didn't see the injuries?'

'He says not, sir. I believe him. I think if he had he would have dropped the coverlet and ran.'

'So this is how you found her? You looked, made your notes and replaced the covers exactly so.'

'Yes, Superintendent, the scene is exactly as I found it.'

'Right.' Now, Thomson stepped closer to the bed. 'Is that blood mark on her forehead a fingerprint?'

'I reckon a thumbprint, sir. I can't make sense of it, unless he cut his own hand. Maybe we shall be able to work out what happened at the post-mortem.'

'Perhaps. But we must do our best to work out the events from what we see here. What else have you observed so far?'

'Her night-clothing is disturbed and stained, and there's a fair pool of blood under the bed; she's lying on her back and her legs are spread out, sir. It looks as though he could have misused her after death, sir . . .

not normal sexual contact, sir, an act of debasement, an abuse of her womanhood, perhaps. There is semen evident on the pubic hair. Perhaps the killing didn't satisfy him, or he may have wanted to abuse her more than he already had. An evil man, Superintendent, an evil, evil killer who wallowed in his debauchery.'

Ann Martha Thomson was seated in her own dining room with Lord and Lady Granville and Colonel and Mrs Henderson, invited as 'James's guests' because of their connection to the Home Office and the Metropolitan Police. The three other couples were Ann Martha's guests, invited for their lively knowledge of the London scene. All were eating an excellent cold luncheon and drinking wonderful French wines, of good vintage and more expensive than police pay – even that of a superintendent – would provide.

Lady Granville had been influential in recommending James Thomson to the police commissioner, the Granville-Thomson link going back to the Smyrna days, when James's mother held her celebrated gatherings in her salon, where any and every passing traveller of any note was certain of a welcome. There, the Granvilles had met more exotic foreigners in one visit than in an entire season in London. Ann Martha had never known whether to be pleased or cross when James was absent on important occasions. Without him, the ambience was more relaxing. James was not good with guests; one always had the feeling that he would not be sorry when they left. But Ann Martha very much liked to entertain;

guests and friends were part of the *raison d'être* for the attention she paid to her lovely home. Without people moving around in it, the house was an empty stage set.

Lady Granville took it as a compliment that her protégé was absent. 'You don't have to apologize to me for James's absence, Ann. I am pleased to know that he is so indispensable to the detection service.' Colonel Henderson, Chief Commissioner, nodded agreement. The Granvilles and Hendersons, if asked, would have to agree that their presence at the table of a detective superintendent, was unexpected – unique, even. But then, James Thomson's origins were exotic and unique, and his marriage to a lady with royal connections – albeit distant – set social distinctions on their head. It allowed them to pride themselves on their open minds and living at the hub of the universe. London, this could only happen in London.

Mrs Henderson asked whether Ann's niece would be joining them. 'Is she with you for Christmas?'

'Until tomorrow. She likes to walk in the snow – I expect she has lost all sense of time. Now, I do recommend this walnut pickle . . .' Her friends, all being fond of excellent food, were easily distracted from the subject of Josephine's absence.

The young men staying in Kroll's Hotel some distance from the St Pancras area of Great Coram Street, and from the house beside the Thames, enjoyed a meal of good German food and Rhenish wine. Not to all tastes, but this group of young people were all Germans.

Some of them had been out and about on Christmas Eve, and one complained of having caught a cold. His wife, whilst enjoying her food, cast dark looks at her husband.

Yesterday he had treated her despicably.

He had gone off with his friends into the city; at what time he had returned to his room she had no idea. All that she knew was that he appeared to be making amends by suggesting that all of them might go together to an entertainment. She knew how short of money they were, and hoped that there would not be another embarrassment about buying the tickets. At least the hotel bill would be paid for by the ship's agent. It would be sensible to stay in the hotel, where they did not have to find money. But . . . She became persuaded that the men were right. They would be many weeks at sea, and who knew whether there would be any civilized entertainment when they arrived at their destination in Brazil. And the ship might easily be blown off course again. Enjoy a civilized city whilst they could. Next week they might be back in their cramped quarters being tossed around by heavy seas. Enjoyment whilst it lasted. He'd had his pleasure last night; she would take her own whilst she could.

Watching the super's perusal of the room, picking up things here and there, moving objects, opening pots and bags, Sergeant Kerley noticed that he did not replace a rosary where it had lain, in a tiny porcelain dish, but kept it in his hand, fingering the beads absent-mindedly, rolling them between fingers and thumb. Eventually, he clenched his fist about the rosary and transferred it to his pocket.

What was he to make of his superior officer? They had viewed many bodies together, some bruised and battered, some knifed, some decomposing or bloated by Thames water, but the super was having difficulty viewing this one.

'Peel back the covers carefully, Sergeant.' James Thomson lowered his gaze to the dead woman.

Yes, he did know her. *Had* known her, before those gaping wounds had all but severed her head.

How had she come to end her life with her body set thus, so suggestive of abandonment and lust? He recollected how small and sweet her voice had been, so much at odds with the surroundings in which he had heard her sing. Each of her blood-drained hands cradled one of her own breasts beneath her bodice; her legs, bent at the knees, spread apart, gave the appearance of disgusting lewdness.

'He's a madman, sir.'

'No, Sergeant, he doesn't get away with that. Decadent and debauched, yes. Insane, no. Capable of planning – men don't just happen to have a surgical instrument in their pocket. This man came here with every intention of killing. I don't know about positioning her like this – maybe it was an afterthought; maybe he thought he didn't get value for money . . .'

'Semen is running from her, sir.'

'Even so, she may have demurred at further attempts.'

'But her face, sir, as peaceful and composed as if she was asleep.'

'I have no doubt that she was asleep, Sergeant, maybe a little gone in drink, dozing. Those wounds are so clean-cut that she may not have known she had been cut. You must have cut yourself a dozen times with a razor and not known until you saw blood.'

Frank Kerley nodded. 'It couldn't have happened any other way, sir. Had she felt even the slightest nick, her reaction would still have been there on her face.'

Thomson nodded. 'How did he deflect the blood from himself? Arterial blood gushes.'

'Naked, I would guess. Kept his hands under the bedclothes whilst he did it?'

'Which might show that he knew what he was doing blindfold, as you might say.'

Frank Kerley nodded. 'A surgeon perhaps?'

'Certainly somebody who would know that arterial blood gushes, and how to steer clear of it until it subsides . . . it doesn't take long.'

'A veterinary surgeon . . . It won't be a butcher; those cuts are done with a razor or scalpel. You notice that she had had a child, or children.' Frank Kerley gently touched the woman's wrinkled belly, with white stretch scars here and there.

In life her breasts, within boning, had appeared bouncy and high, but unsupported were the looser breasts of a mother who has suckled a child. Although she had, before death, the appearance of a young and lovely woman, the evidence of her motherhood was in the belly stretched and wrinkled from carrying.

'Motive, sir?'

'Motive, Sergeant? Will he have a motive that we would understand? Perhaps she said something that reminded him of an unpleasant experience and wished to punish her. Or he may not have liked to have other men touch her after him – a kind of desecration. Perhaps he liked knives, carried them, and the idea suddenly came upon him that he must have the experience of using them. He may not even remember what twisted motive he had by the time we reach him. Instead of motive, we'll have to make do with knowing of his cunning, his dissipation, arrogance, disdain for a woman sunk so low.'

'Yes, it occurred to me that he must be disdainful. Mrs Wright says she saw him, so he must have felt cock-sure of himself.'

'Not a man from her past, but a complete stranger.'

'Passing through, knows he won't return.'

'Even so, put a discreet watch on this place. A decadent, perverted and corrupt mind. When we find him I believe we shall discover a debauchee, someone who enjoys whoring, gambling, violence the lot. I'll wager he has been through our hands before today . . . Possibly he pulls the legs from spiders and the wings from butterflies. But he won't have the appearance of Caliban. He shall not get away with pleading insanity, Sergeant, we shall make sure of that.'

'He'll be as plausible as you and me, sir. I mean that

he has two eyes and speaks the Queen's English, and we shall need all our senses to find him. And if I follow your breakdown of his character correctly, then I fancy he's got about as much conscience as Iago.'

The superintendent now withdrew his gaze from the body, and found it captured by the knowing grey eyes of his large, fair detective sergeant. Handsome face, manly frame, and the broad honest features of a man who, one might imagine, would be better riding a shire horse over the ribbles of a ploughed field than riding a London Underground train.

Iago? Never underestimate Frank Kerley. Despite the rural accent, he was self-educated and as intelligent as they come.

The detective sergeant now moved to look out of the window. 'The mortuary cart's arrived, sir.'

'Is she going to have to be carried out through that gawping crowd?'

'The only other exit is through the basement, and that still comes up in the street.'

'I will go back to the station and send out some more men. Christmas Day . . . I know, Frank, they won't like it.'

'I'll remind them that they'll get dinner tomorrow whereas she won't.'

'When they arrive, shut the Wrights in their room, remind the mortuary men that there are ghouls out there. Just keep them off her whilst she makes her last curtain call.'

'Right, sir, I shall threaten them with a charge for

obstructing police in the course of their duty if I have to.'

Frank was certain that the super had recognized the victim. 'We'll get the beggar, sir.'

'We have to, Sergeant. He has a taste for blood.'

Josephine decided that it would be better to make a late appearance at lunch than to leave Ann Martha to find an excuse for her absence. Mr Hood had sufficient material to get his special edition out. If Uncle James came home, she might do better to pick up some bit of information from him; even so, on her way back to the house she had the cabby stop off at the police mortuary. She came away with a prize. The victim's name was Burton. Once she had this, she ordered the cabby to take her to the Alhambra Palace where, on a billboard, she found 'Clara Burton – Songs and Ballads' listed almost at the bottom of the bill.

'I hope you know where you're goin', miss. We been over half London.'

'If you are worried about your fare, tell me what it is so far.' He did, and she paid him, then he drove her to West Central, where she arrived in time to join the gathering round the cold collation and make her apologies. Ann Martha was mollified at having at least one other member of the Thomson family there and, as Colonel Henderson commented, such a bright and sparkling young conversationalist at that.

By the time Kerley got round to taking statements from the inhabitants of number 12, Mrs Wright had changed into a dark red gown, very suited to her colouring. In the living room she placed on the table a tray with best china and a rich fruit cake for the delectation of the good-looking police sergeant. She had taken a few nips of best London gin to stop the shakes.

The thought that she had set eyes upon the killer was terrifying.

Having given the lodgers permission to return to their rooms to dress and hold themselves in readiness for giving statements. Sergeant Kerley questioned Mrs Wright first. He accepted tea and cake and spoke gently. 'I understand that this will be a great ordeal for you, Mrs Wright.'

'I don't care about that, Mr Kerley, you just get him. She was a nice quiet sort, not at all the sort you might think'd get herself murdered.'

Costermonger Flack. He wasn't on his stand, so Kerley went back to Bow Street looking for one of the uniformed men who walked the Great Coram Street beat and who would likely know where Flack lived.

'You come with me, Constable. He'll know you, so he won't take fright at a detective come knocking at his door late on Christmas Day.'

George Flack had the gravelly voice of a costermonger, and his accent was true Bow Bells. 'I would 'a come dahn to the nick in the mornin'. When I heard that one of Mrs Wright's lodging girls had been murdered. I thought maybe it was the one who stopped and bought stuff from me off the late 'bus. Mind, most of the girls was taking fruit home for to eat on Christmas afternoon. But this one, the cove with 'er, he never seemed kosher. Summit about him, if you know what I mean.'

'No . . . what?'

'First off, you tell me if the girl who was killed was the singer.'

'Why?'

'Because, if it was, then you can be sure it was the bloke who was with her. He was shifty – you don't do a job like mine with 'arf London coming and going and not be able to pick out a bad'n. He really didn't want to buy her no fruit. A real miser. He was counting out his pence as though they was pieces of gold. She really wanted a pineapple. I mean, a pineapple at Christmas, what a treat.'

'But he didn't buy her one?'

'Did he hell-as-like. "Enough!" he said. "Too much cost." So, there's a clue for you, Mr Kerley. He never spoke proper English. Any ordinary sort of cove would'a said "It's too dear, you have the apples." Something like that, you know what I mean. He could speak English, but not proper.'

'Can you describe him? What he was wearing?'

'Oh yes, that's another thing that makes me think you've got to look for a foreigner. He had queer sort of clothes . . . and boots.'

Flack gave an even better description than Mrs Wright. The two of them together would give the artist as good a picture of the man as was possible.

'Sometime tomorrow, Mr Flack. I will send a message for you to attend at Bow Street and look at some sketches an artist will be making. Other people have seen a man of similar description to the man you saw, so together we should get it right.'

Boxing Day 1872

In the first hours of Boxing Day, James Thomson was seated in his little study, hardly tasting the single malt whisky, a gift from Josie who always had the good sense not to give the trumpery that young women often thought men would enjoy. Deep in thought, the wood stove burning hot, he had the letter that the victim had not posted, and the one from her sister, pleading with her to spend Christmas, spread out before him.

The letter that 'C. Burton' had written but not posted read:

My dear sister, Your letter came safely to hand. I have not answered before I have been in a great deal of trouble. I have left Mrs Hillerton and am living at the above address. I am sorry I cannot accept your kind invite for Christmas. I have so much to attend to or I would accept it with pleasure. With kindest love to all wishing you a Happy Christmas & Happy New Year to you all, from your ever affectionate sister C. Burton.

But where was the letter that had come safely to hand? Mrs Hillerton? He hoped that Kerley would have been able to get to her before she heard the news of her sister's death from the daily papers.

His conscience was troubling him. The rosary. He and Frank Kerley had worked together for a long time. They were like a long-married couple, opposites who complemented one another.

He couldn't remember any other occasion when he had not been entirely honest with Kerley. It distressed him. He should have said something the moment he recognized the woman, but he had been confused seeing the death-mask features that he had once known as animated. The moment passed and he was now faced with how to tell his sergeant. Kerley was as sensitive and cerebral as any of Thomson's own exalted circle who thought that their own class had a monopoly on such gifts. Kerley wouldn't have missed the pocketing of the rosary. It lay now on his desk; delicate pink beads linked with a chain and hung with a small plain cross.

Never underestimate Frank Kerley.

It couldn't be left. He must see Kerley first thing. If I become emotional, then so be it. There is no shame in tears. But there was indignity. Not at the station. Kerley must know before they met to organize the investigation.

There was a soft knock on the door. 'Who is it?'

'Me, Josie. Uncle James, may I come in?'

James opened the door for her; dressed in a cashmere shawl over a flannel nightgown and sensible slippers, she came in and he kissed her cheek. 'What are you doing roaming around at this ungodly hour?'

'I am going home in the morning, and I guessed that you would be away early. I wanted to give you this before I left.'

'But you have given me an excellent Christmas present,' he indicated the whisky. 'Truly to my taste, as you know.'

'This one is supplemental, and I am delivering it at midnight away from the curious eyes of my guardian angels.' She handed him a flat parcel that held no mysteries.

'A book? Thank you, Jo, my dear. Something to look forward to reading when the first rush of this new case slows down.'

'No, I should like you to look at it tonight. It contains something that I want you to know.' She felt nervous. 'I chose the binding and endpapers myself.' She paused. 'Could I have a nip of whisky?'

Quite taken aback, as she had expected, he exclaimed, 'Whisky?' Shaking his head ruefully, and reaching for a flat-bottomed glass, he said, 'Since when have you taken to strong drink?'

'Since I stopped having the guardian angels around. A little water please.'

James wondered if this was more of a gesture of proof

of independence than a taste for spirits. However, when she took a sip and held it in her mouth, savouring its flavour, he changed his mind.

Since she and Hani had arrived on their doorstep, each with few belongings, he and Ann had had many firm exchanges of view as to how Josephine was to be brought up, to say nothing of Hani's input. Often it was the two women against his decision, but when he thought it right, he overruled, because he thought he knew what Jo's father would have wanted for his daughter. There could be no argument about that.

As he looked at her now, confident, balanced, well-educated, and apparently happy, he thought that the four of them had done pretty well. She had come into his and Ann's life at a time when the prospects of a family of their own had been pretty bleak.

'Was the cold collation a success?'

'Yes, it was.'

'I am sorry that I could not be there. Thank the Lord for a wife like Ann who understands my duties.'

'Uncle James! You aren't at all sorry, you hate cold collations.'

'It is not the cold food, it is the artificiality of such occasions.'

'You like Lady Granville.'

He smiled over his spectacles as he picked at the red string knotted around the parcel. 'I do.'

'But not the Hendersons.'

'Josephine, do not put words into my mouth. Chief Commissioner Henderson is my superior by far, and it is not usual that a police commissioner will eat under the roof of a lowly super. It is an honour not extended to others of my rank.'

'He likes to hobnob with blue blood, and he knows there will always be some around Aunt Ann's table. I like Lady Granville. I shouldn't mind it if I grow old like her.'

James Thomson laughed. 'I am certain that you can become imperious if you set your mind to it.'

She held her glass out. 'A tiny nip, please. I need a bit of Dutch courage.' When he didn't respond she started, 'There is something that I've wanted to admit to for months now.'

'A young man?' He tipped a generous tot into her glass.

'Open your parcel.' He did so and looked at her, puzzled that it was a scrapbook of newspaper cuttings. Flicking through them he said, 'What is this?'

'This is everything written by Jemima Ferguson. She used to write for *The Echo* and now she writes for *The News*.'

'Ah, the gossip sheet that likes to "tickle" its readers.'

'There is no need to look down your nose at the gossip sheets, Uncle James. They have readers like Ann, and thousands of other sensible people – Lady Granville too, I wouldn't be surprised. There's nothing wrong with a bit of light-heartedness mixed in with the serious and heavy stuff. I know that you don't take *The News*, but have you ever sat down to read it from front page to back?'

He smiled, 'Ah, so this is your method of enlightening me. A woman newspaper writer? Well, I must say you have captured my interest. If you think this lady has something to say of interest, then I am sure that she has.'

'Don't be so patronizing, Uncle James.'

He raised his eyebrows. This was the first time that the child who had brought joy into their marriage had spoken to him as an adult, as an equal. It was very late. He was very weary. He wasn't sure he knew how to respond or handle her.

'Jemima Ferguson is a good journalist. Though she writes about minor events, she tries to draw attention to all kinds of injustices. I know that they are short pieces, but if you read them you will see how concerned and serious-minded she is.'

'Josie, my dear, I am sorry if I'm not responding as you hoped, but I am at a loss to know what you want me to say, or why you have gone to such trouble as to make a collection of cuttings.'

She finished off the dregs of the whisky, placed the glass firmly on the desk and looked directly at him. 'Because, Uncle James, I am Jemima Ferguson.'

James Thomson looked closely at the pasted cuttings as though he had never encountered newsprint before, and then at Josephine.

'What made you think of doing this? Journalism is not exactly a world for women.'

'Which is *such* a good reason to enter it. You're behind the times, Uncle James. In America . . .'

'Ah *America*.'

She heaved an exasperated sigh. 'Oh what a put-down. They are centuries ahead of this country where women are concerned. Women can be *anything* they choose.'

'A slight exaggeration, Josephine. One or two women, *maybe*, have broken into one or two professions—'

'One or two women are enough to break open the gates and let in other women. Well, I intend to break open the gates to the newspaper empire here. If you read the next edition of *The News* you will see my name – Jemima's name – on the front page, and again in the Obituaries.'

'You should have told me . . . us.'

'I wanted to make something of myself in the newspaper world first.'

'Did you think that I wouldn't approve? Well, I tell you this, Josephine, I don't.'

Josephine was dashed. 'Not approve? There is nothing not to approve of. I do good work. If you will read those pieces, you will see that.'

'I see reporters every day of my life. I don't have great regard for them.'

'Why?'

'They can be like vultures over a kill, each of them scrabbling for the best bits before the rest. I don't want you to be part of that, Josephine.'

'I am already part of it. Except that my methods are not to scrabble. Don't underestimate me, Uncle James.'

'Since you came to us, I have always been guided by what I thought your father would have wanted for you. I hardly think that he would have wanted his only daughter to work for a newspaper.'

'What my father would have wanted has nothing to do with it. And, I have to say this, Uncle James, what you want for me has nothing to do with it. You and Ann have given me everything, I love you for it, and shall always be grateful. But I am on my own now. I can now pay my own way. I have an income and received a twenty pounds bonus from my editor. *He* thinks I am good at what I do.'

'Because of this?' Indicating the cuttings.

'Because of that and the fact that *The News* wanted to employ women on their staff. I am the first. It was important that I do well. And I have done that. As you will see when tomorrow's edition arrives on the streets.'

Pausing for moments before he did so, he moved aside a pile of documents, and pulled out a fold of newsprint. 'You mean this?'

When she saw the distinctive head, she snatched the paper from him. Mr Hood had done it. Following the Duke of Wellington's attitude of 'Publish and be damned', he had got the special edition onto the streets ahead of the rest.

MURDER
ACTRESS KILLED ON
CHRISTMAS MORNING

Josephine quickly scanned the brief account. Most of her words had survived the blue pencil. But George Hood had not kept his promise: there was no byline giving Jemima's name, just the anonymous, 'by a *News* crime reporter'. Disgusted, she flung the paper down. 'He promised me . . . he actually said that I had broken the news ahead of everybody and deserved my name on the front page. And I do. Have you read this, Uncle James? Every word about the murder was written by me.'

James Thomson seized the paper and scanned the report. 'By you?'

'As Jemima Ferguson, yes.'

He read aloud, '". . . the man seen leaving the house in the early hours of Christmas morning was described to our crime reporter as young, of average height, wearing a short topcoat, pull-on boots and a billy-cock type of hat. He walked away in the direction of Great Coram Street."' James lowered the paper and put his head in his hands.

'How did you come by this information, and that he went in the direction of Great Coram Street?'

'In the way good reporters do – I went to the obvious place, and asked.'

Holding his head in his hands, he was silent for long moments. 'Josephine, I would be well within my rights to take you to Bow Street for questioning.'

'I might not mind that, Uncle James. Experience.'

'It is not amusing to me, Josephine. You have plastered across the front page evidence that the police might not like to have the general public know. He may well not be the murderer, and as a consequence the police will be inundated with sightings of a young man wearing a short coat and a billy-cock hat.'

'And one of them may well be the man who killed the singer.'

James was confused. Outside 12 Great Coram Street, only Kerley and himself knew that the victim was a singer. 'Josie, the police can only make two and two facts make four pieces of evidence – never three, or five or seven. *That* way we get to the truth.'

'Are you saying that *Harriet* Burton is not the victim, or that *Clara* Burton is not a singer?'

'I am saying nothing about anything, Josie. I am on dangerous ground here. As you must realize, our relationship could be damaging to the investigation. If it becomes known that *The News* crime reporter is the niece of the senior officer investigating this case, I should be compromised.' Long moments of silence fell between them. 'I have to be up and about early, and as you are several hours of rest ahead of me, I am going to bed. I'm sorry, but I can't leave you here as I have evidence that I must lock away. Sadly, I cannot trust you.'

'I would never look at evidence like that. I might keep my ears open to get a clue as to where you shot off to when we came from church. but I would never—'

'Who told you about the man in the billy-cock hat?'

'Uncle James!'

'Urgently, Josie. I must verify this sighting.'

'Who have you interviewed so far?'

'The inhabitants of number 12.'

'Including the skivvies, Mrs Wright's girl and Edith who works on the opposite side of the road?'

James stiffened. When Mrs Wright had assembled all the inhabitants, there had been no scullery maid, just a maid-of-all-work who he and Kerley had assumed was the bottom of the Wright's household pile.

'Her name is Daisy, and she is quite friendly with Edith, who lives opposite. I interviewed Edith.' She turned as she was leaving his stuffy study. 'Now you won't need to take me down to Bow Street for questioning. Goodnight, Uncle James, I expect our paths will cross tomorrow – well, actually it will be today.'

'Josie—'

'Oh, don't worry, Uncle James, I would never embarrass you by letting it be known that we are in any way connected.'

'Nothing to do with embarrassment, Josephine; it can never be known that I have the slightest connection with news reporters. Already I am compromised.'

'How? I made sure that I kept well away from where you and Sergeant Kerley were.'

'How did you know where to go?' His voice was not gentle.

Neither was hers when she said, 'I have good hearing. You mentioned "Coram" to your cabby, so I went to Coram's Fields, and saw the spectators in Great Coram Street.' If it was not the exact truth, it was only to save the young constable from a dressing-down.

*　　*　　*

James Thomson left the house very early, leaving a note of apology to Ann and a little box containing a necklace of jet that she had admired.

Having made a decision regarding Harriet Burton's rosary, which he had taken from the scene of crime, he now strode out with purpose to Bow. The air was still frosty and snow had rutted in the gutters. It was perfect weather for clearing the head. Should he tell Kerley about Josephine?

'Francis.' Elizabeth Kerley called from the back kitchen door. 'You said you wanted to be about early. It's nigh on six forty-five.'

'I'm not so deaf I can't hear the bells, and there'll be no pies if I don't give the rabbits their turnip-tops.'

His wife was the only person who had never dropped his given name. He liked that; it was something close and personal between Elizabeth and himself. He could still recollect the thrill of the first time she said, 'Oh, Francis,' as they broke away from their first passionate embrace. They had married soon after that, each knowing that, when they were in the presence of one another, they could easily snap together like magnets. They had laughed loudly when Elizabeth had said, 'I think we should go for consummation as quick as possible, Francis.'

'You mean consummation as in you and me getting wed?'

Elizabeth, with her arms around his neck, and smiling up at him, said, 'I was thinking that, or something.'

'We could have the first banns called on Sunday.'

'And get wed after three weeks.' She had kissed him hard. 'Because I tell you, Francis Kerley, consummation with you don't hardly leave my mind since you walked me home – for my safety's sake, wasn't it?'

Having found the bare small of her back, he had slid his hands down until he had one firm cheek in each hand. He had laughed into her neck, making her squirm. 'Three weeks is a long time, my lover?'

Without coyness she felt his erection.

'What say to the banns on Sunday?'

She had kissed him close to his ear and whispered, 'Marriage end of August, and prenuptial consummation here and now.'

It had been August, warm, the smell of straw and corn on the air, and the brook chattering, bats flying, nightingales and owls calling, full cows lowing for the milkmaids' tugging fingers. As they lay side-by-side, astonished at what they had discovered, Elizabeth had said, 'Oh Francis, do you realize that we have just consummated?'

Frank Kerley knew a score of other words, but for a reason not understood by them, the word, and the act, were destined to become an important part of their married life together.

The following May, their daughter Frances had been born.

And to an extent their marriage had continued like that. Their physical enjoyment, cementing their growing respect for – and liking of – one another. It would be hard to find a better marriage than that of the Kerleys. It was seldom now that they needed to say the word they had once found so amusing: a look was enough. Their physical attraction for one another had never waned, but had grown full and satisfying.

Frank came into the kitchen, washed his hands, and sat at the table, where Elizabeth put a proper breakfast before him. Plenty of meat and eggs, and bread. Plenty of tea in a large covered pot.

'I'll go up and wash and dress. I'll be down by the time you've finished.' She kissed him lightly as he began to eat.

'Elizabeth.' She looked back at him from the doorway. 'I'm sorry I was sarcastic about . . . when you reminded me about the time.'

'Francis Kerley, you went out and didn't come back till late yesterday, and I reckon it won't be any different today. You're weary and will be even wearier before you sort out this terrible case.'

'They will write her up as a prostitute. She was just a poor young woman, trying to keep her head above water.'

'Isn't that what all of them are?'

Frank looked at her. She was a woman's woman, always turning things on their head, siding with women, defending their actions. 'She picked a bad'n, and he did for her.'

'More likely that he picked her, wouldn't you say, Francis. Oh Lord! There's the front door. You answer it, I'm not respectable.'

*   *   *

116

Josephine's two guardian angels hovered around Josephine as she made ready to return to her other home. ''osie, I have fetch your overshoes from shoe cupboard. These are warm for you.'

It was no good protesting, and it was sensible because snow had fallen on snow overnight. Josephine stepped into the waterproofs whilst Ann wound a silk scarf about her throat. 'There is nothing like silk to hold the body's warmth.'

Josephine smiled and allowed the scarf to be knotted artfully. 'You taught me that, the first winter after we came to England. In the East silk is for airiness, in England for warmth.'

Hani ran to answer a sharp rap on the front door. 'Cab is here.'

Josephine said her warm thanks and goodbyes.

'You know that you can stay longer, Josephine.'

'I know that, Ann, and I appreciate it, but I believe that Liliana will have returned by now, and we promised ourselves a visit to the shops to try for bargains.'

Ann Martha waved that thought aside. 'There are no such things as bargains, Josephine, only out-of-date fashions and soiled goods. If you want a new hat, buy one, not a thing that has been on a hundred heads before yours.'

The cab driver collected her bags and waited with the cab door open ready. 'I promise that I won't buy a single hat.'

'Good, and I am certain that your friend who spends

time in Paris would never dream of such a waste of good money.'

The three women hugged and kissed goodbye, and the cabby was away before Josephine could wave at her guardian angels.

James Thomson sat with Kerley whilst he finished his breakfast. The cup of tea was very different from the China he usually took in the morning, but this was good, Indian; it had a lot of body and taste.

On his way to Bow, his mind had dwelt upon his meeting with the girl he had always remembered with warmth and gratitude. She had been a kind person, and he had gained the opinion that – given different circumstances – she would have made a fine wife. Perhaps she had done; so far, all that they knew of her as a resident of the Wrights was that her life as a singer did not bring in enough to keep a roof over her head so she had been forced to take men home. Men? Perhaps not men, perhaps just this one man. Perhaps because it was Christmas and she was being the good-natured and sympathetic woman he had known briefly. He tried to conjure up an image of her last night. Perhaps she had been singing. A man had complimented her on her sweet voice, as he himself had once done. She would have glowed with gratitude. The man, a stranger, a foreigner, and she had been kindly to him.

He was greatly troubled by Josephine. He and Ann Martha and Hani had given her more freedom to make decisions than most children would have been given.

He and Ann Martha had discussed such matters of her upbringing on many occasions. His brother had had many unusual ideas regarding the disciplining of young children, and encouraged them when they were old enough to make their own decisions and their own mistakes. But he himself was not her father. Quite possibly, because he was endeavouring to—

Frank Kerley's voice broke into this preoccupation. 'Is the tea to your liking, sir? Not too strong?'

'Oh dear, I am sorry, I was miles away.'

Frank Kerley could see that, all right, and the expression of pain and trouble that flickered across his brow.

'Would it trouble you if I were to use your first name when we are not on duty?'

'I should be glad, sir.'

'The tea is excellent. What is it?'

'The tea? It's just ordinary breakfast tea. We don't ever drink any other, except when Elizabeth has some of her delicate artist friends to visit her.'

James at once wanted to ask about the artist friends, but this was neither the time nor the place. And it was possible that there would never be a good opportunity. Their lives were set well apart. How sad that the rules and proprieties of their profession prevented a close friendship. He had no friends to speak of. Some acquaintances, people whose company he and Ann Martha invited, but most of them were Ann's friends. No one close, except Gwendoline Granville, who had known him in Smyrna when he was a youthful palace-aide in a fanciful uniform. Frank Kerley would be

119

a good man to count as a friend. This visit was likely to be as close as they would ever get.

'This would not have been so difficult for me had I spoken yesterday.'

To help his super, Frank cut himself a generous slice of cheese and indicated that the super should help himself.

Absent-mindedly, James cut a small crumbly corner but did not eat it. 'Unless I have underestimated you, I suspect that you already know why I have come before we both start work today.'

'The victim was not a stranger to you.'

James nodded. 'Though I did not know her, except as a singer.' James handed Frank the large envelope containing the letter and the rosary. 'It's all there.'

'I am sure it is, sir.'

'But you will check against your list.'

Frank grinned. 'You wouldn't keep me on as your DS if you thought I wouldn't. Trust is one thing, evidence is another.'

'The woman, Burton, was once very kind to me. Perhaps at a more appropriate time and place, I shall tell you more, but I swear – on oath if you like – that my meeting with the victim has nothing to do with this investigation.'

'Very well, sir. Let's leave it at that, shall we?'

Frank got up from the table and took his plate to the sink, where he scraped the leavings into a dish. 'I'll just take these to the chickens, if you don't mind. Should you care to take a look, I'm proud of them.'

Frank Kerley led the way to the bottom of the long, narrow garden. Brussels sprouts grew in straight rows. Spinach, too, and other brassicas that James didn't recognize in their growing state. 'What's that with the leaves?'

'Curly kale. We like it, but mostly it goes to the chickens and rabbits.'

'Rabbits too?'

Frank snapped off some leaves and held them to the cages. Several fat rabbits came to feed. 'And the chickens are through the gate.'

'You brought a bit of the countryside to London to remind you of it?'

'No, Mr Thomson, this isn't remotely like rural England. Nobody keeps animals boxed up like this. They roam free and take their chances with predators. In London, all of us is in boxes.'

'So why . . . ?'

'Food, fresh food. We know where they come from and what they've been fed on. If we could keep fish, too, then we would.'

'How do you find time?'

'Elizabeth. I like to feed the animals when I can, but she's the one who grows our food.'

'What good use she makes of her time.'

'Time, sir. We should be leaving.'

James nodded.

'About the rosary, sir?'

'It had been mine, I gave it to her, I don't know why, in the nature of a token of . . . I am a Roman Catholic,

Frank, and she acted as a confessor would. I told her something that I could never tell Ann. Nothing bad, Frank, just sad . . . very sad.'

A short silence ensued, after which James again took up his rank. 'Did we get a statement from Daisy, the scullery maid at number 12?' It was obvious from the sergeant's expression that they had not. '*The News* has brought out a kind of penny sheet. It's all on the front page. It's my guess that the sighting must have been from the house opposite, and the only person likely to be about at dawn must be the scullery maid.'

'Mrs Wright didn't say that she had a scullery maid . . .'

'You didn't interview one?'

'No, sir, Mrs Wright said she had assembled the entire household. Dammit, she didn't consider a scullery maid worthy of attention, I'll be bound. And I am as bad not asking.'

'Well, see to it, Sergeant.'

They were well on their way to the police station when Frank Kerley said, 'You say *The News* published details of a sighting? We should have them for withholding evidence.'

'Nothing was withheld, Sergeant: I told you, it's spread across the front of *The News*.'

At Bow Street Police Station, Frank Kerley gathered his squad of trained detectives and a few from the uniformed branch who would be working on the case.

'Notebooks, men. On the cover write "Harriet Burton, sometimes known as Clara Burton and Mrs Brown.

Murdered Christmas Day Eighteen Seventy-two. Page one you head with the name "Miss Burton". Write it in large letters. Whenever you refer to this victim you will use her *name* – not "dolly-mop" or "prossie" or "doxie," or any of the names you are inclined to use when referring to women who have nothing to sell but the parts of their body that they would much prefer to keep to themselves. Understand?' There was some embarrassed mumbling. 'I said "Understand?" That loud enough for you?'

There was a sibilant reply, 'Yess, Ssargeant.'

'You, DC Morrisy,' he indicated a detective standing at the back of the room. 'I want you to be present when the first three of our witnesses arrive to describe a suspect to the artist. I know that some of you think that sketches are a waste of time, but we have nothing better. This time we have two witnesses who saw the suspect clearly, so what I want is for you to oversee each of the attempts of the artist to catch an image, and then to see how each witness responds to the other sketches. By this means, we should get a good likeness. As we gather more information, we may amend the likeness. See that our witnesses are well taken care of, don't leave them hanging around in cold rooms, and remember they have work to do, same as you, and they won't be earning whilst they are here. I know I've said it before, but I'm saying it again – witnesses are our best evidence. Make them feel comfortable. We should all look pretty stupid questioning an empty witness box.' As usual this got a bit of a smile.

His longest-serving men were well used to Kerley's thinking: witnesses aren't keen to come forward, so make them glad that they have, make them feel important, which they usually are.

'The rest will be detailed off to make enquiries about the victim's movements from when she arrived at the Alhambra Palace on Christmas Eve to the point where she alighted from the late omnibus passing through Coram Fields and bought fruit from one of the witnesses coming in today. One last thing, put your hearts into this one. Superintendent Thomson says our murderer has a taste for blood . . . yes! He will do it again if we don't get him soon. He killed yesterday in the early hours, his trail must still be warm. You find him. As soon as we have a likeness, you shall have it.'

DC Morrisy paid close attention as he listened to the Wrights and Flack the costermonger, and watched the artist.

'He wasn't no more than average tall. Early twenties. Darkish. Rough complexion like he needed a shave . . .'

'I think he was a bit spotty . . .'

'He didn't have a beard but he wasn't clean-shaven.'

'He might have been a bit feverish, blotchy like . . .'

'He wore a queer sort of hat.'

'He had on a round billy-cock hat, but with a narrow brim.'

'He wore a round hat dented on the crown.'

'His topcoat was short.'

'He wore a short topcoat . . .'

'He had on a warm coat, but it only came to his knees.'

'His boots was like seamen's boots, or maybe elastic sided . . .'

'I can't really say about his boots except that they was pull-ons.'

'Sea boots, I remember definitely sea boots.'

'He looked a surly cove.'

'He wasn't English . . .'

'He had a distinct foreign accent.'

'He was a foreigner.'

As the detectives spread out across the area of Clara Burton's known activity on Christmas Eve, more and clearer descriptions came in. A sketch was printed, which all of the witnesses agreed was a fair likeness.

It was very early, but as on any other day in Fleet Street, reporters and editors, sub-editors and copy-writers were already working, providing the copy that would begin rolling off the presses that night, so that people could devour news and their breakfasts at the same table.

Although it was so early, George Hood was already seated at his desk. 'Ah-ha, the young woman of the moment. Come in, come in, Miss Ferguson. Sit down, sit down. I am very pleased with your piece. Very enterprising. You have the makings of an excellent reporter.'

'The makings? Excuse me, Mr Hood, I am an excellent reporter. You all but promised me that I should get my byline on the Great Coram Street Murder, and what is there? "*The News*'s Crime Reporter." All of our crime reporters are men: they will take the credit. I feel really let down. Really! Really! If any of the men had come in with this, the credit would have been given, front-page name.'

'I don't remember actually promising that your name would be on the piece.'

'Oh don't you, Mr Hood? Well I remember exactly. I may be a woman, and I may be one of the first to get a foot in the door as a serious reporter, but I will not let you or anyone try to put me down. I *earned* my name on that story.'

He held up his hands, palms out. 'Miss Ferguson, just sit down and let us talk about this.'

'No, Mr Hood. There is nothing to talk about. I got this story before anyone. What happened between my story and its publication?'

'Nothing. But we did discuss the problem of crossing the church.'

'Oh, so?'

'On reflection, I thought that *The News* should not try for too much notoriety at one go.'

'Do you mean that having a woman scoop up a story before anybody, and giving her credit for it, would be construed as *notorious*? I cannot believe it! I have always thought you to be more advanced in your thinking than the rest.'

'*The News* has plans to take on more and more women. On reflection I thought it might be too much of a poke in the eye having a woman reporter scoop the rest. That could well disrupt our plans to feminize our staff.'

'To have a successful woman reporter? That could push your plans ahead five years.'

'I'm sorry, Miss Ferguson, I daren't risk what we are achieving here.'

'Oh, and just what are you achieving – the double-crossing of a really good reporter because she wears skirts? I had a better opinion of you than that. I shall resign.'

'If you do that it will be *you* who will be putting the clock back.'

'You are turning this on its head.' She flung her hands in the air in despair.

'You *are* a good reporter, you have the instinct, the flair and such a way with words,' George Hood insisted.

'Not a lot of good if nobody reads them. Not even the police knew that the killer walked in the direction of Great Coram Street.'

'How do you know that?'

'You don't really expect me to tell you that, Mr Hood.'

Hood looked puzzled, possibly trying to fathom how she obtained police information. Maybe conjecture. She was bright enough. 'I don't want to lose you, Miss Ferguson. Quite possibly I made a slight miscalculation in not giving you the byline.'

'Not slight, Mr Hood. I have more information, a lot

more, but there's no way that I will give it to *The News* unless I have a guarantee that my name will head every word of mine that appears in print.'

Sudden inspiration. A book! Make Harriet Burton the heroine. The plot is there, I have only to research the detail of her life. No, a biography. A good, readable biography.

She knew that she could do it.

After Mrs Wright had approved the artist's sketch, she told the uniform keeping control of the front of house at Bow Street Police Station that she wished to see Sergeant Kerley. 'What's it in connection to?'

'With – in connection with. It is in connection with the murder of Miss Burton.'

'You're a witness, then.' He recalled DS Kerley's warning about witnesses.

'Of course I am, haven't I just come from the artist?'

'Please wait, ma'am. You can sit down if you care to, come round here, we have a little stove going. Your name?' He poised his pen to make an entry in the log.

'Wright, Mrs Frank Wright of 12 Great Coram Street. Near Russell Square, London.'

Tomorrow she would be in the London papers.

Sergeant Kerley came into the little public office. The constable hadn't been able to say what she wanted. 'You always say we should look after witnesses, and by God, sir, she's a top one. I reckon she must be the landlady.' Kerley was cautious because there were always people who, having had a taste of celebrity, wanted to hold on to it. There was no doubt that Mrs Wright liked to be up front; it occurred to him that she might have been on stage herself: she did tend to strut rather than walk.

'Mrs Wright, thank you for coming to the artist's session. I believe that we have come up with a very fair sketch of him. Were you satisfied?'

'All of us agreed that it was a good likeness, but disagreed a little as to detail.'

'Oh, please, tell me.'

'I thought that he was a little rough about the chin, and maybe a little shabby, but George Flack – I've known him for years, honest as they come, but maybe, being a man and a little rough himself, he might not have judged the murderer as a woman would.'

'Suspect, Mrs Wright, we mustn't make assumptions.'

'I'm a very good judge of character, Mr Kerley, and I would put money on him being the one. He was very shifty, that we did agree on. Mr Wright never had such a clear a view as I had, but he wasn't in no doubt that the man in the sketch was a very good likeness.'

'That's good, that's good. The constable said that you wanted—'

'Oh I do, Mr Kerley. I have discovered you a witness who can vouch to the time he left – give or take, you know. My Daisy ... Saw him creep downstairs and let himself out of the basement door, and then up the area steps.'

'Mrs Wright, I requested yesterday that you assemble your entire household.'

'I know, but I never thought at the time . . . Well, you know how it is with scullery maids, you don't think of them as a member of the household, do you?'

One of his super's new-fangled methods of training his men was to put on a little scene – such as the one Frank was now involved in – and learn how to control the situation to the advantage of the interrogator. There were times when a fist banged on a table, combined with a threatening voice, could work wonders with, say, a law-abiding clerk. Mrs Wright, however, needed to believe that, as a main witness, she was held in high esteem by the police. 'I don't have a scullery maid, but I should have been more specific. So, tell me about Daisy.'

'Not a lot to tell really. I would say she might be about twelve, but she is bright, and I have never had any trouble with her. She's a useful little thing, and I've taught her to be honest and truthful, so you can believe what she tells you.'

'Mrs Wright, what I should like is for me to get a cab and for you to come with me to your house. I don't want her prompted at all, but I should like you to assure her that she has no need to be afraid.'

'Little scullery maid' is often the term describing the lowest of the lowly below-stairs domestics, but Mrs Wright's Daisy was just that. Not reaching five foot in height, she was dwarfed by the detective's mass. He smiled, a smile he knew how to use and varied according to whom he was questioning. Charming and friendly, 'Well, miss, I near forgot to come and talk to you.'

Her eyebrows shot up and she blushed.

'Is it all right with you, ma'am, if I question Miss Daisy on her home territory so to speak?' and he indicated to Daisy that she lead the way below stairs. In many houses, the below-stairs arrangements could be most comfortable. This was usually the case in an affluent household with a good mistress, but here the only sign of comfort was an old-fashioned day bed that had seen better days, and the glow from between the bars of the kitchen range, the surface of which had that sheen which only daily black-leading can achieve.

Frank Kerley took one of the four wooden chairs arranged around a bare wooden table upon which various utensils were obviously being used for the making of something very floury. 'Sorry if I interrupted your work, I shan't keep you long.' The little thing was scared half to death; he'd never get more than a word if he couldn't get her over that. 'That's a beautiful bit of black-leading. Mrs Kerley'd be quite jealous if she could see that.' She quickly looked up at him and then returned her gaze to somewhere about his elbow. 'Mrs Wright said you saw somebody.'

Daisy nodded apprehensively, not certain whether she should have seen him, or told her mistress that she had done so.

'When did you see him?' With the blunt end of his pencil he drew a funny smiling snowman face in the film of flour.

A little smile came upon her lips, enough to relax her throat and permit her voice to come whispering out. 'Morning.'

'Where?'

She flicked a forefinger quickly in the direction of a door that appeared to lead outside. Frank went to it and lifted the latch, which made the familiar sound of an iron latch being lifted. 'Were the bolts shot home?' She nodded. He slid both bolts back and forth – they were oiled but grated a bit when moved, then returned to his chair. 'I'd feel a lot easier if you'd sit down, miss. Men aren't supposed to be seated whilst ladies are standing.' He indicated the chair nearest the range, and she slid into it. There were times when he quite despised himself for the acts he put on. Until now, he had overlooked her possible presence in the house, and now he was behaving like a blooming dancing master. But she was hardly more than a child, and he knew no other way of persuading her that he was not about to cuff her, which was likely to be her more usual experience of authority. 'That's better.'

'So where were you when this man came through and let himself out?'

'I'd a just woke up, but I wasn't out of bed and I watched him come down the stairs.' A very long sentence for Daisy.

'Was there any light?'

She shook her head. 'On'y through the window.'

'From a streetlight?'

She nodded.

Frank walked where anyone coming from upstairs

would walk to reach the back door, looked at what he might see of the room, then went to sit on the edge of the worn and seedy day bed. 'I'm surprised he didn't see you from there. Doesn't the light get as far as this?'

'I wasn't there. I was abed.'

Making assumptions again, Frank Kerley. 'Perhaps you wouldn't mind showing me.'

She indicated a walled space about a couple of feet wide, between the kitchen range and the kitchen wall; a space usually used for the drying out of damp fuel or for sweeping brushes and the like. 'It's the warmest part of the house. The walls gets nice and hot.'

Frank saw that, from Daisy's point of view, this lobby-hole might well be preferable to the old day bed. 'Ah,' he said, 'I can see it must be.' He grinned, 'Bit of a tight squeeze for me I reckon.'

She lowered her lids as she grinned back. Had she been a little braver she might have said, 'Oh, go on with you.'

Frank saw that he had won her over. 'So, then, tell me the whole thing.'

'Well, I hadn't been awake more than a minute or two. I was hoping the clock would strike so I wouldn't have to get out of bed to see the time, an' I heard the landing creak. And then the bottom stairs, they creak and all. I never took no notice, really, because quite often there's gentlemen as goes out in the early hours.'

'Out of the front door?'

She nodded. 'That's why I was surprised when I heard somebody come on down the back stairs. Nobody don't usually, not unless they got like gripes or something and they have to go out there in the night-time. So I just holded on because I never had on . . . I never had on my skirt and that.'

Frank added a top hat and collar to the face in the flour as he waited until she continued. 'I thought he was going to the pantry because he got a-hold of the latch. Then he must of realized it was the wrong door. Then he looked at the basement door and went on to that. He tried the latch first, then found the bolts. Only the bottom one works, the top one don't meet proper. He put down his coat and that and worked it open, then he picked up his things and lifted the latch and opened the door.' She looked at him apparently for approval or permission to continue.

Frank nodded encouragingly, 'And . . . ?'

'He put on his hat, then his coat. I tell you it was cold, the air don't half whip round that area, but it never took him more than a minute, then he shut the door, quiet.' She stopped. Frank hesitated before speaking in case there was more, but apparently not.

'You heard him go up the steps?'

She searched around in her memory. 'No, I never. I'll tell you why, I think he was in his socks and carrying his boots.'

'Did you see?'

'No, but he stopped and it sounded like he was pulling on his boots, grunting like, not loud.'

'Daisy, you are a very good observer. I have a very clear picture of what you saw.'

She blushed. 'It's not really very clever just to watch people.'

'Oh, you'd be surprised. So many people watch people but they never really see what's before their eyes. Not many would think to say about the putting on of his boots.' He grinned. 'Too much to hope for that you know what kind of hat?'

Had she known how, she might have preened with pleasure. 'Nearly like a billy-cock, only it wasn't just the same. And his coat wasn't a proper topcoat . . . well, it was, I mean it was a *top* coat, only it didn't come right down long.'

He went back upstairs to tell Mrs Wright that he had finished.

'Sergeant. I remembered something. She come from a place called "Wizzbeach". Queer sort of name, I remember thinking that when she told me.'

Well, my girl, you are on your own now. Although Josephine did not utter those exact words, this was her sentiment. When she had expected to cover the Great Coram Street murder, she had concocted a plan. This, now that she had no one to tell her otherwise, she could develop in more concrete terms. She would seek out the women amongst whom Harriet had lived and worked. David Wilde would know who to ask. If the poor and desperate prayed anywhere, it was where David Wilde was minister.

First, though, she must go to Harriet herself.

*   *   *

This was the second time in a few weeks that she had requested entry to the mortuary, the last being to look at Jane who had died of hunger. Although that had been the first time that she had seen a dead person – at least the first time that she had seen a dead white person. When she was a girl there had been several occasions when a native beggar had curled up waiting for her father, but had left it too late for any kind of medicine to help. That had not seemed so very bad: those people always wore clothes, were curled up and appeared to be asleep; but Jane and other corpses, awaiting a coroner's verdict, or to be claimed by a relative, were stiff and pale and unmistakably dead.

'You a relation?' The man guarding the entry shoved a piece of paper across the counter and, knowing from her last experience that relations were waved through on a signature, she said, 'Yes, distant.'

'She hasn't been here very long, you're the first, but I dare say there'll be plenty more once it gets around what happened. Are you going to do the identity?'

'No, I've just come to pay my respects before she is taken to be put in her coffin.'

'She was cut real bad . . . well, good in a way, quick for her. Don't remember seeing anything as clean and neat as that. Must have been a lot of blood.'

Josephine felt her cheeks burn with indignation, but bit back a scathing comment about her being a person not a curiosity. She had wanted to ask whether the wounds would be covered, but could not bear to be with the keeper any longer.

Harriet Burton was one of several corpses displayed for identification and the ministrations of a coroner. A raised walkway with a painted iron barrier surrounded the viewing area. Covered by a sheet, with only her head showing, she lay on her back in an odd position; her knees appearing to be bent outwards. Josephine frowned at what she feared might lie beneath the sheet. All the other corpses were as one would expect: toes turned up, tenting the covering sheet. A shiver ran through her – not the stark chill of the mortuary, but someone 'walking over her grave'. This could be Liliana or herself, a young woman who might have had another forty years of her life left.

Panic whirled in her chest, then anger. This was the second time in only weeks that she had stood and looked down at a young woman dead. 'Jane' and Harriet, dead because they were women. Dead because they were poor. Dead because nobody really cared enough to make changes. Better-off people would lose their servants and skivvies. Quite unexpectedly she found herself in tears. Sadness and frustration. Waste, loss, of women . . . children like little Micky 'Smiff'. She and her friends might talk the hind leg off a donkey about the conditions of the London poor, but what good did that do? They were talking to the converted.

A conversation that had happened only recently came back to her. Some of them had gathered round her kitchen table, drinking soup and airing their views and agreeing that 'The problem of "The London Poor" is holding back progress.'

'Of course something must be done.'

'But the very fact that even *we* can refer to "the London poor" is part of the problem. They are not "the" anything. They are individuals.'

David Wilde had said that. And he was right. Harriet was a pretty woman who could sing. She had talent, but not enough to give her a living. And so, being a woman, she had taken a man to her room.

That man had been so depraved and arrogant that he had not thought of her as a human being at all, but as a thing, a device to use to gratify his lust. Suddenly she understood what the strange angle of Harriet's legs indicated, and felt hot with guilt and shame.

How was it that a rather serious-looking young woman was able to contemplate depravity, or to consider lust? How could she understand the significance of the position of Harriet Burton's knees? The answer lay in the part that Hani had played in Jo's life long before they came to live in England, where girls and women were unenlightened about their own nature; where ignorance was considered to be innocence, and it was felt that unmarried girls should be kept that way.

But, perhaps in the whole of London, Josephine was unique: a young woman, raised in high society and not in the stews, who knew that men and women copulated, and did not think that a cab-horse with its organ engorged was losing its entrails. When the girl Hani had been taken in as nursery help by Josephine's

138

mother (who had expected to give birth to one baby and got twins), Hani was well prepared for her future as a married woman, which, although at the time she had not reached puberty and thus bride age, was not distant. But, poor Ann Martha when she discovered the uncomfortable truth, who can imagine the problems she faced at the time? There was such a wide gulf between what was expected to be known by girls and women and what – in their case – must be forgotten. But as happened when Pandora opened her box, once knowledge is out, it cannot be put away, though years passed before Ann Martha could assure herself that Hani and Josephine were not damaged in any way by the extent of their knowledge.

Just a short time ago Jo had been shouting at her editor because he had omitted to give her credit for reporting this woman's murder. Like all the other news vultures, she had wanted her pound of Harriet's flesh with her own name upon it.

She said silently what she would have wished to say aloud. I am so sorry, Harriet. Truly, sorry to have used you. But I promise, no matter what comes to light during the police investigation, I will discover the rest of you. Not Harriet the singer who was killed on Christmas Eve, but Harriet the young woman who had family, friends, had a childhood, had dreams. When they are picking over the unclean parts of your life, I shall look for the rest.

Superintendent Thomson went into his study and closed the door. Ann, he knew, had been disappointed at his absence at both Christmas Day lunch and dinner, and her forbearance was, as he so often found it to be, unbearable. Had she discharged her feelings in some normal display of feminine emotion, the domestic atmosphere would have soon cleared; as it was, her reasonableness pushed him further into withdrawal. The truth was, as he knew only too well, he withdrew because he felt culpable. It was true that one Bow Street detective had been on duty but had been taken home with a high fever, so had been unable to undertake the enquiries at Great Coram Street, but it would have been no great difficulty for James to have handed over to another inspector. The truth was, though, that James liked being at the centre of an investigation. It was what he was trained to do, it was what he was very good at doing, and what he liked to do. A good murder enquiry depended upon efficient organization. He was an organizer. Recently he had successfully organized the amalgamation of the 'F' and 'E' divisions at a saving of £1,000 per annum. But the satisfaction of having achieved this did not compare with the stimulation he experienced in organizing a murder investigation.

He finished the writing he had come to do and crossed to the window. A winter garden. Spare elegant skeletons and white trunks of silver birches, a small border of the newest shades of species azalea, beneath which bloomed the snow-white heads of the Christmas hellebore, and the yellow jasmine, which he liked so much for its colour and perfume that reminded him of the sun. He loved the sun. He had been born and raised with sun overhead for months on end. In six months, if there was a favourable late spring, he and Ann would be sitting on the stone terrace taking tea on Sunday afternoons, or cold lemonade of a morning. And later, in July and August, there would be small gatherings of friends listening to piano-playing and enjoying the last of the sun before a light supper. In no way approaching his mother's salons, but pleasurable. Very pleasurable.

But not today. Today, he saw neither bird-bath nor brilliant firethorn berries. That scene was obliterated by another. A cluttered bedroom, discarded clothing scattered around, scent bottles and powder boxes, bits and pieces of cheap jewellery. He saw the counterpane and the hair jumbled upon the pillow, the closed eyes, the peaceful expression. He felt in his jacket pocket for his rosary, but was hardly conscious of the thanks he gave for that look of peace. What if it had been horror? Or terror? He had seen that often enough on the face of a murder victim.

A flight of sparrows busily pecking crumbs caught his attention for a moment, but they soon dissolved into the image of a rosary in a small porcelain bowl. Did its separateness indicate that it was special? Perhaps above all he wanted to know this. Did the rosary merely happen to find a home in the bowl, or had the girl placed it there?

Turning away from the window, he made a decision that he would continue to act as senior officer in this case. He had done good work since he had been in 'E'

141

division, but had been too long involved in matters of administration. Having straightened his desk, he went to find Ann to tell her not to wait any meals for him, that he would be perfectly content with a plate of something cold.

The doors of the Alhambra Palace were ajar, although the bars were not yet open. On the list of attractions the name 'Clara Burton' still appeared. Here was a place that Josephine had often wanted to see, but for an unaccompanied woman to enter was to be misconstrued. A youth pushing a broom stepped in front of her. ''ello, sweetheart. Can I do anythink for you?'

In her London street-voice she said, 'I want to talk to somebody who works in the bar here.'

'Depends on which side of the bar you mean. The girls who works this side won't be here till the first show starts.' He grinned. 'If you're looking for that sort of work, you're a bit early in the day.'

'Are there any barmaids here yet?'

'Alice and Tryphena, but I haven't seen Alice yet.'

She followed him through the dimly lit interior of the famous music hall. The stage with its curtains drawn aside was a dark cavern. It must be wonderful to step onto it, into the limelight, and to have the ability to entertain an audience. She paused, trying to visualize Harriet doing that and to see her walking amongst the tables until a man stopped her. Was that how it was done?

'Are you coming, miss? I ain't got all day. You there, Tryphena?'

142

Just one lamp was burning behind the bar. A young woman appeared from behind a display of exotic drinks. 'What do you want, Billy?'

'A girl here wants you.'

Josephine engaged Tryphena's eyes. She was a striking-looking young woman who held her back straight so that her bosom was high in a close-bodiced frock of dark green. Over that she wore a waiter's long white apron tied snugly around her neat waist. Josephine held out her hand, which Tryphena shook firmly. 'I won't keep you long, Miss . . . ?'

'Douglas. All right, Billy, I'm quite able to talk to somebody without your ears flapping.' Billy went off, whistling shrilly. 'I haven't got a lot of time.'

Harriet or Clara? Clara or Harriet? If she chose wrongly she wouldn't engage the trust of this woman. 'I've just come from seeing Harriet.'

The barmaid clenched her fists and tightened her lips. 'Are you trying to have me on?'

She had chosen the right name. Tryphena obviously knew Harriet under her own name, and not just as one of the acts. 'No, no, I mean that I've just come from the mortuary. She looks very peaceful, and I wanted to talk to somebody who probably knew her.'

'My God! How could you do that? I shouldn't want to look at a cadaver.'

'I wasn't looking at a cadaver. I was looking at Harriet Burton and feeling angry at what had been done to her. If you saw her, wouldn't you feel like that?'

Tryphena Douglas's intelligent eyes engaged Josephine's,

and she nodded thoughtfully. 'I can feel like that without the need to look at her corpse. I could do with a drink. Do you want one?'

This reception was better than Josephine could have hoped for. 'Thanks, but nothing that's going to make me too tipsy. I've got a lot of work to do.'

'Gin and pep?'

'Thanks.' Whatever that might be. Experiences were tumbling over her. Even as she waited for Tryphena to mix the watery-looking drinks, Josephine was filled with certainty that her plan to write a book about Harriet's life could be done. The ease with which she was able to gain entrance to Harriet's place of work, and probably much of her life, and now her acceptance by the barmaid, gave her confidence. Tryphena took the drinks to a small table, whilst Josephine uprighted the two chairs cleaners had placed on it. 'Take the weight off of your feet for five minutes – it's all I can spare.'

'Busy day?'

'Every day's a busy day here.' She lifted the drink to her lips and took a small sip.

Josephine, not knowing how gin and pep might taste, did the same. It was a surprisingly pleasant drink, probably easy to get to like for the sweet peppermint stinging its way over the tongue. 'Look, Miss Douglas – may I call you Tryphena? My name's Josephine, but I get called Josie.' Tryphena nodded, and Josephine continued with what she hoped would appear open and honest, which it was. 'As I told you, I went to see Harriet this morning, not because I knew her, I didn't, but because I was so

144

shaken up by what happened to her I wanted to write a book about her life.'

'A book? What d'you mean? A book that would go into libraries and shops and that?' Josephine nodded. 'Who'd want to read a book about poor girls. You might just as well write about my life – fat lot of interest to anybody there.'

'It would interest me.'

'Of course it would.'

'Do you reckon, then, that if you were My Lady Tryphena that your life-story would be more interesting than this?'

'It's got to be.'

'My Lady Tryphena gets up, chooses what to wear, dresses, goes out, comes back, changes her dress, goes out again to another house just like her own, talks about the same things over and over again, comes back, changes her dress, eats her dinner, goes to bed. End of story. Don't tell me that Lady Tryphena's life is more interesting than yours. Ladies like that get so bored.'

'Easy life, though.'

'You think boring is easy. I tell you, I've seen quite a bit of it. I wouldn't have that life for anything. Behind your bar, you see hundreds of people every day, some of them very strange, I'll be bound. Things change every day, you . . . well, you do things like this. My Lady could never go home at the end of the day and say, "D'you know what? I had this mad woman come to see me today, and she thinks my life would be more interesting to people who read books than the lives of the gentry".'

Josephine had her hooked. Had she wanted, she could have taken Mr Hood two thousand words that would be perfect for a Jemima Ferguson piece. But, no, this project was infinitely more serious than a couple of column inches.

'What do you want to know?'

'About Harriet, about you, how she lived, what goes on here. I know that she was Clara Burton the singer, but I also know that she took a man home with her that night, and he killed her. Now, I can do nothing about that, but I can string words together so that people want to read what I write, and I want people to read it who know nothing of how a young woman like Harriet manages to keep going. She took a madman to her room, and he killed her. All those "My Ladies" who you think have stories worth telling, are kept women, but not in the kind of danger that the women who are picked up here must be.'

'Well, that's different.'

'What's different about it?'

'Husbands. If I had one, I'd be out of here like a shot from a gun.'

'Of course you would, but you'd still be a kept woman.'

'I'd earn my keep by cooking and cleaning.'

'And taking him to bed?'

'Of course.'

'But at the moment you are independent, like me.'

'How do you earn your keep then?'

That was the trouble with half-truths, one half could catch you out. 'I work in an office.'

'I often think I would have liked to do that. Another gin and pep?'

'Not now, but I would like to come back again, if you don't mind.'

'Why don't you come when we're open? It's always nice to have somebody to talk to when things are a bit slow.'

Coming here when the place was open was exactly what Josephine needed to start her research into Harriet's life.

'Come back early evening, you can stand at the end of the bar, and I'll talk to you when I can.'

'That's really nice. Why? I mean, why are you willing to help me?'

'I don't know, really. Probably what you said about toffs not knowing about what goes on. The men do, of course. A lot of the men who come here to pick up girls are toffs, lawyers, doctors, all that sort.' She grinned and downed the last of her drink. 'I shouldn't mind people knowing about that. They'd pay a girl to open her drawers, but give her a proper job in an office? Not in a million years.'

'Would Harriet's man have been a toff, do you think?'

'No, average. Mean with his money.'

Josephine chilled and, trying to keep the shock out of her voice because Tryphena appeared to be so nonchalant, asked, 'So you saw him, the man she took home?'

'Oh yes, he was in here some time. Had a drink, smoked a cigar, taking his time about who would get the privilege of him. That's what I thought, anyhow; thought a lot of himself.'

'What happened, do you think, to make him settle on Harriet?'

'Don't rightly know. I did see him watching her change from her old street boots to the little slippers she wears when she goes on stage.'

'Did she go on stage on Christmas Eve?'

'I can't say as I remember. I've seen her perform so many times . . . but I think she did a turn.'

'But you remember that he was watching her change into her slippers?'

'I have to say, the thought passed through my mind that he might have thought she would be cheap, her boots being so down-at-heel. Probably thought she was really down on her luck, which she was. He was a real mean sort. You quite often get them. Come in here, buy one drink, watch the girls parading, never buying them nor anybody a drop of anything, and then clear off back home to give their wives what for. Anyway, I was wrong about him.'

'Did he buy her a drink?'

'I think he did, but it was so busy, it being Christmas.'

'But you saw him throughout the evening.'

'Pretty much . . . you know, off and on.'

'What about when he left?'

'She, Harriet, asked for her boots which was under my bar, and put them on, just about here where we're sitting now. She was taking her time, I reckon he was anxious to get going. I said as much to her, and she just winked at me. "Oh, let him wait." She was like that with men. She was really nice, though. Never moaned, and if she was flush she'd always say, "And one for yourself, Tryphena." A really nice sort.'

'And then they left?'

'They did. She often takes a glass of something before she leaves.'

'And did she?'

'No. "Sorry, Tryphena," she said, "but I'm going to get handsome there to buy me a few at the Cavour."'

'The Cavour?'

'Restaurant. Just here in the Haymarket. It was Harriet's favourite place when she got somebody to foot the bill.'

'And was he handsome?'

'Depends on what you fancy.'

'And you didn't.'

'I don't like foreigners, and I don't like mean men, and he was both.'

'Suppose he comes back? He must know that you would recognize him.'

'Me and half a dozen more. He won't come back. One thing I'm sure of. The police will be round here soon, so he won't risk coming here once they get his description.'

Josephine was again astonished at her nonchalant attitude. 'I'd better not keep you any longer. You've been really helpful.' She put a florin down on the table. 'Will that be enough?'

'More than enough. Thanks, Josephine. And you'll come back?'

'Oh yes, I want to be here about the time Harriet would have come.'

'See you this evening then. And thanks for the drink.'

Billy came clomping in. 'Police is here. I told you they would.'

'Well, it's obvious that they would.'

'Oh, Lord. Is there another way out of here?'

Tryphena grinned. 'Not keen on the blue-bottles then? This way. Lets you out onto the unloading yard.'

'Don't say anything about me.'

'Why would I do that? Now get going.'

As Josephine went through a door behind the bar, she heard the clomping of feet and a voice she recognized well.

There wasn't much information that Sergeant Kerley obtained from Tryphena Douglas which Josephine did not have.

Tryphena and her sister Alice had travelled home on the same omnibus as Harriet Burton and the foreigner. He had looked very sour-faced. He had objected to having to pay for her ticket as well as his own. It was very late. The last bus to Coram Fields that day.

'Would you recognize him again?'

'No trouble, Sergeant. I'd pick him out of a hundred men if you asked me.'

She gave him a signed statement.

Frank Kerley left feeling immensely satisfied that he

had found such a witness. Miss Douglas would be excellent giving evidence.

All they had to do now was to find a foreigner and put him in an identification parade.

How many foreigners were there in London? Whittle it down to young men. Whittle again to men with the spots on their face that several witnesses had mentioned. But at least they now had several positive descriptions of the man seen with the victim late on Christmas Eve. Here at the Alhambra Palace, on the omnibus, buying fruit from a coster-barrow, and going upstairs in number 12 Great Coram Street.

Even for an officer with a rank as high as Superintendent Thomson's, there were few comforts in Bow Street Police Station, but the room in which he worked did have a blazing fire, and a constable did bring in tea and biscuits. Frank Kerley appreciated both as he sat with his superior and informally reported his findings.

He had come to the end of what he had to say and waited respectfully for the super to comment. Thomson supped tea and gazed inwardly, his eyes no longer moving as they had when taking in the surprising amount of Kerley's findings. At last he said, 'The victim went to the West End, performed on stage at the Alhambra Palace. She was seen leaving from there with a man fitting a similar description to that given by the costermonger . . . ?'

'Flack.'

'Yes, Flack, and very similar to the man seen by the Wrights.'

'We have three good witnesses there, especially Douglas, who had him in her sight for a great part of the evening, and then again on the late omnibus.'

'Has the driver been questioned?'

'Even as we speak, sir.'

'Now that we have a good description and his movements on that evening, I have secured permission to offer a reward.'

'That spells a great number of extra working hours. Rewards always do – brings every trickster and hopeful claiming to have seen something.'

The super smiled wryly. 'Especially if one hundred pounds is offered.'

'A hundred!'

'The man was brazen, Sergeant. If he is not apprehended very soon, he will come to believe that he is invulnerable.'

Frank Kerley nodded. 'And then who knows who his next victim might be. Perhaps a woman more respectable than Harriet Burton.'

As she opened the door to her rooms, the evocative smell of oil paint and turpentine drifted up her nose.

'Jo? Is that you?'

'It had better be or someone else has a key.'

Liliana Wilde, in a large white cook's apron, offered her cheek. 'I thought I'd try some little cakes. Madeleines. They are very French. I learned how to concoct them from a real patisserie-maker.' Liliana appeared as frail as Josephine did robust. This apparent frailty was brought about because her complexion, pale and smooth as alabaster, was framed by a wildness of flaxen curls that neither she nor any nursery maid had ever been able to control. In any gathering of women, Liliana Wilde was outstandingly beautiful. She cared very little for her appearance but, as Josephine had said, she had no need to. Her appearance cared for itself; there was little that could be done to make her an unattractive woman.

In looks they were in some ways similar, although Josephine's hair was a darker shade of blonde and not so spectacularly out of control as Liliana's. They were also similar in being above-average in height for women.

Josephine threw down her bags, unlaced her boots and followed Liliana into the tiny kitchen. 'And what were you doing that a cake-maker would give you lessons?'

'Making a drawing of him. Such a head! He must have a hundred jowls down to his shoulders, an enormous drooping moustache, and the wickedest eyes you ever saw. I have plans to make him the centre of an exhibition I have arranged with the Soho Gallery for this summer.'

'My, you have been busy.'

'Café?' Assuming that Josephine would always drink coffee made in the French way, in an enamelled pot, Liliana poured two breakfast-cupsful. 'There! They aren't a perfect shape, but they are good.'

Josephine ate one cake in two bites. 'Very good. I hope you have made dozens.'

'They are supposed to be a dainty delicacy.'

'But I am so hungry. I haven't found time to eat

anything except a pie from a pieman, and I had to eat that in a church doorway.'

'How did your piece on "Jane" go? I thought it exceptional. Did the great Mr Hood like it?'

'Don't mention his name to me.'

Liliana opened her very large, very long-lashed eyes wide, 'Oh?'

'I have resigned from *The News*.'

'For heaven's sake, Jo, did the man take liberties?'

'Had it been that, I could have slapped his face. Worse than that, Lili, I got the best story ever, before any of the opposition – I'm sorry, I absolutely must have another cake. Christmas Eve, a man picks up a girl from the Alhambra, wines and dines her. She takes him back to her room, he slits her throat and walks off early Christmas morning. I scooped up the story first.'

'Why, Jo, that's splendid. Not a resigning matter – go on take another, they are pretty scrumptious, and I can easily make more – yet you resigned.'

'Hood went back on his word to put my name on the piece. It was front page, but no byline, just by "A *News* Crime Reporter".' Eating with 'mmm's of appreciation, she related the duplicity of her editor and the unfairness heaped upon women who were in general more talented than men. 'I was so furious, I just walked out. After he had promised.'

'Oh, Jo, I am so sorry. Well, they are the losers.'

'He says that he is a forward-thinking man. Oh yes! Going to take more women on the staff . . . that kind of thing, big innovator, going to turn Fleet Street upside down.'

'Why do you think he reneged?'

'The shire MPs and bishops and police commissioners? I don't know ... I only know that, between when I handed in my story and its publication, he had taken my name out.'

'And we do like fame, don't we, me and you?'

'Nothing wrong with that. Power can go with fame. *That's* what I want most of all. I want to dictate terms. I want to show everyone that women are every bit as good as men, in *everything*. It is true, Lili, throughout history there is not a single profession in which at some time a woman hasn't excelled or surpassed males, and yet look at us!'

'We have been over this so many times, haven't we?'

'I know, I know – our problem is our wombs.'

'Of course. Wombs tell us to have babies. And we do. We create an amazing painting, and a child comes along and takes over any talent we might have.'

'Not you, I hope.'

'No, not me. I don't take notice of my womb. If it tries to make me notice it, and I have a lovely young man to hand, I send him away, and paint until it all settles down again. I expect it will get me in the end. I took to a kitten in Paris, but that didn't work, it just grew into a disgusting tom-cat and went off. I don't know where, and I don't care.'

Josephine just smiled. Liliana could always be relied upon to be entertaining on the subject of herself and her work. She was a very good artist; Josephine hoped one day to have one of her paintings on her bedroom wall, but Lili needed to get the highest price possible, so an L. Wilde painting was beyond her means at present. And possibly for some time to come.

'What will you do?'

'I have decided to write a book based on the life of Harriet Burton.'

'And what is she famous for?'

'For being young and pretty and dead. The murdered girl.'

'Can you do this? You have always said that you couldn't do it.'

'Because I never felt that I had a story to tell. But this, Lili . . . Harriet has got beneath my skin, and I shall not be able to leave it alone until I have discovered the story of her life.'

'It sounds to me as though you are becoming as absorbed with this person as you were with "Jane". Why these two? You have written about any number of incidents.'

'I looked at Harriet and "Jane" when they had been killed.'

'"Jane" wasn't killed.'

'Of course she was killed. She had no means to help her survive, and *we* were not willing to give it.'

'There are charities; I wonder why she didn't ask for help instead of starving to death?'

'Charities for women and children expect appeals to come from people without pride – ha! – and in my

"Jane's" case not to sound like an educated woman. That is wrong. No one should be without food and shelter.' She crammed a whole cake into her mouth and spoke through it with a lack of eating manners that Ann Martha would have despaired of. 'Oh, Lili, it makes me so angry!' She bit another dainty cone in half. 'This is the wealthiest city, in the richest country in the world, and women are dying needlessly.'

'And men and boys?'

'Yes, little boys too.' Josephine's face lightened as she remembered. 'On Christmas Eve, I met a little street urchin, trying to be a real passenger-help at my omnibus stop. He was tiny. Micky "Smiff", as he called himself. I gave him my muff to wear as a hat.'

'He's probably sold it by now . . . but you did a good thing there, Jo.'

'You are such a cynic.'

'Some of us have to be if they happen to be close to people like you and my brother. Have you been to any of his "rantings" since I have been away?'

'Yes. He doesn't rant, he speaks in a language ordinary mortals like me can understand. I let him see my piece about "Jane" before I handed it in.'

'And?'

'He complimented me on its sincerity.'

'He's very keen on sincerity, is David.'

'Isn't it about time that you stopped taking pot shots at him? Maybe you and your family had plans to see another Wilde as a great barrister. But David's who he is, and you should be proud of him.'

'You can do that, and I'll keep taking pot shots. Tell me more about the woman whose life you intend making into a book? Why this particular woman?'

'Like "Jane", you could say that she presented herself to me. On Christmas morning, I overheard my Uncle James's constable giving an address to the cabby taking him to the scene of a murder. So I went there. And I discovered that a young woman had been murdered. Later I discovered that she was Harriet Burton, a singer, known at the Alhambra as Clara, and that Clara was a heroine to some scullery maids who were saving up money to go to watch her perform.'

'That's so sad.'

'After that, I went to see her. At the mortuary. She was just a woman about our age, like you and me, except that she could neither write nor paint. But she could sing. All that she had was her voice and her body. Can you imagine how that must feel? Instead of getting recompense for doing something interesting, to have to wait until some man chooses you, and to have to take him home and let him do whatever he wishes.'

Liliana ruffled Josephine's hair. 'I do like being your lodger. Life here is never dull.'

'Tell me that when we get home tonight.'

'Where are we going?'

'I'm meeting someone at the Alhambra Palace, and it would be better if you came with me.'

James Thomson's team of investigating officers spread out through the heart of London, from Piccadilly and the Haymarket, and along the omnibus route from there to the Coram Fields area. The superintendent's tried-and-tested method was well-conducted police routine. Frank Kerley presented a report early enough in the day for James Thomson to order reward notices to be placed in newspapers.

'Sit down for a moment, Sergeant. I'll read your report later,' Thomson said, placing a hand on the sergeant's page of fine and clear handwriting, which was very different from his own heavy and, he had to admit, florid hand. 'Tell me.' Most of the investigating officers would have to face the super like this. On the page of a report, there were no inflections in speech, no hand movements, no facial expressions. 'Tell me.'

'Well, sir, if we ever get to putting witnesses on the stand, the barmaid at the Alhambra will be superb. She speaks well, is very clear in what she says she saw, and is a likeable personality.'

As ever, when he entered the gaudy portals of the Alhambra Palace, Frank Kerley felt the mixed emotions of guilt and elation. It was scarcely fair that the pleasant emotion that lifted his spirits and over which he had no control was spoiled by the other, which was equally out of his hands. A married policeman had no business feeling enjoyment at being in a place of low life and tastelessness. Yet, on the occasion when he had taken the trouble to analyse the nature of his relish for this particular theatre, he saw that it was perfectly reasonable to be reminded of days when he was a youth and had first ventured into a music hall. Gilding, plaster mouldings and heavy textiles, gold leaf and the smell of smoke and beer and brass polish, and, over it all, stale perfume. If it wasn't pleasant, it was certainly evocative. Not that he ever yearned for those days after he had met Elizabeth.

In some ways Miss Tryphena Douglas was typical of the kind of young women often found serving behind the bar of a music hall, in that she had an easy manner and was pretty and curled and smiling. She was, however, he soon discovered, well spoken and intelligent.

She was also, and this pleased him, elegant in her figure and restrained in her dress. So many of the girls in this line of work sought to catch the eye with necklines so low that one expected at any moment to discover a bare bosom escaping, which of course was their purpose, for no gentleman will count his change when this prospect presents itself. Tryphena, though, drew the eye more by a line of many neat buttons running from abdomen to neck of a bodice that covered her finely shaped bosom like a skin. A bosom such as Elizabeth had possessed – still did possess. She did not, as did so many fashionable women, ape the queen by wearing unnecessary black and jet. Women were best suited to colour. Well, that was Frank Kerley's opinion, which he omitted in the telling of his interview with the barmaid.

'Who is next on the list of possible witnesses?'

'Flack, the costermonger.'

'I can do that, Sergeant. By the bye, now that we have so many witnesses testifying to his possibly being German, I have ordered handbills to be printed giving notice of the reward, and showing the artist's impression of the suspect. There is always a chance that he may try to slip out of the country, so a printed letter from me, together with the handbill, will be sent out by tomorrow to police in Germany, France, Belgium, and to all the Channel ports.'

Frank Kerley knew the super would have translated the notice into the relevant languages, and was certain that the grammar in each of the letters would be impeccable. Anyone who could speak another tongue got Kerley's admiration, and the super spoke many.

After much discussion about what would be appropriate to wear, Josephine and Liliana set off by omnibus to the Haymarket. They had piled up one another's fair, curly hair into fetching topknots, attached long earrings to their lobes, and chose the only pretty hats they had that matched their bustly skirts.

'What shall we do if we get picked up, Jo?'

'Say that we are meeting someone. Though, of course, I wouldn't impose that on you, Lili, should you find some nice young man who takes your fancy! But I suppose we shouldn't make jokes. Harriet got herself all dolled up like this, and it wasn't for fun.'

'Oh, I know that, Jo. Just because we have a bit of banter doesn't mean that we are insensitive. I think that you are more apprehensive than I am.'

The two young women alighted from the 'bus and joined people who were pouring into the music hall. Since Josephine's earlier visit, the Alhambra had been transformed by light and colour. A band was playing lively music, accompanying the display of a group of contortionists dressed in glittering spangles, each spectacular climax being accompanied by a drum roll, a clash of cymbals and cheers from the noisy audience.

'I say, Jo, this beats baking cakes. I've been to halls in Paris, but never in London.'

Tryphena Douglas beckoned them to the end of the bar. 'Ladies, what can I get you?'

'This is my friend, Liliana. I think she should try your recommendation, gin and pep.'

Liliana spoke up, 'Have you absinthe?'

Tryphena raised her eyebrows. 'I have, but not many asks for it. Rots your socks, I'm told.'

Liliana laughed. 'I know, and I drink it with due respect.'

'Liliana spends quite a lot of time in Paris.'

Tryphena leaned across the counter, full of interest. 'Is it as bad a city as they say?'

'Worse. But not as bad as London.'

Josephine refused absolutely to take absinthe, but paid for Liliana's and her own gin and pep and one for Tryphena. Whenever she was offered a drink, the barmaid always chose something clear that would take peppermint, so that she could drink with customers but not actually become affected by alcohol. This showed a nice little profit for herself.

The two friends placed themselves at the far end of the bar where they could watch the passing scene, and to where the barmaid could return to sip her drink in between serving.

'You two look like sisters.'

'People have said that. Liliana's an artist.'

'Do you sing or recite or what?'

'She paints pictures.'

'And people buy them?'

'Some people, but others wouldn't have them to line a garden shed.'

'She paints light.'

'How do you do that? Could you paint the lights in here?'

Although the barmaid was not familiar with the term 'painting light', Liliana looked around at the gilding, and at the etched glass and mirrors reflecting numerous gaslamps: light as Tryphena saw it. Liliana's eyes sharpened with interest.

'I'd like to try. That huge mirror behind you, and the sparkling glass of the bottles and glasses; there are so many different kinds of light in just this one area.'

'I expect they wouldn't mind if you came when the place was empty.'

'But the light wouldn't be here then.'

Tryphena nodded in sombre agreement. 'I might be able to get you in.'

'Oh could you? Will you try?'

'Lili, just think, if you could do some pictures to complement my book.'

'Oh, Jo, it's not really my style, too figurative.'

'But think what you'd be doing: a picture is always worth a thousand words, isn't it? People would see your paintings and read my book.'

'That is David's territory – ranting, reform.'

The place was filling up now, and Josephine was concerned that she wouldn't get as much time from Tryphena as she would like.

'So, you and your sister went home on the same omnibus as Harriet?'

'We left here about a quarter-past midnight. It takes less than five minutes to get to Regent Circus, and we caught the last 'bus.'

'Is this where Harriet was waiting too?'

'That's right, we had to wait about five minutes for the omnibus. She was walking up and down, arm in arm with the man I told you about this morning. Well, the 'bus came and I got on with Alice, and Harriet and him followed right behind us and sat down.'

'Could you see them from where you were seated?'

'Oh yes, they took seats right opposite me and Alice . . . well, not exactly opposite me, Alice was opposite Harriet, I was in the first seat. Listen, let me go and get Alice, she can tell you.'

Alice Douglas was a slighter version of her sister. She too took a gin and pep.

'And the man?'

'He sat next to Harriet.'

'Which gave you a good view of him?'

'Oh yes, I could see him clear as I see you now.'

'Did you recognize any of the other passengers?'

Again she shook her head. 'Strangers to me, all of them.'

She broke off to serve a man porter, calling him Mr Pragnell and asking him if he was better of his cold. Having indicated that he might be once he had his porter, he took his drink away with the air of one who was familiar with the place and expected to take his usual seat.

'Please continue, tell me anything else about that journey. Anything at all.'

'Well, Tryphena was wide awake as she always is, but I was dog tired, and was leaning forward, drowsing. Harriet tapped me on the knee and asked if she could hold my parcel, as it seemed I was likely to let it fall. I said no. Then she asked if it was a turkey. I said no, but it was a goose, and we talked about a properly cooked goose being better any day than turkey.'

'Did the man take part in the conversation?'

'No. He never said a word. I asked her if she was doing anything for Christmas, and she said she thought she might go to the country next day with some friends. Then we talked about some occasions when we'd given the conductor the wrong money. I said I had once handed up a sovereign in mistake for a shilling, and Harriet said she once paid a Strand conductor ten shillings in gold for a sixpenny fare and the conductor was a bit off with her. It was only chit-chat, like you do on the 'bus.'

Alice went off for a few minutes serving quickly, bantering with girls and men, some of whom hung around close to the bar, others who took their drinks to the small tables. She came back and addressed Josephine. 'Tryphena said you was going to write a book. Does that mean that we might be in it?'

'Would you mind?'

'Depends.'

'If I get the book written, I will come back and talk to you to check that you agree with what I've had to say.'

'All right then. I'll have to go back to my own bar soon, but I'll tell you up to when I got off. I began to nod off again, and I dropped the goose. I looked across at Harriet, and she looked at the man, but he wasn't acting the gentleman, leaving it to Harriet to hand it to me. I think it was somewhere about the Tottenham Court Road area when Harriet nudges the man and said something. I didn't hear what he said, but I heard her say "sixpence". He gave her a black look, but dug into his trousers pocket and found a coin.'

'What was it the man said?'

'I never heard, leastways, I never took notice. I can't say I was very interested.' She smiled, 'He couldn't have been the sort I find attractive, else I might have.'

Tryphena came back. 'Maggie's just come on duty, so you're all right for a couple of minutes.'

'Thanks, 'Phe. So, there was people getting off at the different stops, everybody saying "Merry Christmas" and all that. Next day, it was all over everywhere that one of the Haymarket girls had got herself murdered. I couldn't hardly believe that it was Harriet. We'd only been with her a few hours before. It was a real shock to us, wasn't it, 'Phe?'

Tryphena Douglas acknowledged that it was. 'It makes you see how easy it is to get yourself killed. I can't say that I've ever thought of it happening to us, but there's plenty you hear of getting robbed and even worse. It's why Alice and me always try to work the same shifts.'

'Aren't there always policemen about at that time of night?'

'Oh yes, plenty,' Alice said, 'but no chap's going to try to rape you with the beat copper looking on. It's in the dark and lonely places, alleyways and such, that they'll get you. A lot of places like that between here and Islington. I'm not complaining about the police, they can't be everywhere at once, so girls who work late have to take their own precautions.'

'Except,' said Tryphena, 'a girl who makes a living picking up men don't have that choice. They have to keep away from the regular coppers' beats. No sort of precautions you could take against a monster with a knife in his pocket.' She wagged her head and frowned, sincerely disturbed at the dreadfulness of it all. 'I still can't hardly credit it. She wasn't the type to play up, in all the time she's been coming in here, I never knew her to have so much as a bruise or a black eye.'

'Is there much of that: women being hit?'

Alice gave her sister a wry smile. Josephine said crossly, 'You'll have to forgive my innocence, Miss Douglas. I can't help it that I don't know what goes on in a world that is strange to me, but I must learn as much as I can if I am to get truth into what I write about it. So tell me, then I shall not ask questions that make you smile.'

Tryphena answered. 'There's some that practically asks to get knocked about, they lead a man on so just to get maybe a glass of spirit. But Harriet? Never! She was the sort of girl people took to. A nice, friendly sort.'

'You liked her.'

'Well, I didn't really *know* her, it's too busy in here to do more than pass the time of day, but I reckon if I had a got to know her better, I could say "yes", she was the sort of girl I would like.'

Liliana asked, 'When you saw her that night, was she alone?'

'Yes, she came but joined three other girls.'

'Do girls often go about together?'

'Some do, but you got to realize, it being Christmas Eve, people were cheered up with each other, going about arm in arm. Usually she wasn't one to drink much: just a stout, which she didn't drink quick.'

'And is that what she drank then?'

'No, she took an Irish whiskey, which one of the others paid for.'

'You have an excellent memory.'

'Well, you know how it is, you remember some things, others just pass you by, but I do remember her taking a whiskey. She was in here just about as it was beginning to fill up, but there was not so many as I was rushed, else I probably wouldn't remember what she nor anybody else had. It was quite lively, as you'd imagine, being Christmas Eve.'

'What time would that be?'

She frowned. 'Hard to say. The only time I ever really notice is when it's close to closing time. But I do remember her asking me if I wouldn't be glad when I could put my feet up. This job's very hard on the feet. And I said that my toes was hurting after being on them for so many hours, so it was probably about tennish, I'd say.'

Once Josephine and Liliana had overcome any awkwardness about posing as bar-butterflies, they began to enjoy the experience, and when Tryphena and Alice Douglas became used to being close-questioned, they tried to anticipate what Josephine wanted to know, pointing out or calling over women who had been particular friends of Harriet.

'This is Madame Margaret.' Tryphena introduced a woman, probably in her thirties, notable for her red hair and ample bosom. She accepted a port and lemon.

'I've known Harriet since she first come to town. She was in the family way, by the coachman where she had been in service. I seem to remember it was in Finchley, or somewhere like that, I don't rightly recall, but I do recall that his name was Burton. That's why she took it, probably thinking he might do something about the baby. Ha! Wasn't she the innocent country girl? He soon cleared off.'

'What year would that be?' Liliana too was being drawn into wanting to know, not just about Harriet, but about these other women who were part of the daily life of the hall and its bar. Jo might be right . . . women of light and dark . . . something to think about.

'February Eighteen Sixty-four.'

'That's very precise.'

'It would be, because I was living in the same lodgings as her at the time. Pleasant Row, Islington. Not only that, it was me and Mrs Atkins – she was the landlady – and Harriet's sister who delivered the baby.'

'Harriet was a mother?'

'Has been for eight year now.'

'What was it, the baby?'

'A girl. Kathryn. I was hoping she might of named her after me, but she never. Nobody ever called her Kathryn, always Katy.'

'So Katy would be eight years old now.'

'Nearly nine.'

'She didn't live with her mother, though.'

'Not of recent time, but back then Harriet had a real bit of luck. There was this Major Brown who took to Harriet, and he set her up in lodgings in Blackfriars Road.'

'Did she have Katy with her?'

'Far as I know. Oh yes, thanks, I will have another. Kind of you, I'm sure.'

She got the second port and lemon under false pretences, because she really didn't have anything more to tell Josephine. 'The thing is we sort of drifted apart after she left Mrs Atkins's. We'd see each other from time to time, and we'd gossip for a bit – you know how it is, nothing much, only vague bits about where we was both living, how things were going and that.'

'Was she still at Blackfriars Road when you last met her?'

'Don't think so. The time when she was living with Major Brown, she didn't have to work, but I know she still kept pally with Patty Lydney and Eliza Cavendish. They might be able to tell you.'

Josephine thought that she was now getting somewhere. Names were tumbling out; real people were attached to those names. Katy, Major Brown, Patty, Eliza. 'Do they come here?'

'No, don't need to now. Patty always had her head screwed on the right way. She and Eliza got some decent rooms together, and they're very choosy who they let in.'

Liliana wrote down Patty's address as Madame Margaret gave it to her. Madame Margaret tapped the side of her nose. 'Don't ever get in no trouble with the police – very respectable is Patty and Eliza now. I don't envy them . . . well, I sort of do . . . what I mean is, good luck to them. They had the sense to put a bit aside while they were young.'

'Do they take in lodgers or run a brothel?' Liliana asked.

Madame Margaret looked offended and, picking up her port and lemon, stood up. 'I can't tell you nothing else.'

Liliana turned to Tryphena, 'What did I say to offend her?'

171

'You used the word that the police use. It's a bad word to the likes of Madame Margaret.'

'I'm sorry, I didn't realize. There are plenty of brothels close by where I live.'

Josephine said, 'London's not Paris, Lili.'

Tryphena said, 'I don't think you'll get any of the other girls to talk to you now. Best you leave. You could always try Patty. She would have had Harriet in her house, but for the little girl.'

As they made ready to leave, Josephine said, 'I hope that I can write this account.'

'You have to, Miss Ferguson, not one of us knows if it won't happen to us.'

Josephine felt slightly uncomfortable. She and Liliana were not 'us', not part of the world of the girls of the Alhambra.

'These girls – Harriet, and the ones you've been with this evening, like Madame Margaret . . . they didn't start out dreaming of a life picking up men and letting them do it for money. There's some that probably was born to girls who did, knowing better than any what was the score, but they wouldn't have said to themselves, "That's what I want to do, pay my way in some side street with any man who has the price of it." I'm sorry if you think I'm being coarse, but that's what goes on here, night in, night out, year in, year out. In the end they nearly all end up the same: drunk, babes, disease, beatings. Alice and me, we're all right, this is hard work and long hours, but it's a good position. Another one of our sisters is in service, and I wouldn't want her life, but worst of all is when a girl gets so desperate that she has to get on the old game . . .'

Josephine nodded.

Tryphena drew her eyebrows together, 'You don't believe that, do you? You don't think you could find yourself so down on your luck that you didn't have anything left except your own self.'

'That's true, and I count myself lucky enough to have family.'

'You might not always have; they might chuck you out . . . I'm not saying they would, but things happen.'

'I am also fortunate enough to be good at stringing words together, interviewing people. I can write things down very fast . . . reporting, you know.'

'As long as you hadn't got your fingers broke or something like that. I'm not saying that you might be one to go down, what I'm saying is that a woman is always at risk of finding herself having nowhere to turn to, and, high or low, town or country, women has the mucky end of the stick.'

Jo and Lili were transfixed by Tryphena's earnestness. A feeling of inadequacy overcame Josephine. She was embarking on the writing of a book about the lives of women about whom she knew nothing.

'Look, Miss Ferguson, this is all new to you, and I have to say that I admire you for wanting to tell people who talk about "fallen women" what their life is like. If you tell Harriet's life, then you'll be telling the life of all of them.'

'I shall do my best. The last time you saw Harriet, where was she, what was she doing?'

'Getting fruit from George Flack's stall. She picked up a pineapple and put it back.'

'Where is this stall?'

'Coram's Fields. He'll be there now till after midnight, but if you want to ask him about Harriet, you'd best go daytime, to his shop in Brunswick Square.'

Ann Martha had to learn from a daily newspaper that the detective in charge of investigating the case of the woman found so horribly murdered on Christmas morning was her own husband. Skilled herself at making deductions from her observations where James was concerned, she had already suspected this from two days of early risings, late returnings from duty and the alacrity with which he dressed in the morning.

Something was exercising his mind and body, and from past experience she knew that nothing did this half so well as tracking a murderer. When Hani said, 'Mister Jame, must be catching killer again,' Ann Martha could only smile wryly. 'Mr James is not easy to live with when he has a murder case.'

'I know. I speak to him, ask him if I tell Cook to make salt biff for supper, he look up, and I am not there.'

'Oh, Hani, you know him well enough by now to know that he means no disrespect to you.'

'Of course I know. But how shall Cook know to make salt biff for supper?'

'If he makes any complaints, we can always tell him

that he chose it. He never knows differently when he's absorbed in his work. I know that this is a very puzzling crime. Mrs Henderson told me that James has requested the commissioner to allow a big reward to be offered, and that hundreds of handbills are being printed and distributed, and to foreign cities as well.'

'Is good that wife of commissioner is friend to you.'

'Absolutely. Mr Henderson must tell his wife everything that he does. Lord, Hani, can you imagine how dull their conversation must be?'

'I hear him now, MisAnn,' and she clip-clopped away to welcome James home, handing him his slippers.

Ann Martha followed. 'You spoil him, Hani. He should receive a reprimand for neglecting us so shamefully. You are looking pleased with yourself, James.'

'Apples! I got them from an excellent witness.'

Hani took the bag. 'These pretty apple, make nice arrangement. Not so nice for eating.'

A meal was quickly assembled for him, and the two of them sat together for the first time since Christmas.

'The daily papers are referring to "The Great Coram Street Murder".'

He didn't respond, but helped himself to plain boiled potatoes with butter, a dish he would eat with almost anything, hot or cold.

'You might as well say something about it. I have to hear from friends that you are sending out handbills all over the world.'

'A slight exaggeration.'

'James! You are so infuriating. Perhaps we could do

it this way. An actress (so called) was murdered on the night of Christmas Eve. On Christmas morning, very early, you are collected from outside the church by a constable with a waiting cab. You jump in and rush off. I perform my duties as hostess *alone* – about which I am not complaining because I knew about policemen long before we married. You realize that you missed seeing Josephine off.'

'I know. But I did see her in the early hours of Boxing Day morning. Did you know she likes to drink whisky?'

'I try to gain your attention by expensive perfume, Josephine by drinking whisky in your presence.'

'Annie, my dearest . . .'

'Be sensible, James.'

'I will try. Yes, I am in charge of the investigation into the murder of Harriet Burton. She is . . . was, not an actress "so-called", she was a young woman who went on stage and sang. She got very little in payment. She had pawned everything decent she had owned. She owed rent. So that she would not get turned out of her room – one room – she took a man home and made him pay a sovereign. Woman of the world as you are, you have no need of me to explain further.'

Ann Martha pushed her winter salad around with a fork, looking very contrite. James was a good man, a truly good man. 'I do give generously to several of the charities for fallen women, James.'

'I know, Ann, but you should realize that such women

176

are not fallen, they are usually pushed by poor circumstances and by men. I am not suggesting that you should not give, but to make a difference an Act of Parliament and a change of heart in the British people as a whole is necessary.'

He rose from the table, wiped his mouth on immaculate linen and went to fetch his coat. Hani, working in the inner hall on an arrangement on a dish of the red apples, holly and spotted laurel, said, 'You find this man, MisaJame.'

'I will, Hani, yes, I certainly will.'

Similarly, Elizabeth Kerley waited for her husband to tell her something. Unlike Ann Martha, however, Elizabeth knew better than to question Francis when he was obsessed by an investigation. This was not the first of its kind he had been involved in. Each killing of a girl cut him to the quick. It became almost personal because of his love for their daughter, Frances. Knowing his girl was living at home, healthy and well, Francis found it necessary to double his efforts to find the killer of another man's daughter and see him on his way to the gallows.

He ate quickly, picked up the bowl of scraps and went down to the chickens. After he had been gone for ten minutes, Elizabeth took a bag and followed the path down to the chicken coop.

'These oats have gone weevily, Francis, the birds will like them.'

He nodded and flung some handfuls into the run. 'Where's Frances?'

'In her room, looking through a new piece.'

'I didn't hear her.'

'She's just reading through the music at the moment.' Their daughter was a talented musician who, having done well with the violin, had decided to take up the flute, too. Until this investigation was over, both Elizabeth and Frances knew that he would have less to worry about if he knew that his wife and his daughter were safely together. It was something unspoken between the three of them.

'We are on to him.' He flung oats at the scrabbling hens.

'Good.'

'We know what he looks like, how he dresses, how he speaks – he's a German.'

'All that so soon.'

'Right. All we've got to do now is to find him and it's all plain sailing.'

'Have you got some good witnesses?'

'The very best. Articulate and firm about what they saw.' He threw oats, bag and all, which sent the hens squawking and fluttering. 'They are firm about his description because he was a cocky bugger, an arrogant bugger. Every time I take a statement, I see him. Young bloody German, strutting around London in his bloody felt hat, his velvet collar, his jacket, his short coat, and, for God's sake, even his short boots. I see him. He came prepared for what he did, I'm pretty sure of that. Her throat was cut with something as sharp as a razor or a surgeon's scalpel. This was no spur of the moment act of madness. Nobody just happens to have a scalpel in their pocket.'

Elizabeth held back on her usual, 'Language, language, Francis,' knowing from years of experience of her husband's passionate nature that, where some men possessing such dominating presence and strength become physically violent, in anger and in love-making Francis Kerley was vocal but gentle. He had investigated many violent murders, but occasionally one would touch him in a way that was personal. Usually because of violence done to a woman; why one in particular rather than another she never knew, only that he became obsessive and withdrawn until the perpetrator was arrested.

'Why was he so brazen?'

'He just didn't care. It's as though he's cocking a snook at us . . . not just us, at everybody who saw him with his victim that night.'

Elizabeth put one hand over his large one. He turned hers palm up and kissed it tenderly, both still watching the chickens peck the brown bag and eat it. Suddenly he laughed, and squeezed her shoulder. 'What daft creatures they are.'

Elizabeth stood close, enjoying the warmth of his large body, then said quietly, 'Francis . . . I don't think you are going to find him in London.'

After a few silent moments, Frank Kerley said, 'No, nor do I.'

To the ever-increasing collection of files in which were contained information pertaining to the death of 'Harriet

179

Burton, sometimes known as Clara Burton', was added a daily shower of claims to the £100 reward. Each piece of information had to be recorded and evaluated.

Frank Kerley knocked and entered. 'I could go through some of these with you, sir. Maybe weed out the absolute cranks.'

'Excellent, Sergeant. So far in the cranks pile I have foreigners of all kinds, from a Swiss travelling band to Chinese and black Africans.'

'And the problem is, as always, that being a crank doesn't necessarily rule out possible evidence.'

'Which is why I wouldn't trust anyone but you to help sort the good from the dross.'

'And there'll be an abundance of dross, sir.'

Frank Kerley seated himself on an upright wooden chair that looked as though it might not uphold his bulk for long. Even in the most senior police offices, the furniture was nothing more than rough and functional. Not much at all to do with the police was of quality.

Ever since he had achieved his senior position three years previously, James Thomson had fought for better uniforms and conditions for his men. Possibly to keep him quiet, he was asked to write a report, which he did with his usual straightforward honesty and fearlessness. 'The stations are prison-like: cheerless and akin to military barracks.' It was the lack of care for the men that most concerned him. 'The men are clothed and shod and clean, but wanting in "finish" – but perhaps I am fastidious. If our men are to be respected by the public they serve, then they must be elevated above the common labourer. If they are to have authority, then respect and care for their well-being must come first.'

'You were correct in your prediction, Sergeant. Some of these claims are obviously a chance to point a finger at a neighbour, or enemies settling old scores.'

However, one or two pieces of information looked as though they might lead somewhere.

There was a firm knock and a uniformed policeman entered. 'Inspector Cruse, sir, it's about the veterinary surgeon.'

'Come in, come in. My sergeant and I were trying to make some order here.' By way of explanation to Frank, James Thomson said, 'A man came into the station reporting a veterinary surgeon who lived at the same address as himself had disappeared overnight. Carry on, Inspector.'

'To paraphrase, sir. The man reporting was Mr Nurse, of Wrotham Road, Camden Town. There had been a veterinary surgeon, Mr Studdert, living at the same address, and on Christmas Eve he disappeared. Nurse also said that Studdert consorted with prostitutes, one of whom he believed was Harriet Burton. He referred to her as Clara Burton, the singer. I visited Nurse today and asked for a statement. He said that maybe he was mistaken, and that it might be another veterinary surgeon who knew the victim, and that Studdert might have gone to Ireland. I pressed him as to why he had reported Studdert's disappearance. He said that he had seen Studdert come home with blood on him, and that he, Studdert, had said that he had been to the Alhambra music hall and had got into a fight.'

Frank Kerley said, 'Sounds to me as though he realized that one hundred pounds wasn't so easily had, and he changed his tune a little.'

'More than a little, Sergeant. When I asked him if he was certain that this had been on Christmas Eve, he said that it might have been, but he couldn't be certain.'

'Did you get a statement, Inspector?' the superintendent asked.

Cruse replied, 'He declined to give a statement, or to give Studdert's address in Ireland, although I am certain that he knew it.'

James said, 'You should have charged him with wasting police time.'

'I still might, sir. However, I did think that a veterinary surgeon who disappears on the very day of the murder was a good prospect. After all, we are looking for a man who knows how to use a scalpel. So I went to the Veterinary College. They have no address in Ireland, but said that he would no doubt be in London at the end of the week as he has to attend college on Monday next.'

'Good work, Inspector, keep with it. Get in touch with Ireland. I wouldn't confuse an Irish accent for German, but who knows?'

And so the investigation went on and on, hour after hour, day after day, chasing sightings, following leads that went nowhere. It all had to be done, but it all ate into the men's time. They all worked extra hours, but there were times when a conclusion appeared hopeless.

James and his senior officers spent time keeping the men's morale high in spite of the pages and pages of reports they had to make.

Josephine's early attempts at making her way into the newspaper business had taken her to many parts of London that her life as an educated young lady would not. To Ann Martha and her close friends, the merchant and trading areas were another country, whose inhabitants spoke an idiosyncratic version of English that Josephine understood perfectly well.

She enjoyed buying from street vendors – flowers, fruit, pies, boiled sweets, muffins – and enjoyed going back to her rooms with purchases in paper bags or wrapped in newspaper. Once she had told Hani about some of her favourite foods, and how it reminded her of the street-vendors of her childhood, but Hani had been scornful. 'You are lady now; my mistress your mother never buys eating food in market. She teach me, "Many bad things on food, girl: flies, dirty fingers, disease. Wash hands, boil water, Hani, make food in own house."'

Her sharp retort had shocked Hani. 'A lot of good it did her! Perhaps if she had allowed market food into our house we might have got used to the bad things, and they wouldn't have died.'

'That fever came on winds.'

Josephine continued buying delectable cooked eels, hand-raised pies, and spicy bread-pudding slices. Liliana liked to experiment with cooking, mostly French dishes, but Josephine loved to collect an assortment of street foods and assemble them into a meal. As a consequence, she knew several street-vendors. She certainly knew George Flack, but not that he owned a shop.

She discovered George Flack's small, open-fronted Brunswick Square shop was only a little better than the covered stall in the Strand where he stood on Saturday mornings.

Flack was typical of his kind, quick witted and apparently good-humoured, though Josephine wondered whether a costermonger's constant good humour was a skill acquired to be a successful salesman. The cry, 'Apples a pound, pears', and double-meaning jokes about peach fuzz and feeling melons, never failed to raise a smile.

He recognized her at once. 'Hello, luv, what you doing down here? Bit out of your manor.'

'Hello, George, I've come down here specially to see you.'

Continuing to serve other customers, asking, weighing, bantering, he said, 'Nah, nah, I'm a respectable married man.'

'Oh dear, and I hoped that you'd give me a few minutes of your private time.'

Leaving the shop to his apprentices, he bowed exaggeratedly to his customers, 'Sorry, ladies, duty calls,' and conducted Josephine to a cubby-hole at the back of the shop.

They were obliged to stand to drink the sugar-loaded strong tea that Flack pressed upon Josephine. 'Nice cup of tea, George, just as I like it. I won't take up much of your time. It's about the singer who was murdered.' She related briefly her interest in Harriet.

'Mrs Brown. That's who she was when I first knew her, some years back now.'

Flack looked pleased at the interest he had aroused. 'Ah, so you didn't know she was sometimes known by that name. I've known her years: Harriet Buswell, Clara Burton, Harriet Burton and Mrs Brown. Same girl, told people she was an actress. She did turns in the halls.'

'When was the last time you saw her?'

'Early hours of Christmas morning, same time as she often comes to my Coram Fields stand.'

'To buy fruit?'

Flack winked, 'Not for nothink else. I ain't got that sort of luck.' The little man became serious, 'Now don't get me wrong, no disrespect, that's just me . . . sort of just comes out without thinking. She might of been an actress, but she was a proper lady, like yourself, miss, decent and friendly, always had a smile and passed the time of day. She knew about my veins – never was a stall-holder that didn't have veins. She'd say, "How's your legs today, Mr Flack?" She knew I only had one foot, but I got a lot of pain in the one that has gone, and I'd have a bit of a joke about being fast enough to catch a hare in Hyde Park . . . you know? Sometimes we'd have a word about us coming from the same neck of the woods, and she'd put on that funny accent of hers.' Momentarily he stared off with a sad expression. 'She was just a nice, pretty kind of young woman. Not one to make you think you could take liberties.'

'What neck of the woods are you from then, Mr Flack?'

'Oh not me, I'm a proper Cockney, born within the sound of Bow Bells. No, it was my grandfather came from close to where she was from. Norfolk. Recognized it as soon as she opened her mouth, even though she had learned to speak more city-like.'

Josephine perched herself on a bench piled high with crates of fruit. 'What do you remember about the last time you saw her?'

'Like I said, it was about her usual time when she comes in at night. She comes off the last 'bus, as a rule. I was quite busy, it being Christmas Eve . . . well, Christmas morning by then. She was waiting, looking over everything, deciding what to have. She says she'll have a bag of Christmas apples – that's the big red ones. "Ain't the best ones for taste," I said to her. "That don't matter," she says, "I like their looks, real Christmassy." (I did have them all polished up nice.) So I weighed her out the ones she wanted, then she turns to this cove that was standing there—'

'You could see him?'

'A course, like I told the detective, I had two lamps burning, real bright, and they was standing full in the light. He wasn't very old, probably younger than Mrs Brown. He was clean-shaven, but a bit rough, as though he hadn't shaved since morning, or his whiskers grew quick, you know how a dark beard comes through late in the day. And he had spots, like he was getting over some kind of rash. Maybe he had been drinking, I myself

186

get a bit rashy if I take spirits – and my nose too. His coat was pretty short, I do remember that, and I think he had on some kind of boots. I seem to remember thinking they wasn't town boots, but he was walking off before I could see proper.'

'Did he take her arm?'

'I never realized he was with her till he spoke, because he never said nothing when she was choosing. When it come to paying, she sort of nudges him to cough up and he baulks at that, but she jokes him into it – well, shames him really – and he makes a to-do about not understanding what coins she wants. But that was all my eye – he knew all right how much they cost, though he made out he didn't. Probably testing her to see if she'd take more than she should.'

Suddenly, Flack slapped his forehead. 'Blimey, I nearly forgot the funny hat. I never seen one like it before. It was a soft felt, round, with a kind of fold down the centre of the crown. Not a hat I'd like myself, but there, him being German, I suppose that's why.'

'German? Are you certain?'

'Oh yes, miss, I can give you any accent you want. I know German when I hear it. I used to work down the docks until I lost my foot.' He stamped his wooden foot.

'What about your boys, did they see him?'

'They told the detective they did, but after he was gone, the young one says he wasn't so sure. I told him, "You got to be sure, because when they capture him we shall have to stand up and say so." I think he just wanted to boast a bit.'

'George, you're a wonder, thank you.'

'No thanks needed, miss. When they catch him and you write this book of yours, it's going to open people's eyes to how the other half lives. I never read a book, but I would have a go with that one.'

The Boot Street rooms were a hive of industrious activity, Josephine bent over her desk, writing furiously, whilst Liliana, whistling like a baker-boy, applied oil paint. When Josephine had written up her interview with George Flack, she went to find Lili to ask a favour.

'Please come with me, Liliana.'

'No Josie, *no*, absolutely *no*. I hate funerals. And a funeral in midwinter of someone I have no interest in? No, thank you very much.'

'You do have an interest in her.'

'A slight one, but not an obsession as you have.'

'Lili, it will be a workhouse funeral. Isn't that bad enough, without the fact that there will be no one concerned enough to be there.'

'She had friends who knew her when she was alive. How about Patty Lydney and—'

'All right, Lili. I will go without you.'

So Josephine went by omnibus alone to Brompton Cemetery.

Josephine had attended few enough funerals, and had expected, because of Harriet's poor circumstances, that, as she had told Liliana, this would be a 'parish funeral'.

Surprisingly there was an undertaker in attendance. A hearse arrived carrying a fine elm coffin, followed by a mourning coach from which stepped four people: a young man, and a woman – older, but not by much – leaning on the arm of a man who must be her husband. There was also another man who, Josephine estimated, was perhaps another relative. The younger man and the woman were much alike, and, even though she had seen Harriet only in death, there was a family likeness. Brother, sister and sister's husband, and a well-dressed man.

Superintendent Thomson and Sergeant Kerley were present at the premises of the undertaker in Drury Lane when the hearse and coach left. Although it was not late in the day, December gloom was descending into darkness. A small crowd of a poor class of people watched. These were mostly women, some of whom Frank Kerley recognized as women who had been brought in for questioning as to their whereabouts on Christmas Eve.

The brother. Appearing no more than a youth, although James knew him to be a young man, he looked pale and lost; beside him, an obviously well-to-do older gentleman made up the foursome of the chief mourners. Frank Kerley did not go into the chapel, but waited in the area of the open grave, standing well back and at a discreet distance from where the graveside service would take place, to observe who was there. He agreed with the super: such a murderer as they were looking for might well get satisfaction from watching the outcome of his handiwork.

And for James Thomson there was the added draw to Brompton Cemetery, because of the small part that Harriet Burton had played in his life some time ago. Arriving late for the chapel service, he was glad now that he had come alone. He spotted Kerley almost hidden by headstones and crosses.

When the mourners emerged from the chapel, he was glad to see that they had not brought the little girl with them. Although by now he was aware of the identity of the mourners, he had not yet spoken to any of them. This had been Kerley's role. From the sister, her husband and her brother, he transferred his attention to the third man of the party of mourners. A gentleman, tall and fair, and with an open, honest face. His bespoke apparel had been created for him by a tailor, a hatter and a boot-maker working in establishments the like of which a sergeant in the Met. would never see, except perhaps in the line of duty.

James Thomson was glad that in Harriet Burton's last appearance centre-stage, so to speak, she was attended with dignity by people of some refinement, even of quality. He was glad that he had come himself, too, and that he had troubled to dress appropriately to the occasion.

When Josephine had arrived, she had gone unobtrusively into the chapel and sat at the back. A surprising number of people were already gathered. Who were they? Why had they come to mourn Harriet? Having come this far, Josephine determined to follow the other mourners to the graveside. Still standing well back, she observed real grief in the brother and sister, the sister having to be supported by her husband and the youth unable to stop his streaming tears. Suddenly she saw herself as an interloper, a voyeur – yet she could not make herself leave. Within only a week, Harriet Burton had become important to her; every new piece of information was insight into her life. Who was the tall fair-haired gentleman? Could he be one of her gentlemen? She longed to know. Was Liliana right? Was she becoming obsessed?

No. She argued her own cause. Harriet Burton had been used and killed by some man who thought that her life was worthless compared with gratifying his own lust. It was not obsession to wish to open up to the public such a life as hers. And if she could do it, she would open his life as well. No matter what, she would write the account of Harriet.

A voice at her shoulder made her jump. 'Hello, Miss Ferguson?' She recognized the voice, but could not place it until she turned slightly. 'Oh. Yes, hello. Sergeant Kerley, isn't it?'

'It is. Are you here for one of your journals?'

Confused at having been discovered by one of her uncle's close Bow Street men, she blurted out, 'Oo, no, I am here on my own account, Sergeant. I have been writing for . . . other newspapers since you so kindly allowed me to interview you.'

'I thought it turned out rather well. My wife has made

a cutting and my daughter insists on showing it to all and sundry.'

'Thank you.'

'Well, it's not that often that the Force gets much recognition. So, what is your interest in this unfortunate woman?'

Any answer she gave would sound lame. 'General interest; a writer always needs to observe unusual occasions.'

The graveside service having ended, mourners were beginning to disperse. She and the sergeant stood respectfully, heads bowed.

'Josephine?' For a second time she jumped at a voice emanating from behind her. 'Sergeant Kerley. What is going on here?'

Josephine closed her eyes and prayed that this was not true. Her uncle had appeared as if from nowhere.

Speechless, she knew that embarrassment was flushing her cheeks, and hoped that the late afternoon gloom hid it.

Frank Kerley looked mystified. 'Sir?'

'Is this young lady persuading you to give her an interview, Mr Kerley?'

'No, sir. No.' Sensing that something was amiss, and not wanting to add anything to the situation, Frank Kerley thought on his feet. 'We just happened to find ourselves together.'

Josephine answered quickly, 'I was saying how surprised I was that there were so many well-dressed people present.'

'What did you expect, miss, a rabble?' And, turning on his heel, her uncle tipped his hat at her and left.

The sergeant, not knowing what was going on, said, 'Excuse me, Miss Ferguson. Nice to see you again,' and hastened to follow the superintendent.

Streetlights shone across the sleety pavements as Josephine rode the crowded omnibus. She really had intended to go and visit him and say that she was sorry for having said hot-headed things. But she had been too caught up in Harriet's life and too many days had gone by.

Uncle James could not stand finding himself caught on the back foot.

Nor for that matter could Josephine. She felt that she had come out of that meeting very badly. What on earth must Sergeant Kerley have thought?

Frank Kerley was puzzled. The super knew that the young woman he had made jump at the sound of his voice was a newspaper journalist, yet he had called her Josephine, and she had responded. It took hardly any time at all for an experienced detective to come up with a solution. He had a vague recollection of the name Josephine. Josephine Thomson – Jemima Ferguson? It fitted. He kept his counsel. If the super wanted him to know, then he would tell him.

That evening, when he was eating supper with Elizabeth and Frances, he asked, 'You remember me once telling you about Mr Thomson and his wife taking in his brother's child?'

Elizabeth nodded. 'That was years ago, but I do remember, it being so unusual for him to confide in you. A terrible tragedy, if memory serves.'

Frances, home from music college for one last meal before she returned to her studies, perked up. 'What, Ma? Tell us what happened.'

'I don't know. Anything I do know is what your father said at the time.'

'Mr Thomson had a brother who worked abroad – some kind of missionary.'

'Oh, Pa, how could he be *some kind* of a missionary. He was or he wasn't.'

'Don't always be so pedantic, Franny, let your father have his say.'

Frank continued. 'The brother and all the family was wiped out in some sort of plague, but the little girl had gone up-country in the care of a servant. Only the two of them survived.'

'That's tragic, Pa. What happened?'

'It's what I am trying to say. The child in the care of the servant was sent to England – the super being next-of-kin – and he and Mrs Thomson took them in and brought the girl up as their own.'

'What happened to the servant, Pa?'

'How would I know that? We work together, we aren't social equals.'

'Doesn't he talk about her, Francis?'

'He is my superior officer, Elizabeth. It's not my

place to ask about his family matters. Too personal.'

'But he came here only last week. Isn't that personal?'

Frank Kerley heaved a great sigh. 'A simple question, Elizabeth. I wondered if you remembered the girl's name.'

Elizabeth Kerley gave her husband what he would have described as a self-satisfied, cocky kind of look. 'As a matter of fact I *do*, but only because it was the same as my mother's.'

Franny said, 'Josephine.'

Frank Kerley said, 'I do believe you are right, Elizabeth. Not that it matters,' and said no more.

The morning following the funeral, when Frank Kerley reported, his super. handed him a sheaf of letters. Frank read.

'To the Coroner:
  Dear Sir,
  Could you not dispense with my servant's attendance at the inquest of his poor sister today and future days? An account of what goes on in a brothel does not tend to edification and brings him into a class of people he has not been used to. He is a very well-disposed lad and I want to keep him so.
  This is the third time I have troubled to write a letter. But you will, I am sure, understand and

excuse my anxiety. If you can spare him, please send him back here.

Faithfully yours, C. Knight Watson'

Frank raised his eyes and eyebrows questioningly.

'That was to the Coroner. Now read this.' This letter was anonymous, and sent to Bow Street Station. It drew the attention of the police to the fact that, with the connivance of Mr C. Knight Watson, Harriet Burton's brother was sleeping on the premises of the Society of Antiquities against the rules of membership.'

'Who is this Mr Knight Watson, sir?'

'Savile Row tailoring, Malacca palm cane with silver at both ends. Ring any bells at the funeral yesterday?'

'The gentleman of means.'

'Christopher Knight Watson, one of the mourners at the Burton funeral.'

'And do we suspect Mr Watson?'

'Not unless the man for whom we have put out a description changed his appearance at midnight. Mr Watson is, as you saw, as fair and tall as yourself. But we should call upon the gentleman. Discover what you can about his link with the Burtons.'

Frank Kerley held up the anonymous letter. 'I think I recognize this one's style. One of our regulars, sir. I'll have a word with the desk, but I think we shall find that this is not the first time he has tried to stir up trouble within the Society of Antiquities. He has some kind of axe to grind.'

* * *

Christopher Knight Watson might be as fair as Frank, and he was tall, but not quite equal to the sergeant's height. Nor was he the product of a village school, but most likely of one of the most ancient public schools followed by a favoured university. But not the services, Frank decided; there was nothing of the military or naval in him – more clerical, if anything. One thing was certain, he had wealth.

His greeting was gracious. 'It is not necessary to apologize, Sergeant Kerley. We all have our tasks, and where should we be without the police?'

'Nice of you to take it like that, sir.'

His manner changed subtly, soberly. 'This devil must be found, Sergeant. How can I assist?'

'It's only a matter of routine, we have to contact anyone who might be able to shed light on this dreadful crime. I believe you know the family?'

Watson smiled, 'And you have, no doubt, received a letter suggesting that you investigate my movements because I am a patron of young Buswell – you realize that his sister took the name Burton, of course.'

'My superintendent thought that I might speak with you about the concern at young Mr Buswell's presence in the coroner's court, as you expressed in your letter. I'm sorry, sir, but I'm not at liberty to say anything about such matters, or any other letter.'

The other man held up his hand, 'Of course not. All I meant was that my action in a small act of charity towards the Buswell boy has upset a certain member of the Society, who has done nothing but raise the matter with other members. And, as for the coroner's court, he is a young man who is suffering greatly at the death of his sister, and to be forced to sit in court and listen to details of the kind of life she . . .' The idea of the hurt to the young man was obviously painful. 'I have sons of my own. I should not like it if they had such grief and ignominy to bear, Sergeant.'

'Right, sir. I don't have sons, but I have a grown daughter.'

'Good, Sergeant, good. Pity the man who does not see descendants.'

Whoever had written the cranky anonymous letter suggesting that this man had anything to do with the murder of Harriet Burton was as mad as a hatter. Frank Kerley was convinced that Mr Christopher Knight Watson had not a violent bone in his body.

A gentle man. The kind of man Frank often wished himself to be, occasionally believed himself to be. His grandfather would have said that it is no hardship to be gentle if you have wealth; it's poverty that makes men harsh. There had been a time when Frank accepted his grandfather's beliefs without question, but not so much now. Now he believed that gentleness is something of the spirit. 'I'd agree with that most heartily, sir.'

Christopher Watson started. 'I doubt that what I know will be of any assistance, except, of course, that it was only Harriet who was known as Burton. The family name is Buswell. Certain members of the Buswell family are known to me through the young man.'

'How came you to know him, sir?'

'He came to the Society as an employee, which he is still. Having nowhere to lodge, and little money, I permitted him to sleep in the building. It harms no one; indeed, if our offended member who takes such exception to the boy's presence did not search him out, then no one would be aware that this is where he lays his head.'

'He lives on the premises of the Society of Antiquities then?'

Watson nodded. 'He's a good lad, and the Buswells are a respectable family. Three of them left home to come to live in London . . .' He trailed off, and a pained expression crossed his face. 'The elder sister, as I am sure you must know, now lives in Sussex and the younger, Harriet . . . well, she is why you are here. This business has been devastating to them, Sergeant. They had been close and caring siblings.'

'Did you know Harriet Burton?'

'No, I did not know that poor unfortunate.'

'You knew her to be called Harriet and not Clara, sir?'

Watson nodded. 'She was never referred to by any other name as far as I know.'

'Clara was her professional name, I mean the name under which she appeared on the list of music-hall performers.'

'You know, of course, about the child?'

'Yes, sir.'

'Kate. Poor child. I don't know what will become of her. I believe her aunt hopes to take her, but for the present she is in a boarding school.'

'A rather expensive one, by all accounts.'

'I pay the fees, but perhaps you know that already also?'

'You pay the school fees, even though you have never met the mother? That is very generous of you, very charitable.'

'Do you ever give to the African mission charities?'

'When I can.'

'Yet you have never met the recipients? Very generous of you, Mr Kerley, very charitable. Read nothing into my wife and me helping the Buswell child. We are not poor people, our own sons are grown and want for nothing, and, if one is honest, the satisfaction one gets from any act of charity is something a Christian should admit to. Our consciences are salved by such acts, are they not? When we say, "There but for the grace of God go I", in our inner hearts we are relieved that God had the grace to stay his hand.'

'I'd agree with that in essence, sir, but even so I would say it is generous of you and your wife. I am sure that for the present, a good boarding school is the best place for the little girl. Away from everything. It will never be easy for her, a thing like this, for the rest of her life . . .'

'You are a most unusual policeman, Mr Kerley.' Frank raised his eyebrows, at which Mr Knight Watson hastily added, 'Impertinent fellow, that Knight Watson! I meant only that, when one relies on the daily press for one's acquaintance with other professions, I am afraid that one is apt to pick up the prejudices of the journalists. Perhaps you are not at all unusual, Mr Kerley. Perhaps all policemen are intelligent and compassionate?' It was a rhetorical question, and he went straight on. 'Well, what else can I tell you?'

'To eliminate you from our investigations, sir, your movements.'

'My movements. I was in the company of my family and friends on Christmas Eve. We played at cards till the early hours. We could vouch for young Buswell, too, if you wish. I shall be glad to give you details of those present.' He smiled, 'I could no doubt also give you the name of the member of the Society who objects to poor young Buswell sleeping on the premises.'

On the streets again, a short piece of poetry, straight from his youth, sprang into Frank's mind. Mr Knight Watson had been reading the poet, Frank had noticed. 'Ellen Brine'. Had Mr Knight Watson been reading it because he saw a similarity between the 'childern all in black' and the plight of the child Kate.

September come, wi' Shroton faer
But Ellen Brine were never there!
A heavy heart were on the maer
Their father rawd his homeward road
'Tis true he brought zome fearin's back
Ver them two childern all in black;
But they had now, wi' playthings new,
No muther ver to shew um to,
Ver Ellen Brine of Allenburn
Would never more return.

*　　*　　*

Liliana had been baking again, this time light but extremely oddly shaped croissants, made deliciously crispy by layered butter. By the time Josephine came warm from having a hot, soapy wash all over, Liliana had a dozen pieces of pastry cooling on a tray.

'Oh, Lili, I have died and gone to pastry-lovers' heaven. Will you marry me and bake croissants every day?' Josephine yanked her fair frizz to the top of her head and skewered it with a length of tortoiseshell.

'Peace-offering, Jo. As soon as you had left, I felt myself to be no end of a pig. I would have run after you except that . . . well, it was so cold and gloomy, and the omnibuses appeared all steamed up, and I hate cemeteries and . . .' She laughed and gave her friend a quick peck on the cheek, 'and it was so much nicer toasting in front of the fire.'

'Pass the butter, and I'll think about forgiving you.'

Having eaten, Josephine sat before the kitchen fire and pulled on thick stockings. 'You *are* coming with me to David's midnight meeting aren't you, Liliana?'

It was clear that Liliana had forgotten the promise to her brother to listen to his New Year message at the church where he was a preacher.

'Of course I'm coming. I've only to put on my boots and I'm ready.'

They set off walking to St Giles, where Liliana's brother was gaining a reputation for himself as a free-thinking preacher. The first time Josephine had heard him speak to his congregation, she discovered a human being in the guise of a preacher. If the *Telegraph* had a vendetta with him, this was more than compensated for by *The News*'s favouritism. The Reverend Wilde was a people's preacher. It was from hearing Mr Hood's good opinion that Josephine had gone to hear him. And from then to David Wilde mentioning that his sister was visiting and looking for accommodation. After which, finally, Liliana had become Josephine's sub-tenant and close friend.

David Wilde had eliminated from his ministrations anything that could be construed as confusing to the people of the area. No tolling bells, no high-flown ideals or language, no threats or warnings that his God was one who turned against the poor and favoured the rich. His God knew that it wasn't difficult for the wealthy not to steal. Over the period that he had been minister in London, those who had been offended by his speeches – which could not be called sermons – had dwindled away, but were replaced threefold by the poor and hungry. The better-off who did stay were stalwart and sincere, and doubly generous with donations.

So that by the last day of the year 1872, the people streaming into St Giles would hear him bring in a new year with a prayer and words of hope and advice, as well as a simple explanation about how the material world could be changed. When he was accused of preaching politics, he would ask where in all holy writ was there a single word that said that he was wrong. So ridicule and denigration were tried, but this was water off a duck's back.

Inside the atmosphere was more partylike than Christian service. Along the side-aisles trestle-tables had been erected, on which were piles of fresh loaves, large dishes of brawn, and dozens of meat pies. It was obvious that the parishioners knew that there would be tea to drink, because each had brought along some kind of mug or cup. Those who might have expected anything stronger were disappointed, because David was much against alcohol.

Josephine and Lilian heard him before they saw him in the throng. Leaning over the pulpit in a very un-cleric-like manner, he was trying to make himself heard. Gradually the hubbub died down.

'Good friends, I had hoped that you would come tonight and thank God for having let us live through another year – hard and bitter for many though it has been – but nevertheless we have come through. In about five minutes' time, we shall hear all the bells of Bow ring in another year – of pain and pleasure, of sadness and happiness, of want and very infrequently, of plenty. But, for a few minutes now, let us think of those whom we knew and loved, and those we hardly knew at all, but who will not be of this world in Eighteen Seventy-three. None of us can be certain of what lies ahead, or even whether there is another world waiting, but we can be certain of the here and now, and thank God for it. Our good neighbours – the grocery merchants, and butchers and bakers, oh, yes, and candle-makers – have contributed food and tea and light enough for us to celebrate the beginning of another year. Bless you all, and I hope that you will bless me.' Loud amens and hundreds of sibilant blessings filled the body of the church.

Josephine drew in her breath. Had he really said that?

That none of us could be certain that another world is waiting? That was agnosticism. If that was repeated, he would lose his living. The *Daily Telegraph* would blare out 'Blasphemy.'

Suddenly the distant and distinct sound of the bells of St Clement Danes, Whitechapel and Bow rang out, soon to be joined by others from all the bell-towers in London. Not all could be heard in Bow Street, but the sound of ringing was in the clear frosty air.

It was some time before Liliana could get to her brother. Josephine followed, wanting to speak with him again. Even if she could not speak with him, to be in his presence. The Reverend Wilde excited her, even more tonight when he had seemed to speak as an agnostic.

All the while they were talking, people were coming up to him and wishing him a Happy New Year, and thanking him for the 'eats'.

'Come on, Jo.' Liliana tried to lead her towards the generous tables. 'Let's try for some food.'

'All right, I'll be with you in a minute.' But Lili waited. 'David,' Josephine said, 'I realize that now is not the time, but I wanted some information from you.'

'She is obsessed by that singer who was killed. She is going to write a book about her life.'

'Lili! I wish you wouldn't interfere. I am quite capable of talking for myself.'

David said, 'Lili, go and get food like a good girl,' and to Josephine, 'Did you know Clara?'

Josephine shook her head. 'Only since her death, and

I find that I now know quite a lot about her – as Harriet, not Clara.'

'What is it you want from me?'

'To meet people she knew.'

'She knew me.'

That night, James Thomson too attended the night-watch service, not at his own church, but at St Giles, where he knew from past, secretive visits, he would come out refreshed and exhilarated. His visits to St Giles to listen to young Reverend Wilde were part of a life he kept separate from Ann. Ann was conventional and afraid to think otherwise than in the manner of her upbringing. It was not that he set out to have secrets from her, it was rather as a means of protecting her from his own upbringing in Turkey, which was, to say the least, cosmopolitan. 'Foreign,' Ann said of it.

He sat with his hat between his feet and watched as the church filled, not with the bonneted and well turned-out congregation he was used to – although there was a fair sprinkling of such – but with working men and, in greater numbers, working women and their children; people who, until Rev. Wilde came to St Giles, did not believe that such places as churches were for them. But they trusted this young clergyman; he did not frighten them with incense, and ritual, and robes and words that had no meaning. They came in crowds from London's infamous Baldwin's Gardens and its environs, London's poorest, to listen to the young clergyman who said things that had relevance to their mean lives.

Enemies called him the 'Ranting Priest', thinking it to be insulting, but James guessed that the young man himself would take it as a compliment, for he meant to raise these people up. This might be the only service in the year that they attended, but then what the clergyman said in his simple language was such rich fare that perhaps they were sustained for much longer than they would be by the thin stuff James and Ann were served weekly.

Certainly it had relevance to James's life at Bow Street.

He wondered where, and how frequently, Frank Kerley attended. Certainly he was Low Church – hadn't his father or grandfather been a preacher? Certainly radical. James wondered what his junior officer would think if he knew his superintendent supported such 'ranting' preachers as young Rev. Wilde. For that matter, he wondered what Ann would say, what Colonel Henderson would say, what Lady Granville would say. Earlier that day he had placed fifty sovereigns in the St Giles collection box.

It was inappropriate to finger a rosary at this unaffected watch-night service, so he sat as he had done on other occasions in this church, with his hands linked across his lap, allowing the easy atmosphere to deal with his anxieties.

He thought about Frank Kerley and what he might have made of Christopher Knight Watson, and admitted to himself that he had sent his sergeant out angling, but, even though he felt that there was nothing to be caught in those waters, James never made assumptions.

Never? He had assumed that Josephine would develop into a woman whose character would be much like Ann's; instead she had developed a character too much like his own to sit comfortably in a woman. How pleased he had always been when he had told her of his plans and hopes for a literate and modern police force trained in sciences and she had asked intelligent questions.

He had assumed that a girl as pretty as Josephine, with Ann Martha to guide her, would not develop ambitions that could never be fulfilled in a world as it now existed. Women were now pushing for places in universities; even Gwendoline Granville had been outspoken in her belief that Ann was as capable of voting as any man. Perhaps so, but not in their lifetime would it come about, and not until she understood that 'Fallen Women' needed more than charitable institutions to keep them off the streets.

With head bowed, he offered a silent prayer for Harriet Burton.

He stood and joined in the singing of a hymn.

He must find time to visit Josephine. He had been full of consternation at the thought of the kind of low life she would encounter if she continued to follow her mistaken dream that she could be a reporter. He realized he had allowed this anxiety to prejudice him. He had read her Jemima Ferguson cuttings and been moved by her sincerity and facility with words. He was optimistic that he might persuade her to make use of her talents by writing biography, perhaps, or even fiction.

Had Harriet Burton ever attended this service, so simple and cleansed of ritual? The rosary he had given her appeared to have religious meaning for her. What did it all amount to? She had been around the Bow Street district for something like six years; she had been a casual singer and a casual streetwalker; she had accepted a rosary from a stranger and a half-sovereign from another. She had died in a welter of blood with a peaceful expression. His instinct was to thank God for that peaceful expression, yet the fact of it somehow made the killing worse.

She had been no threat to her killer, and yet he had taken some razor-sharp instrument and drawn it twice across her throat.

James Thomson was aroused from meditation by the pealing first of Bow bells, then of St Clement Danes, then Whitechapel. He fixed his eyes upon the altar, crossed himself, and vowed that he would not rest until he had her murderer in a cell.

Josephine, standing in the crowd listening to David Wilde, let her gaze wander over the many, many faces looking towards him, and started when, to her great astonishment, she saw her uncle. She drew back, even though the oil-lamps did not, she thought, illuminate the gathering sufficiently for him to be able to see her in an aisle lit only by candles. But, from where she stood, she could watch him. On Christmas morning, when she attended church with him and Ann, she had thought his eyes were glazed with boredom by the long mass in Latin. But not here in St Giles; he sang the one hymn with gusto. Here, he reminded her of what she could remember of the full-hearted singing that had gone on in her father's mission. Uncle James, she thought, why aren't you more easy with yourself?

It was not until she had watched him leave that she had gone to speak to some women who Liliana's brother had said might be glad to talk to her. He was known to them as Young Father David. He had said, 'This is my sister's friend, I hope you will tell her what she wants to know about Clara.'

'What's to know, Father David? She did some singing, and picked up a wrong 'n.'

'People who don't know you as I do have no idea how difficult life on the streets is.' He smiled, 'You are "Bad Lots", and you have only yourselves to blame, isn't that the general opinion?'

'You are a sweet man, Father David, but I don't see what writing up Clara's life is going to do.'

Josephine interrupted, 'Listen, I'll be honest with you, a biography of Clara might not do much, but isn't that better than doing nothing? She had a daughter, didn't she?'

'Yeah, little Katy. Remember her from when Clara lived in Nelson Street. Katy wasn't very old then.'

David Wilde said, 'Josephine, these girls need to get back to the Haymarket. Maybe you could meet tomorrow.'

'Yeah, do that, about four o'clock. I always go to O'Sullivan's for me breakfast then.'

Josephine made an appointment to meet Violet on the following day.

January 1873

O'Sullivan's was a new experience for Josephine, and she liked it. A small eating place, made more accommodating by having long tables and benches. At the long serving hatch it seemed possible to request anything one fancied. Breakfast in name only. Everything from cold cuts to thick soup was written up in chalk on a large board. Items were deleted, others added. It being four in the afternoon, Josephine chose Welsh rarebit. It being Violet's breakfast time, she ordered ham and eggs and fried bread. When Josephine was about to ask for tea, Violet said, 'Have some stout, it's the best drink in the world.' And, once having got used to its bitterness, Josephine agreed.

Violet ate quickly, then sat back and sipped her stout. 'Look, I don't know what you want to know about Clara, but I'll tell you what I can remember from when I knew her. Her best times, I should think, was when she lived with Major Brown. Now, I don't know whether he rightly was a major or not, but he wasn't short of cash and he treated her really nice. Used to call herself Mrs Brown then, didn't have to go out to work. Twice she got in the family way by him, but both times they was stillbirths. If you ask me, that's a bad thing for a woman to suffer. Abortions and miscarriages are everyday things, but to carry a child full-term and then it be dead makes you think that, if there's someone up *there*, they a'nt very fond of women.'

'Did she have any live children with Major Brown?'

'Nah, he went off abroad. I think he died, but I can't remember who told me that. Anyway, the next one she takes up with was a different kettle of fish. He was lovely, good fun, had been living abroad. Falls head over heels in love with Clara, used to come and listen to her sing every time she was on. He had a nice place in Regent Square, and he set her up there.'

'Living with him?'

'Yes, but not taking his name as she did with the major. She knew all along that there'd come a time when he would have to go back to China, but he told her that he would send for her and they would live together out there.'

Josephine ordered Violet another glass of stout. 'I expect that you're going to tell me it was the old, old story – out of sight, out of mind, and she never heard from him again.'

'Well, that's where you'd be wrong. She heard from him regular.' Violet handed over a packet, a large, used envelope bulging with papers. 'I did wonder if I ought to hand these over to the police, but . . . well, what would they do with love-letters except have a bit of a laugh? So you have them.'

Josephine was stunned at being presented with such an insight into Harriet's life. 'How did you come by them?'

'She asked me to keep them a few weeks back because she was on the move such a lot and she'd had stuff go missing in the past, and Willie's letters were more precious to her than her bits of jewellery. She knew with me they'd be safe from prying eyes because I can't read – never could.'

With the new year came a flurry of activity. The reward notices brought forth scores of people who, for the sake of a visit to Bow Street or the price of a penny letter, thought they would try their luck, no matter how little their statements fitted the details. Every type of foreigner was offered, from Japanese to a German travelling band, all members of which wore moustaches and all of whom had to be sought and interviewed. Neighbours seemed intent on settling old scores, and reported their suspicions. The working days of the detectives of 'E' Division were stretched at both ends. DCs and inspectors were sent out in all directions to check on every reported sighting. Each day, when the reports were assembled on James Thomson's desk, Frank usually found himself in the senior man's office, where he was often handed a report with the Met. heading. But they were getting nowhere. James's greatest hope was that the 'Wanted' notices spread throughout the country would produce a lead. But days slipped by, and, although there was a great deal of activity generated by the '£100 Reward' posters, there was little real progress.

New witnesses came into Bow Street who had sight of Harriet Burton and a man on Christmas Eve. Their reports added weight to the description they already had. He was young, surly and German.

Frank Kerley, and the DCs assigned to the case, went on wild-goose chases all around London, and for his own satisfaction Frank went over and over the ground between the Alhambra and Regent Circus. At last he came up with something that seemed to be part of the story and went gladly back to report to the superintendent, who for the first time bade him take a chair and warm his legs.

'She calls herself Madame Margaret, and she says that on the Friday before Christmas she and her friend met a foreigner in Leicester Square. It was the man who started the conversation.'

James Thomson raised his eyebrows.

Frank Kerley smiled, 'I know, that's what she would say, but it doesn't matter really . . . The three of them went for a drink at The Falcon in Princes Street. Then, according to Madame Margaret, he asked if she and her friend would go to a coffee house with him and spend the night. He offered to pay them ten shillings.'

'Did they take it?'

'Apparently they didn't like his appearance. I reckon

it was more that they were huffed at five shillings a head for depravity of that kind.'

'What sort of price do you suppose she puts on herself then?'

Josephine was beginning to have insight into the kind of woman Harriet was, and she liked her. Tryphena had obtained a billboard picture of 'Sweet Clara Burton'. She could not possibly have been as demure as depicted, but her features were dainty and pretty. Josephine could see how she must have captivated men, especially if her voice was as appealing as her looks.

At Somerset House in London, every birth in Britain was on record. Josephine spent a productive few hours there, and returned home to find Liliana stretching a new canvas with her brother David helping. He was in his shirtsleeves and looking very un-clergyman-like. And certainly not as 'brotherly' as she had considered him heretofore. Her feeling of elation surprised her. Even so, she knew that she could never be romantically interested in a clergyman. Since having heard an outdoor speaker on Humanism at Hyde Park's Speakers' Corner, she felt more at home with those views than any religion that offered rewards in Heaven for behaving well.

Liliana asked eagerly, 'Did you find Harriet?'

'I have Lili, I have. My coster friend was correct she was born in Norfolk, at Wisbech. I found two other siblings: one a sister three years older, and a brother, much younger.'

'What next then?' David asked.

'She plans to go to Wisbech,' Liliana said. 'Right, Jo?'

'Of course, what else? I found the last address of their mother and father on death certificates. I shall start there – there are bound to be other Buswells. If not, Wisbech is a small town; I shall find someone who knows the Buswell family.'

David said, 'That's a tall order, it could take a while.'

'I hope not, but I have to do it. Birthplace and early conditions are what makes us who we become as adults.'

'Would you like some company?'

'You want to come with me to Norfolk?'

'If you'll have me, and you would be doing me a kindness.' He smiled wryly, 'I need someone to be kind to me.'

'Listen to the man, he has only himself to blame,' Lili scoffed.

'What is this about?' Josephine asked.

'My church seniors have come down on me like a ton of bricks, and I'm in limbo until they decide whether I am fit to continue to be a clergyman.'

'I'm not surprised,' Liliana said. 'You practically announced yourself an agnostic.'

'I didn't mean it like that. I said that we should live as well as we can in the present.'

'And the *Daily Telegraph* quoted you. "The Ranting Priest".'

'Ignoramuses! I am not a priest. Just a clergyman . . . a preacher if anything.'

'It's strange, I can never think of you as a clergy-man.'

He responded with a burst of laughter. 'I can never think of myself as a clergyman either.'

'Perhaps you are a politician.'

After a long pause, he gave a wry, lopsided smile. 'I am, Josephine, I am, but that doesn't preclude me holding Christian views.'

'Perhaps we might discuss those views and my own on our long train journey to Wisbech. Go and put some things in an overnight bag, David. I should really like to have your company.'

They arrived in Wisbech the next day.

Wisbech turned out to be not as small as Josephine had supposed, and they wasted an hour wandering around wondering where to start. David's idea that they should go to a vicarage gave them what they wanted.

Mrs Burnett was the best sort of woman for a vicar to have as a wife: welcoming, interested and helpful. David, being a churchman himself, established Josephine's bona fides as a serious and concerned person. 'My husband is away from home, but I might be more helpful to you – I am born and bred local. Known the Buswells all my life. A nice, hard-working, respectable family. In a way, with all this scandal about Harriet, it is a blessing that her parents have gone on to a better place. There is only one Buswell left now, on either side of the family – Harriet and Mary's uncle. He's a poor soul, and has taken it hard – the Buswells have always been a respectable family.'

Mrs Burnett insisted that they leave their bags and stay

the night, and that it was no trouble for her to take them to Albion Place and introduce them as people sincerely concerned in the Buswell tragedy.

Josephine was grateful to have found such a mediator, but Mrs Burnett's naiveté was concerning. Josephine might easily have been going to write a column for a London newspaper.

Harriet's uncle might be a poor soul, but he was articulate and educated, and by no means as naive as Mrs Burnett. It took some direct questions about motive and an assurance that he would see what she proposed writing before he agreed to talk.

'Would you ah wrote about our Harriet if she hadn't got herself dead in the manner she did?' Both his accent and phrasing were intriguing.

She answered him honestly and told him that she had been a newspaper reporter. 'I might have written something, but not a history of her life.'

'That seems a mighty undertaking for a bit of a girl like Harriet.'

'Mr Buswell, your niece had a child . . .'

'Ah, Katy, so I'm told.'

'When she is older, she is bound to want to know about her mother. I think what I will write is going to be better for her than newspaper articles. When was the last time you saw Harriet – when she left home?'

'No, since then. Five years. She and Mary came and stayed a week. I was surprised to know that she had had a little one. What has happened to it?'

'She's well cared for. In a boarding school at present.'

'That's for the best. I don't see our Harriet making much of a mother. She wasn't the type. I don't say she was the black sheep, but Harriet's mother was a trained machinist, and my brother had a very respectable living. He was a seaman.'

'How came your nieces to leave home?'

'Well they both died, didn't they? First my brother and then my sister-in-law. That was when the girls decided they'd try their hand in service in London.'

'Was Harriet in service before that?'

'Ah, she went as a servant to a man who lived near here.'

'Can you give me the address?'

'I could, but you won't get no change from him. He's been up the graveyard this four years.'

'I was hoping Mary might come. I wrote to her, but I haven't heard back yet. You haven't seen her, I suppose?'

'At a distance. I attended Harriet's funeral.'

Tears welled but did not spill over. 'I should ha' like to be there, but I can't make distances these days. What sort of affair was it?'

'Very dignified. Your other niece and nephew, several well-to-do people, I don't know who they were, but they were comforting your nephew.'

'That would be the Knight Watsons. Mary once wrote to tell me that there was a philanthropic gentleman who had provided for the boy, and had offered to pay for Harriet's child to be schooled.'

'Is there a connection between your family and these people?'

'Mary's husband, I believe. Good, charitable people Mary believed them to be. Have you spoken to Mary?'

'No. She will not want any more questioning, what with the police and the newspapers. Now that you have been kind enough to speak to me, I shall probably not try.'

'Lately, I've been wondering if there was something I could have done for the two girls, but I don't know what. It seemed at the time to be the best thing for them to get away from here with the deaths of their mother and father hanging over their lives.'

'Mary has stood by her sister, even though it couldn't have been easy.'

'Oh yes, I think there were times when Harriet pushed Mary to distraction, but being the older, she felt responsible. When they came here I asked them straight, how Harriet managed to get herself into trouble and Mary didn't. I wasn't finding fault, what was done was done, and it weren't no business of mine.

'Harriet said, so innocent, "I believed him, uncle. He was a coachman." When he found that he had got her in trouble, he said it would be all right, that they should go down to London where coachmen were always wanted. Once they got to London, he disappeared.'

There being no other person Mrs Burnett could think of who could help Josephine, they caught an early train next morning.

Josephine thought to herself how pleasant it was to have a male companion. Independent as she liked to be, she enjoyed having her bag taken from her and handed to a porter, having a daily paper and a box of jelly sweets purchased for her, having a window seat found for her. When she was settled, he sat beside her.

'Shall we go over your notes together?'

'You mean the Wisbech or the London ones?'

'All of it.'

It wasn't easy to talk about the life of a murder victim with other passengers within earshot, but by reading together and each making pencil notes for the other to consider, they managed very well. When at last Josephine returned her sheaf of notes to a document case, he placed his hand over hers. 'I have to say that I am very impressed, very, very impressed.'

'Really? What impresses you?'

'Your tenacity for one thing – perhaps dedication is the better word. Your passion for your subject. I read the "Jane" obituary: that must have touched many people who read it.'

'But for how long? Until the newspaper is used to light a fire?'

'Mr Gladstone's words must end up like that, too.'

'Maybe that is no bad thing . . . but Jemima Ferguson's words, now that's another matter entirely.'

He now took full charge of her hand in both of his briefly, 'You are incorrigible, Miss Ferguson.'

'I don't know whether to take offence at that,' she grinned, 'mostly because I don't know exactly what incorrigible means. Incurable?'

He smiled, 'Unrepentant?'

She shrugged, still not taking her hand from his. 'That

will do. I repent of nothing. My work, my beliefs, my views.'

'Good. I am glad that you and Liliana found one another.'

Slowly he released her hand, which remembered his for the rest of the journey.

Liliana, very taken with her new-found creative interest, had prepared coq au vin, the aroma of which pervaded the entire floor as her brother, David, in company with Josephine, went through into Josephine's apartment. David deposited two small travelling bags in the hall.

'Ah, the wanderers return. Was it worth the journey?'

'Josephine is the judge of that.'

'Well worth it.'

Liliana served the melting pieces of chicken floating in its flavoursome sauce in wide earthenware bowls. As they ate with the appetites of the young, healthy people they were, Josephine related what they had discovered. 'We seemed to get at some true picture of Harriet.'

Liliana looked up from dipping bread into the remains of the crock of sauce. '*We*, David? *We* get at the truth? Have you appointed him, Jo?'

'No I have not. But whilst David is wallowing in free time until his fate is sealed . . .'

'My fate will not be sealed. I intend to carry on my crusade to improve conditions . . .'

'Yes, yes, David,' Liliana interjected, 'I know all about that.'

'Lili, listen,' Jo said. 'At the moment, David is being very useful to me. He knows who to ask what. It could take me hours of questioning and researching to discover something that David has at his fingertips. He's such a help . . . knows most of the prostitutes in the Haymarket . . .'

Tapping the table with a spoon to make himself heard over Liliana's unladylike whoops and laughs, he said, 'Josephine, I don't think that you will help my quest to be given back my living if you praise me like that.'

Frank Kerley had also visited Mr Buswell. His report on his visit to Wisbech was thin, as James Thomson had expected but, just as he had sent his sergeant to Christopher Knight Watson to 'fish' so Thomson had sent him to discover the only remaining member of Harriet Burton's family not to have been questioned.

'She came from a nice family who lived in a nice town. I visited the graveyard, sir, she would have been better buried there. Used to work for a man with almost the same name as yourself. Spelled with a P. He's dead. I went to look at the headstone.'

That was what James himself would have done. Dotted the i's and crossed the t's. Turnstone. The closer he worked with Kerley, the more he had come to admire him and acknowledge his character and intelligence. Kerley was open in his opinions, yet understood protocol and recognized the proprieties that adhere to rank. In other circumstances, James would have been delighted to have Ann invite the Kerleys socially. But then, why not? He and Ann Martha had often been received at the Hendersons'. Until recently he had imagined Mrs Kerley to be the daughter of an apple-cheeked farmer's wife. Now that he had met her, if only briefly, he felt that she and Ann would get on splendidly. One day he hoped to find a suitable opportunity to ask the sergeant how a Dorsetshire farmboy came to have an artist wife and a musical daughter. Or was he perhaps no less prejudiced than many of his own class, who thought that to be from the working classes was to be lacking in taste and sophistication.

'Have you considered applying for higher rank, Sergeant? You know that I have always been impressed by the way you work, and I like the way you think. I should be pleased to give you a recommendation.'

Kerley smiled. 'Thank you, sir, thank you very much. I will give it some thought, but I reckoned time enough when my feet give up. I like to be out and about.'

'Don't leave it too late. You're a good man to have on a murder investigation – *any* investigation at all.'

'Thank you, sir. I might not have got a trip to Wisbech if I was an inspector. I'd have been a sight too expensive.' Then, seriously, 'I'm a happy man, sir. My philosophy is, "Don't change something that don't need it".'

'You might find that you were happier, or at least more fulfilled, with more authority.'

'"Might" is the important word there, sir. To my

224

mind, happiness and fulfilment aren't always inter-changeable. Mrs Kerley might be fulfilled if she'd stayed single and been a full-time painter, but she'd tell you herself, she wouldn't have been happier.'

Frank Kerley was beginning to feel that they were losing their quarry. Time was running out. No German answering the description had been seen in the dockland area, or Soho, or any of the other places foreigners tended to gather. He found himself checking and rechecking, realized that often he was reading a report hurriedly, as though that would speed up the discovery of a vital piece of information that would allow them to pounce on him.

Every dark-haired, sallow-skinned, clean-shaven man of twenty-five years he passed in the street was a possible suspect, yet it was impossible to stop every man who fitted the description to discover whether they spoke with a German accent. He read every report from every investigating officer and, as did his super-intendent, made notes and chased up every line of enquiry.

He read and re-read the antecedents. And the reports that were still not cleared. He noted in several of these that the investigating officer had been told of the victim's reported indifference to the men she brought home. 'Let him wait' was mentioned more than once.

This was not something helpful to the victim's char-acter. The newspapers would soon hint – or worse – that she had brought it on herself.

*   *   *

Josephine gave a lot of thought about how to persuade Harriet's landlady to talk to her.

Liliana had the answer. 'Money, Jo. Don't be subtle. Offer her a decent sum and she will tell.'

'How mercenary, Lili,' she smiled, raising her eyebrows. 'How much is a decent sum?'

They decided that five pounds sounded mercenary, but five guineas was a more respectable fee.

Josephine used a little flattery, and the suggestion that a place in history in a book was a much better thing than the Wright name in newspapers, particularly as she would get a fee for her time. In this way she achieved her interview with Mrs Wright, who, given the option, chose to meet Josephine at one of London's most expensive tearooms.

There was no doubt about it, Mrs Wright had presence. With an erect posture, full, swaying skirts and a high, complicated hat, she allowed herself to be conducted to where Josephine was waiting, at a table that was beautifully laid up for tea, with dainty sandwiches and little cakes highly decorated with sugar and cream. Josephine was not insincere when she said, 'If you don't mind me saying so, you have a wonderful way of making an entrance.'

'Thank you, Miss Ferguson, it's on account of my theatre training. It's something that comes natural once you're trained.' She was obviously not intimidated by her surroundings, but unbuttoned her gloves and turned them back on the wrist, and adjusted the folds of her skirt. 'This is nice, very nice. It's quite a while since I was entertained to tea. I must try to come up West more often, I'm glad of you suggesting Claridges, Miss Ferguson.'

'It occurred to me that you might like to talk away from . . .' Tailing off, not wanting to mention Great Coram Street directly.

Accepting milk for her tea and some small triangular sandwiches, Mrs Wright said, 'Did you know that my name's Harriet too? She called herself Clara for her act because it's a modern name. Which always seemed queer to me because her act was real old-fashioned.'

'In what way?'

'Well, she never tried to put any spice into her act. She had a pretty enough voice, but no . . . ?' Mrs Wright raised her chin and pouted provocatively, 'She never tried to be fetching.'

'So she wasn't the sort of girl to . . . act provocatively on the stage.'

'Not any time I saw her. I don't think she had it in her. No, what men liked in her was that sweet kind of girlishness. It wasn't false, she was a kind person, would give away her last sixpence. Which wasn't a good idea when she had to find her rent.'

'Did she get behind with that?'

'She may have done before she came to me, but I never let my girls get behind. It's no good to anybody to have debts dragging them down. No, when she went out on Christmas Eve, she owed me rent and I reminded her.'

'When she went out to go to the Alhambra Palace?'

'Yes. She was the only one of my girls who had an

act there last Christmas . . . you understand that many of my girls are on the stage.'

'No, I didn't know that.'

'I like having them around. Most of them haven't got people of their own. You see, when a girl gets stars in her eyes about treading the boards, a lot of them just ups tracks and comes to London. What they don't realize is that, even if they're good, it don't last. I was lucky, I didn't need talent, only this.' She ran her hands down her curvaceous figure. 'I was always the sweetmeat in the magician's box, the distraction whilst he moved mirrors and panels. Of course, I was only a little bit of a thing, and a real contortionist inside those boxes.'

'You say that you didn't need talent, but that is what you had. I would say to do those things you must have had amazing talent.'

'Well, thank you, there's not many who's ever seen it like that.' She smiled, showing that she had all her front teeth and that they were very good. 'What I did have a talent for was money. I saw the writing on the wall when I was very young, so I lived quite simple – not meagre – and always put money aside, bought good stones that would keep their value. Diamonds and gold always keep their value. It's what I try to tell my girls. It's why I don't like them getting into debt.'

'And Harriet?'

'She'd known good times; she had decent protectors she lived with for long stretches at a time. She'd had several good pieces given to her – modern stuff, but stuff to hold their value. One in particular, Major Brown, she was with him for quite some time. Trouble with that set-up is that, although Harriet still did her turns on the halls, she never looked at that as her income. To my mind, if he wanted her to be Mrs Brown, then she ought to have lived off of him and put her own earnings to one side.'

'And didn't she?'

Mrs Wright shook her head. 'I dare say she expected to be the major's lady for ever.'

'What happened?'

'She never told me that. But I know people who knew her then, and they say he went abroad. Twice that happened to her. The second one, I don't know his name, he was young, never gave her anything to salt away.'

'I hope you don't mind me asking, but was she in debt to you?'

'She had been behind . . . not much, but when she come home that night, first thing she did was to pay the rent she owed, and she give us a bag of apples for Christmas, just took a couple for herself.'

'Does that mean she made the man she brought home with her pay . . . I don't know how to put this . . .'

'Pay up front of what he was expecting?' Josephine nodded. 'Wisest thing, and to hand it over for safe-keeping if it's possible. In Harriet's case, she got the money off of him and paid her rent arrears with it. My girls a'nt whores, Miss Ferguson, not at all; there's thousands of girls out there having to do what they can to keep body and soul together.'

'I know, but before I decided to take an interest in Harriet's life – well, and death really, I didn't know how many girls have to go with men on the streets. It's a terrible thing.'

'Miss Ferguson, you won't know the half of it, I'll be bound. Girls by the hundred, come in from country places into service, like Harriet. Gets in the fam'ly way by some man who tells her a tale about better'n herself because he's got a position in the household, like Harriet, or it could be by the master, or the son of the house. It's often the innocent country girls who come off worst.'

'So, I suppose they are turned out.'

'To fend for theirselves and the young one. Nobody cares a tuppenny toss.'

Mrs Wright sounded so resentful that Josephine wondered whether Mrs Wright's own story had been similar. 'But you care, I can tell.' Josephine called for fresh tea to be made and another selection of cakes.

'I can't do much. But at least a dozen girls out of hundreds who would have been going up dark alleyways with any Tom, Dick and Harry, could have a place with a family.' Tears welled in her eyes and she blotted them before they fell. 'I always thought they wouldn't be in any danger living under my roof. Yet she was; she wasn't no safer there than if she had gone with him like . . .'

Josephine tentatively rested her hand upon Mrs Wright's. 'I hope that you are not feeling guilty or anything like that. You have no reason to, none at all.'

'Not guilty, but useless. What men do to women don't bear thinking about.'

'There are good men.'

Mrs Wright nodded. 'Oh yes, but sometimes you can't tell which ones is which until it's too late.'

Josephine decided that she must hand over to the police Harriet's letters that Violet had given her. Before doing so, though, she began recording them as part of her research, and as she did so read them aloud to Liliana.

> 'Point do Galle (Ceylon)
> Sunday 13 November 1870
>
> My Dearest Harriet,
>
> I have travelled as far as Ceylon in safety, and next Sunday hope to be in *Singapore*, and *there* to receive your *first* letter before going on to my Hong Kong home. Not a day passes that I do not think about you many times, regretting that I do not possess the *original* instead of the photograph you gave me, not at all a flattering one – and I often wonder if you have had resolution enough to fly from London associations to the shelter of your sister's roof. My anxiety about you, dear Harriet, is very great, and *if* there is no letter from you at Singapore when we arrive there next Sunday, I shall not know what to think, and I shall fear all sorts of mishap have befallen you.
> My chief dread is that the quiet, perhaps monotonous life of Hurst Green with your

sister may soon weary you, and that then the temptations of your old friends – female as well as male – with the attractions of London to your excitable self, may have led you back to a life from which I would gladly preserve you. Though a month has passed since I left you. I am not a bit more reconciled to my solitary banishment than I was before leaving London, and increasingly regret that time did not permit me to have arranged for you to have accompanied me, as you sometimes said you would like to do. I should then have felt that my best days were not spent *alone* in acquiring wealth without myself to expend it upon selfishly. Indeed, after living so pleasantly in London, I *do* feel that I want a companion to love and be loved by. I do so *much* fear your being left in London.'

Josephine lowered the long, finely-written letter she had been reading aloud to Liliana. 'I've just thought, how would Willie ever get to know that the woman he loved is murdered? It's not as though he's kin or family or betrothed or anything? Imagine what it would be like for him receiving a newspaper from England and reading that his sweetheart is the victim of the Great Coram Street murderer?'

'If he had not abandoned her, then she would not have been the victim. Are you going to hand over the letters to the police?'

'I have to, Lili, it would be withholding evidence or something if I didn't, and I don't want to get on the wrong side of Uncle James any more than I already am.' She continued reading and writing as they huddled around the kitchen range, which was almost red hot against the chill of the bitter January fog that seemed to be able to creep into any house.

'Now, before telling you more about my voyage, let me remind you of your promise to write to me everything about all your arrangements and plans for the future. Do, my dear girl, tell me everything about what you have been doing and thinking. Tell me, too, what arrangements you can make with your sister about keeping you, I mean remuneration for your board and lodging. I think you should not pay more than a pound a week, if so much. *I must know all your circumstances* before I can decide what to do when I reach Hong Kong. So, Harriet *mia*, pray keep nothing back from me. You may really confide in me.

'Men! Even when they say they are in love, they cannot leave women alone to be themselves. Listen to this . . .

'Another thing, my dear, I must remind you about. You promised to make some attempt at improvement in your writing and reading. You are so quick, intelligent, yet so young, that you need not despair of overcoming any defects.

'Defects Lili, defects! Such a man, to have no defects of his own.

'I know you would be a very good docile pupil, if I could only be near you to assist or direct your studies.

'After writing to you from Alexandria we crossed the desert by daylight on Saturday the twenty-ninth of October in very good railway carriages – can you fancy a railway laid in the midst of miles of sand? We reached Suez in time for dinner at seven. We got on board the rail steamer on Saturday morning and started down the Red Sea (you know it is the place you read of in the Bible whence the Egyptian Host were overwhelmed when pursuing the Israelites) . . .'

'Jo, the man's a monster,' Liliana chipped in. 'Who does he think he is, commenting on her defects, telling her how to live, and now geography and Bible lessons? I hate him, Jo. And so should you, writing in such a tone to Harriet. She was obviously sweet and nice to him. He was never going to bring her to China.'

'Just let me finish before you pass judgement. There's a lot more yet, and several other letters.'

'Mercy.'

'Aden is in Arabia, a dusty village without a tree, nothing to be seen but long strings of camels laden with dates, and half-naked Africans and Arabs. I went as hire to see the English soldiers' barracks and you would have laughed to see the black Natives with very little more clothing than father Adam's primitive fig leaf diving in the deep seas to pick up the money we threw in for them, quite fearless of the sharks abounding there.

'Another evening we had some "Christy's Minstrels", who gave us much fun. All this goes on, on the fire deck, with such a glorious *Moon* over us. (By the way, my dear, the *Moon* will, I suppose, be full with you again.)'

Josephine lowered the letter again. 'You realize what he means by this?'

'Of course. He hopes that he has not left her with child. Full moon!'

'And he mentions it so casually. How could he have gone off to China not knowing? He couldn't have loved her. "By the way," he says after he's related all that about entertainment. And that, "I suppose". Can you believe, Jo, that a man who is physically implicated with a woman can ever *suppose* that he had not left her carrying a child? Go on, let's hear it to the bitter end.'

'I try to banish thoughts of my pleasant evenings with you by chess-playing and reading, but I am now a believer in the saying, "*'tis not good for man to be alone.*"

'Now, my dearest, goodbye, write me in return. May God bless you, and keep you out of harm. I shall expect your answer to my Alexandria letter after we reach China.

'Again, Harriet *mia*, Good-bye. Yours as ever, Willie

'There is such a glorious Moon just rising on the sea – it reminds me of my *disappointment* in number thirty-four when the Moon (I mean *your Moon* came to the *Full* a couple of days sooner than was agreeable. W.K.'

'And how very inconvenient of her,' Lili said crossly, 'to have a full moon when it did not agree with her lover.'

'He wasn't all bad; he was sending her money.'

'Josephine, I dislike being coarse, but she probably cost him a lot less putting her up in his rooms than if he had to go out and pay . . . whatever it is women ask.'

'It's a half-sovereign, Lili, for a nice lady such as Harriet.'

'Jo!'

'What?'

'How on earth can you know such a thing?'

'I asked the girls.'

Josephine was now very busy looking into every corner of Harriet's existence. She went to see George Hood, who greeted her warmly. 'Miss Ferguson, I hope that this is to tell me that you are ready to return to us.'

'No, but I have come to say that I should have been a bit more mature about . . .'

'If I am honest, I should have done better. Come and sit down, tell me whether your project is proceeding well.'

'Better than I ever supposed it would.'

'Excellent. In what way better?'

'Well, although my story is the biography of Harriet Burton, I find myself being drawn to writing about her world and other girls in it. Thousands find themselves in Harriet's predicament, and nobody, except a few limp charities, is interested. Charity is worse than useless.'

'Why do you think that?'

'Those people who *do* have some concern are misled into believing that if they give money that is enough, but that if the girls don't *reform* then they only have themselves to blame. A prayer meeting and a dormitory doesn't come near helping. It is the other end of the problem that must be tackled. The reasons *why* they have to take to the streets.'

'Come back to us, Miss Ferguson. If you will, then I will promise you a regular place and you can write on any subject you choose.'

'Really?'

'One proviso: that your pieces will be short, but not very sweet. I would want you to prick consciences, stir up trouble, but always based on irrefutable facts.'

'My Harriet work keeps me very busy. I doubt if I should have time, even if I did want to come back to *The News*.'

'It might be easier working from here. You could have your old desk back, and an assistant – a female.'

'A woman assistant?'

George Hood nodded. 'She is very good, sensible, well-read, intelligent. Mrs Fisher. You probably wouldn't be able to have her all to yourself, but . . .'

'All right, I will give it a try, but you must understand that my Harriet work comes first.'

'Understood.'

'Also, I have had to do quite a bit of travelling and will have to do more.'

George Hood grinned. 'Are you bargaining with me, Miss Ferguson?'

'I am asking to be able to claim expenses. I wouldn't be unreasonable, or unfair.'

'Anything else?'

'The archives. I might want help in researching back numbers.'

'Mrs Fisher can do all that.'

'Now?'

'If you wish.'

When George Hood took Josephine into the general office to speak to Mrs Fisher, the lady was reading copy through wire-framed eyeglasses. She looked up and nodded. 'Yes, Mr Hood?'

Mrs Fisher was a slim, straight-backed woman of perhaps forty years. It was not until she removed the pince-nez that it was possible to see her striking features to advantage.

Large eyes with laughter wrinkles, long nose – noble or Roman or just big, but well suited to her bony face and high cheekbones. Most amazing of all was her hair. Many men wore their hair longer; it was dark and shiny as coal but had grown white at the temples where there were two badger-like streaks. Her facial bone-structure, short hair and white temples might have given her a masculine appearance, but it was not so, for everything was softened by her long-lashed eyes and plump, pink mouth that had a natural smile curve.

'Mrs Fisher, this is Miss Ferguson, she will be using *The News* offices for a scheme she is working on.'

When Mrs Fisher stood up with alacrity and held out her hand, she proved to be a very tall lady indeed. 'You are Jemima Ferguson?'

'She is, Emmeline, the very same.'

'George knows what I think of you. We're old friends –' she smiled at him – 'good friends. He knows how downcast I was when he said that you were no longer with *The News*.'

'Well, now she is. Not reporting, not yet, but having use of all the facilities that *The News* can give her. This includes some of your time and research expertise.'

Taking Josephine's hand again, Mrs Fisher pressed it. 'Better and better. George knows how much I am in favour of women being represented in all the professions, and he has given me the title of "research assistant".'

'I'll leave you to get acquainted, and for Miss Ferguson to tell you Emmeline how you can best help with her current scheme.'

Josephine drew a chair close to Mrs Fisher's desk. 'I wasn't expecting help, merely a desk, and access to *The News* archive. I have one friend who helps me when he can, but not in the way I need it.'

239

'You must have found it difficult being the only skirted reporter.'

'I was never a reporter, but it was always my ambition to be.'

Indicating over her shoulder in the direction of the room where *The News* reporters worked, Emmeline Fisher said, 'They must know that their monopoly of this profession will end soon.'

'Did you hear that they refer to me as the "She-Radical"?'

'I hope that you took that as a compliment.'

Josephine smiled. 'It rather got my hackles up, but now that you mention it . . .'

'My dear Miss Ferguson, I am *so* pleased that George persuaded you back.'

'Not exactly back.'

'Ah, but working here, that's the important thing. Can I tell you something in confidence?'

'It's not necessary to ask that.'

'Of course, but it concerns George, and he's a long-time and loyal friend.'

'I understand that. I owe him loyalty, too.'

'George knows that he made a big mistake over that story you wrote enabling *The News* to be first on the streets with the Great Coram Street tragedy.'

'I think so too. He lost his nerve.'

'He did; he had said as much to me, but with the best of motives . . . Well, perhaps not the best, but sincere motives. He took fright at the last moment. He knows that you should have had your name on the front page.'

'I should have, but I understand what he is up against – proprietors of other papers are envious of our growing popularity . . . and he *did* produce a newsheet to beat our competitors.'

'Miss Ferguson, I should very much like to work with you, if you agree.'

Josephine found herself smiling broadly. 'Deal done, Mrs Fisher.'

'Shall we start right away?'

Josephine claimed a desk by the window and placed her notebooks on it. Mrs Fisher took a box of new pencils, notebooks and some packets of paper, and arranged them neatly before Josephine. 'If those fellows call me the "She-Radical", they must have a name for you,' Josephine observed.

'"Brock". Oh, how original and clever.' Mrs Fisher strained her hair away from her face, emphasizing her white streaks. 'Water off a duck's back – my husband has been calling me "Brock" for twenty years. Now, tell me what you would like me to do.'

'It may be clutching at straws . . . on the other hand . . . I thought, the personal advertisements . . . I don't know what I expect to find, but a morning spent reading back over the month or so before the murder. Perhaps she met this man through the small advertisements.'

'Ah, yes. What a good idea.'

'I don't hold out much hope, but skip through all the likely newspapers leading up to Christmas. One never knows . . .'

Mrs Fisher smiled widely, 'One never does.'

At the end of her first morning, Mrs Fisher laid some notes on Josephine's desk.

'These all refer to "Clara" in some way but are no use to us. However,' she pointed to a copy of *The Echo* – 'this jumped out at me. German Gentleman . . .'

Josephine read the small advertisement. 'GERMAN GENTLEMAN. The lady who met German Gentleman near St Pancras Church last week regrets failing in her evening appointment and would arrange another interview – 172 Caledonian Street.'

Josephine smiled as she scribbled down the address. 'Mrs Fisher, would you care for a walk?'

The door at 172 Caledonian Street was opened by 'Madame Margaret', the woman who had left the Alhambra Palace bar in a huff.

'It's you again.'

'Yes, it's me, and this lady is Mrs Fisher. I'm sorry if what I said at the Alhambra—'

'What d'you want?'

'Firstly to say that I'm sorry.'

'How did you find me?'

'That's the other reason why I've come. It's this.' Mrs Fisher showed her the newspaper clipping. Madame Margaret became uneasy. 'Can I talk to you?' Josephine asked.

'Not in here you can't, there're too many nosey parkers.'

'How would it be if I were to buy you breakfast at O'Sullivan's? Would you talk to me there?'

'You know O'Sullivan's?'

'Of course, Welsh rarebit and stout is my favourite.' She said this with such assurance that Madame Margaret began to feel that, although this was a strange woman who talked posh, she might be all right.

This was a test of whether Mrs Fisher would be of use in Josephine's investigations; in the event she proved to be entirely at ease, as if she was used to breakfasting with a prostitute and a young woman who did not stand on ceremony.

Over a seven-item breakfast for Madame Margaret, and for Mrs Fisher and Josephine a repetition of the meal she had had with Violet, Josephine waited for Madame Margaret to talk. Eventually, when she was enjoying a second serving of fried bread, she spoke. 'About the German. Well, it was like this. My friend and I was picked up by this man, and he asks us to have a drink with him. So we took him to The Falcon, the pub. We thought we'd have a bit of a day off. Well, what happened, this German says would we go with him to a coffee house and spend the night with him – the both of us for a half-sovereign. At least, that's the coins he showed us.'

'A coffee house?'

'We reckoned he meant a hotel, but didn't know the right words. Anyway, we wasn't too keen. So he said, "I will give you each two gold pieces."

'Well, to us that's a decent bit of money, so we said

we would meet him where we met him before, outside St Pancras Church.'

'But you got cold feet.'

'Sort of. We said maybe he wanted ropes tied and that kind of thing.'

Josephine didn't, but she was fast learning about the Haymarket women.

'I've never had nothing to do with that kind of thing, I leave that to them who don't mind. I don't like being hurt any more than is normal, so we didn't turn up.'

'What made you change your mind?'

'Debts. I said to my friend, as there's two of us, we're not likely to come to harm. So we decided to put that in the paper.'

'Did he fit the description the police have put out?'

'Oh, yes, he fits.'

'And you think that your German was the one that came back and picked up Harriet?'

Madame Margaret's hard face began to crease, and she gripped her lips together to hold back tears. 'Of course I bloody think that. It was my fault that Clara got done in, wasn't it?'

Mrs Fisher handed the other woman a handkerchief. Josephine said, 'No, it was *not* your fault. It was the fault of the man. He killed her, not you. Now you just stop thinking like that.'

'If I hadn't put that advert in the paper, he would of stayed away.'

'You do not know that. He . . .' Josephine had been

about to say that he had come prepared to kill and would have done so anyway.

'Yes, miss . . . he was going to kill one of us, wasn't he?'

David Wilde gathered his cloak about him and held it close to his chest. Fog and smoke created a thick air, yellow as tallow and hard to breathe. St Giles was but a few hundred yards from his home, not a traditional vicarage or manse, but a two-storey house in a row of similar houses. Although he was not permitted to preach, he could go into St Giles and talk to anyone who needed him. He liked his life and had no complaints. Today's dinner-time broth would have a ham-bone as its base. On other days there were pigs' feet, marrowbone, onions or leeks as the stock. Bread, pearl-barley or dumplings were additions in rotation. Mrs Chapman, the woman who cleaned and cooked for any minister living in the church's tied house, might not be an imaginative cook, but she was an excellent one.

He was so hungry he could scarcely wait to get home. 'David.' He at once recognized the voice calling him as Josephine's. He looked around eagerly and saw her hurrying towards him out of the fog's yellow gloom. 'Jo. What a treat. Are you in a rush?'

'No, but if you are I'm sorry to hold you up. I wanted to ask your advice. Could I walk with you?'

'Better than that, you could join me in a bowl of Mrs Chapman's soup. I can assure you that it will be wonderful, it always is.'

So, unexpectedly, Josephine found herself seated with David and his housekeeper in a comfortable below-stairs kitchen, eating thick broth and chunks of bread. She had never imagined him living like this; in fact, she had never envisioned his home life at all; until now he had always been part of the public supper rooms' group of would-be reformers, or a visitor to hers and Liliana's kitchen.

'Good, isn't it?' he grinned. 'Ham-bone and chicken broth with cider. Not Liliana's *coq au vin*; Mrs Chapman is a country cook ... the very best, aren't you, Mrs Chapman?'

'Giving out prizes, then, are you, Young Father? You don't get round me so easy. Going out like that when I told you there was a hole in your sock.' She wagged her head in mock exasperation, but it was obvious that she enjoyed caring for David. Jo knew that he disliked the popular name he had been given – Young Father David – but he let it go.

If Mrs Chapman was a country cook, then the country must be situated within the sound of Bow bells. 'I would give you a prize, Mrs Chapman ... in fact I would like to ask if you would give me the receipt for the women's page of a journal I write for.'

'I'm glad you like it, miss, but my soups don't never have a receipt. I wouldn't want it always turning out the same. My soups grow out of what gets give by people in a small way of business who can't always give money to the church.'

Josephine was glad that David was looked after so

well, and by such a nice friendly woman who didn't stand on ceremony.

Mrs Chapman cleared the table and took the dishes through to the scullery.

'You remember that you introduced me to Violet?' He nodded. 'We met, and she gave me these.' Josephine produced the packet and placed it on the table. 'Love letters written to Harriet. Violet had been keeping them for Harriet whilst she, Harriet, was moving to new lodgings. Violet was trusted because she could not read. She says that no one else has seen them, and I believe her. However, I *have* read them. They are from a man with whom Harriet obviously lived for a while: Willie Kirby.'

'I remember Willie.'

'You do? Ah, that is just what I wanted to know.'

'He was yet another of Clara's – Harriet's – ships that passed in the night. Each of them, I'm certain, she believed to be her knight in shining armour, who was going to take her away from her life here. I think he was on leave from somewhere in the Far East.'

'Hong Kong. The letters were written whilst he was on board ship returning there.'

'Liaisons such as these are not so uncommon. Young men come home on leave, set up with a pretty young woman for six months or so, even a year. The young women can scarcely believe their good luck and see a bright future for themselves. I never know whether to be pleased that young women have had a period in their lives when they are off the streets, or angry that they have their hopes dashed.'

'He did write her very many letters. Do you think that a good sign? That he did intend to send for her? He says so . . . but promises are easy to put in a love-letter aren't they?'

'Unfortunately I've never had occasion to write one.'

'Never? Poor David, you must be at least twenty-eight . . . you'd better hurry or you'll be left on the shelf.'

Giving her a mock pathetic smile, 'Twenty-nine. I couldn't even hazard a guess about his intentions. Harriet did bring him along to our meetings on occasion, but he didn't impress me as being the kind of man who would saddle himself with a wife.'

'I think one doesn't have to read between the lines to come to that conclusion.'

He left the table, took down a brown earthenware teapot from a shelf and proceeded to make tea. 'I'm sorry, we don't run to coffee here.'

'I prefer tea.' That wasn't quite true, but she was fascinated to watch him move about the kitchen, able, without searching, to lay his hands on any utensil necessary. A man who could fend for himself in a kitchen was rare. She doubted that Uncle James would have been able to find a spoon. The more she got to know David Wilde, the more he grew in her estimation. 'So, tell me, what must I do with his letters? I wondered if you would take them. If he ever returns . . .'

'No, no, even if he did return, they are not *his* letters. They are part of Harriet's estate, and they might even be evidence. I think you must take them to the police.'

'I did think about doing that, but what good are they to the police? Willie Kirby isn't a suspect. From the dates on the letters, he is still in China.'

'The police will be trying to discover as much about Harriet as you are, and who knows what information or evidence they may have that you do not.' He fingered the package. 'And there must be a great deal of information in here.'

'There is, but nothing that would help discover who killed Harriet. They do reveal a lot about Willie Kirby, though, and about the way that men in general think of girls like Harriet.'

'And what do "men in general" think of girls like Harriet?'

'I'm sorry, I didn't mean to imply *all* men.' She felt flustered. 'I meant . . .'

Smiling at her discomfort, he said, 'No, no, maybe you are right, but I cannot agree or disagree with you if you don't explain.'

'It is obvious from the start of our lives that boys are led to believe that their lives are more worthwhile than their sisters'; mothers favour sons over daughters, daughters learn to defer to brothers, sons model themselves on their father. Little boys learn, by osmosis if not by explicit lessons, that the world is fashioned to suit the male of our species, and that they are entitled to any advantage given to them.'

'I can't deny that.'

Wrong-footed by his acceptance, she said, 'Oh.'

'What, specifically, does Willie Kirby write that makes

him an object lesson on men's attitude to the Harriets of this world?'

'I don't know how they met, but we can make a good guess at that. He takes to her – more than that, I believe that he is fascinated by her, he certainly liked mixing with her friends: "the sisterhood", he calls them. He enjoyed that world, and yet he picks at her constantly to change. He wants her to dress differently, to be more sober and sensible in her ways, to stop being flighty, to read seriously, to practise her spelling and writing. He begs her to leave London and go to live a more proper life in the country when, for goodness' sake, it was her very impropriety and carefree life that he found so engaging.'

'She did leave London for a short while after Willie left.'

'Did she? I would guess that it *was* for a short while.'

'She went to her sister. I believe that her sister was as intent on improving Harriet as was Willie.'

'That doesn't surprise me; in fact it upholds my belief that women must be moulded to what men believe they should be. I have seen Harriet's sister; she appeared the epitome of properness. Willie Kirby found a light-hearted woman like Harriet, and liked her enough to have her live with him, then proceeded to try to make her serious and ladylike; to force her to work at her grammar and spelling.'

'In many ways, Harriet already *was* a thoughtful and serious woman. She might have lived an unstable life, but she always cared for her child and tried to keep her away from the Haymarket scene. Whilst the child's father was off and away, Harriet did what she could for the child in the only way she knew how – to entertain.'

'I hadn't realized that you knew her so well.'

'I didn't, but like so many of the people who live and work in my part of London, I know *about* them. I get to know their circumstances and usually their problems. Harriet Burton's greatest problem was trying to bring up and educate a child. And you are right about Willie Kirby. He was willing to keep Harriet, but not her daughter . . . She was sent to the country, perhaps to Harriet's sister, I really don't know.'

'I suppose you are right about these letters.'

'I am. As part of Harriet's estate they belong to her child, or her sister.'

'I didn't think of that.'

'You would have.'

She rose from the table and put the packet of letters into the document case she always carried. 'Thank you for the soup and advice. Come soon and visit Liliana and me. I will persuade Liliana to continue with her French cuisine.'

He grinned. 'I'm not sure whether that is a threat or a promise, but I will take a gamble.'

She had met many young men at Ann Martha's soirees, luncheons and dinner parties, but not one with whom she had felt as comfortable as she did with David Wilde. Best not tell Ann Martha, or she would start making guest lists and choosing wedding clothes.

*　　*　　*

251

James Thomson was seated in his office when the front desk sent in to say that a *Miss* Thomson wished to see him. James was up and out of his chair at once. They had not met since Harriet's funeral, and he was wondering what to do about it.

'Josephine, my dear, come in, come in.'

His expression was so kindly and welcoming that she felt assured that they were back in one another's good books again.

'Uncle James.' She kissed him on the cheek. 'Lovely fire. It is so cold out there. More snow on its way, I shouldn't wonder.'

'I will get some fresh tea made.'

'Don't trouble on my account.'

'No trouble,' he smiled widely. 'What is rank for if it is not to have the privilege of having tea and biscuits brought to one's desk?'

The tea having been brought and poured into heavy institutional cups, Josephine pushed the envelope containing Willie's letters across his desk. 'These were given to me.'

'Letters?'

'Love-letters, from a Willie Kirby. You may have heard of him in your investigations.' His expression was closed. 'She was kept by him for a while, and I believe that he sent her money until very recently. That is only gossip, but I've been told that it stopped, which was why she was forced on the streets again. I brought them to you because I don't want to be charged with withholding evidence.'

'Josie—'

'Uncle James, you may not like what I do, but I am determined to do it. I am back working as a correspondent for *The News* and I am writing a biography of Harriet Burton. I have interviewed very many of her friends. I think they trust me more than they might a policeman.'

'It is not surprising that they respond to another woman.'

'Then you should have women in the police force, shouldn't you?'

'Josie, let's not get into a discussion again about the place of women in the world. I agree, women could have a greater role to play than they have at present, but I don't make the rules.' He emphasized the last four words.

'I know. I know. I am just sounding off to someone who I know will not call me a madwoman.' She paused for a few seconds. 'And, Uncle James, as well as handing over the letters, it did occur to me that you might like to read what I have written of Harriet's biography so far.'

'That is very generous of you.'

'Ah, but the offer has strings.'

'Dearest girl, you know that you cannot make bargains with me regarding this investigation.'

'How close are you to catching him?'

He didn't reply.

'Not close at all?'

'I cannot answer that.'

'Do you know "Madame Margaret"?'

'Madame Margaret's name has been mentioned as one of many of the girls who frequented the bar at the Alhambra Palace, that I can tell you.'

'And The Falcon public house?'

'I don't recall that place in connection . . .'

'Madame Margaret and a friend took a German there before Christmas. The description of the man tallies with that of your suspect.'

James Thomson was all attention now. Nothing of this had come out in Kerley's report on his interview with the prostitute. 'Do you intend telling me, or do you intend dragging out your story?'

'All right, Uncle James, I was going to make a bargain with you. All the information contained in my manuscript for a promise to let me meet him – all right, at least see him – as soon as you have made an arrest.'

With the lack of success they had had so far in apprehending the suspect, he thought he was pretty safe in telling her, 'No promises, but I will try to let you know somehow.'

'That is all I ask. And I promise that nothing I will do will compromise you or give any clue that you have any connection with "Jemima". Give Ann my love, but don't you dare tell her what I have been doing.'

'You may be sure of that.'

'And you will send me a telegraph as soon as you find him?'

'Josie, I said that I would do my best to at least give you a hint, but certainly not telegraph you. That is the best I can offer, and maybe that is not exactly within the rules of the Met.'

She hugged his shoulders and placed a kiss on his thin, plastered-down hair. 'I am the last person in the world to jeopardize your career, Uncle James. I expect you to be commissioner one day.'

He held on to her hand. 'Don't you dare wish that upon me! I'm a Scotland Yard detective, and that is all that I want to be.'

Only days after Josephine had extracted a half-hearted deal with her uncle, there was a dramatic breakthrough in the investigation that slowed down every other line of enquiry.

It came from Ramsgate in Essex, a seaport on the eastern coast of southern England, not a hundred miles from London.

A sergeant in the Ramsgate force was so eager for promotion that he perused every piece of paper that passed over his desk. As he was contemplating what to keep and what to discard, several things came together: the £100 Reward notice that had been pinned to the station notice board for weeks, the artist's impression of the wanted man, the description mentioning that he might have a German accent, and a report of yet another incident connected with a German vessel named *Wangerland*.

The *Wangerland* was an emigrant ship en route from Danzig to Brazil, blown off course by a violent storm and onto the treacherous Goodwin Sands. The vessel had been tied up for repairs for weeks now, and from time to time trouble had broken out – not from the poor devils kept on board, but from the officials and agents who were living ashore in Ramsgate. Only minor incidents, except for the letting off of a firearm from a hotel window, but collectively a nuisance that the Ramsgate police could do without.

He took his suspicions to Superintendent Buss, who at once saw that there might well be a connection – it was a relatively short train journey between Ramsgate and London.

'Well spotted, Sergeant. Make a telegraph connection with Bow Street.'

Josephine was about to leave after making a short duty visit with Ann, Hani and Uncle James, when there arrived the same eager young constable who had been waiting for James Thomson with a cab on Christmas morning. He stood respectfully in the outer hall, awaiting an answer to the note he had carried here.

'Right then, Constable, I shall be no longer than two minutes.'

A maid was sent to fetch the small overnight bag he kept ready for such quick departures. 'I am sorry, Ann, and you too, Josie, but I must go to the station at once.'

'Is it him, the German?' Ann asked.

James Thomson flicked a glance at Josie.

'You know that I cannot tell you that, Ann. I am sorry that I could not enjoy an entire morning with you both but—'

'I know, I know, duty calls.'

Josephine saw the eagerness on her uncle's face and knew at once that the note contained dramatic information.

'I was about to send for a cab, so perhaps I could ride part of the way with you.' She hastened to take her kapok-lined jacket and hat from the hall stand, gave Ann Martha and Hani a quick hug and joined her dismayed uncle in leave-taking.

With the constable on top with the driver, James at once set about admonishing Josephine in a low voice. 'What do you think that you are doing, Josie? You simply cannot impose yourself like this.'

'All I want is a ride in your cab. You haven't forgotten your promise that you would let me see him?'

'For heaven's sake, Josie, I have no idea whether I am going to be seeing *him*. I cannot emphasize enough that if it gets known that I am closely related to a member of the newspaper fraternity then I could be compromised.'

'We have been over this. You know that I would never do that . . . Don't you trust me, Uncle James?'

'That's not the point, Josie.'

'Do you or don't you have faith in my promise not to compromise you in any way? You have to do what you must, and so must I. If there is one thing that I absolutely must do, it is to see the monster who ended Harriet's life.'

He withdrew into his thoughts, looking out at the busy London streets as the cab forced its way through the congestion of the centre. Josie knew that she had said

257

enough to prick his conscience a little. And he *had* said that he would do his best. Eventually he said, 'I did say that I might find some way . . . but I tell you this most seriously, Josephine. You must never, ever, try to extract promises of that nature from me, ever again.'

'I do understand, Uncle James. And really, honestly, I shall never ask such a favour again.'

'The best that I can do is to say that I shall be catching the afternoon train to Ramsgate. You are *not* to try to do the same. If at any time you do arrive in that town, you will keep well away from us.'

'Uncle James, I have said that you can trust me, haven't I?' He continued to look out at the traffic. 'Look at me, Uncle James. I am serious. And thank you, thank you. You understand that I *have* to do this.'

The cab stopped and he got out. 'Bow Street, Josie. Do you wish to take the cab on?'

'I think I shall, Uncle James.'

Touching her hand, he said, 'I do understand, Josie. I was very touched by what you have so far written.'

Good as her word, Josephine did not try to travel to Ramsgate on the same train as her uncle, the sergeant and some of the most reliable eyewitnesses. Instead, she went straight to the railway station and caught a much earlier train to Ramsgate.

The spirits of the two detectives and the entire 'E' Division lifted, as would the spirits of any team of detectives whose suspect is a German who killed with a 'scalpel or similar thin-bladed instrument' and is offered a German surgeon.

The constables had been very successful in speedily rounding up the witnesses, and awaiting the two detectives were Oscar Philippe and William Stalker of the Cavour Restaraunt, Tryphena Douglas, George Flack and his two assistants.

'I didn't call Mrs Wright; she is still overwrought at the thought of confronting the suspect, nor the two scullery maids.'

'Those six will do us well enough.'

They were now on their way to Ramsgate in a first-class 'reserved' compartment. In another, but third class, accompanied by two constables, were the witnesses.

Superintendent Buss of Ramsgate was waiting at the station with three cabs, and greeted the two detectives warmly. 'It is fortunate that the repairs to the ship have taken longer than expected. It was thought to have sailed directly after Christmas.'

'So, if this surgeon you suspect is the one, then we have our only bit of good luck in weeks.'

They were now travelling in a cab from the railway station. Thomson asked, 'What is the story behind these people who came to London, Mr Buss?'

'I have to admit that it is one of mishaps and coincidences.' He related how an emigrant ship, the *Wangerland*, came to be tied up in a Ramsgate ship-repair yard.

'How long has she been there?' Frank Kerley asked.

259

Superintendent Buss was much more concerned with protocol than his Bow Street equal. 'My sergeant and I have worked together for many years. I encourage him to ask questions,' James Thomson explained.

Unused to such a relationship, Buss's answer was still directed at the senior officer. 'November. The damage proved greater than first expected.'

'So, what have they been doing, these people who suddenly found themselves in Ramsgate instead of en route for Brazil?'

'They *are* still en route, merely delayed some two months. You can hear all this yourself via an excellent translator I have engaged, but, to paraphrase, this ship has just one cargo – emigrants. I tell you, Mr Thomson, a more sorry lot you never saw in your life. They have invested everything they possessed to sail away to a new land. There is to be a German colony in this place, Bahai.'

Kerley asked, 'How do they think they are going to set up there?'

'There is an agent, Mr Hermes. Herr Hermes, whose job – as far as I can ascertain – is to arrange the practicalities of the settlement.'

'Ah. And they are taking along their own surgeon, sir?'

'Right. Our suspect, ship's surgeon Karl Wolebe. There is also a doctor, Franzen, and a pastor, the Reverend Hessel and his wife. I don't know what would possess anyone to take on such a venture. The emigrants are mostly families, but the others – the professionals, so

260

to speak – are all young people. None of them thirty, I would say.'

'Idealists?' James Thomson asked. 'See themselves as present-day Founding Fathers, like those who sailed to America?'

'I speak frankly, and I have no evidence to support this: I believe that this is nothing more than a money-making venture, using the poor wretches below-decks for the purpose.'

'Poor wretches?'

'They have not been on dry land since they sailed. We have no jurisdiction over the arrangements on board, and it appears that they have no papers which give them the right to be in England – so there they stay, in the most degrading of situations.'

'And the others?'

'They all have passports, which is how Wolebe and his friends were able to travel to London.'

'Do they live aboard?' Frank asked.

'Oh no, they all have rooms at Hiscock's Royal Hotel, along with the ship's captain, Captain Wilken, and others. They come and go as they please. Others come to visit them – agents, vice-consuls, officials from Danzig – which is where this venture all began.'

Superintendent Buss and the entire entourage of police, witnesses and the prisoner were conducted to where the chairman of the bench of magistrates and twenty other justices were assembled, plus a formally dressed group of three august gentlemen. Superintendent Buss

261

introduced the second group who were (as Frank Kerley would later describe them to Elizabeth) most definitely important as well as being self-important. But for the present Frank's mood was in no way frivolous, but entirely correct and mostly unnoticed by the important gentlemen.

The magistrates arranged themselves to flank the chairman and the august gentlemen, whilst James's witnesses were put into a room to one side of the court. Then a number of dark-haired, clean-shaven young men of medium build were lined up facing the bench.

'You have done well to find so many likenesses to the suspect,' James commented.

'All German emigrants – not difficult to find around the port.'

The line-up was ready. Thomson and Kerley stood with the Ramsgate men. The chairman ordered the surgeon to be brought in and the manacles taken off. 'You may choose your place in the line, Herr Wolebe.' Frank Kerley noticed the respect afforded the murder suspect. A surgeon, well turned-out, of the class of person that commands respect. Wolebe chose a central position. He was thinner and paler than Kerley had expected, but men kept in custody, even though only for a day or so, often appeared altered. Nevertheless, the likeness to the charcoal portrait was easy to see.

'If you are ready then, Mr Buss, bring in the first witness.' However, before this could be done, there was a disturbance. A young man burst in, and said, 'I must stand by my friend. I insist. I am his pastor and must give him my support.'

'Who are you, sir?'

The German consul spoke up. 'This is a countryman of mine, Reverend Godfried Hessel. A clerical gentleman and colleague of Herr Wolebe.'

'He wishes to stand with the suspect?'

Hessel spoke up. 'It is my duty to support my dear friend Karl Wolebe.'

'Very well.'

'Thank you, I will stand beside my friend.'

Frank Kerley felt a terrible, inexplicable apprehension. Something untoward was taking place, but he could not understand what it was.

An usher opened the door to the room in which the witnesses were penned. He allowed Tryphena Douglas into the court.

James was proud of her: she would make the ideal witness with her quiet manner and her bearing. Never mind that her accent was that of a London barmaid, the girl had a refined air about her and she spoke up. Tryphena walked steadily and looked carefully at each man in the line, but stopped only when she reached the suspect. Then, speaking clearly and pointing, she said, 'To the best of my belief, this is the man who met Harriet in the bar and was with her on the omnibus.'

'Please touch on the shoulder the man you believe you saw.'

Tryphena Douglas reached out and touched a shoulder to the sound of gasps being drawn. James and Kerley looked at one another, then at Buss. Frank Kerley felt his spirits plummet.

The wrong man.

She had picked out the friend, the clergyman.

The rest of the London witnesses were brought in one by one. Without exception, they each touched the clergyman and said, as Tryphena had done, 'To the best of my belief, this is the man.'

On arriving at Ramsgate, Josephine, not having any plan, decided to sit in the station tearoom and watch the trains from London arrive. Her stomach turned with excitement when she saw her uncle and his entourage being greeted and taken off in cabs. She had no need to follow on their heels, but waited to give them a head start, then engaged a cab to take her to the vicinity of the town hall. If there was to be an identification parade, that is where it would take place.

Although she had not seen her uncle arrive at the town hall, she did see other comings and goings that led her to believe that she had chosen the right place. A number of uniformed policemen arrived on foot, accompanied by men who were obviously chosen for their likeness to the man on the Wanted poster.

The air carried the smell of the sea, from where came sharp, gusting winds. Josephine was glad to have a woollen scarf and hat on her perambulation around the vicinity of the town hall. Her attention was attracted by two young people carrying on a fierce argument as they hurried along. The woman clutched a shawl about her, apparently oblivious to the fact that she was without a hat and her hair was being torn from its pins by the gusts.

Josephine could hear nothing, but their actions spoke for them. The woman was angrily trying to stop the man from doing whatever it was he intended. From time to time she pulled his arm, making him stop and face her, still arguing. He shook her off. She hurried after him, again pulling at him. He pushed her away. She clenched her fists at him in frustration. As they reached the entrance to the town hall, he twisted away from her and rushed inside, leaving her standing.

Now what was all that about?

It was as much as she could do to hold herself back from entering the building herself. But good sense prevailed: if this was an identification parade to put the finger on Harriet's killer, then she would need to prove to Uncle James that she was responsible, and serious. If she put so much as a foot wrong, she would never achieve what she planned, which was to come face-to-face with the killer.

Had she known that this was the clergyman who was to put the cat amongst the pigeons, she might not have waited so patiently eating a pie and drinking tea to pay for her observation place in a pie shop facing the town hall.

She was lingering over yet another cup of tea when she saw several cabs drive up to a side entrance. The only person she could identify was Sergeant Kerley, his fair head visible as he doffed his hat to climb into a cab.

What to do now? Go back to London and hope that her uncle would do another favour? No. If they had apprehended the man, he would not be happy to see her. Stay in Ramsgate? Try to discover what had gone on?

Having decided to stay, she went to the offices of the Ramsgate evening paper, where she presented herself as Jemima Ferguson, assistant to George Hood of *The News*. Her honesty, charm, and the mention of the well-respected George Hood gave her access to the information she sought. The crime reporters were eagerly writing copy for the next edition.

From their office she gleaned nuggets of gold.

There had been a startling outcome to a parade where a Great Corham Street murder-suspect was to be viewed by some London witnesses. A man – a clergyman, no less – had at the last moment thrust his way in and insisted that he stand beside his friend – the suspect – to support him in his hour of need. As he was a clergyman, the magistrate allowed it.

Then, what happened? The London witnesses had identified him, the clergyman, as the murderer, and *not* the surgeon. There had been two London detectives in attendance, but the arrest had been made by a Ramsgate detective. The suspect would be taken to London.

The scene of the arguing couple came back vividly to Josephine. The incident appeared to fit the facts. Better far than returning to London, having ascertained where the Germans involved were staying, she found a modest emporium, purchased a small leather bag and a few items that would make her a bona fide visitor and took a cab to the hotel where the Germans were putting up.

The arrested man had been taken by cab to Bow Street, but James Thomson chose to travel back by train.

For the first while he and his sergeant travelled in silence, each within their own thoughts about the startling outcome. 'He fits, Frank.'

'He does, sir. A gambler, even with his own life.'

'A gambler, certainly, but an arrogant one who believes that he can outwit the rest of us. You may be sure, Frank, that he knows what he is doing.'

'It could have been collusion on both their parts: his and the surgeon's. How did he keep quiet so long and not make a statement about the visit to London?'

'I believe that we shall find that this party of young people have been living in a hotbed of intrigue.'

'But to be accused and not say what he must have known about the clergyman?'

'It is possible that the surgeon has his own secret.'

'Each has a hold over the other?'

'It would make sense. Which has the better chance of escaping a charge of murder: a bachelor surgeon or a married clergyman?'

'No, sir, he's not going to escape. He did it, clergyman or not, and he will get the rope. No magistrate is going to ignore the evidence of six witnesses – plus Mrs Wright and the two scullery maids if necessary . . . and who is to say what will be found out in Ramsgate?'

'I hope that you are right, Frank. Buss agrees that you

should go back there tomorrow when his men examine Hessel's possessions, and they question the rest of the London party and the hotel servants.'

They fell into a thoughtful silence.

Frank's thoughts went back to what had troubled him since it had been mentioned in the early days of the investigation. His senior's connection with the dead girl. Although it appeared that the investigation was drawing to a close, he wished that the super would come clean about his relationship with Harriet Burton.

Suddenly, the super leaned across and tapped Frank on the knee. 'You have something on your mind, Kerley?'

'Have I, sir? Mrs Kerley tells me she can read me like a book.' He smiled.

'No doubt she is more astute than I, but although I have yet to see you reveal your mind during an interrogation of a witness or a suspect, I think I know you well enough.'

'I have no reason to hide my thoughts from Elizabeth.'

'But from your superior officer? A colleague of long standing?'

'Sorry, sir, I never intended to imply that.' Frank could not avoid the shrewd scrutiny of the dark brown eyes. 'You would not thank me for revealing the nit-picking nature of my concern.'

'I won't ever be patronized, Kerley. Particularly not by a man under my command, and most particularly not by an officer for whom I have high regard and whose character and intelligence I esteem.'

'I'm sorry if my reticence smacks of condescension,

sir. It springs from an equal regard for an officer under whose command I hope to remain.'

'Thank you, Kerley.' The two men did not unlock eyes. 'And will you now kindly tell me what this is all about?'

Frank paused only long enough to try to assemble the right words, then, grasping the bull by the horns, said, 'It's been at the back of my mind what you once said about having at some time spoken to Harriet Burton. You said at the time that you once saw her perform. Then there was the matter of the beads. I am sorry, sir, but you won't be satisfied with less than honesty.' James gave a nod in acknowledgement. 'Had you been any man other than my superior officer, I might have questioned you further on the occasion when you first saw the body and revealed that she was known to you.'

Don't ever underestimate Frank Kerley.

James Thomson pulled from his pocket an expensive leather case containing two cigars and proffered it to Frank.

'I can't get on with them, thank you, sir. I use a pipe.'

The superintendent indicated that he should go ahead if he wanted, and Frank made a long job of filling a pipe and tamping the tobacco.

'You can be assured that, had my meeting with her had the slightest bearing on the case, then I should have added that to the evidence, but you are right to ask. It has no bearing, but I am glad to have the opportunity of telling you.'

This was an extraordinary turn of events. Hitherto James Thomson could never have conceived of an occasion when an officer of lower rank would speak with such candour to his superior officer, and that officer himself had so trampled down the barrier of class and rank as to put himself at a disadvantage.

'In the antecedents, as you no doubt recall, there is a list of lodgings and people with whom she lived, which includes a Major Brown?'

'Of course, sir, they lived at One hundred and seventeen Stamford Street, and before that in Blackfriars Road – Forty-eight Nelson Square. Not likely to forget, sir, I must have read them a dozen times lately. That's when she started calling herself Mrs Brown – she had a stillborn child by him.'

'She had two.' James Thomson leaned forward to unstrap the window a little to expel the accumulating tobacco smoke. 'Has Mrs Kerley had such an experience, Frank?'

'Thank God, no, sir.'

'Then you and she are fortunate. It is the most grievous experience one can imagine. Not only for the woman, but for the man also – a thing few people think much of. It is fearful to see one's wife experiencing anguish and misery and be quite unable to do anything to assuage it. He must be strong and give her hope, make her believe that she will bear another child. Yet his own heart is broken. Whilst the woman is surrounded by her comforting relatives and friends, the man's grief is not seen. People do not expect a man who has had his hopes of fatherhood dashed to be anything but supportive, strong and brave, yet he feels none of those things, he feels weak and greatly in need of comfort.'

Frank Kerley took in the expression he saw in the superintendent's eyes, and saw that the man had experienced an inexpressible pain.

James Thomson continued. 'It is a little while since this unfortunate occurrence. She had been passing herself off as the wife of Major Brown. I hardly know now how I came to find myself seated in a music hall. My wife was still lying-in and the house was filled with women bent on drawing her out of her despair. If I am to tell you the whole story, then I must say that I most likely went in the direction of the Haymarket, bent on trying to deal with my own despair in whatever manner took hold of me. Nothing seemed to be worth a thing without the little children I had seen laid in the ground. Unconsecrated ground, Frank! Unconsecrated because they were twins who never drew breath. Yet these were my children. My wife has never realized that they did not receive a Christian burial. I have always persuaded her not to visit their resting place – if resting place it is.'

He stood up and, pulling at the leather strap sharply, shut the window again against the cold air and soots from the engine.

Frank, with the happiest of memories of his own daughter's birth, would have done anything not to have been the recipient of this sad tale, but he had been the reason for its telling, and must suffer whatever consequences came from it.

'Where I found myself eventually was seated in the bar of the Alhambra Palace, a bottle of brandy before me, staring without knowing what was passing before my gaze until eventually this sweet, unusual voice penetrated my dull brain. I had never heard quite that kind of voice before.

'The ballad was poignant and sentimental. Not the kind of song I am very partial to, and I hardly think it was the sentimentality that affected me, but that sweet voice spoke of vulnerability. She may have felt unconfident in that place where voices are most often strident and coarse, I doubt hers always reached the back of the theatre, but perhaps it did not matter, she was a most feminine and pretty young woman. She looked no more than nineteen, although she was of course older than this. If you were to question me as a suspect, then you would be right to suppose that what I say is not true, but I was not attracted to her . . . to her physically. During the entire encounter I never once wanted to experience a sexual relationship with her.'

To spare his senior officer embarrassment, Frank knocked the ash from his pipe into the little brass cup attached to the side of the door for the purpose. It was notoriously unsuited unless one was most careful, so the operation provided a distraction.

'I don't know where my thoughts had been – they may have been in a stupor from the brandy I had been drinking – but suddenly I looked up and there she was, seated beside me, the curtains on the stage pulled and the lights gone up for an interval. She said, "If you want me to go away, you have only to say so." I think I probably indicated that she should stay, and offered her some of the brandy. "A lemonade, if you please, and I'll take a dash with it.'

'She was with you for the evening?'

James Thomson nodded. 'Until quite late. After the first drink of brandy and lemonade, she drank only lemonade, and I joined her in drinking that too. The waiter seemed not to mind, I paid him for the bottle of brandy which he would be able to sell a second time. Once she began to draw out of me the reason for the melancholy she had observed when she came from the stage, a table in the Alhambra stalls was hardly the place. So we walked. Nowhere in particular. Her discretion was touching; she did not enquire a thing about me except to ask when we looked for a place to take refreshment whether it was a place where I would be recognized, as she was sure I would not wish to be seen in her company. (I shall never know, but I do believe that she may have recognized me.) But I tell you sincerely, Frank, I don't think I should have minded much at that moment, for I had discovered a fellow human being who recognized my suffering and my absolute need to talk of it.'

'And you talked of stillborn children.'

'We did, for the entire time. She said that she had experienced that grief not just once, but a second time. I asked her what it was like for the woman, and she told me of the sense of having failed her husband (she called him that) and the longing, at first, the woman has to replace the lost child. "But you see," she said to me, "I soon found out that a baby isn't replaceable. It is itself and is unique, and its parents must mourn it and then get over it." She said, "People will tell your wife to have another child quickly and she will forget the first, but that is not true. Each child is remembered for itself, no matter how long it lived or whether it lived at all."

'You have no idea how wise that girl seemed to be. What a comfort it was to be told something by one who was an authority on the subject which no one else would talk about with me. She was open and honest. I have to confess I admired her strength of character and despised my own weakness, but she assured me that it was no weaker for a father to grieve for a dead child than for its mother. She said that I would find it a painful experience, but that she was certain that I would survive it, as she had herself. She told me about her daughter and the circumstances in which she herself had been at the time she put the child out to foster. "I have even survived that," she said.'

Again he met Frank Kerley's eyes full on. 'That really constitutes the entire story. It was late when I walked with her to Russell Square, where she had been living since Brown left her to fend for herself. I did not go to her room, nor had any desire to do so. She had done more for me that evening than any relative or friend had done. She gave me hope that I would arise from my state of despair and soon see that the future would lose its bleakness. It could not have been easy for her to spend an evening with such a grim companion, to say nothing of having resurrected her own experience. I felt that I must pay her but felt clumsy when it came offering money for something that money really cannot buy. However, her straightforward manner when I broached the subject swept away any awkwardness. "I have no income at present, and my voice is not exactly my fortune. I have to eat and clothe myself, and landladies do not give free lodging." She refused the five guineas I offered, saying that she would take a sovereign, though when she left, I slipped the rest into her pocket. She kissed me on the cheek.

'She was right. From that day I began to return to the real world, where the twin children who should have been did not exist. I might have sought her out and told her this, but I did not. Wounds heal, and more often than not one forgets to bless the means by which they are healed.'

'That's a common human trait, sir.'

'Thank you, Frank. You cannot imagine how much I wished myself a better person on that morning.'

'Sir, may I ask you something?' Thomson nodded. 'Were you and I working together during that period, for I can think of no time when you appeared anything but professional.'

'Yes. That too was my salvation, I could leave home and immerse myself in "E" Division. That was the time when I worked on the orphanage.'

Frank hardly knew what to say. Superintendent Thomson had received great commendation for the months of work and donations he had contributed to the setting-up of a police orphanage. 'And the Police Reward Fund. You were the first person to understand the lives of ordinary policemen.'

James Thomson gave a wry smile. 'Commissioners and ministers are rewarded – titles and the like. It was difficult to get anyone to see that ordinary people too need to have their exceptional deeds recognized . . . and their orphaned children cared for.'

'It made you enemies, Mr Thomson.'

'Small-minded people are not worthy of being recognized as enemies. The enemy in "E" Division is still the awful poverty and degradation under which the greater portion of the people live.'

'I often think, sir, that if we could house and feed children as is only right, our job would be to catch the real villains, grotesques like the one we nabbed today.'

They were now racing towards London through the flat and featureless countryside of Kent. The composure of both men regained, the matter that Frank had raised was done with, but it would be a thing that would link them to the end of their careers.

After two nights away from home, all the pleasures of coming back to her own rooms returned to Josephine. A clutter of animated voices came from within, making her return doubly pleasurable. She dropped her bag and put hat and jacket on a hall peg.

Without so much as a greeting, Liliana said, 'Here's Jo, she will agree with *me*.'

The door that linked the two parts of the accommodation was propped open, as it often was when Liliana wanted to keep at work but not miss anything going on in the kitchen. Christine Derry, the promoter of new art, was stirring something on the newly installed gas stove; David Wilde was placing spoons and dishes on the table.

Briefly she took in the scene. This was the kind of homecoming she had envisioned whilst she was still trying to break out of the cocoon spun by her guardian angels.

Smiling broadly, she said, 'Jo will agree with nothing nor no one until she is given a cup of chocolate.' Chocolate, always warm and ready to drink, was served dark and thick, in the European style that Liliana had introduced.

David Wilde stepped forward and offered to shake her hand. 'I hope you don't mind us rabble invading your territory like this. My sister said that you would not.'

'I already said that I hoped you would come. I'm pleased. And Christina, making your amazing hotpot?'

Christina, who had stopped stirring to pour chocolate, said, 'You have arrived at the exact moment of readiness. I must say this new stove is a marvel, from a flame to a glimmer in an instant.'

Liliana, who had been intent on entering whilst still cleaning her hands with turpentine, was shooed back to wash with soap. In five minutes the four young people were seated around the wooden table, ladling meat and vegetables from the central crock and breaking bread from a large loaf. Not at all in the style of Ann Martha and Hani. They would be dismayed at their casual manners, but that was the point: they would never see Josephine's new way of living.

What it was that Jo would have agreed with Liliana about was forgotten in their eagerness to hear – and her own need to share with somebody – the extraordinary happenings at Ramsgate. She began by telling them how she had rushed to the railway station and arrived ahead of the Bow Street detectives and the witnesses.

'How did you know to go to Ramsgate?' Christina asked.

'Professional secret, and anyway it doesn't matter. Only that I did the right thing. It was a strange feeling stalking the police. When I saw them arrive with the witnesses in tow, I knew that something important had happened.'

'You didn't go prepared to stay,' said Liliana.

'No, but as soon as I knew that the suspect had been released and another arrested, I had to. I bought a few things and took a room at Hiscock's Royal Hotel, where this party of Germans had been staying for the two months since they arrived in Ramsgate.'

'What were they doing there?'

'Shipwrecked, apparently, and waiting for their ship to put to sea again. Don't interrupt me, Lili, and I will tell you the whole thing, most of which I got from the staff at the Royal. Particularly Somers, a girl on the hotel staff who I engaged as a personal maid.

'As you can imagine, the staff were agog as the news

leaked into their life below stairs. They see everything. Know all the gossip. And I am not an amateur at engaging in gossip.'

'Is that an inherent trait in you, or can it be learned?'

'You don't need me to tell you that, David. I see you doing it every time I come in to hear you talk to your audience.'

Christine said, 'I think it is being at ease with oneself and with the other person. I confess, I haven't that skill.'

'And so . . . ?' Liliana prompted.

'And so, from what Somers said, there were several of these young shipwrecked Germans travelling together. They were quite rackety, always falling in and falling out. One of them, the man who has been charged with Harriet's murder, always carried a revolver, and had already received a warning from the police for firing a shotgun from his bedroom window.

'However, all of this was minor compared to what happened a few days ago, when the young surgeon was arrested on suspicion and taken into custody. Jane Somers said that it was as if the public rooms had been turned into a disturbed beehive. The German consul and the ship's agent were back and forth, talking and arguing with the captain, the ship's doctor and some of the other passengers.'

'"Never act up before the servants" was my mother's advice,' Christine said.

'And never act up before your mistress if you are a servant,' Liliana retorted. 'That way you are out and no reference.'

279

'As far as I am concerned,' Josephine continued, 'I should have been lost without Jane, my fount of all knowledge where these young Germans were concerned. So, she told me that they had acted up from the very beginning. However, what happened on the day that I arrived was beyond anything that had gone before.

'The surgeon, whose name is Karl Wolebe, had been arrested on suspicion of murdering Harriet, and was to be put up for identification by the London witnesses. The consul was going to the town hall as his representative. Before he left, he, plus the ship's captain, the agent, the ship's doctor and two others – the ship's pastor and his wife – had foregathered in one of the Royal's public rooms. And, as my informant Jane put it, "there was a right ding-dong", a lot of it in German, but that didn't stop the servants getting the gist of it as one of the porters had been with a family who lived for years in Germany.'

'So what was the "ding-dong" about?' asked David.

'It was about the consul insisting that the ship's pastor – one Reverend Hessel – should support the surgeon at the identification parade, to which the Reverend Hessel apparently replied, "Very well then, if you insist." Then the wife was supposed to have said in jest, "If you are accused, a wife will not be allowed to vouch for evidence." I assume she meant that she wouldn't be able to give evidence against him.'

'Why would she even think that she might be called to do so?' David asked.

'Unless she knew that he was in danger of being identified,' Liliana said.

'Or,' said Christina, 'that the surgeon *was* likely to be identified, and she *could* give evidence against him.'

David said, 'That's a tortuous kind of conspiracy . . . all three of them would have had to be colluding.'

'Who is to say that there was not something more?'

Josephine looked sceptical. 'What, Lili, that the wife was an adulteress?'

'Have you thought that both men might be implicated in Harriet's murder?' David suggested.

'I have thought of that. And it may still be a possibility. You remember, David, that you introduced me to Violet and some of her friends? Well, there was one, "Madame Margaret", who had met a German prior to Christmas and had been offered money to—'

Liliana looked quite gleeful. 'Both of them? Lord help us! London gets more like Paris every year.'

'Lili,' David chided, 'let Josephine continue with her story. Facts not conjecture. And did he go to the identity parade?'

Josephine gave a gleeful grin. 'He most certainly did. What happened in the town hall is almost unbelieveable, but true. Just as the line-up was formed and the witnesses ready to come in, Mr Hessel came bursting in and demanded loudly to stand by his friend. Of course, there were no members of the public at the identification parade, except for those brought in to stand in line. It was from these that my friends in the local newspaper office paid for the inside story. Anyway, in short, dear friends, the clergyman has been arrested and brought to London, and the surgeon released.'

'Heavens!' The other three were hanging on Josephine's words.

'How extraordinary,' David said, 'how came this turnaround?'

'Simple. After being allowed to get in the line – by now his attitude was one of magnanimity rather than his earlier reluctance, "I shall stand by my friend!" – he was identified by the six witnesses as the man who had been seen in any number of places in the company of Harriet on Christmas Eve. I know some of these witnesses, and if they say it was the clergyman, then I believe them one hundred per cent. You remember, Tryphena and Alice, Lili? You'd trust their word wouldn't you?'

'I would, especially Tryphena. I was greatly impressed by her, I even have plans to ask her to let me paint her – all that dignity and posture set before the array of bottles of spirits and liqueurs.'

'Well, once this news got back to the hotel, all sorts of gossip came my way.'

'Such as?' Liliana asked.

'Such as the vicar having a separate bedroom from his wife and sometimes getting up in the middle of the night to sleep on board – there was some nose-tapping about that. Such as the two of them strutting about arm in arm. Mrs Hessel flirted with every young man.

'It was generally agreed, according to Somers, that *something* had happened in London. Because when the party returned, there was odd behaviour. First, Karl Wolebe (the surgeon, you remember) gave up his room at the Royal and sent his bags on board, saying he was going back there to stay until the ship sailed. Then he changed his mind and said that he was going to sleep in the hotel. Then, to cap it all, after everybody's in bed and asleep, he starts kicking up a fuss and getting servants out of bed to let him out. He went off only half dressed, rushing out in the middle of the night and demanding to be let on board to sleep there.'

Christina intervened, 'Did you see the wife?'

'Only outside the town hall when she was making a spectacle of herself trying to stop her husband going in.'

'What about when she returned to the hotel?'

'She didn't actually return there before I left, but had gone on board the ship.'

'Go on,' David urged.

'Well, on the return from London of this rackety group, Somers recalled that Reverend Hessel sent down for a large bottle of turpentine to clean his trousers of some blood from a nosebleed. He used an entire quart bottle.'

Liliana said, 'Turps is no good for removing blood.'

'Which is as Somers said. And the laundress – this will make spectacular evidence if she is ever called as a witness – in the Hessel's bundle of washing on return from London were a great number of blood-soaked handkerchiefs, and some petticoats. Again he explained the amount of blood away as a nosebleed.' Josephine smiled. 'You realize of course that no comment was made by Jane Somers or the laundress at the time, except that it must have been a mighty nosebleed.'

'With hindsight then,' Christine said, 'the saturated handkerchiefs suddenly became evidence that the man could be a murderer.'

'I believe that is what he is – Harriet Burton's killer.'

The prisoner Godfried Hessel was once again brought to stand in an identification line, this time at Bow Street police station.

James Thomson, tense with his wish to get it over, watched as the two overawed scullery maids, Mrs Wright, Madame Philippe from the Cavour Restaurant, and Alice Douglas walked the line of men. Again a positive identification was made, but Hessel appeared to rise above the proceedings – cocksure, disdainful and self-important.

It would not be professional for James to feel triumphant, but it was hard not to.

'We've got you!'

When earlier Mr Buss ordered the prisoner to empty his pockets, James had shared with Frank Kerley that most satisfactory moment. One gold coin, some silver and copper, a gold watch, a corkscrew, a penknife with sharpened blade, a fine, slim, steel fisherman's gutting blade, and a long, spring-loaded knife.

Hessel had not expected to be arrested, so had joined the line-up carrying what was normal for him. One could only surmise that he never went out without them. What kind of clergyman is it who carries a sharpened fisherman's blade and a spring-loaded knife?

All that he had to do now was to select from the many witnesses who had identified Godfried Hessel, those best suited to face the questioning of the likes of the Mr Polands and Magistrate Vaughans of the world of the London courts.

Before David had left, he asked whether she would be interested in meeting a friend of his. 'You won't have heard of her yet, but you will. Her name is Isabella Varley and she has written a book. I thought that she might be of use to you in telling you how she managed to get her own book published.'

'Really? Do you believe that someone might be interested in publishing "Harriet"? That will be my title: "Harriet – The Biography of a Country Girl in London". Is Miss Varley's a novel? I should think that fiction is much more likely to find a publisher than the biography of an unknown woman.'

'You could ask her.'

'Thank you, David, you really are a nice, thoughtful man.'

'Oh dear. How dull that makes me sound.'

'I don't think you dull at all. Quite the opposite. You are all fireworks when you speak in St Giles. What you say is not only true, it is inspiring. When I have been listening to you, I want to go out and make the world better. I expect that is how the Knights of St George went off to the Crusades.'

He laughed, 'Do you see yourself on a charger?'

'Not me. I am scared to death of horses.' Shaking his

hand to take leave of him, she said, 'Thank you for offering me your friend Miss Isabella Varley. When I am ready, I may ask you to let me meet her.'

Still holding her hand, absent-mindedly it might seem, as he had done on the train, 'Very well, but it leaves me disappointed. I had hoped that I had found a reason to ask you to go somewhere with me.'

'Lord above, David, you don't have to stand on ceremony with a woman who has your eccentric sister as a sub-tenant. I should very much like to go somewhere with you.'

'Really?'

'Better still, would you come out with me tomorrow morning?'

'I would.'

'You have church duties to perform, don't you?'

'No longer. I have parish duties – there I am my own master. I will go with you.'

'But you don't know where it is.'

'Then it shall be a surprise.'

She grinned, handing him his thick scarf to wind twice around his neck. 'I would rather not surprise you. Tomorrow morning, Harriet's killer will appear in Bow Street magistrate's court to answer the charge of murder.'

'And you would rather not go alone?'

'Oh no, not in the sense that I am apprehensive – no, I should like to have another person there to give an independent view of the man. I think I have been too involved with Harriet to be impartial. Also, I would like

Madame Margaret to be there, and I wondered if you would ask her.'

He laughed, 'Margaret going voluntarily to Bow Street court?'

'Which is why I hoped that you might persuade her. She was propositioned by a German, and I want to know if she recognizes the man who's been arrested.'

The court was crowded, as was usual if a murder case was to be heard. Josephine, David and Madame Margaret sat squashed together, high up at the back in the public seats. Madame Margaret had been reluctant to get out of bed so early, but Young Father David was a favourite of hers, so she was in court, almost unrecognizable without her extravagant dress and cosmetics. Only her red, red hair, partly covered with a shawl, distinguished her.

'I don't like this, Father David. I don't like this at all, miss. What if it's *my* German bloke? I don't know why you would want to know, miss.'

Josephine decided not to try to explain, but to rely on a promised payment for Madame Margaret's trouble in getting up so early. After three short cases she became quite absorbed in watching the court in action from a different perspective, away from her usual place in the dock on charges of soliciting or disturbing the peace.

There was a short recess and a great deal of bowing and scraping as the chief magistrate retired. 'Pee and tea,' Madame Margaret explained. 'I've often wondered what's behind that door. I always imagine there's probably a really nice comfy room.'

The chatter subsided as a door opened and two uniformed policemen, not wearing helmets, appeared one each side of a manacled prisoner.

Instantly, Madame Margaret hunched down, pulling her shawl well down over her sweat-beaded brow and covering her mouth and nose with her cupped hands. She had no need to whisper, 'That's him.' David was seated between the two of them so that Josephine could not give the other woman's hand an assuring squeeze, but she was moved to see David take one of the prostitute's hands between his own and try to calm its trembling.

They were so wedged in by others in the crowded public gallery that it was impossible to leave, so they sat on and heard Josephine's Uncle James give evidence as to the circumstances of arrest, the victim's brother-in-law as to the identification of Harriet, and listened to the prosecution and defence cases in outline.

It was only at this point that Josephine discovered that Reverend Hessel's defence would be that, although he had been in London at the time of the murder, he had been taken ill on 22 December and been confined to his room at Kroll's Hotel in the Minories, well away from the site of the murder, and that Herr Kroll and his servants would give evidence to that effect.

It was well past noon when Josephine and her companions stepped out into snow that had fallen in the streets during their absence.

'I can't stop shaking and feel right sick,' Madame Margaret complained.

'O'Sullivan's,' Josephine commanded. 'Take her other arm, David.'

Once in the humid warmth of the breakfast rooms, and having taken a double shot of rum, Madame Margaret's cheeks regained some colour. 'Do you mind fetching us some food?' she asked David. Pulling a wry face he said, 'I'm sorry, Jo, but I don't have any money with me.' Which raised a laugh from the prostitute. 'You and me both, Father David.'

Josephine felt wretched at her assumption that all people carried money when they went out and, pulling a half-crown from her pocket, she passed it to him. He was not at all embarrassed, as many men would be, but picked it up and went to the serving hatch. 'Are you feeling better, Margaret . . . may I call you by your name?'

'It's as good as most things I've been called in my time, though my true name isn't that, it's Bella, but I don't use it except only when I'm not on the street. Call me Bella if you like.'

Bella, with a face clean of cosmetics, and seated hunched instead of displaying her usual projection of chin and bosom, was a different woman. So vulnerable that Josephine felt some guilt at having subjected her to the confrontation with the German. But she had really wanted to know whether the clergyman had been in London prior to his Christmas jaunt.

* * *

Following Hessel's remand, Herr Kroll called at Bow Street and handed in a written statement for the attention of Detective Superintendent Thomson. A voluntary written statement was unusual, and so promptly delivered. James read, 'I voluntarily tender, as suggested by my legal representative, a written statement of what was asked by your detectives as to what could be proved at the hotel.' There followed a detailed account of the comings and goings of the party from Ramsgate. It was a precise list of rooms, occupants, times, registrations, and everything else the owner of a first-class hotel might keep account of. Solid alibis. Irrefutable evidence by Herr Kroll and his servants.

This was to be Hessel's entire defence. He was not there. He could not have been there. He was confined to his rooms. He was heard to cough. His boots were put out for cleaning on Christmas Eve – he had no other boots than those.

James's earlier spirits dropped. His witnesses against Hessel's. Low-class witnesses against wealth and respectability.

There must be more to be uncovered in Ramsgate.

Frank Kerley returned to Ramsgate at once and went to Hiscock's Royal Hotel.

Although Superintendent Buss was nominally in charge of the questioning here, he was quite willing to give way to Frank Kerley in the questioning of Hessel's wife.

In all their weeks of speculation about Harriet Buswell's killer, neither of them had seriously considered a wife for him. But here she was, a young woman, who in other circumstances must have been lively but was now bewildered and strained at the turn of events at the town hall. And, Frank observed, she was angry.

Although she spoke reasonable English, Frank was correct and to the letter, and insisted that someone from the German consulate be present at all times.

'I regret, madam, that I must ask you to accompany me on board to examine your husband's chests and boxes.'

Through the consul, she said that these contained nothing but wearing apparel and dirty linen and that she would not wish this to be examined.

'I assure you, madam, that in any other circumstances but these I would avoid having to do so, and the consul will, I am certain, advise you that you do not have the right to prevent this happening.'

In sympathetic, gentle words the consul confirmed that this was the case – in English, after Frank had requested that he do so.

'You cannot make me go there,' she said. 'There is smallpox aboard the *Wangerland*.'

The consul retreated from her as though she might be a carrier of the dread disease. 'I had not heard of this.'

'Ask Captain Wilken, ask Karl Wolebe, ask Doctor Franzen . . . They know it.'

And so it proved true. The agents and captain were trying to prevent the discovery of the disease, hoping, Frank assumed, that they could make their escape before it was discovered. He was under no illusion as to what would happen to any of the emigrants found carrying smallpox.

Karl Wolebe, the original suspect, was not to be found, but Captain Wilken and the doctor agreed to accompany Frank Kerley aboard the vessel in order that he carry out his search, the kind of demeaning task he loathed. As it turned out, what she said about dirty linen was the truth. Crammed into sea-chests without laundering or care, silverfish and insects were nesting. The smell was repugnant.

'I noticed that Dr Hessel was wearing what appeared to be a new suit of clothes. Where are those he wore to London?' The search continued. More trunks were opened. Sergeant Buss came aboard as a cabin chest stowed in the Hessels' accommodation was opened.

It was obvious that the Germans were ill at ease, whether from the close proximity of smallpox below decks, or from discovering the contents of the cabin chest. 'If you are willing that the superintendent and myself list and take away some of the contents of this chest, we need not detain you any longer.'

With the captain and doctor gone, Kerley and Buss listed the items. 'One black dress coat, one black cloth vest. A quantity of clean and dirty linen consisting of men's shirts, collars and cuffs, two woollen shirts, some papers and books written in a foreign language, one worn suit, a six-barrel revolver, three packets of cartridges, two cases containing scalpels and other surgical instruments, a minister's black gown and cap, one black mackintosh, one pair of patent-leather side-opening boots.' All of which were later carried ashore by some of Buss's men.

'Mr Buss, sir,' Kerley said as they made their way along the dockside, 'I believe that someone should make a report on the conditions aboard this ship.'

'I am not sure that I should be the one to make the report.' The superintendent looked ill-at-ease. 'I understand your concern, but at least aboard the ship any disease is contained. A report might mean that the infection could escape and ravage the whole of Ramsgate. Do you understand my concern?'

'Sir, I also understand the plight of those poor wretches huddled in such poor conditions as I saw on my last visit.'

'It has not so far been confirmed as the smallpox. It might not be that.'

'What are those two doctors doing?'

'I really don't know.'

'Well, sir, if I might suggest—'

'Sergeant Kerley, you may have a less formal relationship with your own superior than my men have with me, but I am not open to suggestions from lower ranks.'

Frank felt his blood rage through his body. However, he knew better than to oppose a man of superior rank, and one who might well report insubordination. Frank Kerley wanted above all to continue as a detective and do what he did best. One of the many moral dilemmas he faced. He tried to draw on his grandfather's wisdom, but he was unable to find an answer there. So he was circumspect in his reply. 'I apologize, sir. I did not intend overstepping the mark. It is true – as you will remember Mr Thomson saying – he encourages comment. Sorry, sir, I shall think before speaking in future.'

Buss nodded his acceptance of Frank's apology.

'May I suggest something, sir?'

Buss nodded again.

'That you put pressure on the agents and the captain to insist that the doctors attend to their passengers by way of better food and medications.'

'I shall be pleased to do so, Sergeant. These people have been here long enough causing mischief and making trouble for my men.'

Frank raised his eyebrows questioningly, for he could only have been referring to the upper-decks passengers, the ones putting up at the Royal, but Buss did not enlighten him as to what mischief and trouble those passengers from the *Wangerland* had caused.

The vessel itself appeared as sick and wretched as its below-decks passengers. No wonder it had been damaged in a storm. If its present state was that of a repaired vessel, what had it been like when it sailed from Danzig? Those poor creatures below decks. Who would care to risk life to a tub like that?

That question puzzled Frank Kerley all the way back to London.

Ann Thomson had seen so little of her husband, and he appeared to be having so little sleep or proper meals, that she planned a strategy to make him have at least one evening at home.

Consequently, the Sunday after Hessel's arrest found James in the comfort of his own home, entertaining again, among others, the Granvilles and Colonel and Mrs Henderson. He was under no illusion as to Ann's reason for inviting the chief commissioner: he would not be able to absent himself from the dinner table pleading urgent papers awaiting him, no matter that this was true. Nor was he under any illusion as to why the chief of police should accept Ann's invitation – it was always 'Ann's invitation', her blood being of the very blue kind and not to be refused. Daily, since he had headed the Great Coram Street murder investigation, James had reported formally to the commissioner. The daily facts as they were reported to James himself. Tonight, however, James knew that Commissioner Henderson would want an unofficial briefing. In particular he would want to know why 'E' Division had been so rash as to arrest a respectable clergyman – a German at that, knowing that the queen was still mourning one of that same nationality.

The ladies eventually retired from the table, no doubt to discreetly sympathize with Ann on the dreadful things in which James's work involved him, and hoping to hear some of the more interesting details of a case involving a clergyman and a prostitute. James was assured that they would get nothing out of Ann Martha, even though she had tried to squeeze every last bit of scandal from him.

Still seated at table, Ann's cousin the Honourable

Hammond Proctor-Lazenby opened at once, saving Commissioner Henderson the trouble. 'What's this thing about you arresting a clergyman, James?'

'Landed yourself in something there, old chap. You'll never make anything stick,' added his brother Maurice. 'I mean, the royal household is half German; the country will never stand for it.'

James was able to appear sociable with the aid of the port bottle and a cloud of cigar smoke. He endeavoured to sound amiable. 'The man has only been remanded pending further enquiries. Scotland Yard doesn't give us carte blanche to choose our suspects.'

'But how could you even suspect such a man? A clergyman and a German to boot! Men don't come more respectable than that.'

'What does he look like, James?'

'He fits exactly the description we posted – young, dark, solid.'

'Does he wear his dog-collar when he goes about killing the odd dollymop after matins?' This got a laugh that the women must have heard.

James kept his equilibrium and refrained from what he wished he could say, 'You may as well save your breath to cool your porridge.' Instead he said, 'Why don't you find yourself a seat on the public benches – better yet, one of the reserved seats.'

Maurice said, 'No fear, James, I once tried that. Good God man, the smell of it. All the Lysol in the world cannot disguise the aroma of Mr and Mrs General Public.'

Hammond nodded in agreement. 'I have never been able to understand how a man of your refinement can stand it, day in and day out.'

James worked hard at keeping his good humour, if only for the sake of Lord Granville, who was an old friend, and Colonel Henderson, his superior officer, who might hold James's future in his hands, so he puffed more smoke-rings into the already clouded atmosphere before laughing and slapping Hammond on the shoulder. 'I reckon Mr and Mrs General Public might find this room a bit ripe.'

Good joke. James passed the port.

James Thomson was no fool; he was well aware that his own attitude was unusual to say the least – very unusual in his profession. Society, high and low, was rooted in prejudice. Although he had been nurtured in Smyrna's ex-patriot society, and for a while served Prince Tipo in his palace, his mother's influence had been strong. Bohemian was the current word for such nonconformists. In England they were few and far between. The example of Victoria and Albert had changed two generations. Having conquered such a huge part of the world, British people had become narrow-minded, certain that they were right in everything, examples for the rest of the world to live up to.

He had been glad to see that Josie had a mind of her own. She was problematical because of his own position, but he realized now that the problems were his, not hers. She was intelligent, and brave, and strong enough to see off the Proctor-Lazenbys of this country.

When the last of their friends departed, James went straight to the bedroom. Ann came up looking pleased with herself; he was already in his nightshirt.

'There, my dear,' she said as she stood with her back to him for his help in unpinning her hair. 'Don't you feel the better for an evening in civil company?'

It was over now, and she had arranged the dinner believing that it would do him good. Even so he could not answer her warmly. 'My dear Ann, in spite of what your cousins might think, I do not work among barbarians. Sergeant Kerley is quite as sensitive and intelligent as many who come here to dine.'

'I am sure that you are right, dear, but the Sergeant Kerleys of this world would hardly know how to tackle turbot.'

'Sergeant Kerley might well surprise you, Ann. He often surprises me.'

'Thank you, James, I can manage now.'

'No, let me brush it for you, I always find that very soothing.'

'I know very well that our code of behaviour is not the only one, James, but it is the only one that I know how to deal with.'

'The most alien code must surely have been Hani's when she first came here – you dealt with that wonderfully. *And*, I believe that we may have been the better for having her with us.'

'Absolutely, James. Hani is the most civilized of people.'

'Yet she had been a servant out there. Except for Josie, the woman closest to you, then, is a servant much lower in the pecking order than my Frank Kerley.' She did not reply but gazed into the mirror at the reflection of her own eyes. Moving to more neutral ground, he said, 'I thought that the food was excellent; you know how I love turbot, and the lemon soufflé . . . delicious, light as a feather. You certainly have the flair for planning an original menu.'

'I tried to give you your favourites.'

'Thank you, my dearest, you are my bright flame in a dark world.'

Elbowing him in the stomach, she laughed. 'A dark world, James. It's not at all dark, and spring is just around the corner.'

'Ah, spring. I do look forward to the light days when we can eat and drink alfresco again. I like seeing our friends best in small, informal groups.'

As he lay in bed waiting for sleep to come, he wondered what Kerley would have thought had he been able to spy upon them this evening, but James did not like to speculate further on that. What he had seen of Kerley's private life showed it to be very different. Not worse, and probably not better, but very different. Perhaps that was why they had become such good partners. They came at problems from different directions. Before he fell asleep he wondered whether Kerley had found anything of significance in Ramsgate.

*　　*　　*

George Hood summoned Josephine into his office.

'Hessel wants us to buy his story.'

'Confessions of a murderer?'

'No, he is offering a column exposing the conditions under which an arrested person is held.'

'Oh, doesn't he like his conditions, poor thing?'

'Under the law he has not been convicted of a single thing. He is there awaiting a hearing.'

'On suspicion of having slit the throat of a young woman.'

'It is not for us to sit in judgement – Mr Vaughan will do that. In the meantime I am offering you the opportunity of meeting Hessel.'

Josephine was stopped in her tracks. 'Oh, Mr Hood, there is nothing in the world that I should like better at this moment.'

Hood gave a self-satisfied smile. 'You will be no more than a messenger. A contract must be made, so I thought that you could take it to him.'

It was arranged that she would collect the contract and go to Bow Street and meet the solicitor after Hessel's appearance tomorrow.

James knew that from here on he would be bound to his desk, but he did not mind half as much now that he had the stimulating and exacting task of setting up the evidence and depositions for the prosecutor's case at the hearing. It was beginning to come clear that Hessel's entire case would rest upon an alibi, and the prosecution's upon the circumstances in which he was seen with the murdered girl (he still thought of her as that, in spite of it having been confirmed that she was twenty-six years old).

He was at his desk early in the day, wanting to deal with a whole pile of files before his next appearance at the court. First, he had letters, which Kerley had had translated in Ramsgate and brought to Bow Street.

Reading in order of date, James Thomson became increasingly disturbed by what was revealed, not only about the Hessels, but the whole enterprise. Even without suspicion falling upon two of their number, the cabin-passengers on the *Wangerland* were stirring up a hornet's nest. These people were trouble.

Frank Kerley knocked and entered. 'Do you want me for anything, sir?'

'Yes, go back to Kroll's Hotel and question the porters about Hessel's boots. Sit down a moment.' James put down his wire-rimmed spectacles and waved Frank into a chair, where he sat with his ramrod-straight spine pressed against the chair back and his long legs spread out at angles. 'We've had a visit from Mr Mullins.'

'The instructing solicitor?'

James nodded. 'He asked for Wolebe's diary.'

'That's still with the translator.'

'I know, I don't believe that is why he came; he knows that Wolebe's diary won't be relevant to the case. He was letting me know that they are going for an unshakeable alibi.'

'How can they make it unshakeable? Hessel wasn't seen between eleven on Christmas Eve and midday on Christmas Day.'

301

'He was heard to cough and his boots were outside his door.'

'Those damned boots, sir.'

James smiled behind his straight face. Kerley hadn't even realized he had said that they were 'damned' boots . . . but they *were*. 'I agree.'

Frank continued. 'Hessel said, "I will wear my boots and stand by my friend" when he was persuaded to join the ID parade. Why make a point of telling all and sundry that he would wear his boots? What else would he wear – his carpet slippers? And when I asked Wolebe to be witness to what I was listing to bring away from Hessel's cabin, he said, "Those are the boots he wore in London," indicating the patent-leather boots.'

James followed Kerley's line of thought. 'And the hall porter at the Royal Hotel said, "He took his open-sided boots to London." Is that right?'

'Yes, sir, and the boot-boy said, "I cleaned his sea boots the day after he returned." Alice Douglas said he wore sea boots on the bus.'

'And Daisy, the Wrights' scullery maid, said he carried boots . . . and the maid opposite saw him pull on his boots outside number twelve. Pulling on indicates elastic-sided boots or open-sided boots.'

'*Or* sea boots, sir.'

'Right, Sergeant. Had he been wearing patent-leather, then Alice Douglas would not have called them sea boots.'

'Which were what the Kroll's porter says were put out

for cleaning when he went to bed early on Christmas Eve . . .'

'As early as seven, sir.'

'. . . and on Christmas Day did not get up until one o'clock, when, one assumes, he put on his cleaned boots. Boots, boots, boots.'

'Ah . . . how about this, sir? His alibi stands on the fact that his only pair were seen outside his room door by pretty well everybody, and that they were described as sea boots.'

James nodded. 'Yes . . .'

'But next day a whole lot of them went out to the Crystal Palace and Covent Garden. Glittering venues, both.'

James shoved his glasses back on his face, as if to follow the saga of the boots. 'Wearing his only pair . . . sea boots, Frank? I think not. This was a band of stylish young people, the men were dandies – wouldn't have been seen dead wearing sea boots to Covent Garden.'

'That was my line of thinking, sir.'

'It wouldn't break an alibi on its own, Frank, but it certainly throws doubt upon it. And added to the circumstantial, and eyewitnesses . . .'

'I'll be off to Kroll's Hotel then, sir.'

'It will do no harm, but don't give them any opportunity to say that they are being harassed by us. Mr Mullins has already suggested that Herr Kroll is very important and a man of substance.'

Frank Kerley kept a straight face when he said, 'I am something of a man of substance myself, sir,' ducking his head as he went through the doorway.

*　　*　　*

The sun shone brightly as Josephine walked to her office. It was still too early in the year for ideas of spring, but the clear, frosty-blue sky and sunshine was in tune with her mood. Liliana was busy making last-minute decisions about small paintings for her exhibition, which was imminent. 'I wish I could take you with me, Lili.'

'So do I. You must take in every detail of him: his cell, the amount of light – I doubt there's much, what items he has, how they are placed, the condition of the walls; you must fix them in your mind so that you can dictate them to me. I have never painted except from life, but this must be from your mind.'

'I am going to look at Harriet's room later.'

'Never!'

'I asked Mrs Wright what it was like and she's said that I can go there.'

'Take me with you, Jo.'

'I can't do that. It would appear too insensitive. Mrs Wright is very protective of her girls.'

'Your book could have illustrations. How interesting would that be to your readers.' It wasn't a question. Lili, carried away with enthusiasm, was aware that people loved a few illustrations in any factual reading. 'Harriet's room, the bar at the Alhambra Palace, with Tryphena, and then the murderer in his cell.'

'Not the hanging?' Liliana appeared to be considering this. 'No, Lili! I was being facetious.'

'But, yes, Jo. Think how much more dramatic that would be than simply writing "The End".'

'The book won't need that illustration. Everyone has a picture in their mind of the gallows.'

'At least consider it, Jo.'

'Lili!'

'Then at least take me with you to Mrs Wright's.'

Josephine went with Mr Mullins, Hessel's lawyer, into Bow Street station. James and Kerley had both left, so it came to Inspector Cruse to study the papers Josephine carried and question the lawyer until he could find no valid reason to keep them from visiting the prisoner in his cell.

'Five minutes only, sir,' Cruse said authoritatively.

'My client is entitled to confer with me as long as he reasonably wishes and without a jailer present.'

'I know our own rules, sir. I meant the young lady. She does not have your privilege with the prisoner.'

The prisoner Hessel of the Bow Street cells was very different from the Reverend Godfried Hessel of the magistrate's court. There he had been ramrod stiff and had raised an eyebrow superciliously at the court clerk, who had had the audacity to ask him for his plea and to state his name. Even 'Madame Margaret' – Bella – had picked up on that. 'Who the hell does he think he is? The clerk don't have any say in what goes on.'

Here he was an uncombed, dishevelled, nondescript young man, huddled in a grey prison blanket.

Without thinking she remarked, 'It is very chill in here.'

He raised his head and stared straight at her. She might have recoiled from looking into the eyes of the man who had slit Harriet's throat without compunction, but she did not; instead she stared steadily back at him.

A slow smile. 'Yes, Fräulein, perhaps you might mention this to my jailers: the food is for pigs, the walls are damp, and I have asked for reading matter that I have not received, and my clothing has been taken away.'

She spoke up clearly, not intimidated. 'The creature comforts of men such as yourself are no business of mine.' Her stance was challenging, unfeminine.

Hessel looked up at Mullins. 'Why is she here?'

'She—'

'Thank you, Mr Mullins, I am perfectly able to speak for myself. Mr Hessel, you have offered to tell your story to the readers of *The News*?' Making a question of it and waiting for an answer.

'*Ja.*'

'Then here is a contract for you to sign in the presence of your lawyer.' He held out his hand, but she handed the paper to the lawyer. Petty, not wanting to give Harriet's murderer even the slightest courtesy.

'Your name, Fräulein?'

'I am *Miss* Jemima Ferguson.'

Hessel took the document and turned it to where some light came in through the bars of the cell door. 'You see what shall be my first page of Pastor Godfried Hessel's Diary, Fräulein Ferguson. Bad food, no reading material, no warmth, poor bedding, little light. A dog would be better housed. All this I shall write in my daily column.'

'You do understand that, depending on what you

write, much of it may not be published until after your trial.'

Again that slow, sly, disturbing smile. 'I shall not go to trial, Fräulein, and be assured I shall write nothing that will give reason for censorship. Your ill-educated and untrained policemen may try to play tricks and bring their so-called evidence, but none of it will stand up against me.'

'You would not be the first one to underestimate them.'

'It is good that you advocate their cause.'

'"Advocate" is not the word you are looking for.' Another petty dig, but petty or not, she relished it. She wished that he would stand because he would be shorter than herself. '"Champion" is a more apt word.'

He didn't take his eyes from hers. She wouldn't be stared down. Or intimidated. She only wished that she could say how much she hated and despised him, but *The News* wanted him to sign up with them, and whatever she might think of that, *The News* was still her paper.

'I am forced to tell you that you are ill-informed about the Metropolitan Police. The truth is that they are estimable men. They are well-trained, relentless, and not ill-educated. One of the detectives who arrested you speaks four languages.' Had she scored a hit there?

He returned his attention to the contract. She doubted if much of what she had said had dented his inflated opinion of himself. Never mind, there would come a day when he would be brought down. Whatever happened, she determined to be there when the judge donned the black cap. '. . . that you be hanged by the neck until you are dead. May your soul rest in peace.' May your soul burn in hell.

He took his time reading each clause. The lawyer tried to bend over to offer help, but Hessel waved him away.

Josephine used every second to examine him. But she could not do it impartially. No matter how objective she tried to be, she felt her scalp growing tight on her head, seeming to draw back her ears. Her teeth were clenched tight. So were her hands, her nails dug into her own flesh. She could scarcely bear to occupy the same space as Harriet's killer.

Yet this would be the only chance she would ever get.

Suddenly he looked up and said in his fluent but accented English. 'What is your concern with me, Fräulein Ferguson?'

Her mouth was dry. 'I am just a representative of *The News* – the kind of thing I deal with on a daily basis.'

You are nothing special. Petty. Satisfying. She would have demeaned him further if she had been able.

He shook his head. 'With *me*. You, pretty fräulein, are curious to see a man who can kill a woman, *ja?*'

'No, no. It is nothing like that. And you are only here on suspicion.' How she managed to say that in such a conversational tone . . .

He smiled a little and shook his head, then returned to reading the contract, leaving her trembling inwardly.

Holding herself together.

At last she had a glimmer of insight into what he was.

He was doing with her what he had done when he had taken no trouble to conceal his identity on Christmas Eve. And again when he had pushed his way into the identification parade when he had no need to. She had seen the determined way he had thrown off his own wife when she had tried to stop him placing his life on the gambling board. Dicing with his own life.

This would not have been the first time he had played for high stakes. It must be in his past. She would find a way to discover it. Where had he been before he joined the Brazilian venture? Mr Hood would surely be able to uncover that.

Writing his signature with a flourish, he handed the contract to her and said to his lawyer, 'I wish to speak privately with Fräulein Ferguson.'

'That is not possible.'

'Make it possible. I am no threat chained to the wall. Tell the jailer,' he ordered.

'I am sure Miss Ferguson has no wish to hear what you have to say, Mr Hessel.'

'You are wrong, my friend, the fräulein does wish so.'

He was so arrogant that her instinct was to turn and give her answer by leaving. The lawyer looked perturbed. 'I don't advise this, Miss Ferguson, even if the jailer agrees.'

'Don't ask him,' Josephine said quietly, 'just wait outside. If the jailer objects, I am sure that you can hold him off for just one minute. One minute, no longer.'

Reluctantly, the man exited from the cell, leaving the door open.

Josephine's inner trembling had ceased. She felt strong and much superior to Hessel, shackled in chains and huddled against the cold and damp in a stale blanket.

'You want to know if I am capable of killing the prostitute.'

'I know without doubt that you are.' If he thought that his sly smile intimidated her, he was wrong. 'Harriet was not a prostitute.'

'Taking a stranger to her room for money is not prostitution?'

'Harriet was a decent woman trying to keep body and soul together and provide for her child.'

'A child?'

'Mr Hessel, I am not here to gossip about Harriet's life. You put an end to it, and I know that.'

'You believe that it was I who killed your friend?'

Why had he called her that?

'No, not *believe* that you murdered my friend – I know that you did it.'

Amazingly, he nodded in agreement, even as he said, 'That cannot be proved.'

'Don't underestimate our police force. You are going to the gallows.'

She often wondered what his expression had been, but she would never know, for she had turned on her heel and strode out.

*   *   *

As she was making her way up to the police station, she heard the voices of Sergeant Kerley and her uncle James. There was no way of avoiding them. She nodded to Hessel's lawyer and said good afternoon to him.

'Josephine?'

'Uncle James, fancy meeting you here. Sergeant Kerley, very nice to meet you again.'

Her uncle looked somewhat fed up. 'Sergeant, as you are my best detective, you will have discovered that Miss Jemima Ferguson is my niece and ward, Miss Josephine Thomson.'

Sergeant Kerley looked ill-at-ease and went off as soon as he had said something polite.

'In here,' James Thomson ordered.

Again she found herself in the office with 'Superintendent' painted on the door. 'What are you doing here?'

'I am on legitimate business. Your prisoner will be writing a daily column for *The News* and I came with his solicitor so that the contract could be signed.'

'I had heard about that. There is nothing that I can do to stop *The News* paying him money, but they will not be able to publish a word until the hearing and the trial are over.'

'He will not be writing anything about the trial – only a day-to-day diary without comment. *The News* doesn't mind waiting. It has stolen a march on all the others: the murdering devil will write exclusively for us.'

'Oh yes, the "tickle".'

'Guilty or not, Hessel will make a great deal of money out of his writings.'

'And much good may it do him.'

'Uncle James, can you think of no harsher words than that? I told him plainly that he was going to the gallows.'

'Josephine! Did you have to be *The News*'s messenger? Or did you persuade your editor that he would get a Jemima Ferguson article?'

'Neither. Mr Hood knows about the Harriet book, and had the generosity to offer me the chance to ... to see him face to face. You would never have let me near him.'

'I would not!'

'He did it ... you know that, I know that.'

'Germans are very good at ...' He trailed off, realizing that if he said something of the work Hessel's fellow-countrymen were putting in to give the murderer an alibi, then Josie would leap on it. 'I thought that you had come in answer to my note.'

'I haven't received a note, when did you send it?'

'By hand earlier today.'

'And ... ?'

'I asked if I might talk to you about Harriet.'

Josephine was very taken aback. This was the last thing she had expected from him. 'Yes, of course you may. I shall be very glad of it. What ... ?'

'Not here. Could we walk to your rooms and talk there?'

'Absolutely! I should love you to come. Of course

Liliana is painting away like mad ... an exhibition quite soon; things get a bit slapdash.'

'Josie, I won't be inspecting, just visiting.'

'With luck she will have been baking. Yes. She bakes when she needs to get a new perspective on her work in progress, if that means anything to you. I'm chattering away, aren't I? Nervousness.'

'We would be private there?'

'Of course. We live quite separate lives – except for use of the cooking stove.'

'Separate' must have been hard for her uncle to believe, for when they arrived Liliana, Christine and David were on hands and knees, either painting frames or tacking canvases into them, and the work had spread into the hall and kitchen. Lili leaped to her feet. 'I am *so* sorry, Jo, I had thought to be finished before you came back.'

Normally, Josephine would have waved the apology away and helped out. 'Oh, Lili! I have always told my family what a good thing it was that you came to live here ... but I can hardly say that now.' She held a hand out indicating her uncle. 'This is—'

David, to the surprise of the three women, leaped to his feet and went towards James, offering his hand. 'Superintendent Thomson! What a pleasure to meet with you again. Josie, you never said that "Thomson of the Met" was your uncle.'

'I don't think I knew that my uncle *was* "Thomson of the Met"!'

Again a surprise as her uncle grasped David's hand

warmly. 'Wilde. I had every intention of asking if we could meet, but at the moment I have no time to spare for charitable work.'

'Of course, the Great Coram Street Murder.' He glanced at Josephine, unsure as to whether he should say anything about them having gone with Bella to the remand hearing.

James felt it incumbent upon himself to explain. 'Mr Wilde and I have spent some time working to raise money for charity. And he has helped me with the work establishing the police orphanage. He is very knowledgeable about how to be charitable without condescension. Which is why we get along together.'

Josephine was very taken aback at how pleased her uncle appeared at seeing David. Perhaps the mutual admiration went some way to explaining why she had seen him at the St Giles night-watch service at New Year.

'Mr Thomson, we are really sorry to have overflowed into Josephine's territory. Come along, Lili, back in your own room.'

All affability, James said, 'Don't trouble yourselves, what I have to say to Josie can be said in any public room in any hotel. Come along, Josie, I'll take you to a very pleasant place in Half-Moon Street.' Nodding politely he said, 'Miss Wilde, Miss . . . ?'

'Derry, Christine Derry. May I put you on the gallery's list, Mr Thomson? You should really see Liliana's work as a collection.'

Josephine would see to it that this would not happen. She did not want her two worlds overlapping any more than they already were. What had happened here today was enough.

As they were leaving, Liliana said, 'Jo, I almost forgot, a policeman called with a note for you. It is on the kitchen mantelshelf.'

In the cab, James Thomson said, 'How do you know Wilde?'

'He's Liliana's brother.'

'Of course . . . and what does he think of his sister's life in Paris?'

She thought that she heard disapproval in the question. 'Probably what you think of mine in London. Liliana might have rooms in the artists' quarter, but that doesn't mean that she lives any differently there than here.'

It was obvious from the greeting by the doorman that her uncle was known at the Half-Moon Hotel. He asked if he might use one of the rooms and be served tea and sandwiches. They were only too happy to oblige. The small smoking room.

'I'm impressed, Uncle James.'

'I solved a small crime. Small, but important. A Dutch master oil painting, worth a great deal of money, disappeared. People might scoff at my meticulous method of keeping records, but I often know just where to enquire when such items are stolen.' A well-laden tray was placed on a low table before them. Josephine, not having eaten for hours, ate her way into the sandwiches.

'The hand-delivered note, Uncle James. Why do you want to talk to me?'

'I want to show you something. But first I must ask you to be sworn to secrecy.'

'Uncle James.'

'I am serious, Josephine. If it were to be known that I have shown you these,' he placed a package on the table, 'I should be reduced to the ranks – or worse.'

'Then why show me?'

'Because you need to see them.' She frowned in puzzlement, but did not respond. 'I have changed my mind about your wish to document the life of Harriet Burton.' She relaxed her frown and raised one eyebrow. 'You know that there is no possibility of you getting any closer to Doctor Hessel than you did this morning. And there is no way that I can help you with anything other than what is available to the general public, to anyone who wants to understand more of the circumstances of the man who killed Harriet Burton, and the kind of man he is. They are not the original letters, but translations. You will not be able to use a word of them.'

'Are they evidence then?'

'No, at least not to his guilt. Josie, if you give me your word that you will never reveal anything of what is contained in them, you may read them.'

'You mean to take away?'

'No, no. The fact that I have not left them under lock and key at the station is enough. No, I will sit here until you know their contents.'

'Very well, Uncle James, you should not need to ask, but I give you the assurance you ask for. No one shall ever hear of them from me.'

Ignoring the jibe. 'Good.' He spread out the bundle of letters on the table. 'They are in date order.'

'Why are you doing this?'

He sipped tea before answering. 'I hardly know, Josie, except that what I read of the book you are writing made me think about how little people know about women like her. Wilde and I and people like us are hard enough put to raise money for orphans. It would be impossible to do likewise for all the Harriet Burtons of this world. There are charities who try to do something for "fallen women", but not very charitably, nor with much understanding. Such women are always seen as architects of their own misfortunes, and until the public's eyes are opened to what lies behind their lives, little will change, and men like Hessel will prey upon them.'

'If you are not able to use the letters in evidence, what will happen to them?'

'Scotland Yard and the Home Office will bury them in their archives, and they will probably never see the light of day again.' He sat back comfortably, lit a cigar and waited for her to read.

The letters, as shown by their dates, had, around the middle of December, flown back and forth. Mrs Hessel accused Dr Franzen, the ship's physician, of neglecting passengers; Mrs Hessel was insulted by Dr Franzen; Reverend Hessel demanded an apology; Franzen hauled the captain before the consul to declare that he had treated between-decks passengers with care and that he had not accused Mrs Hessel of untruthfulness and refused to ask her pardon. The captain was unwilling to be drawn into such disputes and Dr Franzen demanded a higher salary to keep quiet about what was going on aboard the *Wangerland*.

Josephine looked up and raised her eyebrows. 'Blackmail, too . . . nice people.' James hunched his shoulders in reply. 'What do you make of this letter, from a Louis Hermes?'

'Oh, he's the agent.'

'He's asking Hessel to get signatures from "other passengers and intelligent between-decks passengers" to say that there are no problems.'

Taking the letter, he flicked a finger at the page. 'It is all contained in this paragraph. "You know yourself how emigration is visited by hostile attacks and especially that to Brazil. It is our *duty* to do all we can to *keep our backs free against unjustifiable attacks*." What I have discovered is that this is one of many ships exporting people to the other side of the world in very dubious conditions.'

'So the attacks are not "unjustifiable"?'

'I am afraid that is so.'

'So no honest and self-respecting doctor or clergyman would have anything to do with it.'

'That is my opinion.'

'Can't you use these letters to show that he is not the god-fearing man he is being made out to be?'

James shook his head. 'When the case goes to full trial we would have to call all these people. They would be hostile; we should get nowhere. The letters are only evidence that this is a particularly nasty group of avaricious people without a scruple between them. And, with the exception of the physician, they were all cavorting in London last Christmas.'

'Why do these people do it, Uncle James? I'd have to be in a pretty bad way to leave my country.'

'Many of them sell everything they have to pay for the passage, thinking they are going to the promised land.'

'But the others, Uncle James? Franzen, Wolebe and the Hessels. Are they all running from something?'

James shrugged. 'Avarice? There are wealthy and powerful people behind these colonization enterprises. A mere doctor is no threat to them.'

Josephine neatened the pile of papers and returned them to the original package. 'What a dirty business, Uncle James.'

'True, and whilst we have got one man in the cells for murder, these businessmen get away with many. People die like flies on these emigrant ships.'

'Is there nothing to be done then?'

James shook his head. 'Had the *Wangerland* not hit the Goodwins, we might well have thought that emigrants were going on a brave adventure, to start life in a new land.'

'Thank you for letting me see these. I understand why they are no use to you in Hessel's trial.'

'But they might stimulate interest in a journalist who likes to tilt at windmills – no, that isn't the right analogy. Jemima Ferguson is interested in reality. I thought she might like to look at the scandal of emigration.'

She got up, crossed to where he sat, put her arms

around his neck and kissed him. 'You are a good man, Uncle James'.

He patted her hand. 'I try to be, Josie, but I don't succeed.'

It appeared now that the defence's strategy was to place as much importance on the position and the respectability of Hessel as on his alibi. The hotel records were not to be depended upon.

In an interview with Herr Kroll himself, James saw that they were likely to admit to bad record-keeping. 'Superintendent, you must have like problems with your people. You explain six times how a thing must be done, five times it is done correctly,' he had waved airily at the corrections and errors James was querying, 'on the sixth they forget, or do not take trouble.'

'So these are not alterations to dates and times?'

'No, no, these are corrections made. You understand that at holiday times I am forced to take on extra staff. Kroll's is a most popular establishment for the more refined class of German. I try most hard to obtain servants of the very best calibre, but it is not always possible to obtain Germans. Local people do not always understand my orders. Mistakes are made. I do not suffer this – incompetent servants are dismissed.'

'So, you are saying that there were mistakes made in recording the comings and goings of your guests?'

'Also in the recording of room-services, yes, and what you see are sad attempts to recompense some errors.'

'You are prepared for the honest reputation of Kroll's

Hotel to suffer if you are forced to admit that alterations were made to your records?'

'It must be done. It is more honourable to admit that one's employees have made mistakes than to do otherwise.'

That was when James realized that, although the prosecutor, Mr Poland, would question Hessel's alibi that he did not leave the hotel, the defence's Mr Straight, would raise doubt in magistrate Mr Vaughan's mind. This respectable hotelier had perhaps been over-zealous in presenting correct records – nothing more sinister than that.

Hessel's defence would then rest largely on his character, respectability and being a man of the highest reputation. If Herr Kroll were to take the witness stand, he would be impressive in defence of his countryman.

So, in search of more background to Hessel, on the day prior to the hearing, Frank Kerley went back to Ramsgate to delve further into the life of the cabin passengers during the months following their being stranded.

He did not feel very sanguine that the murder weapon would ever be identified: all of the knives and scalpels discovered in Hessel's chests were clean and polished. But it was necessary to be meticulous, leaving no stone unturned.

Superintendent Buss's enquiries had uncovered something interesting. The young Germans were frequent visitors to Wheeler's, who were dealers and cutlers.

Frank's spirits were raised when he interviewed Mr

George Wheeler. On being shown the artist's impression of the murderer, Wheeler said wearily, 'I know him all right, and the rest of his gang.'

'Gang?'

'I don't mean a gang of villains, but there were always four or five of them who came in here together.'

'Often?'

'Not as you would say *frequently*, but often enough so that I began to feel unsettled when they came into my premises.'

'In what way did they unsettle you?'

'Difficult to say . . . they were boisterous, taking things from cabinets, asking to look at handguns and cutlasses. They would inspect them closely and then proceed to take aim at one another in jest, or swing a cutlass. I tried to point out the foolhardiness of this without putting them off making purchases . . .'

'Did they make purchases?'

'Oh yes. On one occasion one of the men – the one in the drawing – brought in a revolver and asked to have it cleaned and said he wanted to buy cartridges for it.'

'And did he?'

'It's not something we sell at Wheeler's, and when I told him this he said, never mind, he was going to London in a day or two and he could get them there.'

'When was this?'

'I could look it up . . . probably sometime last November.'

'Not December?'

'No. But they did come in again sometime close to

Christmas – there was snow about, so that's when it must have been. A minute, and I'll look it up.' He leafed through pages of a daybook. 'Ah yes, it was December. His name was Mr Hessel, the one who wanted cartridges. He must have got them because he brought the revolver in again to be cleaned. This time he was dressed like a clergyman. He was carrying a dagger at his belt and asked me what I thought of it, and I said that it was a very fine piece.'

'And was it?'

'Oh yes, new I should say. He asked to see similar dagger-knives, which I showed him. He was very much taken by a white-handled dagger-knife and asked the price. I said it was a good blade and not overpriced at five shillings.'

'And did he buy it?'

Wheeler made a wry face. 'He did . . . eventually. He was one of the mean types that's never satisfied unless they can do you down for sixpence. He bought cases of surgical knives, so I let him have it for four-and-six. I remember my brother who was in here at the time, saying, it's a queer sort of vicar carries a dagger and buys cases of surgical knives. I said perhaps he was a surgeon as well as a clergyman, but my brother said, no, the other man was a surgeon, as he had been buying surgical knives as well.'

'You didn't see the "Wanted" posters?'

'No. The other police officer asked me that, but, as I told him, it's not often we leave our workshop, and we live above.'

'Did any women come with the "gang", as you call them.'

'Oh yes. A rather pretty young woman – married, but I couldn't say to which of the young men she was married. She was for ever giving them the benefit of her advice and making gay with them.'

'In what way "making gay"?'

'Like a girl, making flirtatious comments. You must know the kind of thing I mean, Sergeant.'

From Wheeler's, Frank went to the Royal Hotel, and once more questioned some of the servants. Here again, Frank was seeing a similar picture emerging as the one that Wheeler had described. None of the servants said so directly, but they hinted that there was a lot of 'coming and going' among the cabin passengers.

'The clergyman's wife almost always kept to the same room, but some of the men never appeared to settle. Sometimes one or the other would take off and have their bags sent aboard the *Wangerland*.'

'And did this go on from the time they first arrived?'

'Not so much at first. But after a whole party of them went up to London, there was a lot of fidgetiness.'

'Fidgetiness?'

'Mostly with the men.'

'Which men?'

'The captain, Mr Hermes the agent, the ship's surgeon Mr Wolebe (the one who was the first suspect), and the clergyman – who's been arrested and took to London – and his wife. They had spats and arguments. None of them thought to keep their voices down.'

'Do you know why?'

'No, they all spoke in their own language, but there's no mistaking that they were at odds with one another. Which wasn't surprising, seeing how long they were kept hanging about, what with the repairs to the brig taking more and more time. It could be that the agent was at fault.'

'The one, perhaps, they could take it out on?'

The porter who was being questioned nodded. 'The physician sometimes came. He lived in town with his family, but he came here to see the others. There was an occasion when the agent arranged a supper and dance for the cabin passengers, when the doctor and Mr Hessel near came to blows over something Mrs Hessel had said.'

'Did they exchange blows?'

'No. The captain and the agent sorted them out, and the doctor went off flaming with anger.'

'What did you think of them, as a whole?' Frank asked. 'This is just out of interest . . . not to go into a statement.'

'Well, at first, when the surgeon was took away by the police, everyone was saying how shocking and that it was, but then some said they wasn't surprised. There was often a lot of drink taken . . . gambling often . . . the clergyman had let off a revolver from one of the windows and the police was called, the young men – not the captain so much – were always showing off that they was armed one way or another.'

*　　*　　*

On the morning of the hearing, as James Thomson had anticipated, a crowd gathered outside the police court long before it was due to open. What with the repeated examinations in the coroner's court, then the Ramsgate hearings following the arrest of Karl Wolebe, then the dramatic arrest of Hessel and the almost daily newspaper coverage for over a month, interest increased greatly. As always when a murder was committed, one might believe from the press that London was awash with blood. True, the city and the river gave up many bodies that had known a violent end, but murder by someone outside the victim's immediate circle was a rare occurrence. So a murder trial like this one was an event arousing intense curiosity.

That morning, a letter had appeared in *The News* berating the police for being so ignorant and uncultured as to have arrested a man of the cloth – shipwrecked, and having been near to death, this respectable man had been arrested on suspicion of having murdered a prostitute. The nation should bow its head in shame . . .

Before he left for the magistrate's court, James ordered Kerley to assemble as many men as were on duty in the station yard.

'Men. We have all read this offensive nonsense in the papers.' Boots shuffled and little snorts of acknowledgement were made.

'Many times in the past the police force has been called ill-educated, badly trained and rough men – or worse, but usually by drunks and regular criminals. I think that the writers of those insulting letters might ask

326

themselves who they would call upon if their homes were burgled, or their wallet stolen or their watch snatched by a foot-pad. Would it be my ill-educated, badly trained and rough men? No . . . you would at once become men of "E" Division, and very pleased they would be to talk to you. Rough men? Do they think that we are rough men when we patrol their streets and keep cat-burglars from entering by way of windows left invitingly open?

'As you know, questions are being asked about the arrest of a distinguished German pastor, "a visitor to our shores". "Outrageous", "ludicrous", it has been said. It is my opinion that we – and the general public – need to think on this. "E" Division and the force at Ramsgate did not hold back from apprehending this distinguished German because of his rank and class. No, there was very good evidence indeed. It was he who was seen with the victim on numerous occasions on the night that she was murdered – to say nothing of his being seen leaving the house of the victim in the early hours.

'We and you have been meticulous in our searches, both here and at Ramsgate. We have taken many dozens of statements. Today, this "visitor to our shores" will again appear before Chief Magistrate Mr Justice Vaughan, to answer to the charge made against him. You have worked long and hard. We have the evidence. We have the man. Do not allow these mean diatribes in the papers concern you. It is only the opinion of the senior officers of "E" Division that should concern you; our opinion of you is a good one.'

With murmurs and the tramping of marching hobnails,

the men who had scoured London from the Haymarket outwards over the last many weeks left to go back to their beats.

Frank's next enquiry was with Captain Wilken, whose statement was simply confined to the going-aground of his ship and her towing into Ramsgate and subsequently to dry-dock in London where she was repaired. When Frank asked what he knew of the sleeping arrangements of Hessel, the captain said, 'He used to sleep at the Royal, but since we came back from London, he's been sleeping on board the greater part of the time.'

'Why do you reckon this was? I mean, his berth on the *Wangerland* is cold and damp and it's January. And not only that, wasn't smallpox supposed to be rife?'

Captain Wilken shrugged his shoulders.

'It's what I was told when I wanted to make a search, you remember? Didn't he ever say why he chose to leave dry and warm quarters for something so uninviting?'

But the captain, even if he knew something, was not saying. He merely spread his hands and shrugged.

Frank, well aware of the absolute necessity to tread most carefully where these touchy foreigners were concerned, retreated. He had no wish for the German consulate to become even more involved than it was. He already felt hemmed about enough, what with the shrewd band of lawyers, barristers and consul officials, to say nothing of the stonewalling alibi being offered by Hessel's fellow countrymen.

He again questioned William Clement about Hessel's

suits, and Mr Hiscock, the owner of the Royal, about the arrangements whereby Hessel and his wife occupied rooms at the Royal, but could get nothing more than he had previously, which was that Hessel always wore the same suit, except sometimes he wore dark trousers, and that when they first arrived they shared room number 17 and on returning from London, Hessel asked for Number 16 for himself and number 15 (for which he did not pay rent) for his trunks. These people would probably be called upon as witnesses when the case went for full trial, so it was vital that nothing was left to chance.

So yet again he went over the statements from Jane Somers and two laundresses who had found the bundle of linen saturated with blood. This bit of evidence might be argued down. The defence could simply ask them whether they had been told where the blood had come from. Mrs Hessel had sent them for washing, had she not? And Mrs Hessel, a young woman caught unprepared for menstruation in a strange place . . . might she have taken her husband's handkerchiefs in emergency? Wouldn't that explain, too, Hessel sleeping apart from her? Perhaps she had miscarried; the laundress had spoken of blood-clots and saturation. But no, she was out and about celebrating . . . Covent Garden theatre, the Crystal Palace. Mrs Hessel was not a woman suffering any kind of female indisposition.

No one statement was sufficient of itself to convict a man of murder, but collectively, and together with the London eyewitnesses pointing to Hessel being the man with the victim, meant sufficient evidence would be stacked against him to convince a jury.

The journey back to London seemed endless to Frank.

For one thing he would again be very late home, and he had hoped that once the hearing started he might see something of his wife more than of late, but he had seven or eight reports to submit, and although he wished to see Elizabeth, he wished more to see Mr Thomson and hear what he had to say about the first day. Elizabeth had started painting again, and this pleased him . . . perhaps not so much pleased him, as made him glad that she was filling spare time exercising her talent, and he therefore need not be too concerned for the long hours of duty, the spoiled meals and late nights. There was nothing to be done about the lot of a policeman's wife: it was an inevitable part of the marriage contract that she must be prepared for disruptions and disappointments. It was true, as she had occasionally pointed out, that he had not been a detective when they married, nor were their lives then circumscribed by Scotland Yard regulations. But Frank liked the companionship of his wife and, in normal circumstances, would have spent time discussing her work and encouraging her.

He looked out of the murky windows at the bleak January landscape, and felt suddenly tired and dejected. It could all fall apart. He had a presentiment that if they were not very careful indeed, the case would be lost. That was unthinkable. He was as sure as he had ever been of any suspect that, clergyman or not, this was the man who had slit Harriet Burton's throat. The prosecution would call her a 'gay woman', a prostitute, a 'woman of the night', a 'woman of low life' – all terms he had himself used at some time in describing a 'dolly-mop'.

He closed his eyes and wished that he could have slept, but this time he was not travelling first class and the compartment was so full that he felt uncomfortable at the space his large body and legs took up. In trying to keep to the space of a man of normal size, his limbs became numb. He hoped the numbness would not turn and seize his muscles with cramp, when he would be forced to leap to his feet and bend the arches of his feet.

Frank Kerley was not to see his super that day as he had hoped. The day in court had proved to be unbelievably exhausting to James, so he had gone home to eat dinner with Ann. That, and hearing first-hand what had gone on that day, pleased her so much that she did not object when he had begged her pardon and, pleading hours of work, gone to sit at his desk in his study, where the hiss of gaslamps and the crackle of a coal fire were the only sounds in the velour-deadened atmosphere.

His notes spread before him, he began to place them in the order in which he would write his report to Colonel Henderson, and for the writing up of his personal journal. Of the two assignments, only one was a duty. The daily entries to his journal were one of his greatest pleasures, whereas police reports were written in a style peculiar only to his profession. Supposedly concise and unambiguous, it was however thought helpful to include such unnecessary niceties as prefacing every address to one's superior with, 'I beg to report that' or, 'I beg to request permission', as though one was a humble petitioner asking a favour rather than doing the work one was engaged to do.

James occasionally indulged in the fanciful thoughts of, 'If I were commissioner of police . . .' and had already subscribed to a list of changes to practice that would make the force more efficient and productive and the men more efficient and content, a thing he knew them not to be at present. And who could blame them? Poorly paid, yet with all of society's troubles thrown at their door; unarmed yet sent on the streets to face whatever violence lay in wait for them; long hours of duty, yet, when things didn't suit it, receiving from society only brickbats. And at the moment, for all the hissing at James's prisoner by the hoi polloi, James also smelt the professional class pack at his back.

Having completed his report, he laid the quarter-bound accountant's book before him. He had a momentary, not-uncommon vision of himself in the future, when he would take up a sheaf of paper and begin writing his autobiography based upon this journal in earnest. He did not deceive himself that he was any great sort of an author, but his material as a Scotland Yard detective would be of interest: he was sure of this from the number of people who were always eager for him to hear the 'inside story'. Even though he was no Dickens, James always tried to give a background to his entries.

'Twenty-ninth of January, Eighteen Seventy-three. There is no doubt of it, I wished many times today that Frank Kerley had been beside me, for over the past four weeks I have seen in him all of those qualities a senior officer looks for in a junior officer, and most of those a man could hope for in a trusted friend. From time to time throughout today I admit to having felt doubts as to the outcome of the Harriet Burton murder case, and I wished that Kerley had been there to give reassurance that my doubts were unfounded and that the man would be put up for a full trial and would go to the gallows for the dreadful deed he has done. But I had sent Frank off to Ramsgate. No doubt Cruse could have gone, but if anyone is to uncover evidence that is firmer than the dozen eyewitnesses to H. and the girl being together on the night she was murdered, then I could trust no one but Frank to try.

'The hearing began with the usual preliminaries. Mr Justice Vaughan, the usual Bow Street Court stipendiary magistrate presided over the hearing. Mr Poland prosecuted, Mr Straight defended. This being a hearing of evidence before bringing the accused to full trial, there was, of course, no jury. Perhaps it was this that has made me feel uneasy, and what I should have liked to have heard Frank Kerley's opinion on. With a jury, one is not relying on the fallibility of a single man, with all his incipient frailty and prejudice. That is not to say that eleven men may not also be frail and biased, but to put such judicious power into a single pair of hands has always seemed to me to be a dangerous thing to do. But I digress.

'In choosing the order in which the witnesses should appear, it was not easy to decide whether to get the greengrocer's boys out of the way early and chance giving a poor opening impression, or to open with Miss Tryphena Douglas, or to have her come last to the witness stand and leave the magistrate with her dignity and assurance in his mind. In the event, as it was necessary to follow the course of the evening of the twenty-fourth in sequence, it was Miss Douglas who appeared first. Another digression, but now to the setting of the scene and the playing-out of the first act.

'Bow Street Court is mostly wooden: wooden floor, doors, forms in the public gallery, wooden pews and seats in the well of the court where sit the main protagonists, a wooden witness stand, and wooden dock in which the prisoner sits upon a wooden chair, and wooden "thrones" upon high where sit the magistrates and county officials, such as the lord sheriff and members of Parliament associated with the case. Although a magistrate's court does not have the pomp of a court of full hearing with a judge and jury, it is no less a court of procedure, where each taking part must do so in a prescribed manner. Thus, although in this country justice must be seen to be done in the presence of whoever of the passing throng cares to watch the law take its process, these representative overseers too are expected to abide by the rules, and will soon be ejected if there is any unseemly behaviour. (This does not stop a good many of them, if the case looks likely to be entertaining, bringing along small hampers to sustain them, and friends to fight over their seat should they need to leave it for nature's purposes.)

'Today, when I entered, the pungent smell of oranges was already apparent, and mixing with the ever-present haze of dust that seems to hang in the air of Number One Court. And as the lamps are seldom out when the court is in session, they too added to the general confusion of smells that are particular to a police court. My timing was right, for having ascertained that all the witnesses for the prosecution were present in an anteroom and overseen by my men, I took my place in seats on the wing of the courtroom, almost at the moment when the usher called for silence and for all to be upstanding.

'I have been upstanding in that court on many and various occasions for Mr Justice Vaughan, but each time we face one another with an unknown and untried set of circumstances between us. This time, as it seemed to me this morning, the situation was of great seriousness, and I had a feeling that I am sure a soldier must experience as he is about to go into battle. Yet I should not think of bringing a case before Mr Justice Vaughan in such terms, for the battle is not betwixt the two of us, the battle is between the wits of the other two protagonists, Mr Prosecutor and Mr Defence. I can but pray that our Mr Prosecutor has the wit to use my long line of foot soldiers in such formation as to defeat the line of confident German generals and their auxiliaries. (Perhaps that is unfair to those other witnesses for the

335

defence, yet I have felt that the statement by Kroll's night porter is not safe. But he stands by it, as does the maid, who swears she saw Hessel in his bedroom on Christmas morning. She could *not* have done so, unless it was *much* later than she says, or it was *not* on Christmas morning at all. This is a possibility, I must consult Poland on this point. What occasioned the maidservant to remember weeks later that it was this *particular* morning and not another? Herr Kroll is a man of very strong character, who might easily suggest to his underlings that what he tells them is the truth. They remember such and such, and it needs only the hint that yes, it was on Christmas morning that this occurred, or that it was on Christmas Eve that the door was locked, so that . . .'

On this occasion, James not only digressed but fell asleep over his journal. He awoke at three in the morning, cold and cramped, and was forced, feeling quite guilty, to creep in beside Ann.

Tryphena Douglas would never forget the day that had just passed. It was the first time she had ever entered a police court, and it had proved to be quite as frightening as she had supposed it would, but she knew that she had conducted herself well. Even Mr Thomson had taken the trouble to see her outside and tell her how impressed he had been with the way she had given her evidence. Nobody would ever know how terrified she had been. She had been the first of 'their' crowd to be called. She had been shown to a door which, when opened, led directly into the court. It had felt as though everyone in the world was looking at her. Thank the Lord Mr Thomson had seen to it that all the witnesses knew what to expect and to know who was who. 'Remember,' he had said, 'all of you are only doing your public duty. Everyone in the court knows that. There may be times, especially when your word is being questioned, when you may wish that you had never admitted having seen the accused, or to knowing the victim. But remind yourself that it is the job of the defence counsel to question the truth of what you say. Keep in the front of your mind always that there is not a single person in the court of whom you should be afraid. Each one is a person doing his work or his duty. Each one is a human being. Except perhaps one, and it is that one you must think of when you swear to "Tell the truth, the whole truth and nothing but the truth".'

Mr Thomson had been wonderful reassuring, and when it had come to holding the Bible she had not flinched. She had heard her answers echoing clearly around the court. Mr Straight had been the first to question her.

'Give your name.'

'Tryphena Douglas.'

'Miss Douglas, do you work as a barmaid at the Alhambra Palace Theatre?'

'I do.'

'And, in the course of your work, I believe you came to know the woman, Harriet Burton.'

'Yes, sir, she was a singer at the Alhambra, and she came in sometimes for a drink at the bar.'

'Miss Douglas, will you please tell the court what you remember of the evening of the twenty-fourth of December, and the early hours of Christmas Day, the twenty-fifth.'

'Yes sir . . .' And she had gone on to tell what she had already told Mr Thomson and Mr Kerley and the solicitors. Once she had got started, it was, as Mr Thomson had said it would be, quite easy, as long as she kept thinking that there was nobody here she need feel scared of.

Except him in the dock, and she had not looked at him. Not until Mr Straight had asked, 'And is that man here today?'

'Yes, sir.'

'Will you please point to him?'

Tryphena Douglas would not ever forget the absolute silence there had been whilst she was giving her evidence, and the way it was broken when she pointed to the man who had been in the bar and then on the bus going home. When she had seen him then, she had thought what a mean beggar he was, trying to get out of buying Harriet a drink, and counting over his pennies in the way the mean ones do. And then again on the bus, Harriet had had to prompt him to buy the tickets. Being mean wasn't a crime – if it was, half the chaps who came into the bar would be in clink – but killing a nice, kind girl like Harriet was. She hoped he'd swing for it.

George Flack's experience was a bit more intimidating than Tryphena's. He knew that he was a lowly kind of cove in the eyes of toffs, but he had never seen any reason to be ashamed of that. He knew his cockney accent amused gents. They'd get a good laugh late at night shouting, 'Apples a pound, pears!' as they went off home, stumbling about with a basket of fruit as a peace offering for their mothers, or for some other women who scared the trousers off them. He knew people like them said people like him were common. Well, of course he was common – working men was six a penny. But they thought he was inferior, which he wasn't. He was as proud a man as any of them, and he knew what he knew and nobody would stop him saying so. If they got a laugh off of him, then that wasn't no more than happened most days of the week – it was part of his stock in trade. This appearance wouldn't do his shop no harm, no more than his name in the paper had already done.

Mr Kerley had said to him not to go telling his story to every ear'ole who would come and try and get it off him. 'When it's over, George, if the press offers you a quid for your story, then take it, but until the court, just keep it to yourself. That way you won't find yourself telling a different story in court from the one you've told me.' And George hadn't. He had admitted to any customer who asked that he was *that* costermonger, and joked with them that if they wanted to see the whole show, they'd have to buy a ticket.

And today had been the whole show. He had taken the oath without too much hard work, and he had told his story simple and plain as he had told Mr Kerley.

How he had known her for years, and how that night she had come to his stall and bought some apples; how there was this bloke with her who wouldn't buy her a few peaches or a pineapple when she asked him. George had not commented upon the meanness, but he thought he had put it in his voice when he answered. A couple of peaches wouldn't have hurt him.

After he was told he could stand down, he had gone outside for a bit of a blow. The barmaid Tryphena was there and said he'd done all right. 'I liked the way you said, "That's him! That's the one." I wondered if you'd say for certain, he's got up a lot smarter than he was on that night, didn't you think?'

'I saw through all that. I picked him out. When I went down to Ramsgate for the ID parade, that friend of his was there. A'nt you seen him sitting there in court? Well, you just have a look when you go back in, he's about the same stamp, same colouring, but that's not what you go on, is it? You go on their faces, and how they stands, how they walks. I picked him out at once, no trouble. They must think we're daft. I'll tell you sommat that an't very bright . . . him chancing it like that. ID parades is just voluntary. What made him take a gamble like that? If he hadn't done that, who'd a been any the wiser?'

'Perhaps he's a gambling man.'

'With the chance he might end up being charged when he knows we'd seen him?'

She had smiled, and George had made himself a

promise to go and have a drink up the old Alhambra one day. She said, 'Perhaps he's like a lot of others, who think that because people like you and me have to work for our living, that we wouldn't have the nerve to speak up. A lot of people don't, you know, Mr Flack. They touch their caps and curtsey and think that a person born with a silver spoon in their mouth is a superior sort of being.'

George wouldn't have minded telling her that he thought that if there was a superior sort of being, then she herself was one. But she might of got the wrong end of the stick, and they had all got on pretty well together on these trips they'd all been obliged to take. Mr Thomson's people.

'I hope he stands trial and swings for it.'

With that, William Stalker appeared. The waiter from the Cavour restaurant had gone through a similar ordeal. He lit up a cigarillo that gave off a pungent smell. 'Well, people,' he said, 'I should like to stay, but I'm on duty soon as I get back. I suppose the next time we do our act it will be before a judge in full fig.'

As they parted, Tryphena stunned the two men by asking, 'You think it will get that far?'

'Why not?' George Flack asked. 'A whole parade of Mr Thomson's people, one after the other, pointing to him and saying, "That's the man who was with her," and then Mrs Wright who saw him, and the girl who watched him putting on his boots . . . He'll stand trial all right, Miss Tryphena, don't you lose no sleep on that score.'

And neither did Tryphena lose sleep on it, because she returned to court and heard depositions read giving evidence of blood on washing sent to the washerwoman, and a whole bottle of turps being used up when he got back from London. Until today, Tryphena had not realized that there were so many of Mr Thomson's people; she had only met those with whom she had travelled to and from Ramsgate.

The next morning, the second day of the hearing before Mr Justice Vaughan, Frank presented himself before the night-duty men had signed off. 'Gawd, Francis, didn't you go to bed?' This particular desk sergeant never tired of what he thought was the joke of using Frank's correct name, a name Frank had felt too milksop, so had rejected when he became five years old and started school. His grandfather, who had been mother and father during Frank's formative years, had not himself minded being named Francis, but had agreed to the small boy's whim and thereafter had never once forgotten to call his grandson Frank.

'Bed? What's bed? A copper who sits on his backside all night might know that, buggered if I do!' and strode off down the passage to place his reports of his previous day's enquiries at Ramsgate on the super's desk. He knocked and went straight in, only to find that, early as he was, James Thomson was at work before him.

'Sorry, sir. I didn't expect you'd be in. It's just the reports. You all right, sir?'

'Thank you, Sergeant, I'm well enough – considering.'

'It's just that you look like you could do with a good night's sleep.'

'I expect we could all do with that, Frank. How about you?'

'Four hours, out like a log. It does me.' It certainly looked as though it did, for Frank was not only closely shaved and his fair hair shining with soft soap and health, but he had a spring about him that was indefinable except that it showed. Only Frank and Elizabeth knew from what spirited and joyful sort of encounter in the very early hours that healthy glow sprang. James thought, as he often did on seeing Frank early in the morning: the man looks as though he's ready to leap on his horse and ride off to market. 'How did yesterday go, sir, if you don't mind my asking?'

The super only barely hesitated before answering, but Frank noticed. Damn it all, the last thing he could do with was for the super to have lost his assurance. 'They did us proud, Frank. Only Oscar Philippe crumbled. I don't know why, he just looked quickly round the court and said he wasn't certain that he could point out the man who had dined at the Cavour.'

'That's only one. And Miss Alice?'

'She said the same as always.'

'I'm glad she did, sir. If she wasn't absolutely sure, then she had to say, or Mr Straight could have torn her evidence to shreds. How was our star?'

'Miss Tryphena? As you would expect. I should have liked to put her up last, and left them all with that air of confidence. She pointed directly at Hessel and said her, "That is the man" piece. Then George Flack, he was excellent, too. "That's him!" he said. "I was never

343

surer of anything in my life." Caused a nice little stir amongst the German contingency.'

'Well, that all sounds pretty satisfactory to me, sir. I don't think we have any need to worry.'

Don't ever underestimate Kerley.

'Are we worrying?'

'I'm sorry, sir, I didn't mean we were actually expecting the worst . . . a manner of speaking, sir, that's all.'

The super sat back and waved Frank into the other chair. 'If we had a single piece of hard evidence, something we could take in our hands and hold up in court . . . How did you fare with the knives?'

'If we could just get him on the stand . . . nothing to do with the knives that we can use, but he did buy a new one when he returned from London. If we could get him on the stand and put questions as to his character. He's presented as a man of the cloth and a man of the highest reputation, greatly wronged by us but, as the man who sold him a dagger said, "It's a queer vicar that fires off a revolver from a hotel window and goes about armed like a brigand" – and, I'd add, who has a friend like Mr Wolebe who hasn't got a very savoury character.' His superintendent nodded thoughtfully but made no reply. 'Have you read the stuff in the papers, sir?'

'No, but I know what they are saying, Frank. It is all the work of the usual ragtag journalists and those readers who haven't a thought, and nothing better to do with their time but to pull something or somebody down. Suggest to the men that they tear the paper in squares and use it for a more suitable purpose than reading it.'

The super's face was so straight when he said this that Frank didn't know whether he was supposed to laugh, but he did anyway.

'Listen, Frank, I've had a thought. It may not be worth much, but we must leave no stone unturned ... I was writing up my journal last evening, when a couple of things crossed my mind about this alibi. Christmas Eve ... Hessel went to bed early, his boots were outside his door, he wasn't seen until next morning.'

'Right, sir, but he was heard to cough.'

'The night porter's statement. He locked up the hotel for the night, accompanied by Kroll, as is said to be his custom. Right? The hotel is shut up for the night. Ergo, even if Mr Hessel had managed to get out, he could not have got back in to be in bed when the maid served his late breakfast. Why?'

'Because he would have had to rouse the night porter and the night porter was not aroused, sir—' Frank gave an almost imperceptible whistle – 'except that Mr Wolebe said in his first statement that he had been out on the town and had picked up loose women and gone home with them and had not returned to Kroll's until the early hours.'

James Thomson nodded.

Frank Kerley was gazing into his own mind as he sorted through the train of thought his superintendent had had a couple of hours to ponder. 'Wolebe came back, found the door locked, and kicked up all hell, according to the staff. So, who's to say that whilst that racket is going on, and they're getting him to his room, they didn't leave the door unlocked, letting our dear clergyman sneak in unobserved?'

'Even if this did not happen, Frank, the story about locking up for the night and there being no chance of getting back in is thrown into doubt. It's not too full of holes, you think?'

'No, sir, it's not as bad as going to sea in a colander. I reckon it's worth another go at.'

'I am not pinning any hopes on it, Frank, but if we could show that there is a crack in the alibi they are suggesting is cast iron, and make sure the magistrate sends the case for trial . . .'

'If you don't mind my asking, sir, is that the way your mind is working? Do you believe that Mr Vaughan might *not* send him on?'

'Oh, no, Kerley, not at all. He's bound to send him on, the circumstantial is too strong to ignore, no matter how strong the alibi is. As I see it, the one balances the other, and justice would not be seen to be done if the decision was made in a magistrate's court rather than before a judge and jury.'

'So what now, sir?'

'I am going back to Kroll's Hotel and shall ask to look at the books again, and see whether I can question Kroll and that night porter. I shall not have a warrant, so he will be quite within his rights to refuse to show me the books, so I shall have to ask him in a friendly way, a favour.

James could not read Kerley's expression exactly, but he thought it was saying, Well, you can but try. Which

was very much his own thoughts as he left Bow Street
Station.

Mrs Hessel was putting up at Kroll's Hotel for the period
of her husband's trial, and, having the keys to the Hessel
trunks still in his possession, James Thomson used the
return of these as his reason for calling there.

'Whilst I am here, I would very much like to have a
word with your night porter – the one who locked up
on the night in question.'

'That is not possible, officer. I am under the instruc-
tion of Mr Mullins.'

'I am aware of Mr Mullins, and I do not propose to
do anything, but I should like to see those members of
your staff who made statements to my officers.'

'I regret not, sir.'

'Then perhaps the rooms occupied by the Ramsgate
party. Merely where they are situated if they are let?'

'No, Superintendent.' Kroll's manner was adamant,
and James wished that he had a warrant. 'I cannot
possibly allow you to view all those rooms.'

'The Hessel rooms then?'

'I cannot do that.'

'Are they occupied?'

'That is not to do with the matter. You must bring a
searching document and I must see my solicitor.'

'Mr Kroll, you are not the man standing trial. Why
should you need to consult your solicitor?'

Kroll went tight-lipped but did not accede to James's
request.

'I can show you nothing, sir, nothing . . . it may be highly irregular.'

'Mr Kroll, I am a senior and experienced Scotland Yard detective. I trust you are not suggesting that I would do anything irregular?'

'I did not mean irregular. Only that . . . I am sorry for this. Officer, I must be in court ready to give evidence for the good doctor.'

'I think, Mr Kroll, that you should talk to Mr Mullins about that. You will be giving evidence on oath to the *court*, in the person of Mr Justice Vaughan. In a trial that may end with a man forfeiting his life, there is no place for witnesses to be "for" the accused or "against" the police.'

Kroll's pomposity was brushing off on James; he heard himself speaking with the same arrogance, and was ashamed, but not sufficiently to stop himself. 'This is not a game, Kroll. When I gave evidence yesterday as to what I saw in the bedroom of the murdered woman, I spoke only as to what *I saw* . . . nothing personal against Mr Hessel – only in so far as he happens to be the man in the dock. Obviously he was arrested because investigations showed him to be the man who spent time with the young woman, but there is nothing personal between myself and Hessel, which is how it should be with you. In this country we go to court – without prejudice – to try to discover the truth. I am sure that is what you want, too: the truth.'

'I do, of course. And I know the truth. It is that Dr Hessel, a fellow countryman of mine, is accused of a crime that if it could be true brings shame on the name of Germany. But this is a good man, an honourable man.'

'Then for you to let me see your books a second time can only help us both get at the truth. I merely wish to see the guest list, the barman's accounts, dates of arrivals and departures. Books are not people to be influenced by me; they answer for themselves.'

But James Thomson came away empty-handed and angry, feeling cast down by the man's arrogance and self-assurance – and chagrined by his own lapse.

Frank Kerley needed that doubt set up by the super to be quelled, and thought he knew how to do it. As Mrs Wright's scullery maid Daisy was not to be called as a witness, Frank got permission from Mrs Wright to take her to see inside the court. Before doing so, he took her to a pie shop and fed her an eel pie and sweet tea. When he thought of his own daughter, well set-up and educated, he'd have liked to be able to do the same for every little girl. Daisy, if she wasn't lucky enough to find herself a decent admirer soon, stood a fair chance of ending up traipsing the Haymarket as Harriet Burton had ended up doing.

With one reassuring hand upon her shoulder, he stood beside Daisy, behind the public benches where one could see the entire court. At first she seemed unable to take her eyes from the grand figure of Mr Justice Vaughan in his wig and robe, then, after about five minutes, during which all attention was upon Wolebe who was giving evidence, he felt Daisy stiffen and look up at him. He squatted so that she could whisper. 'Mr Kerley, you see that man in that kind of box?' She inclined her head discreetly towards the well of the courtroom.

'Which box, the one where the man is speaking from?'

'No, the other one, with the railings round it. Well, the man in there is the one I seen. His hair wasn't brushed and he could ha' done with a shave, but he's the one I seen.'

The super was wrong, Daisy would have made a good witness. The super had said that they would be open to the accusation of scraping the barrel to put the scullery maid on the witness stand. Too late now. He had overstepped the mark there by taking her into court whilst the hearing was going on. But still, he went out assured that they did have the right man.

On the first day of the hearing, Josephine was in Danzig.

The day before, Mr Hood had summoned Josephine to his office. 'Shut the door, Miss Ferguson. Sit down.' He handed her a letter. 'Read this. It arrived this morning.'

Josephine read.

In how far Dr Hessel now undergoing Examination for murder is guilty of that act the examination will soon show, but we think it to be our duty to give a short history of the accused and his wife. It may not bear as a direct proof upon the act but it will show to some extent their former conduct.

Dr Hessel was for about two or three years

350

employed as a Reformed Preacher at the New Peter's Church, the last year of which he also kept a Boys' School to increase his income, the salary for his pastoral duties not being sufficient to keep up his position in society.

By his good address and gentlemanly appearance, he introduced himself into the best society. This could only be of short duration, as he and his wife contracted debts which only could be recovered by legal proceedings. To this we add his profligate and spendthrift conduct, he used to be drunk late at night and early in the morning, which can be proved by his servants and used to borrow money wherever he could. This brought him of course so low that he could not pay his rent and, not having any more articles of worth to pledge, he saw himself obliged to give in his resignation to the College to search for better luck in a foreign country (Baharia).

His resignation was willingly granted as all his behaviour and conduct was fully known and the College granted him his request, the substantial assistance in the sum of 180 thalers to pay small debts of honour. Which he did not pay.

To complete his disgraceful career during the last days of his stay here, he gave a dinner to his boon companions from which he and his wife disappeared and then left them to pay the expenses to his memory.

All that what he and his wife possessed was

principally borrowed, the smallest part of which was paid by cheques so that in all he leaves now a debt of several thousand thalers.

To the truthfulness of these statements which Dr Hessel cannot deny, we refer you to the Senioren College of this reformed parish and also to the Royal Court of Public Examination here.

Signed, Many of the betrayed believers of Dr Hessel.

'Well?'

'A policeman I know once told me that murder is not often a first offence, that there may well have been other minor offences and some while before.'

George Hood nodded. 'I would agree. An early tendency to criminality that is not stopped will escalate.'

'What will you do with the letter, Mr Hood?'

'For the moment, nothing . . . at least until you have been to Danzig.'

He waited for her response, and when she said nothing, he continued. 'And talked to the "Senioren College", whoever they may be, and visited the Royal Court of Public Examination in Danzig.'

'I don't speak German.'

'*The News* has interpreters. We will provide you with one.'

'Could I take my own interpreter? I have a friend who has several languages.'

'As long as the fees aren't too high.'

'Just pay for the boat ticket and a hotel.'

'All right. But there's no time to lose. The hearing is already under way.'

'Thank you, Mr Hood, but why me? Why not one of *The News*'s Young Lions?'

'Because we are publishing Hessel's memoirs, remember? I can't have *The News* riding two horses. In any case, I think this should be yours to deal with. Confirm the information, come back with some statements to back up this letter, and we shall have something substantial to pass on to the police.' He stretched and laughed, hugely pleased. 'Good, isn't it?'

'Just hope that it isn't too good to be true.'

'You know that it's not.'

Josephine nodded. The impression that she had formed of Hessel when she had taken the contract to him in his cell would be vindicated.

'Will you allow *me* to take our findings to the police?'

'I expect you to make a dramatic scene, and later write an article, "My part in the downfall of a killer". Right?'

'Right, Mr Hood.'

Josephine and her 'interpreter', David, had spent an intensive two days, with scarcely any sleep and precious little food.

Now they were eagerly awaiting their landing back in England. Seated side by side in a small cabin, David helped Josephine assemble their notes. The college from which Hessel had resigned under a cloud, and from where the anonymous letter had originated, had given them a statement. Several of his past colleagues had

353

relinquished their anononymity. Several of the men she had interviewed had spoken quite good English, so she could have managed without David's interpretations, except that it was David rather than herself they chose to speak to. In any language it was easy to hear that indignation – his behaviour still rankled; there was embarrassment, too, at having been duped by the Hessels. Very soon, the instigators of the letter to *The News* rattled off any number of misdemeanours, large and small, committed by the Reverend and Mrs Hessel. Profligacy, dishonesty, arrogance, false pride, deception, drunkenness. Mrs Hessel was extravagant, and a flirtatious troublemaker.

'David . . . did you get the impression that they think that Harriet was not the first woman to be killed by him?'

David thought for a few moments. 'Could be. They certainly went into detail about his firearms and carrying knives.'

'Which may be the prime reason for the letter.'

'Not just character assassination out of pique? I think that you may be right, Jo.'

He had slipped so easily into calling her Jo, as Liliana did, that she hardly noticed the first time it happened. Now, she liked that he used her familiar name.

'Did you pick that up, that they believed him to be capable of murder?'

'I don't know, Jo. I may speak German well enough, but I can't get the nuances, the nudges and winks.'

'Never mind the nudges and winks, I wouldn't have stood a chance without you. But I tell you one thing,

I am determined to learn some languages – I felt an ignoramus. I am sure I must have been standing around with my jaw dropping whilst you induced those people to open up about Hessel.'

'They hardly needed persuasion, Jo.'

'True. Even though I don't speak German, I couldn't fail to recognize their animosity.'

'My impression was that they presumed that he was guilty.'

Josephine tapped the sheaf of papers containing the statements they had gathered. 'And this will help see to it that he doesn't get away with putting on a front of religious respectability.'

A silence fell between them, warm, thoughtful and not fraught with the need to say anything. Just the swish as the prow of the ship cut through the sea.

Eventually, David said, 'Jo.' A moment, then a deep breath, 'Jo, I have made a decision, an important one, and I should like to have your opinion.' Another moment of pause. 'I have decided to give up the church.'

'And you want my opinion on that? David, I can't give it. I've heard you speaking to your congregation. You give them hope, they have great affection for you. Where else in London do the likes of Harriet go when they're in trouble? The homes for fallen women such as my aunt and her friends establish? "Young Father David" – people call you that because we all need someone to speak to who isn't judgemental.'

'Sorry, Jo, but you are reading more into me than there is.'

'No, I'm not. You're a good man, David. My Uncle James is another . . . and his Sergeant Kerley. But you're too thin on the ground for London to lose one of you.'

Again, as on the Norfolk train, he captured and held her hand between both of his. 'I can do very little as a clergyman. Look at me now, cast out because I speak out, speak the truth. Our prisons are full of people who have no business being there. The disgusting conditions in orphanages; even more disgusting are the stews and alleyways. Children are born there, grow up, and die there. And frequently they die early and violently.'

'I know that, David, I know, which is why you must not give up speaking out, and it is why *I* want to become a columnist people respect in a newspaper that people can trust to tell the truth.'

He squeezed her hand as he laughed, 'Dear Jo, you know how to make life difficult for yourself.'

'Not difficult, David; exciting, worthwhile, gratifying: a life worth living.'

'But you think that preaching and having the virtuous newspaper owners always on my back is a life worth living for me?'

'You do more than that, David. You help people no one else wants to help.'

'Powerless, Jo. What I do is put a little ointment on ulcers that are never going to heal, that's all. And now that God has left me, I can't even say that I do it in His name.'

'Ah. So what you said at New Year was not taken amiss by the *Telegraph*.'

'I hadn't realized it at the time, but yes, I now think that this is the only life we have, and what we don't do on earth will never get done.'

Josephine fell silent. This was probably the first time he had ever put his thoughts into words. Had he told Liliana about his loss of faith, she would not have been able to contain herself; Liliana had opinions on everything and she wouldn't have waited a minute before telling Jo what she thought about her brother.

'You're very quiet, Jo. Are you shocked?'

'No, no, of course I'm not shocked. But it does put a different slant on the opinion you asked for.'

'Well?'

'Do you remember me saying to you, not particularly seriously at the time, that you should go into politics?'

'I remember. That was what started me thinking. You are right, politics is the only way to change conditions.'

Arrival time was only twenty minutes away. Once they arrived in London, the intimacy they were experiencing would be gone. 'Now that I know what is in your mind, I can give you my opinion – you should stand for Parliament.'

'Thank you, Jo, you're a good friend.'

'And you, David, I could never have succeeded in Danzig without you.'

'You would have found someone ... your Mrs Fisher?'

'Perhaps.' Then, looking directly into his eyes and

smiling, she added, 'but I find you much better company.'

Holding her gaze for a moment, he said, 'If I do try to find a parliamentary seat . . . well, um . . .'

'Come along, David, it's not like you to be lost for words.'

'To become a member of Parliament, a man is required to have a wife. Bachelors are suspect. Do you think that you might marry me, Jo?'

'Oh.' How foolish of her not to have suspected that the hand-holding was more than flirtation. And she had allowed it. Enjoyed it.

He let her hand go. 'You are not going to say "yes" are you, Jo?'

Now she took his hand. 'It is not that I don't want to say "yes", David. I like you enormously, I love being in your company, but my situation is not like yours: members of Parliament need to be married, newspaper reporters – female ones at any rate – need to be spinsters.'

Silence returned, not as warm as before. 'Would you have married me had I stayed with the Church?'

'That has nothing to do with it. It is Jemima Ferguson who can't marry you. She is conceited enough to believe that she can become an equal to any male reporter. Jemima Ferguson cannot be anyone's wife.'

'We can remain friends?'

'I should be devastated if we did not. You and I are an integral part of our rebellious group – all talk, of course, but not if you were to stand for Parliament. With us, you might even have the basis of a new political party – one with a conscience.'

Now they were back in England, back in the real world.

'Shall you mind if I come with you to Bow Street, Jo?'

'Of course not. I expect you to . . . without you, all *The News* would have is an anonymous letter.'

'You *are* going to hand it over to your uncle?'

'Of course. With these statements, the police will have no trouble. Uncle James will send men to Danzig, I'm sure. No stone unturned with Uncle James.'

'Do you know how long the magistrate's hearing will take?'

Josephine shrugged. 'I would think not more than another day or two. But the full trial won't take place for weeks and weeks. Once the police have the letter, though, they will be able to make a lot more enquiries than we were able to. The British consul in Danzig will smooth the way for them.'

What happened next, in London, was something remarkable.

Something so extraordinary and so inexplicable that it was likely to puzzle people generations in the future when, delving in to old public records and archives, they would read the reports of Mr Justice Vaughan's words, and wonder whether British justice lived up to its reputation. They might conclude that justice was not blind, but prejudiced.

* * *

359

Josephine and David disembarked and at once took a cab to Bow Street magistrate's court, where she thought that she might find her uncle. The public gallery was full. Some uniformed policemen were gathered just inside the courtroom. Josephine saw Sergeant Kerley's head above the rest and, standing with him, her uncle. She and David pushed their way towards them.

'Josie,' he whispered, 'what are you doing here?'

Answering in a whisper close to his ear, 'The News received an anonymous letter about the Hessels, and sent me to see what I could find out. David and I are just returned from Danzig – you won't believe what we have discovered.'

He took the letter, scanned it briefly, then handed it to Sergeant Kerley.

Suddenly, Josephine realized that something dramatic was happening. The silence surrounding Justice Vaughan's voice was electric. 'What is happening?'

'Justice Vaughan is summing up.'

'The hearing's over?'

'Stopped. He heard the prosecution witnesses. Then all the defence witnesses gave alibi evidence, and the hearing was over. Listen.'

'And so, to the evidence given by other witnesses. Herr Kroll, a German of the highest reputation, has given evidence as to the accused's alibi over the crucial hours when the murder of Harriet Burton took place. The respected surgeon Karl Wolebe and other professional fellow-countrymen spoke as to the accused's character and told the court of their high regard for the accused. Mr Wolebe told of the accused's selfless and Christian action in presenting himself at the identification proceedings when Herr Wolebe himself had been wrongly arrested on suspicion of being the murderer of Harriet Burton.

'To my mind it has been conclusively shown that Doctor Henryk James Godfried Hessel was not the companion of the murdered woman.'

Josephine watched as colour drained from her uncle's face, and Sergeant Kerley's face became suffused with angry blood. Both were grim-faced and tight-lipped. Josephine reached for David's hand and gripped it tightly. *Not* the companion? Conclusively shown? How could that be, when so many people had identified him as the man who had been out and about with Harriet on Christmas Eve? When he had been seen to go up to Harriet's room and to leave the house in the early hours of Christmas Day? The puzzled frown on David's face was as deep as her own.

Mr Justice Vaughan had the attention of the entire court as he continued.

'As to the evidence presented by the prosecution. This did – at first – undoubtedly point to Doctor Hessel as having been in the company of that unfortunate woman, and therefore the police were perfectly justified in taking the course of action they did.

'This case has been most fully investigated here, and the witnesses on both sides have been subject to a close and searching cross-examination, and I am satisfied that the witnesses who have identified *Doctor Hessel* as the companion of the deceased ... are ... *entirely ... in error ...*'

The hearing was all but over, the crucial statements had been made.

'It is therefore my duty, and a duty that I discharge with great satisfaction to myself, to state that the prisoner is released. As far as I can see, I say that he leaves this court without suspicion.'

The following day every newspaper had columns and editorials and letters around the Hessel Case. And *The News* started to serialize 'Doctor Hessel's Story In His Own Words'.

At the breakfast table, Frank Kerley attacked the pages of newsprint. 'Listen, Lizzy: "Mrs Hessel, racked by torturing anxiety, scarcely ate or slept during her husband's imprisonment, and now that the tension of the strain is over, the revulsion is leaving the poor lady's nervous system in a sadly depressed and shattered condition. It is hoped, nevertheless, that Mrs Hessel will have sufficiently recovered to render it possible that in a week's time her husband and herself can leave England by steamer for Baharia, where they will arrive before the fated *Wangerland*.'

'The sooner they are out of the country and it's all forgotten, the better, Frank, if you ask me.' Elizabeth tried to be neutral and careful about what she said, for Frank was undoubtedly not himself.

The one bit of brightness had been yesterday, before the hearing had collapsed, when he had come home pleased as punch with the news that his super had put him forward for a commendation and a reward.

'Of course,' he explained, 'Colonel Henderson could never agree to putting the super's report forward for the reward, but the words in the super's report are better than guineas, Lizzy.'

Elizabeth herself could not see why the commissioner could not put Frank forward: going aboard a plague ship is as brave as facing a pistol. But that's how they were in the police force. If he had actually got smallpox he might have been rewarded, or if the case hadn't collapsed like that. She felt real pain for Frank, and knew that he felt pain himself. He was a very professional policeman, seldom brought his work home with him, never let all that dreadful stuff he had to do affect his relationship with herself and Frances.

But this case seemed to have got to him right from the start.

One night in bed he had said to her, 'This is a Them and Us case, Lizzy. It's like it was when I was a kid back home, the lord of the manor couldn't ever do no wrong. You could put a monkey in a silk shirt and people would believe him before they'd believe a working man in a fustian jacket.'

Josephine went next day to see George Hood. 'You should have handed the letter over to the police as soon as it arrived.'

'It would have made no difference. His supporters are "Germans of the highest reputation" – isn't that what Justice Vaughan called them? With the queen mourning the German of the highest reputation of all, the riff-raff of the London streets hadn't a chance of being believed.'

Josephine believed that he was probably right in that.

'What did Superintendent Thomson say when you gave him the letter and the statement?'

'Nothing. He read it and so did his sergeant. Small comfort to know that they were right when he and his wife are out there being feted. Some of his fellow-countrymen living in England have started a subscription.'

George Hood nodded. 'The queen has contributed thirty pounds and the prime minister has made a large donation. I've heard that he is going to make an apology on behalf of the people of Britain.'

'Not on my behalf!'

Liliana read aloud from one of the many newspapers that littered the kitchen table. '"The Sailing of the *Wangerland*. Mrs Hessel's ordeal has rendered her unfit to continue the journey to Brazil at present and she will remain in London until she has rested . . .".'

Josephine snatched the page, crushed it into a ball and threw it at the wall. David picked it up, and sat crushing it into an even harder ball.

'Where were they last night?' Liliana asked. 'Dining at Windsor Castle?'

'Or with Mr Gladstone.'

'Of course, Mr Gladstone is very interested in the plight of prostitutes. He might ask the good doctor about his unique method of clearing the streets of harlots.'

'Lili!' David remonstrated.

'I know ... sorry, a very coarse joke. At least Mr Gladstone does show some concern for "fallen women".'

'The trouble with people who have the power to change things for the better is that they are not *people*, they are *men* ... I'm sorry, David, I don't include you ...'

Liliana said, 'I should stop there before you get yourself in deeper.'

David said, 'A day will come when you will have a say in the country's affairs.'

'Do you mean Jo personally, or women generally?'

'Jo will get her say long before women as a whole do.'

By the time the petals of blossom and spring flowers in London parks had fallen, and the summer of 1873 had bloomed with new fabrics and fashions, the Great Coram Street Murder was all but forgotten. The enthusiasm that book publishers had shown for Josephine's *Life of a Country Girl*, paying her a decent sum of money for its rights, waned. It would be published, but perhaps at a more favourable time.

George Hood let her fume about the capriciousness of publishers. 'Favourable? When would that be, do you think?'

'Do you want me to agree, or tell you what I think?'

'Tell me.'

'Very well, a favourable time will be when there is a similar case of murder. When the murder of another young prostitute is headline news.'

'I didn't write Harriet's story for sensation, I wrote it so that people would become more enlightened about how poor women exist in London, how easy it is for a respectable girl to have to resort to the streets.'

'Of course, but your publishers needed to have your murderer found guilty and hanged. Have they suggested that as a possible denouement?' Josephine didn't answer. 'Of course they did, and you, my dear Miss Ferguson, are determined to be the purist.'

'Don't you see, Mr Hood, my *Country Girl* can't have a satisfactory conclusion – her killer got away scot-free!'

'As I see it, you have two choices: you can insist that your book is published without it ending in a trial and execution, or you can insist that it tells the truth.'

'You think that is a choice?'

George Hood shrugged his shoulders. 'For you? No.'

'The *Country Girl* has not turned out to be what I first intended, a kind of biography told in story fashion. When Justice Vaughan said that he believed the well-off and educated, and that the rest were "entirely mistaken" – *all* of them? *all* mistaken? – my book became a kind of exposé of prejudice.'

'And injustice. Don't forget injustice, Miss Ferguson.'

'Are you laughing at me?'

'Of course not, but where your book is concerned I

think that you are blind to what I thought we agreed upon when you joined *The News*. "Tickle", Miss Ferguson. Have you forgotten why our readership increases daily?'

Josephine fell silent. She had come here believing that she would have an ally in her editor. 'What should I do then?'

'Well, you have already seen that Harriet Burton's life would be more interesting to people in the form of a novel, so write a fictitious conclusion.'

'What?'

'Anything. The truth of your story is in Harriet's life . . . and death.'

'A trial scene?'

'Why not? You could have the accused face all those people who never appeared at the Bow Street hearing, the ones not even the police knew of until the anonymous letter.'

'The Danzig people?'

'Of course. *The News* might start a whispering campaign. "Is this book a true account of what happened?" And put questions in the Personal advertisement columns.'

Jo burst out laughing. 'Oh yes, Mr Hood. What "tickle"!'

Christine Derry put on a splendid show of Liliana's work, the central piece of which was a large canvas entitled "Working Woman", depicting Tryphena Douglas as a kind of proud empress of her glittering bar. As the group

367

of friends walked through the warm streets towards Boot Street. David put a hand on Jo's arm. 'There's something I want to ask you before we get to the Dining Rooms.'

Oh Lord, he's going to ask me to marry him again. Which he was, but not in so straightforward a manner as that.

'I've decided to leave the Church entirely.'

'I can't say that I am surprised.'

'Yes, well, I thought more about our conversation on the boat. I have been approached by some Liberal people and their financiers. They have asked me to allow my name to be proposed for a seat that has become vacant in the West Country – Cornwall, actually.'

'David, that's wonderful – you agreed, I hope.'

'I said that I was interested – very interested, but . . .'

'No buts. Grab the opportunity with both hands. You were born to be a politician.'

'I am so pleased that you think it the right thing. I thought that the other right thing would be for us to be married?

Irritation niggled her. The right thing? Not, I love you to distraction, Jo.

'No response, Jo? You would be a wonderful wife for any politician. Together, we could make such changes in society. This is the time for change, Jo.' He squeezed her hand eagerly. 'I see us in high office.'

Pulling her arm away she said tightly. 'I'm afraid that I don't, David.'

'Jo. I thought we had similar ideas about society, about changing things for the better, a more equal society, the poor better cared for.'

'And you believe that a marriage could thrive on that? Where does love come in, David? Anywhere? Or just after ambition?'

'Love goes without saying. I love you because of all those things I have discovered about you.'

'I am sure that you will find someone who likes the idea – but not me. I should have thought you had realized by now that I am lead violinist, not second fiddle.'

'I am very disappointed, Jo.'

'Don't be, David. Ask Christine, she'd make a much more suitable politician's wife than me.' Did that sound like pique? She hoped not. 'In any case, I have been asked if I would like to join the staff of *The Post* – it's a New York daily paper.' She did not mention that she had sought the position herself. She had sent off a collection of her pieces, and related her part in obtaining the Hessel contract for *The News*.

'You intend going to America alone?'

'I hope that Hani will come too.'

Her almond-shaped eyes almost closed with smiles and tears, Hani said, 'America? Of course I go. MistaJame feel better if I am with you.' She giggled and clasped Jo's hands. 'Oh 'osie, what fun . . . what adventure. There are maybe more Eastern people than in London.'

'You think you might find a husband.'

'I do not, silly gir', but who knows?'

'So you will come?'

'I come . . . of course. This time when you leave home, I take care of you.'

'Hani, no! It will be a rule of the house that you understand that I am a grown-up woman.'

'Of course, 'osie. I not tell you what to do.'

Josephine gave Hani a brief hug. 'I don't believe you, but I am so glad that you will come. Right . . . such fun, such adventures.'

On her last evening, before leaving for Southampton, from where she and Hani would leave for New York, James and Ann Martha took Josephine to dine out at one of Ann's favourite restaurants – splendid, of course.

They were seated in a lounge drinking post-prandial brandy and coffee, when James produced an envelope which he passed across the table to Josephine. 'I could have let you see this before your book was published, but in the end decided not to in case it might prove too much of a temptation.'

Taking the strangely folded document from the envelope, she read.

1873

British Consulate – Danzig
Consular No. 8 Confidential.
By post
copy to The Queen. Mr Gladstone. The Home
   Office.
Confidential information relative to Dr Hessel
To The Right Honble. The Earl of Granville KG,
   Foreign Office.

My Lord

In compliance with Viscount Enfield's instructions
as conveyed to me in His Lordship's Despatch
marked No. 1 Consular Confidential, dated 11th
instant, but which did not reach me until the 20th
instant, on the subject of Doctor Hessel, I have the
honour to report to Your Lordship as follows:–

Unfortunately the person who is the object of
Your Lordship's enquiries, and who has acquired
lately such notoriety, did not leave Danzig
with that high character with which he has been
credited by his friends and supporters in his
misfortune in London.

Dr Hessel came to Danzig from a Parish in
the Rhenish Provinces, and was attached here
to a Reformed Church, and not as has been
erroneously stated to one of the Lutheran
Communion, though he may have been originally
ordained a Lutheran Minister, of this I cannot be
certain.

It is correctly stated in the anonymous letter,
that besides his clerical duties at the Church
of St Peter, in this town, he was also employed
in tuition in a private School, and that by his
insinuating manner he gained a favourable
admittance into Society at this place.

His connection with the private School of Dr
Weiss was suddenly broken off in the Autumn
of 1871, and I understand that the cause of it
has been ascribed to some money transactions of

Dr Hessel's, but I cannot speak with any degree of certainty on this delicate subject as I am not willing to give my enquiries that openness which might ensure a more complete result, nor am I authorized, by Your Lordship's Instructions, to proceed otherwise.

As far as I am able to ascertain anything further about Dr Hessel, a certain irregularity in his habits ascribed to him, and this with increasing pecuniary difficulties assigned as the cause of the cessation of his clerical duties here, and of his determination to leave Europe for the Brazilian Empire.

I am not in a position to establish with any degree of accuracy the extent to which these charges may be proved, but from a variety of sources to which I have referred with the greatest possible caution, I have arrived at the painful conclusion that there must be some foundation for them, and that the description of Dr Hessel contained in the anonymous letter which I beg leave to return as instructed, cannot be considered as altogether incorrect.

Should Her Majesty's Secretary of State for the Home Department deem further enquiries necessary, I think that it would be requisite to make them through the Prussian Police Authorities, as the only means of establishing accurate data.

The charge of having feted his friends on the day of his departure, and of having left by the train without taking leave of them, or having paid

the Bill, is currently believed against Dr Hessel
at Danzig liabilities he left behind him may be
exaggerated, but I am assured by my own Lawyer
Mr Marting that he has succeeded in obtaining
a payment of twenty odd pounds for one of his
clients from Dr Hessel through the intervention of
the German Consul General in London.

I have the honour to remain with the greatest of
respect, My Lord, Your Lordship's most obedient,
humble servant, W. White

'Thank you for letting me see this, Uncle James. What
will happen to it now?'

'It will be secreted away in the deep vaults where other
embarrassing and sensitive documents are buried.'

'This makes me even more certain that I am making
the right decision to start life in a country where there
is no queen sitting heavily on people – and "humble
servant". What does that mean, Uncle James?'

'Josephine, you know that is not to be taken literally.
I am certain that this man is not one bit humble, quite
the reverse.'

'I don't want to be a "subject", I want to be a
"citizen".'

Ann Martha said, 'Josephine, you make it appear that
this is not a free country.'

James's eyes asked Josephine to forgive Ann Martha
her unenlightened views.

'Things will change, Josie.'

'Perhaps, Uncle James, but I can't wait that long.'

Author's Note

My interest in the Great Coram Street Murder started when, researching for another book, I came upon a reference to it quite by chance. The victim's name, being Burton – Harriet/Clara Burton – was the spark that ignited my interest. Then, in a short piece in a collection, there was the comment by an author who, like me, had been intrigued by the story (but abandoned it), that 'it is now known that the murderer got away with it.'

That author's widow generously gave me her husband's research, which didn't give a clue as to why he had come to that conclusion. Now I was hooked, so I spoke to my 'ace' researcher, Elizabeth, who knows her way about the dustier parts of London's archives.

Soon, she had unearthed very many documents, and produced a blizzard of photocopies, police reports, victim antecedents, witness statements, career records of the two detectives, even a photograph of Superintendent Thomson, his will, and a photo of the house in Great Coram Street. In addition there were many column inches of newspaper reports, and a letter from Scotland Yard's Black Museum relating to the clue of the bitten apple found at the scene of the crime. Then there were the long, long love-letters from a Willie Kirby – who one must suspect of stringing Harriet along.

Perhaps most intriguing of all is a confidential Foreign Office report on the suspect, a Clergyman of the Highest Reputation. This was from the British Consulate in Danzig to Earl Granville at the Foreign Office. He passed it on to Queen Victoria and the prime minister to read. Too late! The bird had been released and flown.

One can only speculate on the speed with which this hot potato was passed around. What to do? Obvious, bury it. And so it remained buried until my researcher Elizabeth discovered it. It was the one piece of evidence I needed to justify writing this book, which is not only about the murder of a woman and the man who got away with it, but also about prejudice and injustice. Nothing's new.

The more Elizabeth found, the more interesting became the story of the murder of Harriet Burton.

Chequebook journalism being nothing new, the accused man's 'Story in His Own Words' appeared. Readers' letters, then as now the 'Why-oh-why?' brigade, wanting somebody at whom to hurl abuse, chose to denigrate, insult and berate the police – so ignorant and insensitive that they had arrested a 'Clergyman of the highest reputation'. Add to this that the clergyman accused of killing an actress in her own bedroom was a fellow-countryman of the widowed queen's dead husband, it was enough to ignite the flames of outrage.

After the clergyman was released, donations were called for and money poured in – the queen herself gave £30, a large sum then, and the prime minister was another contributor. A subscription dinner was arranged. A message of abject apology on behalf of the nation was inscribed on a silver dish, which was presented to the young man and his pretty wife before they sailed away to the other side of the world.

Recently, I engaged a profiler to look at this 'cold case murderer' using the same up-to-date methods as would a present-day murder team. The profiler's report confirms what I had come to believe. Godfried Hessel was a psychopath. He enjoyed the 'buzz', such as when he let off a fire-arm from his hotel window. He believed that he was unassailable as, for example, when he forced himself into the ID parade and made no attempt to keep from being seen with Harriet on Christmas Eve. He killed Harriet Burton because he felt like it at the time.

Now, of course, I itch to know what happened to Harriet Burton's killer. Did he continue his journey to Bahai in Brazil? Did he kill again?